FORT

MEL KEEGAN
Fortunes of War

THE GAY MEN'S PRESS

First published in 1995
by GMP Publishers Ltd
PO Box 247, London N6 4BW, England

World Copyright © 1995 Mel Keegan

*A CIP catalogue record for this book is available
from the British Library.*

ISBN 0 85449 211 9

Distributed in North America by Inbook,
140 Commerce St, East Haven, CT 06512, USA.

Distributed in Australia by Bulldog Books,
P O Box 155, Broadway, NSW 2007.

Printed and bound in the EU by Nørhaven A/S, Viborg, Denmark.

BOOK ONE

The Black Sheep
April — June, 1588

Being your slave, what should I do but tend
Upon the hours and times of your desire?
I have no precious time at all to spend,
Nor services to do, till you require.

Nor dare I chide the world-without-end hour,
Whilst I, my sovereign, watch the clock for you,
Nor think the bitterness of absence sour,
When you have bid your servant once adieu;

Nor dare I question with my jealous thought
Where you may be, or your affairs suppose,
But, like a sad slave, stay and think of nought
Save where you are how happy you make those.

So true a fool is love that in your will,
Though you do anything, he thinks no ill.

Shakespeare, *Sonnet 57*

Chapter One

Candle shadows writhed about the walls from tapestry to shuttered window and it was difficult to see, but Dermot Channon knew the man was there. It was Walt Copeland, the brewer, the ambitious one who had wormed his way into the court with dubious services performed for dubious masters. Channon neither liked nor trusted him.

He had hidden, so he was equally aware of Channon. Both men stood against the wall while a guard clattered to duty. It was late. Music and laughter could still be heard but most of Hampton's apartments were shut up for the night.

Why would Copeland hide? Channon smiled faintly. Some clandestine affair, a lady's honour at stake? Honour was as insubstantial as virginity. Palace intrigue had ceased to amuse Channon long before. He turned his back on both Copeland and his business.

Footsteps shuffled away toward the servants' rooms, like the scuttling of a rat. Channon glanced after the man but saw only a flutter of brown cape before Timothy Bevan's voice called his name.

'Channon, is that you? Señor Channon?' Bevan's Castilian was thickly accented.

The use of years brought the language to Channon's lips too. Its vowels came more easily than the barbarities of English. 'I am looking for the physician, John Glover. He is not in his rooms.'

'Are you ailing?' Bevan stepped into the light of a tall candelabrum. He was handsome, young, with a neat red beard. But he was soft, Channon thought, with soft hands, and none of the calluses earned upon the hilt of a sword. He was well suited to the court but in the field he would be carrion, despite Bevan's aspirations.

'I seek the doctor for my uncle,' Channon told him. 'Don Mauricio has seen better days than this.'

Bevan made noises of agreement. 'Aye, I was there. Captain Rothwell was in fine voice and hot temper. The Ambassador, your uncle, answered well.'

'Before being flayed,' Channon retorted. 'He is presently bleeding from those wounds.'

'Frobisher must take Rothwell's part,' Bevan mused as they walked on along the passageway. 'It is not in his interests, nor the Queen's, to stand with Don Mauricio. You heard the rumours?'

'That Her Majesty is Rothwell's investor?' Channon glanced side-long at Bevan. 'There's no proof. Even if there were, what of it? She may yet censure Rothwell, and there the matter ends.'

Censure him, Channon thought bitterly. Sharp words or a repri-mand, for grievous damage done a Spanish warship in the Channel. With a ball through the hull at the waterline the *Alcanzar* wallowed in heavy seas like a pig. Six lads were killed by the shot that pounded the Spanish *galleasse*, or drowned in the flooding — lads for whom Channon felt a seaman's kinship. He could have been among them.

'Her Majesty is not fully accepting of Frobisher's and Rothwell's argument.' Bevan's tone was conciliatory. 'She might chastise the captain. His neck could be the price for it, as your uncle demanded.'

'One life for six.' Who were those dead lads? Channon wondered. Had he known them?

'Six common monkeys,' Bevan argued.

'Six men!' Channon snarled. 'I was taught that all men are born equal before God.' Bevan glared, then had the grace to bow. 'It is for the Queen to decide. Don Mauricio has done all he can, and tonight pays the price for it. Have you seen the quack? Which wilting violet does he attend tonight?'

'Wilting indeed,' Bevan agreed. 'At last I saw, he was with my Lady Anne Page, who was taken ill at vespers.'

The woman was one of those who waited upon the Queen. Channon halted beside a window overlooking the regimented garden. Moon-light silvered the lawns; a guardsman prowled, pike over his shoul-der. The moonlight gleamed on his helmet.

'Will you take a message for me, Master Bevan? I imagine you will be returning to your lady love directly.'

'Directly,' Bevan confessed. 'Ann and I shall wed, by and by. When she is ailing my place is with her.'

'Then impose on the physician to prepare a sleeping cup.' Channon watched Bevan's soft hands fuss with the froth of white lace at his chin. 'I shall be waiting.'

With an elegant bow Bevan hurried away toward the women's apartments. The Queen's rooms were jealously guarded, especially at night. Not even Channon could walk those passages unchallenged, though the guards would be courteous, respecting his rank if not his race.

For some time he stood by the tall window. In the candlelight just half his face was illuminated, reflected in the tiny, diamond-shaped glass panes. Saturnine, he thought. Bored, growing stale in this velvet prison where men smiled politely and clasped hands concealed daggers.

He nodded goodnight to his reflection and walked back the way he had come. The lute and the psaltery called from John Woodland's rooms, where young men gathered for music, poetry... some said for love. Often, Channon heard their pleasures and damned the rank that brought him here and at the same stroke set him apart. The lure of young men's guileless charm was acidly sweet.

But his place was with his ailing old kinsman, till this charade was over. Would Mauricio live to see the end? Channon was less certain with each day the Ambassador spent in verbal combat with men like Drake, Frobisher, Hatton. And Elizabeth.

A fire blazed in the wide stone hearth. In the chair beside it the old man was frail, blue about the eyes with fatigue. The last in a succession of Spanish diplomats, Don Mauricio de Cervallo tussled with an impossible duty. He looked up as Channon entered, and found a smile.

'The physician is with Lady Anne Page.' Channon warmed his hands at the fire. England was damnably cold, damp, though it was almost summer. 'Bevan took a message and you shall have a draught. To bed with you, Mauricio. You are a wraith.'

'I feel like one.' The soft Castilian voice was balm on the ear. Mauricio rose stiffly. In the heavy red velvet robe he looked thin. 'I feel my years.'

He was fifty, no longer young, and in poor health. He had never enjoyed a soldier's constitution, Channon thought as he took the robe from him. Men like Mauricio were tutored for a different kind of battle. His weapons were words and law, but lately English privateers made a mockery of that law.

Verbal battle had ignited over the *Alcanzar*. Was the assault upon her an act of war or piracy? Spanish merchants and diplomats were still welcome on English soil, yet men like Charles Rothwell were free to fire upon a ship keeping to its own business in open water. And the wisdom of Court rumour swore Elizabeth was Rothwell's investor.

The mattress cushioned Mauricio's spine and he relaxed with a groan. Channon drew the bedcurtains and left him with a smile. 'Look to your health, uncle. Will you let these English pirates master you? What of family honour, answer me that!'

Honour was in ample supply within the Cervallo family. Little else was. Like many Spanish households, their purse was empty. Fierce dignity covered patchwork fortunes. Channon sighed as he settled in Mauricio's chair by the hearth to wait for the physician. Philip, His Catholic Majesty, was hungry for this island, at whatever cost. The price was paid by men like Mauricio, and the lads who died on the *Alcanzar*.

The physician was a long time coming. Midnight was an hour past when Channon opened the door not to John Glover but to a young page. The lad was disturbingly pretty, with wide, clear blue eyes and hair like yellow silk beneath his cap. Channon arched a brow, and the boy held out a lidded pewter cup.

'From the physician, sir. A sleeping cup, upon Master Bevan's instructions.'

Channon took it. 'Thank you, boy. If you are returning to the quack, ask him to come personally in the morning. The Ambassador is ailing no less than Lady Ann.' The page bowed politely and enormous blue eyes looked up at Channon with a guilelessness that almost made him mourn. Soon that innocence would be gone forever. 'What's your name, boy?'

'Stephen, sir. Stephen Tanner, in the service of Master Bevan since last year.'

Was he twelve, thirteen? With another bow he excused himself. The soldier lingered at the door to watch him go. He found more beguilement in a boy's beautiful innocence than in the paint-and-powder games of palace ladies, despite their undeniable charms.

'Dermot?' Mauricio pronounced the name with the full, rich accent of Seville.

And Channon was on the point of returning to the bed when he saw, again, the shifting candle shadows betraying a man not so artfully concealed as he hoped. Curious, amused, Channon stepped into the draughty passage and glimpsed a figure in a brown cape. Copeland plying to and fro like a clandestine courier? On whose dubious errand this time?

'Dermot, have you gone?' Mauricio called sharply.

He would be out of bed soon, chilling himself in nightshirt and slippers. Channon bolted the door. 'A lad brought your cup. Drink this and rest.'

The bedcurtains were open. Mauricio held a sheaf of papers, and Channon frowned. 'I've a score letters to write,' the old man protested, gesturing with the crisp yellow sheets.

'Not tonight!' Channon took them and thrust the cup into his hands. 'Master Guido can take down the letters for your signature, and morning is soon enough. I am here to safeguard you. Good Christ! How shall I guard you from yourself?' Mauricio's face creased in a tired smile. 'Drink, and sleep. Fret over Philip's business when you've the health for it.'

The cup was bitter with valerian, skullcap and willow. Peppermint and honey masked their vileness. Mauricio managed a drop and reached for a cup of wine. Channon stood over him like a father with a wilful child, but only a second drop had passed his lips when Mauricio began to gasp and curse.

Then he was retching violently. He heaved himself over the bedside as his belly emptied, and Channon saw blood. 'What is it? Mauricio!' The Ambassador could not answer, but Channon could guess.

Poison. No sleeping draught would empty a man's stomach as soon as a drop was swallowed. Anger and fear took him to the door. The bolt slammed back and he summoned the guard with shouts that would rouse the whole palace. Doors opened at the commotion and a burly young sergeant rushed toward him.

'Fetch the physician,' Channon snarled, 'Quickly. Tell him Mauricio de Cervallo is poisoned, by the very draught Glover sent. While you're about it find the boy, Stephen Tanner, of Bevan's household. It was he who delivered the cup.'

Astonishment whispered along the passage as Channon slammed the door. By morning it would be all over Hampton, and Elizabeth would have the tale at breakfast. The old man lay weakly on the side of the bed. The air stank and blood soiled his linen.

'Mauricio?' Channon lifted his chin to look into his eyes. The pupils were dilated, but they were alive. 'How much did you drink?'

'A drop only,' Mauricio gasped.

The cup was in the bedding, half its contents spilled. Channon held it to his nose, but to him bitter herbs all smelt alike. He would have held his breath and drunk in good faith... he would have been dead. Mauricio was nearly so. His face was waxen, his mouth loose, head lolling.

A sudden battering announced Glover. He had been marched up by a guardsman, and Channon nodded his thanks to the man as Glover hurried inside. He was short, stout, in black robes; and he was frightened. Sweat beaded his bald head despite the night's chill.

'Poison?' Glover panted. Channon stood aside to let him work but never took his eyes from him. 'Are you sure, Señor? I don't understand.'

With the door bolted, Channon hovered over the quack as Glover looked into Mauricio's eyes, counted his pulse. 'By God, if you made a mistake with the cup I'll have your hide!' It was a soldier's warning. Glover's face was white but he swallowed his protests as he saw the steel in Channon's eyes. Spanish eyes in an Irish face, at once compelling and disturbing, as Channon well knew.

He lifted the cup and muttered distractedly. 'Hemlock, foxglove. By God, it did not come from my hands. I mixed the cup in Lady Ann's parlour while she slept, from medicinals in my bag.' He looked entreatingly at Channon. 'I swear, Master Bevan watched me. I don't keep hemlock and foxglove in my bag! Aye, I have them in my apothecary, but not here. I could never make this mistake.'

The claim would easily be verified. Glover's bag lay at his feet, and Channon confiscated it. Its contents would be examined by an authority. Bevan could testify to the doctor's work when the draught was mixed.

Furious knocking took Channon to the door, where the guard sergeant had Stephen Tanner by the scruff of the neck. The child wept abjectly as he was thrust into Channon's hands. He knelt on the Persian carpet by the hearth, and Channon looked down into a lovely face that was pale with fright and bewilderment.

'Please, sir, what have I done?' Stephen begged. 'They won't say what I've done!' He pulled off his cap and twisted it between his hands.

'You brought the cup that poisoned the Ambassador,' Channon said softly.

'I?' Stephen's mouth slackened. 'He is dead?'

'By fortune alone, he is not,' Channon told him. 'The physician swears it was but a sleeping draught when it left his hand. The only other hands to touch it were yours.'

Stephen struggled to his feet. 'I would not fetch poison to any man, let alone a Spanish knight.'

'Yet only you touched it,' Channon purred, 'save Glover and myself.'

'No, sir! I set it down.' Stephen's eyes widened. 'Master Copeland asked for a taper to light his pipe. I set the cup down and had my back to it. When I returned he was by the table. I swear it, sir, I did nothing, nothing to be hung for!' He was begging, as if he expected to be locked away.

Copeland served several influential men; he ran errands, hid in the shadows, scuttled like a rat when he was seen. Anger compressed Channon's lips. His fists clenched as he studied the boy. It could go badly for Stephen. Copeland had friends, he would have doctored the cup upon instructions, and the same enemies of Spain who wished Mauricio in his grave would protect Copeland while a little page was punished.

A sigh whispered over Channon's lips. He set a hand on the boy's shoulder, felt his trembling. 'I saw Copeland skulking earlier. And I told Bevan to send a cup, in clear hearing of anyone listening... leave the brewer to me.'

'You believe me?' Stephen hung his cap haphazardly on his head.

Channon straightened the cap and caressed his soft cheek. 'This face could not lie. You think I don't know innocence when I see it?' He looked into the bedchamber. 'It is past time you set your head down. Off with you. Send servants with fresh linen, and leave all else to me.'

For a moment Stephen clutched his hand, then he fled back toward Bevan's apartments. The crowd of gossips had dispersed but the sergeant who had found Stephen loitered, watching the Ambassador's rooms as if he must slam the stable door with the horse long gone. Channon beckoned the young man closer.

'Find the brewer, Walt Copeland, with all speed. And detain him.

He'll be charged on the morrow, not the boy.'

A Cornish burr answered as the man shouldered his pike. 'I know the man. Handy with bribes, if thee'll look the other way. If he's in the palace, I'll fetch him.'

If he's in the palace. Channon's mouth hardened as he returned to the bedchamber. Mauricio was still retching, but less painfully, with dry heaves. Glover held a bowl at his side and Mauricio bled into it. Glover fussed, mopped his face, gave him water, and blood oozed from his wrist drop by drop as Mauricio lay in an exhausted daze. He licked his lips and focussed on Channon's face with difficulty.

'Who?' he whispered. 'Find him, Dermot.'

'Copeland poisoned the cup, no mistake.' Channon said bleakly. Glover shot him a glance. 'Aye, physician, your neck is out of the noose thanks to Bevan's pretty little page. But who paid Master Copeland?' He watched Glover staunch the old man's bleeding with tight bindings. 'It is a rare kind of compliment, Mauricio. Your arguments carry such weight with the likes of Drake and Frobisher that you arouse Spain's enemies to murder.'

But Mauricio was asleep, and Glover stepped back. 'He will rest now. He should stay abed for several days, then deal gently by himself.'

'He speaks with Philip's voice in Spanish affairs,' Channon said doubtfully. 'He has little time to rest.'

'And what good will it to the King if your uncle is dead?' Glover demanded. He drew the bedcurtains with sharp, angry jerks. 'Guard him from his enemies, but guard him first from himself, his country-men and his King, who will use him till he is worn down.' He picked up his bag. 'Am I at liberty?' Channon nodded. 'Then, good night. There will be uproar when the Queen hears of this!'

Alone, Channon stood by the hearth and watched the embers blacken. He dozed in the chair until he heard the guard change. Dawn had flooded the sky, pink and gold with fragile beauty, when a discreet knock announced the Cornish sergeant who brought unsurprising news.

'Copeland is not in the palace, Señor. We searched everywhere that can decently be searched.'

'So he has fled.' Channon dismissed the man with a nod of thanks. He must bathe, shave, change his hose and linen. Don Mauricio slept on, oblivious.

Just after nine the Queen's private physician came politely to verify the tale, and wrote a curt report. The Queen, he said, would be furious. It was not that she entertained any love for Spaniards or Irishmen, and Channon was both; but integrity had been compromised tonight. Murder was no fit substitute for diplomacy.

At noon the old Ambassador was on his feet, though he was weak and shaking. A liveried secretary ushered him into the Queen's public chamber while Channon tarried outside and listened to the whisper of politely toned voices.

Lady Margaret Trewarne brought him wine and flirted coyly as he waited. Channon indulged her, unconsciously comparing her posing, powder and rouge with the guileless beauty of the manchild, Stephen Tanner. He flirted adeptly to please the woman, and she was satisfied.

He caught a glimpse of the Queen as the door opened. Mauricio bowed and closed it once more, leaving Channon with an impression of turquoise silk, flaming hair and skin the colour of the swan. 'So?' he prompted as his uncle took a cup of wine from Lady Margaret's tiny, ringed hand.

The Ambassador's voice betrayed his ordeal. His face was the colour and texture of old parchment, and clothes that should have complimented a man's figure hung loosely. Flawless hose only displayed legs that had wasted. 'I am to go,' he said quietly.

'To Seville? Home?' For a moment Channon wondered if the embassy had been expelled, if there had been a dispatch from Philip. Had Rothwell's attack upon the *Alcanzar* been taken as an act of war?

'No, to the country, here in England, to rest.' Mauricio sipped the wine, appreciating its tart, acid bite. 'I have friends here. The Earl of Blackstead, Lord Armagh. I have spoken of William Armagh often enough.'

'I know the name.' Channon set down his empty cup. 'And what of the plot upon you life?'

'Plot?' Mauricio's face darkened. 'It appears this man Copeland took it upon himself to murder me. This seems to satisfy Her Majesty.'

'It would,' Channon said bitterly as he led the way out past the courteous servants and guards. 'It wouldn't do to look too closely into the matter. Who knows which head may find itself on the block? Damn!' They stood in the busy passage and he schooled his face to conceal his anger. The old man waited for him to speak again, and a faint, grudging smile quirked one corner of Channon's wide mouth. 'Leave matters to me. There are... ways and means.'

There were spies, and men whose tongues would loosen for a few coins. They went out on Spanish business with a guinea apiece for their efforts. But Antonio Diaz would take no payment for his services. It was enough to find Copeland and see the price of Mauricio's suffering settled, one way or another. Diaz served many diplomats as secretary and spy. He passed freely along the river streets with the look of a merchant, and was often at Hampton with messages. Channon trusted him and needed only to wait.

The afternoon was warm. With his uncle asleep and time on his hands, Channon lingered to watch the young men playing shuttlecock on the lawns. A boy strummed the lute, a sweet, mournful madrigal for another lad whose eyes never left him. They were lovers, and in love, oblivious to the shrill squeals of the girls chasing croquet balls in the sun.

A shadow fell across the low wall where Channon sat, and he looked up at the man outlined against the sky. He was tall, broad and as swarthy as an Spaniard. A signet winked on his right hand; a rapier rode at his left hip. Channon stood and accorded the captain a stiff half bow, which Sir Charles Rothwell did not return.

He was well into his thirties, ten years Channon's elder, with crinkly, dark brown hair, receding from his forehead. His eyes were nested in deep creases, the legacy of many years at sea. Unlike Bevan, who merely aspired to glory, Rothwell had won his spurs. He commanded the respect and fear of his opponents. Save, Channon thought, for Mauricio de Cervallo, whose pedigree was older, and whose honour was not besmirched by allegations of piracy.

'Good day, Captain.' Channon's English was rich with Irish vowels.

Dark blue eyes studied him from beneath lowered brows. Rothwell was silent for some time. His left hand rode the jewelled hilt of the rapier, as if he half expected to use it. He had that reputation. Several men had challenged him, and had died for the audacity.

'A fortunate escape for your uncle,' Rothwell said at last, with spurious blandness.

'Fortunate?' Channon demanded. 'I imagine a certain murderer is not so pleased as yourself, Captain.'

'Murderer?' Rothwell echoed. 'Don Mauricio lives!'

'By chance.' Channon's narrowed eyes examined Rothwell, feature by feature.

Two weeks before he had ordered his gunners to fire upon Capitan Miguel Vasca's *Alcanzar*. If it was not an act of war, Channon did not know what to call it, but Rothwell was a privateer, and Her Majesty was not responsible. No word of judgement on this account had been given yet, but Rothwell seemed unconcerned, as if he knew he had the Queen's favour. Elizabeth was still in conference with Drake and Burghley, while admiral and chief minister argued different sides of a worn-out question. War was inevitable.

The boy with the lute began to play again and Channon turned his back on Rothwell. How preferable it was to watch the boys who sat in the sun at the corner of the croquet lawn, and share vicariously in the love of two handsome young men. Rothwell lingered a while, then stalked away. His heavy tread suggested a fury kept tight-leashed. Channon glanced after him, pleased to be rid of his company. More than once, that privateer had openly savaged Mauricio before the Queen.

It was two days later when Antonio Diaz sought him out. Maids were lighting the candles about the great dining room. From the kitchens came the aroma of venison and boar while minstrels tuned before the revels began. Her Majesty was entertaining privately. In her place, Burghley and Walsingham would argue at the head of the table, oblivious to the flirtations around them.

Diaz stepped into the hall, unnoticed. Channon lounged by the hearth, drinking madeira and whiling away the time as he waited for Mauricio, who could by now stomach a little plain food. Diaz bowed with a rustle of velvet and lace, and one hand offered a slip of crisp yellow paper, sealed with wax into which was stamped a signet Channon knew.

'From Bernard Smythe,' Diaz murmured. 'And you owe me a five guinea bribe, Dermot. Cheap at twice the price!' He was a slender man in wine-red velvet: Channon's height, five years older, honey-skinned and handsome.

The wax split and Channon unfolded the paper. The message was written in a bold, ill-tutored hand. Smythe's origins were as humble as Copeland's but his scruples kept him honest. Channon read the lines and nodded.

'Master Copeland is at a tavern called The Lancastrian. Where shall I find it?'

'In Cheapside, up from the river,' Diaz told him. 'Ask anywhere along the waterfront, it is well known, a haunt of sailors and cut-throats. Copeland must be at home there.' He frowned inquiringly at Channon. 'What is to be done with him?'

'He will die,' Channon said mildly.

'Aye.' Diaz rubbed his chin with one fine-boned hand. 'I will do it, it you prefer. It need cost you no more than the guineas that bribed Smythe to betray him. I would be honoured.'

But Channon shook his head as he slipped the folded paper into his doublet. 'The duty is mine, Tonio. It is better done by my hand. Mauricio is blood of my blood.' He touched the spy's shoulder gratefully. 'I'll see to it tonight, before Copeland flies the coop again. Smythe is sure beyond all doubt that he is at this tavern?'

'He sold goods and chattels to him,' Diaz whispered as servants passed. 'He has dealt with Copeland before, and knows him well.'

'Then the rest is simple.' Channon smiled bitterly. 'I shall not forget your service.'

'As Don Mauricio shall recall these last few days!' Diaz melted away as laughter roared outside the wide, open doors.

The long, mauve twilight had faded before Channon left Hampton, alone in a coach. London seethed about him, fleeting images remembered forever while the greater picture would soon fade. The voice of the water carrier; the dirty face of the girl-child begging for farthings; the cries of strumpets touting for business from upstairs windows; the slender strength of the young acrobat performing tricks for a crowd that only pelted him with fruit.

The Lancastrian was not far from the river. Channon left the coach beside a reeking fishmarket, and the driver was too preoccupied with the whey-faced whores to see which way he walked as he hurried away. The crowd swallowed him. He passed by as an Irishman, a ne'er-do-well soldier of fortune who barely merited a glance as he moved from shadow to shadow.

A signboard creaked in the aromatic breeze off the river. High tide, the pitch and tar of old boats, yesterday's fish and last week's refuse sullied the wind. Channon's nose wrinkled. It took a month on land to teach a man to appreciate the freshness of the sea wind.

The tavern smelt of pastry, smoke and ale. He heard singing, or what would pass for it, ribaldry and coarseness. Under the din he paid for a tankard and inquired after Copeland as if he was on business. The taverner sent him up to a room at the back, far from the taproom. A room where a man's cries would go unheard, his pleas unanswered.

The stairs creaked; the passage was dark. Channon stopped at the door to listen and lifted his cloak over both shoulders to clear his callused, soldier's hands. The rapier rasped out of its scabbard, and then the door banged inward on protesting pivots.

A lamp burned on the table. Copeland sprawled on the bed in his hose and little else. The bedcurtains were askew and a brace of old wheellock pistols lay beside the lamp. Channon saw all this in the split second as the door burst inward, before Copeland was even aware of the intrusion.

He scrambled off the bed and dove for the pistols, but Channon was too fast. He snatched them up and levelled one on Copeland's large belly. He smelt the unmistakable odour of gunpowder and knew they were loaded without looking at Copeland's frightened face. The brewer was small, with brown hair beginning to thin, a flabby body and sparse beard. He backed against the wall, eyes flicking between the weapons in Channon's hands — Salamanca sword in the right, pistol in the left.

Channon kicked the door shut and leaned on it. He spoke in English, his tone as mild as the words were barbed. 'I hope I find you in a state of grace, for you'll die tonight.' He thrust the guns into his belt. 'But first you will tell me who paid you to murder Don Mauricio de Cervallo.'

Copeland shook his head. His gullet bobbed as he swallowed, his eyes bulged as Channon stepped closer. Perhaps he believed someone would intrude, fetch him to safety, for he never spoke a word, though a good deal of his blood spilled.

Shortly before dawn Channon left The Lancastrian with only the bittersweet flavour of vengeance to settle his temper. Walt Copeland took his master's secrets to the grave.

21

Chapter Two

Tara ran like the wind. She was four years old, bred to hunt and race rather than carry men into battle. Ten generations of the finest bloodstock culminated in her veins, and when she was mated to Connaught her colt would be worth a king's ransom.

Or a Queen's, thought William Armagh. He stood by the posterngate of Blackstead Manor, watching the big, red mare run between the river and woodland. Deer scattered into the trees as she thundered by. Her jockey had given the horse her head, and the earl grudgingly credited his youngest son. Robert was good for nothing but he rode well and Tara, who was still young and wary of riders, trusted the boy.

On the edge of the woods Robert turned her. She reared and sprang away again. Her hide shone in the bright May sun as Robert let her run for the joy of it. The earl stroked his bearded chin as he calculated the value of the mare and her progeny. The Armaghs were not wealthy, but they could be. Elizabeth had bought horses from the Blackstead stables twice before. A colt sired by the finest stud in the shire must catch the Queen's eye.

What price the fortunes of Irishmen into whose hands fate had placed an English earldom? William had ceased to wonder. Robert turned the mare again and lay flat over her withers as he headed down the meadow toward the village of Ralston. He rode as well as any man, but praise came grudgingly to William's mind, and never to his tongue.

Beyond the woods he saw the spire of Ralston church; beyond that, the Scar, a hill undermined by the diggings which cut copper out of the earth. The ground had subsided in an odd manner, changing the profile of the landscape.

The boy turned the mare once more but she had slowed and he did not urge her. He knew when enough work was enough. The magic of handling horses was God-given, William thought. It could not be taught, nor learned, but was born in a man. Tara would be in the stable soon, rubbed down, her nose in a pail of oats. She and the stud, Connaught, were the Armagh fortune. Horses were the life's blood of a country. Without them, a man ranged only as far as his own feet carried him, and his trade was limited to what he could carry on his back. It took an Irishman, William was sure, to appreciate this.

He turned as a rumble of wheels caught his ears. A smart coach in blue livery, drawn by matched bays, was approaching from the road northbound, from London. Curiosity stirred. Often there were dispatches from Master Tom Dandridge, whose dissolute nature and appetite for money made him the perfect hireling, and would one day be his undoing.

The vehicle would draw up to the manor's ivy-clad frontage. With a glance at his son and the mare, William hurried back to the servant's door and ducked in beneath the climbing roses. The house was dim and smelt of polish, pastry, tobacco. Old Edward had already opened to the visitor. He wore the Armaghs' emerald green livery, which honoured the family's heritage, and their bloody history.

William straightened his wind-tousled hair and glanced at his face in the hand mirror. A stern face, set in disapproving lines, with silvered hair and ice-blue eyes. He tidied the lace at his throat and smoothed his black velvet doublet as Edward approached.

'There is a gentleman to see you, my lord.'

The servant waited in the hall. The open door admitted the wind, and his blue-cloaked visitor was outlined against the light. The shape of a sword thrust back under the cloak. It was not Dandridge, but a slender Spaniard with the sharp, shrewd eyes of a spy. Armagh knew him, though not socially, and disliked him.

'Señor Diaz, an unexpected visit.' He offered his hand. 'What brings you here?' It could only be business.

Antonio Diaz took his hand briefly. His palm was cool, soft, the hand of a man who knew nothing of physical labour. He smiled politely and accorded the earl a stiff bow. 'I shall not trouble you, my lord, save to water my horses, if I may. I have dispatches for you.'

'From Master Dandridge?' Armagh's pale eyes lit.

The Spaniard looked sidelong at him. 'You have the Irishman's habit of meddling in affairs which are not your concern. One day the English will lop every Irish head for it.'

'An unfortunate day for your King if they do,' Armagh retorted. 'You imagine Spain can challenge England without the freedom of Irish ports, the succour of men who share your Church?'

With a fat chuckle Diaz turned back to the coach. 'I am but a humble messenger.'

23

'Humble spy,' Armagh corrected. He followed Diaz into the warmth of sunlight channelled by Blackstead's gabled wings. 'Who buys your wine and women this year, Diaz? Philip? Or do you spy for Frobisher and Drake?'

Diaz's eyes hardened, his mouth tightened. 'I am a lapdog, but a loyal one, in the employ of a countryman.' He leaned into the coach, produced two sealed letters and slapped them angrily into the earl's hand.

The first seal stamped into the scarlet wax was the Cervallo device, a falcon in whose talons writhed two serpents... a letter from Don Mauricio. William's old friend wrote often, sometimes complaining bitterly of his treatment — he would say, persecution — at the hands of the privateers who were publicly denounced, privately celebrated.

'The other letter?' Armagh examined the second dispatch. 'Ah, Dandridge's signet.'

'Matters of meddling and mayhem,' Diaz said acidly. 'With your leave, my Lord, I'll water my nags and go. I am bound for York. The *Alcanzar* is on the river there.'

'She is a warship,' Armagh said pointedly.

'Under the command of Capitan Miguel Vasca.' Diaz's eyes glittered with mischief which annoyed Armagh. 'She came up the Humber for repairs after she was fired on by a privateer.' He glanced at Dandridge's letter.

The earl stepped back into the house as Diaz's coachman led the nags to the trough by the shadowed west wall. The spy strolled away, moving like a dancer, a swordsman. In his hands, Armagh knew, the rapier was a lethal instrument. The oiled oak door latched, and he hurried to his study for a dirk to split the wax.

He had not seen his son by the west gable. Robert leaned on the red bricking while Tara drank at the trough. Diaz smiled at the boy's windblown appearance: brown hose, white linen shirt, an Irishman's fair complexion and rich auburn hair. 'Good day, Robin. Your father is in an evil mood.' He spoke in his native Castilian, always fascinated when the young man responded in the same tongue, almost without accent. Despite his tousled looks, Robin Armagh was a scholar.

The remark brought a rueful smile to the boy's smooth face. 'When was my father ever in better cheer?' The Spanish language left his tongue easily. 'Is there news?'

'Dispatches from the Ambassador and that fool Dandridge.' Diaz watched the horses drink. Tara nuzzled her jockey's shoulder until Robin stroked her velvet muzzle. 'You would do well to caution the earl. If he meddles in matters which are none of his concern he might easily come to grief.'

The boy's green eyes widened. 'Caution him? I would sooner leap naked into a nettlebed! I can do no right by my father. If I tell the truth, I no longer try.'

The words were regretful and Diaz saw Robin's face darken. The coach's high wheels rumbled over the raked gravel as the vehicle turned, and the driver climbed back to his perch. For some time Diaz studied the boy. He knew two of the other Armagh heirs by sight. John and Richard were at Court; they were not much like this one, and of that Diaz approved.

He offered his hand in farewell. 'If you cannot caution your father, stand ready to flee. Often, they empty the whole nest when they take the eagle.' He dropped his voice. 'If your father thinks to run with the hare and hunt with the hounds, to give Elizabeth lip service and Philip his aid out of loyalty to his Catholic fathers, he could end as the hare, and the hounds will tear out his throat.'

He said no more, and left Robin blinking after him as the coach rolled out and the horses set a good pace for York. Who knew what was in the earl's mind? Little ever passed his lips, least of all in the presence of the son he despised.

The warning of danger quickened Robin's pulse as he stabled the mare and rubbed her down. She had run well, and he told her so as he groomed her. She was dozing when he left. He slipped quietly into the house and listened for his father's voice.

He was upstairs, punishing some unfortunate maid with harsh words and ill temper. The door to his study was ajar, inviting intrusion. Spying? Robin thought of Diaz's warnings.

The dispatches lay on the writing desk beneath an old dirk. The uppermost was from the Ambassador, Don Mauricio de Cervallo, and written in English, in his own hand:

My dearest William,

    I find myself once more presuming upon your generosity, of necessity. This shambles will be the end of me! Not content to lambast me, my enemies and, I imagine, the enemies of Spain, have taken sterner measures. There was poison for me two days ago and I am still weak, in mind and body both. I am under orders, a royal decree!, to vacate my apartments at Hampton and recuperate elsewhere. When last we supped you extended invitations to return to Blackstead upon my pleasure, and I would avail myself of this kindness. I send this letter with a messenger, and will be arriving soon after, with your agreement. Blackstead beckons with its peace and the succour of a Catholic house. 'Til we sup once more, William,

Vaya con Dios,
     your servant,
     Mauricio de Cervallo

How long had the two been nearer brothers than friends? Robin was unsurprised by the letter's affection. Blackstead was an Irish house. Father Michael Doughty heard confession and said mass in the Lady Chapel in the east wing. A Spaniard would be at comfort here as nowhere else in the shire.

The second letter was from Dandridge, written in the man's spidery script, which suggested haste and stealth:

My Lord of Blackstead,
     In the matter of Rothwell, I bid you, say little and await Her Majesty's pleasure. The Spanish Ambassador has been most outspoken, and even Admiral Drake was compelled to yield before him in this instance. To invest in a privateer is, these days, a delicate affair. We must nurture the face we show Spain. Rothwell's ships and mercenary soldiers are judged fine beyond doubt, but there is dissent at Court. Rothwell struck unfortunate prey upon his last voyage. It was he who harassed the *Alcanzar*, and Captain Miguel Vasca wrote to Her Majesty, he recognised Rothwell's ship, *Rosamund*. The Queen is his investor, you may be sure, but there remains the concern of our relations with the Catholic Empire. Rothwell may end on the scaffold without need of your involvement. Let vengeance be furthered without blood upon your own hands, I pray, if only in my Lady Catherine's dear memory. As to the matter of —

'Robert!' The study door slammed opened and the letter was torn from Robin's hand. 'You are a spy as well as a wastrel, are you? As I have long suspected!' The letters were tossed onto the desk and cupped palms boxed the boy's ears.

He cried out as pain pierced both eardrums. Dizziness shocked him and he sagged to his knees. 'Father —'

'Silence, from you, boy! There'll be no lies.' Armagh's open hand smacked one smooth cheek, hard enough to rattle Robin's teeth. 'Now, get you from my sight, and if I see you before morning I shall surely lay the whip across your back. Get out!'

He went, bitter and hurting, hands cupped to his head as his ears ached. He stumbled under the climbing roses, for the hundredth time fleeing from the anger and hate. All love had died. He had ceased to look for affection years before and would have been content with tolerance, but even that was denied him. Bitterness warred with grief, and won, but it was an old bitterness. Its edges were dulled.

When the pain in his ears was only a nagging throb he went out to run over the same course as the mare had raced. He punished his body till exhaustion brought him an hour's escape into oblivion. Inside the walls of Blackstead, for Robin Armagh, there was little more.

Behind him, the old man brooded in the hallway. Anger diminished as he read Dandridge's letter again. Sir Charles Rothwell lived at the Queen's pleasure and might as easily die at her pleasure. The promise of vengeance was consuming.

He gazed across the hall at the portrait which hung below the staircase. The woman's face was serene; a faint smile lifted her beautiful mouth. Catherine Armagh had been just twenty when it was painted. Ten years later she was still beautiful at an age when her peers were growing feeble. The portrait was twenty years old, painted before Robert was even conceived.

Catherine's green eyes, her nose, her lush, sensual mouth, were born again in Robin. To look into the boy's face was William's agony. But if the lad had done much to earn his father's anger, it was Rothwell who bore the brunt of the fury, and it would be Rothwell who bore the vengeance, when old accounts were settled at last.

Chapter Three

The lush English hills slipped by the coach windows but with the fate of Captain Rothwell undecided Dermot Channon's thoughts remained at Hampton Court. Elizabeth was furious, and so was Drake. Past his prime, stout but still arresting, the 'master thief of the unknown world' echoed the angry words of Frobisher and Hatton. Against all this Don Mauricio could do nothing save reiterate the unwritten laws of the sea. Laws which judged Rothwell a pirate.

But if Rothwell was a pirate, what of Drake? So Drake defended Rothwell, and the arguments were transparent and endless. Channon listened for hours as Mauricio debated with them under the Queen's hawkish eyes. Mauricio was the worse for it, while Rothwell was still at liberty.

The old man seemed to fail before Channon's eyes now. He had always been frail but his health had been sound enough for him to be sent to England again. Every man knew it must come to war. The only questions left were when, where, how. These were matters for statesmen, not soldiers. Channon was content to listen while admirals and ministers squabbled.

The Spanish intervention in Ireland had the English fretted. If Ireland took Philip's part, a war with the Catholic Empire might spell disaster. Channon could hardly have cared less who fought, and why, or where. Spain and Ireland were of the same coin in his accounting. The blood of both lands ran rich in his veins.

He liked Drake. Sir Francis was more than twice his age and the brilliant red hair had begun to fade as the stocky figure thickened about the middle, but the bold green eyes were as sharp as ever. Drake was a pirate, and he did not care who knew it. Before the Queen, ministers, admirals and the law, he argued for Rothwell; but it was himself he defended. What Rothwell did, so did Drake — albeit with prudence, and not so foolishly close to home.

He had met Channon's eyes levelly, and the admission was made, one soldier to another. Channon acknowledged with a bow and those green eyes glittered with unholy mischief. Eyes which had seen sighs unimaginable to the average man. Sights Channon also had seen, despite his youth. The mercenary trade took a boy far afield, made a man of him quickly. If he survived his baptism at all.

Vera Cruz. Suchetepec. Guayaquil. To the common man in London and Seville they were exotic names upon a pilot's chart. To Channon they were other worlds, often beautiful, sometimes terrible. Realms where he had sought his fortune after the *tuatha* that should have been his birthright was snatched away, late one bloody summer afternoon not long before his fifteenth birthday.

He remembered the wind in the heather as he lay hiding and watched the English troops from a distance. The sun gleamed on the polished steel of body armour and helmets. The general rode a tall, rawboned warhorse. He led soldiers who came to steal and slaughter, and left behind only ruins. All at once, a heritage that had seemed immutable was gone.

The battle was repeated on other Irish estates, the murder of the ricon's family, the seizure of land that would have been his son's. William of Normandy sent the first soldiers, centuries before; the Irish earls had been French or traitors since that day.

Like Mauricio's friend, William Armagh. The Armaghs had fought alongside the Norman troops and kept their lands. As a boy, Channon was taught to despise traitors. As a man, a soldier, he understood. If his father had bent his stiff neck before an English flag he would have lived, his daughters would not have been raped, his sons would not have been butchered. He might have defeated the English by deception. Lip service to the Queen... loyalty to his heritage.

The old fool fought, and a whole clan paid the price. The memories haunted Channon's dreams. His mother fled back to Spain, to the security of her family, and took Dermot with her. He recalled the sea wind, the ship, and knifing grief; later, his education in the arts of a foreign land, a new language, and new allegiance. He knelt before the colours of Philip II, promised loyalty, even life.

But the Cervallos provided no financial support. Their Irish cousin inherited their fierce honour, but for young Dermot Channon the only future was in the trade he had learned as a boy.

Soldiering came easily. His earliest memories were of watching his brothers practise, the ring of swords, mist and soft rain. Little love for anything English stirred in him, but he had learned to respect Englishmen. They were the best and worst of men, often at the same time. Scheming and conniving on one hand, brave and indomitable on the other.

His thoughts returned to Drake, to the thick Devon accent, the way the green cat's eyes lit as *El Draque* smelt a fight, the white-knuckled grip upon the hilt of the admiral's sword. Sir Francis was under average height and in his forties now, but no one underestimated him, at sea or at Court. When he spoke, Elizabeth listened as intently as she heard Hawkins, Frobisher, the men who had looted Spanish fleets out of the Americas to fill her treasury.

The image of Drake, rigged for a battle of words, made Channon smile in spite of his concern for Mauricio. Mauricio was no match for such men. Philip should not have sent him. He was alone in a den of lions, and when his words proved too keen, his enemies had other weapons.

It was the very reason for Channon's presence here. As the Ambassador's personal guard, the young Spaniard whose name and looks were so Irish was free to move as he would at Hampton, take liberties and be outrageous — the only part of the employment he enjoyed. Lounging in velvet and lace while his kinsman was verbally flayed had soon palled.

He rolled to the sway of the coach and watched Mauricio drowse. Four weeks before, the *San Lorenzo* shipped home from a voyage in hazardous waters. Dermot Channon was aboard: six feet tall, with brown eyes bestowed by his Spanish blood and milky skin imparted by the Irish. Channon, the soldier, the mercenary, who had served with the Spanish privateers and come home with a whole skin.

Seville was bright, his welcome was warm, yet he was at sea again in days and his feet touched English soil for the first time in his life. Mauricio's coach met the ship and, late that afternoon, when April sunlight slanted through leaded windows and cast mosaics across floors worn smooth by untold knees, Channon himself knelt as the English Queen swept by.

Her tiny body was dwarfed by its formal gown. Enormous panniers thrust out her hips; above the ruffled bodice her face was chalk white, her hair the colour of flame. When she laughed she held a fan to her mouth, for her teeth were rotten. This was usual, and Channon attached no importance to it. Elizabeth was not young, and age carried many burdens.

Age did not concern him. He had no reason to believe he would live long enough to bear those burdens. The soldier's trade was too dangerous; already Channon had his share of scars.

Some called Elizabeth beautiful, but if she were, the beauty emanated from the force of her personality. The power of a monarch born. Channon had never been closer to her than a dozen yards. He was presented as Mauricio's kinsman and personal guard, and she nodded without even looking at him. One more Spaniard, or Irishman, was of no interest.

The breeze was chill after Seville's warmth and Mauricio's bones ached. He dozed, wrapped in a cloak, pale as death. The lines were etched deeply into his face and his hair was white of a sudden. Even Elizabeth had seen his deterioration. The order to leave at once, rest and recover, was not lightly made.

Recover, and return to the lion's den? Channon frowned gravely at his uncle's wan face. Every day he jousted with the likes of Drake, despite Channon's regard for the 'master thief', stripped a week from Mauricio's life. A month on a country estate would bolster his flagging health. The companionship of an old friend would put spirit back into Mauricio. But to Channon the prospect of languishing on an English estate was appalling. He chafed at the idleness and longed to leave as his hands and muscles softened, day by day. The sea beckoned. Philip was building a fleet against the hour when he would move against the woman they called 'the Usurper'. Every soldier would be employed.

His half-closed eyes watched the curve of a river go by. He picked out the landmarks Mauricio had described, a spire, a crooked hill, pointing the way to Blackstead.

He knew the Armaghs by reputation. The earl was hardly English, his pedigree was as Irish as Channon's own. The name of Armagh told its own story. The Normans marched in and the choice was bitter: fight and die, or kneel before the English banner. Some Armagh, five centuries past, bent his knee and the earldom was created.

Weeks of tranquillity loomed like thunderheads and Channon took refuge in wilfulness. He would find a comely maid at Blackstead — perhaps several. Or a young groom with velvet skin and a sensual heart. He hid a smile as he saw the church spire. Blackstead lay over the next hill.

Mauricio and William Armagh would closet together, talking endlessly of war, Queen and Court, scandal and gossip, never realising that a juicy scandal was under their noses.

Was there a boy at Blackstead with yellow hair and a warm heart?

Channon was content to dupe his elders shamelessly. The old men, staunchly Catholic, would suffer fits if they noticed a young man's pranks, but a little discretion went a long way. So, a boy, Channon thought, courting lasciviousness to banish boredom.

Long months at sea and in the fetid jungles of the Indies taught a man how satisfying were the arms of a comrade. How much simple comfort was to be found in the loving arms of a man, a male, who understood what it was to be a man and in need of relief, solace, pleasure!

One brow arched, Channon watched Mauricio's fitful dozing. How much did he know? He was no soldier, the furthest he had ever travelled was England and France. What could he possibly know of the ways of soldiers? And of his Irish kinsman. What would he make of the knowledge that his nephew was godless and sodded. Channon bit back a wry chuckle as he recalled the sermons of churchmen, equally sodded, perhaps a little less godless. Mauricio was a faithful son of Rome; better that he never learn of his kinsman's wilful heart.

The coach creaked as the horses threw their weight into the traces and pulled hard up the rise. Channon stirred and Mauricio blinked awake with a start as the vehicle tilted.

'Where are we, Dermot?'

'I saw the river moments ago,' Channon told him. 'Blackstead lies a mile ahead by road. Much less as a bird flies. How are you, Mauricio?'

'Well enough to put on a brave face... but relishing the promise of a soft bed.' Mauricio folded the cloak and stretched his aching limbs. 'I'm too old for this. I shall be sent home soon. I have failed in my office, but I long for home. This duty will kill me if the privateers do not murder me first.'

'Copeland paid that debt with his life,' Channon murmured. 'Still, there is his master to be dealt with. You have your suspicions.'

Mauricio shrugged. 'I offended so many of them, but I find it hard to believe men like Frobisher or *El Draque* would stoop so low as to meddle with an old man's sleeping cup.'

'And Rothwell?' Channon asked. 'You demanded his neck, and even Drake could not argue.'

'Rothwell.' Mauricio closed his eyes as the coach rounded a bed, the approach to the gates of Blackstead. 'I could easily believe it was Rothwell, but before I dare speak a word I must have proof, or I shall be accused of slander.'

'I asked Tonio Diaz to look into the matter.'

'Diaz is still in York.'

'And headed for London soon aboard some ship or other.' Channon looked out, up the road. 'You had no regard for Rothwell even before he fired on the *Alcanzar*.'

'The man has been a thorn in my side for years,' Mauricio admitted. 'Not that he has done the Cervallos any injury, but I share William Armagh's pain.'

Channon frowned at him. 'There was some struggle between Rothwell and Armagh? I know nothing of that.'

'Nor should you!' Mauricio smiled. 'You were a boy at the time. It is ten years now that Catherine has been in her grave.' He looked out toward the gates as the driver called to the horses and the coach slowed. 'There is a portrait, painted when she was in the full bloom of beauty. You'll see it soon enough. That beauty endured longer than usual, and at last was Lady Catherine's undoing.' His face clouded. 'Rothwell is powerful. He must have what he wants. Denied, he is enraged. Time has mellowed him, but then he was young. Foolish.'

'Rothwell had a hand in Lady Catherine's undoing?' Channon's frown deepened.

'Her death,' Mauricio corrected bluntly. 'If you call a blow that snapped her neck like a twig "having a hand in it". He hit her only once, in a fury beyond reason. A servant saw it. William and his older sons were absent. She simply fell to the floor and she was dead. A tiny, fragile woman, like a child in her frail beauty. Rothwell wanted her and she refused him. Sir Charles is unaccustomed to being denied.'

Channon recoiled. 'There must have been a reckoning.'

'Rothwell swore she tripped over a rug, struck her head and broke her neck.' Mauricio rubbed his palms together thoughtfully. 'A physician examined her and Rothwell's story was accepted. But the physician was of a sudden blessed with wealth he could not conceal or explain; and the little maid, Jane, who saw Catherine fall, was just as suddenly dead.' Mauricio's brows rose. 'There was nothing to prove Rothwell's hand in any of it, and he is too powerful to risk making slanderous accusations.'

'One could die for them,' Channon said quietly. 'There is always the direct recourse.' He made a small throat-cutting gesture with one finger. 'An assassin is as sure as the law and twice as swift. Surely

Armagh is not so bound by scruples that he let his wife's murderer go free when a dirk would even accounts!'

'William has scruples, but not that kind. It is not for want of courage that Rothwell is alive and at liberty. The man is surrounded by an army of lackeys and mercenaries. He has been at sea constantly for most of the last decade.'

'And now,' Channon mused, 'he passes his days at Hampton, waiting to be judged on the small matter of the *Alcanzar*.' He stirred as the coach rolled through the gates. 'I asked Diaz to send word of who was killed aboard her. I know many of Vasca's lads. I shall grieve even for strangers, but if old comrades have been wantonly killed I may attend to Rothwell's fortunes personally.'

Mauricio leaned over to clasp Channon's sinewy forearm. 'Have sense, boy! Look to your own fortunes — the English would cut off your head.'

The coach drew to a halt on the raked gravel and Channon held the door for him. The Armagh house was very old but in excellent repair. He saw ivy and climbing roses, leaded windows, roofing slates, gables, polished woodwork. A stone horsetrough stood in the shadows and clipped yew hedges girdled the rose gardens. This was the heart of an English earldom that had found its way, by quirks of death and marriage, into the hands of Irishmen. Channon chuckled wickedly.

The breeze smelt of hay and the river. He took a breath as an old servant came out for the bags. Mauricio addressed him by name, spoke affectionately to him. 'Where is the earl? I had hoped he might greet us.'

'He returns later, sir.' The servant struggled with the valises. Channon's large brown hands took them, and he smiled his gratitude. 'My Lord went to the village to see about blacksmithing.'

A bag in either hand, Channon went ahead into the house. The portrait of the woman commanded the eye at once, and he stood at the foot of the wide staircase, looking into her green, slanted eyes. It was easy to see what a man like Rothwell might desire so keenly that denial enraged him.

'Your rooms are this way, sir.' The servant went on up the stairs ahead of Mauricio while Channon was still held captive by the portrait.

So Rothwell had lusted for Armagh's lovely wife, and killed her with a single blow. So frail was the body of a woman, Channon thought. So fragile, he had hardly dared hold the few he had ever touched. Had Rothwell killed her without intending to, in the heat of his anger?

But Channon rejected that. A man did not strike a woman such as Catherine Armagh. The intention to hurt was damning enough. Rothwell had struck her with the full force of his arm. Fury seethed under Channon's heart as he studied the portrait. If Rothwell was responsible for the deaths of his friends aboard Vasca's ship, it would be a pleasure to make his own accounting, and Armagh's at the same stroke.

Chapter Four

At eighteen Robert Armagh was already disgraced, and the judgement seemed harsher still since his was an 'undesirable' family to begin with. The estates passed to Blackstead's Irish cousins one bloody day in 1455. York met Lancaster; father, sons and brothers were slaughtered at Saint Alban's, leaving one male heir. A black Irish ram who had knelt before the Norman conqueror.

The name of Armagh was ill fitting to Courtly ears, and the disgrace of Blackstead's youngest was new, raw, just three years past. Robin was chastened, disciplined by father, priests, tutors, but the earl still simmered with anger at the sight of him. The sin was irredeemable.

Banished to study and chapel, Robin spent the years with books and prayer, nourishing his mind, purging his soul. At first he worked resentfully but at last he settled, for it was not the education that chafed him, but confinement. Others his age were at war, at sea, while he was shut away with Master Grey, who crammed his memory with Latin and Greek, geography, history and literature.

Every family must have a scholar, Robin agreed. But why not pale, sickly John? Why not quick, clever Hal? John had been sent to Court to lounge decorously in doublet and hose, looking fair and frail, while Hal had left a year before with Hawkins, on a voyage to the New World. There was Richard, too, the eldest, the apple of William Armagh's eye, already a knight while the cosseted last-born, Robin, had been intended for the priesthood.

A breath of summer blew over Blackstead. May was warm, the woods were lush. London lay a day's ride south, and the quiet was at odds with the tumult of the city streets.

Hawkins lingered in the Americas but Drake, Frobisher and Raleigh were back. And Martin Frobisher in particular had news that boded ill for the flimsy veil of peace separating England and Spain. Spanish warships had sunk Her Majesty's ship *Argent*, a week's voyage off the Lizard, so he claimed. The Spanish Ambassador denied it, but Frobisher was adamant. And Elizabeth was furious.

The Ambassador was an intelligent man, but he was not young and Robin knew he was ailing. Don Mauricio spoke softly, careful with his words lest he anger the fearsome woman some still called the Virgin Queen. Annoyed, she was dangerous; angry, she could be lethal. Beneath the platitudes, Elizabeth and Philip were armed and wary. Mauricio de Cervallo was a token acknowledgment of England's precarious kinship with Spain.

For Robin, this talk of great nations and power was engrossing. In three years he had become fluent in four languages and had the skills not merely to read ocean charts, but to make them. To study cartography was the ultimate folly for one who had seen the sea only once, but it was a welcome change from the burden of mathematics and prayer.

But lately his fluency in Spanish and his knowledge of ocean charts had borne fruit. Robin was able to follow the chatter of sailors in the street, and from their unguarded talk often learned more than Hampton's peacocks learned from diplomatic dispatches.

Blackstead was both home and prison. As a boy intended for the Church he had been safeguarded from the world; later, he was confined on the estate of necessity. The black sheep must be hidden, lest his face be seen and people remember. The priesthood rejected him, and William would allow no opportunity for further disgrace. Robin found the mantle of the scholar hastily hung about his young shoulders. Only in the months of summer did Master Grey return to Lincoln for his own recreation, leaving the student at liberty.

The house stood beside the broad, gentle river that curved through woods where Hal and Richard would hunt when they were at home. Their visits were rare now. Hal would only return when Hawkins shipped back, and Richard served the Admiralty.

Robin nursed a great envy of his brothers, but it was a half-formed feeling. Blackstead was the only world he knew. His companions were tutors and servants. What did he really know of the world that began outside the walls of the estate? Often he perched on that wall and his eyes were drawn to the east, where the sea lay far off beyond the mud flats, while he pictured London, the grey, formless city of his imagination.

Soon he would leave. He was almost fully grown and his education was complete. Master Grey had rapped his knuckles frequently to spur him, but not lately. The lessons merely polished his arts. His voice was a man's, deeper with every season, and his body had been hardened by riding and running, which were his only release. It was almost time to go.

The earl would scarcely notice that the black sheep had gone. It was years since he had noticed Robin, save to be vexed over the cost of clothes to be replaced as he grew. William had more important things on his mind.

First, the meddler, Dandridge. He was a secretary to some minister at Hampton and ran errands like a lackey. Then, the Spanish Ambassador, who was at Blackstead again. Spanish visitors were common. A youth in disgrace, Robin was ignored, but from the foreigners' talk he gleaned an insight into the world outside his prison.

He had seen the coach arrive that morning as he escaped from the house and lost himself in the water meadow where he exercised Tara. The vehicle was elegant, the horses fine. Two men alighted, and though Robin knew the Ambassador at once he did not recognise the other. A secretary or valet? Wealthy men hardly lifted a finger when they had scullions to pick up every dropped kerchief, write every letter.

Summer had not yet begun but the sky was clear. Master Grey was gone and Robin was free. Days would pass in which he did not speak to a soul, but he had no complaint. Solitude was his escape, for it loosed his imagination, which would take him anywhere.

He sat on the wall, gazing at the hills as afternoon warmed. Half-made plans charted his future. With his gift for cartography he could find work in Plymouth, Southampton, even London, where the name of Armagh simply meant an Irishman far from home. He had his youth and strength; he had never been ill, save for a brush with the pox that left no scarring, and had never suffered an accident, since a fall from the hayloft when he was twelve. Playing with Hal, he lost his footing and almost broke his neck. He lay abed for a week, hovering between life and death. His father had been at the bedside... the old man was fond of him then. All that changed later.

Afternoon had grown old and he slid to the ground. His hose was soiled, his shirt rumpled. They would say he looked like a ragamuffin but Robin had stopped listening, or caring. The way back took him along the river. Swans paraded their cygnets, shapeless balls of grey fluff soon to be transformed into beauty. He watched them for a time before he walked up from the wide, sluggish river.

A path led through the yew hedges marking the perimeter of the gardens. It was still, the sun had just gone, the air was warm and heavy with the scent of roses. The gardens were his favourite place, so private that his dreams were unfettered. Tall yews shut out the wind and in their shelter rare blooms throve. Robin tarried, knelt on the tiny moss lawn and lifted his face to the sky.

Too late, he realised he was not alone. A quiet footstep alerted him and he blinked up into the amused face of a man a few years his elder. The face was handsome, with deep brown eyes and milky skin at odds with the severe Spanish dress. His hair was almost the same shade as his eyes, reminding Robin of the brown velvet of a doublet. Absurdly, his fingers wanted to touch, so see if it had the same softness.

The stranger's physique was powerful. His legs were muscular, in beautiful hose, his shoulders were broad. White lace framed his jaw and emphasised the breadth of his chest the garb of Spanish nobility. Yet he did not look at all Spanish. Fascination bound Robin's eyes to the man, and he jolted back to the present as the stranger gave a low chuckle.

'What have we here?' His accent was very pure, the finest Castilian, Seville or Madrid. 'A kitten, lost from someone's lap! And a pretty kitten. Whose could you be?'

Robin spoke without thinking. The language came as naturally as his native English. 'I am my own, sir. I belong to no one.'

The stranger was taken aback. 'You speak Spanish! No matter. Many speak it. It is an elegant tongue. A stray kitten, are you, no home, no one's warm lap to sit upon?'

'This is my home, sir.' Robin was deeply disquieted by the man's slow, thorough appraisal. The brown eyes covered his body from face to feet. He knew what they would see. Red hair, a round, impish face, rumpled clothes. 'Am I at fault?'

'Not unless the master comes upon you, loafing among the roses.' The Spaniard laughed softly. 'I shall say I detained you. Comely lad, turn your head this way. And again.' One hand, incongruously leathery, tilted Robin's chin this way and that. 'There is no one to stroke you, kitten?'

'My name is Robin.' He got to his feet, flustered and ill at ease. 'Stroke me? I am not a little cat, as well you know.'

'Yet you would enjoy to be handled as one.' The Spaniard smiled invitingly. 'Touched softly, until you purr. When your work is done I'll look for you, if you wish. This place is bleak. There was no welcome in it before you appeared.' The brown eyes teased gently, sparkled with easy good humour. 'Well, Robin, speak up. Where lies your heart? I am gentle and not ungenerous with those who please me.'

In the space of a heartbeat Robin realised what was being offered and his face flushed. It was an invitation to pleasure. To sin. His body was cold for a second, then blazed with heat, a heady mix of embarrassment, confusion, fear. The mesmerising eyes held him captive, chased every thought from his mind. To lie with a man!

What Robin knew of love was scant. Sonnets, myths. What he knew of love between men was a single word. *Sodomy*. It was the worst of all sensual sins, so he had learned, yet this Spaniard with the face of a lover was smiling at him, amused, inviting, as if it was the most natural act.

'I cannot,' he stammered. Crimson, breathless, he wanted only to take to his heels.

The Spaniard shrugged affably. 'There are maids aplenty to cosset you, no doubt. You've no taste for the other? So be it, kitten... but what a shame. This place is bleak again. I thought to pass the time with pleasure.' His smile was regretful now. 'Be off, before your master finds you idle and sets about you with a stick. I shouldn't relish your pain on my conscience, m'dear.'

At a loss for words in both languages Robin fled, into the house, up the creaking stairs and into the haven of his room. The door slammed, latched, and only then did he stop to breathe. Pass the time sweetly? It seemed a contradiction. He flopped onto the bed, heart still hammering. Two men, loving?

Yet everyone knew the tales of Father Joseph and Father Angelo and the choristers, beautiful lads whose hearts were warm, and who were adored. The scandal was gossip fodder for months. The boys never denied it; the priests were defrocked, banished, but Peter and Edward went with them.

Loving? The proposition was so unexpected, Robin could barely credit what had been offered. He had been invited to pleasure. A casual kind of pleasure. Would he warm the sheets of a Spaniard for a night or two, like a maid chosen for sport?

It was three years he had last been desired. One single night was his shame, and there had been no pleasure to earn the disgrace. Since then he had been attended by servants of his father's age, and the needs of his body were left to his own hand. He knew how to ease himself so as to sleep; he confessed the sin, did penance and sinned again. Desire was no stranger. Dreaming, he saw the faces of women, imagine their bodies and woke in discomfort. Women were a mystery, swathed in skirts, alluring and forbidden.

And men? It was said to be evil for men to bed together, though it was also evil to bed with women unless both lovers were wed; yet adulterers abounded, even the Queen, whose Robert Dudley was her husband in all but the law. Would Joseph and Angelo defy God, consign the souls of boys they adored to damnation?

Robin mulled it over with feverish rationale. He had wondered about the priests and their boys. How was it done, how did it feel to share carnal embraces with a male? His body heated, wilful, disturbing. He had real no idea what the act could be, save that one could be stroked.

The Spaniard's invitation was a blow under the breastbone. Was this the man's intent? Pleasure, the companionship of a shared bed? It was not what Robin had dreamed of love, yet he felt the stab of a hunger he had never recognised before.

He would soon be late. His father expected him to be punctual and presentable before Don Mauricio. Robin stripped, washed in cold water, fetched fresh hose and doublet and hastily dressed. The doublet and hose were green, matching his eyes, though he had never noticed. The clothes were those outgrown by Hal and Richard, costly and well mended.

On the stairs he felt a thrill of terror. The Spaniard would look upon him with lover's eyes Robin could not forget, and he would realise the mistake he had made. He had enticed a boy to bed and to sin... had he known the 'kitten' was the earl's son, he would never have spoken.

Perversely, even in his confusion, Robin gave thanks for the man's ignorance. To be desired was pleasurable in itself, flattering, arousing of a sweet ache in the belly. Robin summoned his courage.

They were in the dining hall. He heard the earl, Don Mauricio, servants, and the soft, deep voice of the amorous stranger. They spoke heatedly of Frobisher, the sinking of the *Argent*. Trouble was brewing, Don Mauricio warned; it would be war. For the first time in years Robin was too preoccupied to care. He came to rest at the open door in the long wood-panelled hall and stood silently until his father thought to perform his introduction.

'Ah, there you are, rascal.' Armagh was indifferent. 'Mauricio, you know my youngest boy. Robert, the gentleman on my right is Dermot Channon, a military officer of some considerable reputation in King Philip's service.'

Robin bowed, produced a smile for the Ambassador, then turned his attention to the soldier.

Channon had turned slightly from him, a glass of madeira in his hand as he looked through the open windows, watching doves courting on the lawn. He turned back slowly, as if he must compose his expression. His face was remote now. The look of the lover had vanished completely. Only a faint, rueful gleam in the brown eyes betrayed him. Robin held his breath.

'Good evening, Master Armagh,' Channon said softly, in his richly accented English. 'It is a... pleasure to make your acquaintance, sir.'

Chapter Five

I t was the kind of mistake anyone could make. The kind that might get a man killed. Channon's only blessing in the moments after the earl introduced his son was that he had never in his life blushed, and his cheeks did not betray him tonight.

The delightful youth who had knelt in the garden, tousled, rumpled, was still before him. The curls were combed, the hose fresh, the doublet immaculate, but the wide eyes and strange beauty were unchanged. In velvet or tatters, it was Robin Armagh himself who would woo and seduce.

The older men were engrossed in conversation. Robin hovered by the hearth, discomfited, stealing glances at Channon then quickly looking away. Was he affronted? But Robin seemed more flustered than offended, and Channon offered a prayer of thanks.

He ambushed the young man at the window and held out a pewter goblet of madeira. 'Take a cup from me, and my apologies. Had I known who you were...' His smile was hardly contrite. 'I thought you a stable lad and wished to court you for pleasure.' Colour flushed Robin's high cheekbones. Channon disguised a smile with his cup. 'I am repentant,' he lied.

'And I bear no grudges,' Robin whispered. 'I was flattered. It was — is a rare compliment.' The lamplight shone full in his face as he looked up. 'To be desired.'

Glib remarks died on Channon's tongue as the light caught Robin's face. A seraph, an angel? Regret coiled through his belly and he sighed over all that was not to be. 'Had you only been a stable lad! 'Tis no matter, as long as you are not offended. I meant you no insult.'

'I know.' Robin sipped his wine. His blush clearly embarrassed him, and the flush deepened. Channon was charmed. 'My father said you are a Spanish soldier, yet called you by an Irish name. You dress as a Spaniard, and we spoke that language in the garden.'

The question struck to the heart of the enigma. Often, Channon gulled men with tall stories, but for Robin there would be the truth. He owed the youth no less after the evening's blunder. The thought of blatantly propositioning an earl's son could make even Channon's fair skin smart. Yet, if Robin had been a stable lad, what nights there would have been. The fantasy taunted him.

'I am half a Spaniard,' he confessed as the servants worked at the table. 'Or half an Irishman, if you prefer. My father was an Irish ricon. His *tuatha* was smashed by the English, but in his youth he furthered his fortunes with a Catholic marriage. My mother, Domenica, was Mauricio's sister. Aye, Robin, the Ambassador is my uncle. I left Ireland for Seville, and then for the sea.'

'In command of a ship?' Robin asked eagerly.

But Channon shook his head. 'A captain of fighting men, though I've fought on many a ship and may soon be master of my own. War stinks in the wind, as you've heard.' He gave the old men a hard look. By the fire, they were drinking deep, oblivious to the young people.

Channon sipped the fine madeira and reappraised his companion as Robin frowned. 'What troubles you?'

'Your allegiance is to Spain,' Robin observed.

'Perhaps.' Channon shrugged. 'Or is my allegiance to myself? The English murdered my family, but my father was fool enough to fight a battle he could not win, and threw away my inheritance. The Cervallos gave me a home, but all I have, I earned with these two hands. Spain gave me one gift: the chance to fight. Still, it is what I was trained for. I was younger than you when the soldiers came to my home, and blood ran like water.'

'I read of it.' Robin turned back to the light, which glittered in his eyes like witchfires as he watched a starch-capped serving woman close the drapes. 'What brings you to England? Surely not the climate.'

The lad had a quick tongue, and Channon chuckled. Robin's voice was soft, sultry, but Channon heard no guile in it. 'My uncle's life is at risk. I am here as his guard, since I've nothing better to do.'

'And how do you find England?' Amusement had begun to replace Robin's embarrassment. His eyes were bewitching, like the eyes of the woman in the portrait.

'England is fair, but cold and damp, with little to divert a man of sophisticated tastes.'

A brief pause, and that sultry voice asked, not quite in jest, 'I was to be such a diversion?'

Channon smiled ruefully. 'Perhaps. Had you wished to play my games. I wouldn't have forced a stable lad, merely courted him.'

'But what of the sin?' Curiosity spurred Robin. 'As an Irishman or a Spaniard, you must be a Catholic.'

'Must I?' Channon regarded his wine with an unreadable face. 'I have no God,' he said at last. 'I've seen and done too much in this short life to have any piety left. The torturer, the scourger and the rapist hardly confirm one's faith. They mock the existence of any gentle God who cannot be God if he approves of such pain, and cannot be God if he is blind to it, yet the pain is permitted to continue, century upon century. He smiled unexpectedly. 'A knotty paradox for you, Robin. If you have the solution, let me hear it!'

Robin's mercurial face was confused but Channon did not see the outrage he had feared. A brass gong called the family to the table, and Mauricio seated himself at Armagh's right. There was no lady to host the evening. Lady Catherine was ten years in her grave, and the only daughters still in this nest were Margaret, a pretty child of twelve, and Elizabeth, a pert maid of fourteen years, soon to wed.

The Armaghs were neither wealthy nor well connected. The house was well tended, but Channon saw none of the suffocating propriety that poisoned Hampton. To his surprise he liked Blackstead, and liked Robin most of all. Flushed, flustered, the youth kept his eyes down. He was perplexed, and Channon regretted his dismay. Robin had done nothing save show a comely face to a stranger. He was beautiful, Channon thought as he watched the young man eat. Robin's curious vulnerability made him much more than simply attractive.

The old men debated politics, privateering and the Queen, and Channon listened idly. The earl's silver hair was tightly curly, his face deeply lined. His nose was the only feature Robin had inherited, but William must have been handsome twenty years before. Even now, strong character endured in his face though it was stern, cheerless. When he was prompted Channon made a wry soldier's comment, but the conversation was too dry to interest him when at the end of the table Robin was stealing covert glances at him. Shy? Channon smiled, and wondered if he might find diversion under this roof after all. Robin's every bone betrayed his fascination, as the candour of his face betrayed innocence. A young harlot would have flirted. This lad risked a glance, looked swiftly away and hid his blush behind a cup of wine.

The daughters were shepherded to bed when the table was cleared, and Robin was plainly not welcome to stay. Surprised, Channon watched Armagh exclude him from the gathering without a thought. Robin lingered for a while, then simply bowed before Mauricio and said good night.

A frown creased Channon's brow as he leaned on the mantle and spun his pomander between his fingers. Lavender dispelled the earthy scents of onions and ale. No love showed in Armagh's face when he looked at his son, only brooding vexation, as if Robin had angered him beyond forgiveness. What could he have done? Some mortal sin? Channon stifled a chuckle. Not the sin of sodomy, surely!

He would learn Robin's secrets, he promised himself as he poured a last cup. Mauricio called his name and he took his wine to the hearth. A letter lay open in Mauricio's lap. He saw yellow paper, spidery writing and red sealing wax.

'From Dandridge.' Mauricio passed it to him.

'The secretary?' Channon read swiftly through the letter. 'Ah, and a spy! He works for Hatton, I believe. Sir Christopher Hatton, the Captain of the Guard... also a rich investor in privateering.'

'And many legitimate endeavours,' Mauricio added. 'Hatton invested in the voyage that took Drake about the globe. Most of his fortune stems from that small wager.'

'Yes.' Channon handed back the letter and studied their host. Armagh's feet were on the fender as if he felt the cold. 'Am I to understand, my Lord, you are conniving at Sir Charles Rothwell's undoing? There is danger in this.'

Armagh grunted. He had drunk a good deal and was near sleep. 'Danger is everywhere. If the country will soon be at war, who shall notice the loss of one more like Rothwell?'

'A man killed in war is one thing,' Channon said quietly. 'Murder is another matter.' He arched a brow at Mauricio, but his uncle shook his head minutely.

'Murder?' Armagh echoed. 'Revenge!'

'In the eyes of the law, murder,' Mauricio insisted. 'Dermot is right. Rothwell is too powerful, too high in favour to be challenged lightly. After the funeral you will deal with his friends, who may prove more vengeful that you imagine.'

Armagh's mouth compressed. 'And what of yourself? All but poisoned! The man, Copeland, is dead.'

'Copeland was nothing,' Channon argued. 'Hanged or executed by my own hand, where lies the difference? I hoped to learn the name of his employer but he was silent till the end.'

'Dandridge might be able to learn that,' Armagh mused.

'I asked my own spy to listen at doors and pay a sovereign here and there.' Channon looked into the fire. 'My uncle publicly humiliated Rothwell, before the Queen. The more I think on it, the more certain I am that Rothwell arranged for the poison, and hoped a little lad from Bevan's household would pay for the crime.'

'Copeland paid,' Mauricio said, 'a life for a life. That I live at all is the will of God.' He was reading steadily through a stack of letters, all in Dandridge's spidery hand. 'Your spy has been into Hatton's papers. He should take care, William. Hatton has Burghley's ear as well as Drake's, and has been a favourite of the Queen for some time.

Dandridge will come to grief if he is discovered.'

'He knows.' Armagh leaned over to stir the fire with sharp thrusts of a black iron rod. 'Walsingham's man returned from Spain with news that does your country ill. Have you read this far through those letters?'

'I have.' Mauricio's eyes glittered ruefully at Channon. 'Do you know the name of Pompeo Pellegrini?'

'Pellegrini.' Channon was about to say no when memory stirred. 'A little man of your age, with a barbarous accent? He was bribing for favours in Genoa, if I have the right man. They told me he served the Grand Duke of Tuscany, in Madrid. I took him for a rustic boor looking for a fortune.'

Mauricio laughed. 'He's a Catholic Englishman in Walsingham's service. He was Mary Stuart's man, when you were born, Dermot. With Darnley murdered he fled to Spain and has played false a good many of his trustees since. He sent back to Walsingham last year, news from a Fleming, some fellow whose brother serves the Marquis of Santa Cruz. The news was, Spain could no more mount an assault upon England than an ass might fly. Now he sends back a truth that should have been kept secret. Here.' Mauricio passed over a letter for Channon's amusement. 'Dandridge heard Hatton and Walsingham talking unguardedly.'

The letter was brief, acid. Pompeo Pellegrini was really Antony Standen, and the barbarous accent that offended Channon's ear was his deception. He had somehow become privy to treasury information: Philip was deeply in debt to bankers in Genoa. The construction of an armada impoverished Spain as surely as English privateers made sport of her ships at sea.

But for the Plate Fleet, Philip's fortunes would have been decided by Genoese money lenders, not English admirals. It would have been ironic. But the fleet came home, low in the water under the weight of bullion, and with sixteen million ducats in the treasury Philip's eyes returned to England.

'The *Alcanzar* was on the King's business,' Mauricio said softly, taking Channon by surprise. 'Pray to God the English never learn this.'

'And her business?' Channon handed back the letter. Walsingham and Hatton should be wiser than to gossip like fishwives. Hampton was full of spies.

'Capitan Vasca was scouting the coast for points that are too well defended, and bays where troops might easily land.' Mauricio held his hands to the fire. 'The work has been done before, but the English are moving. Today's truths are tomorrow's traps.'

'And the Spanish?' Armagh leaned forward.

'Philip is restless,' Channon said tartly. 'The people are paupered. This war is a folly that will cost the country dearly, even if it's won in the end, which I doubt.'

The old men frowned at him. Neither was a soldier. What did statesmen know of the agony of war? A battle was planned by elders and ministers in the quiet of a palace. It was fought in the teeth of a fickle Atlantic gale, where even the run of the tide was uncertain.

'We outnumber the English,' Mauricio prompted. 'I hear, the fleets in Le Havre and Calais are enormous.'

Channon sighed. 'What of the sea, the weather, and men's ingenuity? No battle goes to plan at sea when the wind springs suddenly from the wrong direction! Drake, *El Draque* himself cannot whistle up the wind. Our ships lumber like hulks. The English are faster, and they out-turn us.'

'But we outgun them,' Mauricio argued. 'Firepower will turn the game to our advantage.'

'I pray you are right,' Channon said quietly.

'You have no faith in the scheme?' Armagh asked shrewdly.

'Faith?' Channon got to his feet and stretched his spine. 'I've not enjoyed the luxury of faith since I was a boy. You know where I am from, my Lord! But this I can tell you, out of a soldier's bitter experience. Numbers mean nothing in heat of battle. The French learned this, one wet St Crispin's Eve.'

The old men fell silent. Mauricio fetched a last cup and Armagh brooded over the hearth. He was scheming, Channon saw, but at what? The Armaghs were still alien in England. What turn would their fortunes take if Spain was victorious? The Church of Rome would return, and Irish earls must prosper.

'Your leave,' Channon said as Mauricio settled with his wine. 'This country air fatigues me and I've been about since dawn.' At the door he paused for a moment. 'Tonio Diaz will be returning from York on a coaster, perhaps tomorrow. He will have Vasca's news.'

More likely a harbinger of diaster than of triumph, he thought as he climbed the stairs. His room was at the back, overlooking the river.

Naked, he sat in the moonlight at the casement. He had seen that moon over the jungles of Vera Cruz and Panama, and the glittering seas of the Americas. He would be at sea again soon. Intuition made his bones ache.

Yet he sat at the window, picturing the wood elf he had found in the garden hours before. Robin was no stable lad to be seduced, tumbled and paid in kisses. His sensual curiosity was alight, and noble blood ran hot; he was fresh and ripe for harvest.

What Blackstead needed, Channon judged as he slid between cool linen sheets, was some delicious folly. And he knew no better way to pass the time than to be busy at love. How many nights had be spent beneath the summer stars, in the arms of some comely fellow, long at sea?

Seamen knew the arts of pleasure. Ask any mariner what was sweetest in the world, and some would say their mother's smile, some, the breast of their wife or mistress. Others would say, the flesh of a lad who was warm and forgiving... mothers and mistresses were left far behind, and a year at sea was a lifetime.

How many men met the love of their life at sea? Pain strummed Channon's nerves as his thoughts turned inevitably to Pietro. A lad from Madrid, a sailor since the age of ten, pressed into service and thrust into the beds of his officers. Abused, Channon remembered, until the dice rattled on the deck and he was wagered yet again, won like a prize.

And a prize he was. Fair-skinned for a Spaniard, brown-eyed, fine-boned, with velvet skin. *And I won him*, Channon thought as he pillowed his head on his forearm. *I won him by wagering everything I owned against Paulo, the bosun, when the lad wept in misery.*

Young Pietro was not surprised to find himself in Channon's bed. Fear whitened his lips, pinched his cheeks. Terror turned to lazy pleasure as he was used gently, given delight in return. Affection blossomed then, and Channon cherished the memory. Pietro had been killed by natives in Vera Cruz, two years before.

His bed was empty now. The Cervallos exhorted him to wed, but Channon felt no urge. Marriage would be an inconvenience for one who spent three-fourths of his time abroad and gambled his life twice in a week. What poor woman should be condemned to loneliness, fretting and early widowhood? Channon's fortunes were uncertain.

But he was never alone for long. He was always alert to opportunity, and Robin Armagh was like a shining rainbow trout, luring the mercenary deeper into the water.

Never welcome in William's company, Robin left with a last covert glance at the soldier. A branch of tallow candles lit his bedchamber and the bed was turned down. He was tired after being busy since dawn, savouring his freedom from his studies. The time for decision was almost at hand.

To waste more seasons in study, or seek his own life among people to whom his disgrace was unknown? Leaving Blackstead would take courage, but he had already tarried too long. Dermot Channon reminded Robin of this. He was a bare few years older, but commanded a wealth of experience which made him a man. It was not age but the sum of one's deeds which decided who was a boy, and who was a man.

Envy had prickled Robin all evening. Channon had everything. Position, rank, respect. His dark, handsome looks were like nothing Robin had ever seen. The soft Castilian voice was seductive and the man's eyes were mesmerising. Robin slid into bed, naked as he always slept, and reached for a volume of Latin verse.

But he could not read. Channon wanted him, desired his body, and if his father had been a common coachman there would have been mating tonight. He shivered, tried to fathom how it was done, given the difference between men and women, and arrived at only one possible answer to the puzzle of sodomy. An unnatural act, it was said, yet the Bible told stories thousands of years old, and men mated then, as now.

If it was unnatural, why was it indulged through the centuries? Priests did it! Channon's friendly enticement beguiled Robin and he thought, over and over, *Sweet Jesu, he wants me!* He threw back the sheet and studied his body, a slender sprawl in the candlelight. Channon felt the sweet, barbed pangs of lust for this?

Lust was familiar to Robin; to be desired was not. He imagined Channon's eyes feasting on his nakedness and his loins stirred. The mercenary would not simply look. He would touch, hold, kiss. Lust tingled Robin's spine.

He pulled up the linen, uneager to indulge himself — undecided if a night's pleasure was a fit trade for one's salvation. Yet Channon had no such qualms. The torturer, the scourger, he had said. The voice of experience was usually bitter. Instinctively, Robin trusted him. Channon *knew*, and what could so wretched a creature as Robin Armagh, who had spent his whole life imprisoned here, know?

Sleep eluded him until near dawn, but at last he dozed. Fragmented dreams taunted him, intense but disjointed and almost forgotten as he woke, with the exception of one unforgettable moment when he felt a man's strength crushing him, and a hot, wet mouth bruised his own with kisses.

Chapter Six

Morning was sultry. The sky was stormy but the weather would hold till afternoon. Channon had a sailor's feeling for the wind. He rose with the sun out of long habit and breakfasted in the kitchen on mulled ale, cheese and bread, while he teased the young wench who was raking out the inglenook. He had slept briefly but soundly in an empty bed, while Robin commanded his thoughts with the allure of the forbidden. Channon mocked himself as he finished the ale and swatted the maid's round backside.

The air was crisp and cool. Mist still coiled beneath the trees and he swung on a fur-trimmed cape before he made his way to the stable. The grooms were breakfasting while they tended the nags, and he smelt bread frying in an iron skillet.

He pulled on black pigskin gloves as he turned into the gape-fronted stable, and would have called for a groom, but before he could speak he saw Robin. The reins of a big chestnut mare were looped over his arm. A smile replaced Channon's usual expression of self-confident hauteur.

'You rise with the sun? I hadn't thought to see you before some civilised hour.'

Robin looked up at him and Channon murmured in astonished pleasure. He had never seen the boy's eyes in full daylight. By candlelight they were dark pools, in sunlight, deep forest green.

'I could not sleep. I find myself restless,' Robin said blandly. 'And your excuse, sir?'

'Excuse?' Channon laughed lightly. 'I need none. I am about at this hour every day. The habits of a soldier. Will you ride with me?'

'I will.' Robin led the mare into the yard. Her coat shone with the same burnished copper as his own hair. He was warmly clad in a green cape, leather jerkin and polished leather boots which cupped his thighs and showed off long, shapely legs. He patted the mare's neck proudly. 'Tara was foaled here and will soon be bred to our stud, Connaught. That's him in the stall there. He is the jewel of this stable.'

The stallion was a rare beauty. His coat was almost black, his mane unshorn. Channon had inherited the Irishman's regard for horses and admired the stud as a groom brought him out a spirited bay gelding. 'The nags in this stable would fetch a king's ransom. Even this palfrey would not disgrace the Queen.'

'Her Majesty buys colts from us on occasion.' Pride was rich in Robin's voice.

Channon watched him swing into the saddle, and his admiration then was for a different kind of bone and sinew. He gave Robin a smile he knew was charming and mounted up as the bay was held for him. 'Where do you ride?'

'By the river.' Robin gathered the reins. 'They can stretch their legs safely in the meadow.'

The mare's iron shoes rang on the cobbles like bells. Channon set his heels to the gelding's flanks but he needed no encouragement. They skirted the house and garden, and Channon allowed Robin to lead him through the postern gate.

The horses ran for sheer exuberance, following the river until a copse of elm halted them and Robin drew rein at last. Breathless and exhilarated, Channon shared a smile with his young companion. Robin was flushed with exertion, bright eyed, captivating. It was on the tip of Channon's tongue to say so, but the compliment would have been impertinent and instead he said, 'You ride as well as many I've seen.'

'Long practice.' Robin was clearly flattered. 'I've ridden since I was very small.'

'And had the best nags,' Channon observed. He leaned back and twisted to see the roof of the house. It was out of view, they were alone. 'Will you tell me, Robin? Tell me why your father is at odds with you.'

51

To his surprise the green eyes clouded and averted. 'It need not concern you. A family matter, years gone by.'

'My apologies,' Channon said, frustrated. 'I am merely curious. I saw little paternal pride last night.'

'You saw none,' Robin corrected. 'Still, it does not concern you, Spaniard. The earl has his reasons.'

The boy's voice was edged with bitterness, and Channon frowned at him. 'You have forgiven me for last evening.'

'I told you, I was flattered.' Robin wrestled with the mare as she sidestepped and began to prance, annoyed at being asked to idle when she was out for her exercise. Robin handled her deftly. 'I shall race you to the well, up yonder.'

'Race me?' Channon saw the well, a quarter of a mile away. 'And the stakes?'

'A wager?' Robin's brows rose. 'I have nothing to gamble. I intended only a game.' He looked away, embarrassed.

'But every contest must have stakes,' Channon coaxed, 'else, where is the sport? The prize shall be... a kiss. If I win, of course.'

Colour leapt in Robin's cheeks but he smiled. 'You are bold, Spaniard! And if I win?'

'A sovereign,' Channon offered. 'I'd pay a sovereign to taste your mouth, so I'd make the wager.'

'A high price for one kiss,' Robin judged. His eyes glittered with mischief now.

Channon mirrored the expression. 'Not any kiss, Master Armagh. Yours.'

'Then you had better win,' Robin taunted as he spun the mare on her haunches and bounded away toward the well.

Afterward, Channon would never be sure if the race was won fairly. The gelding slithered to a halt a good length before the mare and he saw no regret in Robin's face as he kicked out of the stirrups. The breeze tossed his hair as he looped the reins over the well's rusted crank. Channon slid down, secured the horse and considered his prize with a thrill of triumph.

Forbidden delight? He was intent on the beautiful, pouting lips, a mouth made for feasting on, not prattling scholarly gibberish. Robin breathed deeply and backed up against the crumbling, mossy stone. His colour was high and he never took his eyes from Channon.

'The spoils of the game.' Channon stood very close and placed both

52

black-gloved hands on the green cape. 'Your mouth is mine, is it not?'

'So I agreed.' Robin's voice was husky with some feeling Channon could not guess, though it could not be horror, or the wager would never have been made so lightly. He was ready to lose, and Channon slipped off his gloves, leaned forward to claim his prize.

A scent lingered about Robin. Clean, male, unforgettable. His face was smooth though he had been shaving for years. Channon felt the faint rasp of his beard. His breath smelt of wine and herbs, drunk hot for breakfast. Channon's bare fingers cupped his chin, lifted it, and he looked into eyes that were stormy.

'Be at peace. I shall not hurt you, I swear it!'

Soft lips twitched as he tongued across them, teased their deep Cupid's bow. For a moment they were sealed, and then to Channon's delight they parted, perhaps in curiosity. His tongue slipped inside, found Robin's mouth hot and wine-sweet, and he pressed the kiss harder. Their mouths welded, a scorching expression of the lust that was an old friend, old enemy to Dermot Channon.

To Robin it might have been a less familiar demon. For one moment he froze, stiffened from head to foot as if he would bolt, but the next he stepped forward and joined Channon in a punishing embrace. Tongues explored, and Channon reckoned he had received his sovereign's worth when he lifted his head at last and saw Robin's bruised mouth.

His pulse hammered and he was unaware he was panting. 'By God, you seduce me!' he said against Robin's hair. 'Your blood is as quick as mine — I judged you wrongly!' He explored Robin's face with his both hands. 'God's teeth, I want you for my lover. Would you deny me now?'

The young man swallowed. 'I should.'

'Afeard of sin?' Channon's fingers knotted into the warm auburn curls and he nuzzled his captive's neck. 'I was seduced and sodded before my fourteenth year, by a churchman of good reputation. It is a venial sin, absolved for a penance. A pardonable sin, sweeting, since priests know better than we the dark pleasures of love between men — and that men will love men, sin or no, hell or no. Are you so fettered by the Church? Why were you not a priest? Had you been, they, not I, would have shown you this face of love!'

Robin sighed. 'I was intended for the Church but I disgraced my family. They wouldn't have me. I would have been a very bad priest.'

'Would you?' Channon hid a smile. 'Will you tell me now, what is this shame you hide, that kept you from the Church, thank God, and gave you to me!'

The green eyes had been clouded with confused desire but they sparkled ruefully now. 'I was fifteen when I was taken visiting to the house of the Countess of Roebury. She was a lovely girl, wed to an old man. She smiled at me one afternoon while her husband was away — or should have been. I followed her to a bedchamber like a lamb to the slaughter. She stripped and kissed me, but before I could profane her husband's honour there was a great commotion.' He looked away, trying to make light of it, but the memory was painful. 'My desire was proud between my thighs, the lady was half clad. I was disgraced forever, for the sake of a few kisses.'

'This is the sum of it?' Channon demanded scornfully. Laughter rose in his chest. This lad was his match. All Robin needed was freedom, and he would take wing. 'There was nothing in it,' Channon scoffed. 'For this, your father chides you, years later?' Robin nodded. 'Then it's past time you ceased to court favour here, where there is none, and sought your fortune elsewhere.'

'One day soon I shall leave.' Robin stirred.

'But not yet,' Channon begged. 'Not while I'm shut up in this drab nest of academics. I want you, Robin, more hungrily now than when I thought you were a beautiful young scullion.'

'Beautiful?' Robin laughed. 'You mistake me for someone else.'

But Channon shook his head. 'I have you rightly placed. Eyes like the sea, the face and body of an enchanter. Will you, Robin? Will you come to me? Forget this prattle about trivial sins. Let me shall show you what delight is about.'

Longing was etched in every line of Robin's face. He said nothing, but caught the mare's reins and mounted up. Channon swung onto his own nag and did not insist. He did not doubt that Robin was his. He must be patient, persuasive, but Robin Armagh was his already.

He could afford to let the lad flee for the moment. Robin must thrash out the misgivings of a lifetime. An afternoon's privacy would be to his service. Channon let the big chestnut outpace him, for Robin was skittish as a colt, best left to himself. Channon smiled after him, and when he ambled back into the stableyard Tara was stalled and Robin was gone.

A lad doffed his cap. 'Master Channon, your uncle is asking for you. He's had a messenger from Colbridge.'

Channon's heart quickened. It must be a lad running errands for Tonio Diaz. He strode quickly back into the house, entered by the kitchen and heard Mauricio in the hall beyond. The old cook, Mistress Lovell, was rolling pastry while rabbits stewed over the fire.

'I tell you, I shall fare better for fresh air and gentle exercise,' Mauricio was saying. 'I'm not yet so decrepit as to need coddling!'

'And the poisoning?' Armagh demanded.'You almost died.'

'Almost,' Mauricio said pointedly. 'There is life in the old hound yet.'

They were in the library, the door was ajar. Channon knocked with one knuckle, a smile of greeting on his lips as he saw Mauricio in his dark blue velvet. He was by the hearth, brandishing a paper as if it were a dirk. Books lined one wall; morning sunlight slanted through the east widow, casting diamond mosaics on the dusty floorboards.

'Ah, Dermot.' Mauricio beckoned him in. 'Diaz is at a tavern, east, nearer the coast. He'll be in Colbridge till tomorrow, waiting for the coach. It is a ride of five miles, by Whiddon Manor. You want to meet him.'

'And you intend to accompany me,' Channon guessed. 'For the air and exercise, if I heard correctly!' He sobered. 'Mauricio, you still look frail.'

The old man sighed. 'Then I shall ride slowly and rest often. On the ride home we shall break our journey at Whiddon Manor — we have a kinsman there, a distant cousin through some mismarriage of a Cervallo daughter, generations past.'

'Then we'd best be moving,' Channon said drily, 'since we'll make slow time.' He glanced at Armagh. 'Where is Colbridge? It'll do Mauricio no good to wander astray and sleep in a hedge!'

'Over the hill by the path, ford the beck by the stepping stones, follow the stream to the village,' Armagh told him. 'You'll see a manor on the other side of the village, but stay well away. It's Halstead Hall, Rothwell's estate, won at gambling a decade ago.'

Rothwell, who broke a woman's neck in his fury... who fired upon the *Alcanzar*, and likely arranged to poison the cup of the man who outfoxed him with words. Channon swallowed the anger aroused by the man's name as Mauricio went up for his boots and Armagh sent a boy to the stable.

Of Robin there was no sign. Channon stood in the hall, studying the green, feline eyes of the woman. She was beautiful. The portrait was done by an English master, and even an untutored eye saw its quality. The artist was in love with his model. To see Catherine was to see Robin also, and Channon was rapt. How could old Armagh be so loveless toward Robin, when Catherine seemed reborn in the boy? Or could Armagh scarcely bear to look into Robin's face, for seeing Catherine there?

Boots clattered down the stairs and Channon stirred. He looked for Robin as he and Mauricio entered the stableyard, but he was gone. Mauricio was in better spirits than he had enjoyed for weeks. He had a little colour in his cheeks, an edge of gaiety in his conversation as they rode up the hill, past the well.

I pressed him against the stone there, and had his mouth. He is mine! He must be. A shiver caught Channon unawares.

He saw the glitter of sunlight on water a mile away. The beck was low at this time of year, and before noon they smelt the chimneys of Colbridge, glimpsed its thatch as they skirted the woods. Yet even here they saw the promise of war.

'See, Mauricio?' Channon pointed to this and that tree.

'The axe markings?' Mauricio peered into the shadows beneath the heavy foliage.

'Trees chosen for felling, for shipyards,' Channon told him. 'Shipwrights choose the best long before they will be needed. Ask the countryman if there's to be war. Shepherds know before the news reaches ports and palaces.'

Colbridge's single tavern was the Black Boar. The woody scents of ale and hearth smoke issued from it, and Channon left the horses with a lad at the door. For a penny they would be fed and groomed in the stable at the rear.

'I thought you would come.' Antonio Diaz said softly from the inn's open door. He had a tankard in one hand, mutton in the other, and waved with the cup. 'Sup with me.'

'Gladly. Mauricio?' Channon ushered his uncle ahead of him into the dim, smoky, companionable tavern.

They joined Diaz by the inglenook. The innkeeper was a vast, stout man with ruddy cheeks and a greasy apron. Pastries, mutton, cider and apples were set before them, before they were alone and Channon turned to business.

'News, Tonio?'

'Capitan Vasca is angry,' Diaz whispered. 'But wary, and not blustering. He was in English waters to spy, and could come to grief for it, as could we all. He was boarded but his charts were hidden.'

'Charts of which coasts?' Channon murmured. He watched the taverner covertly. He and his wife were arguing over the ale.

'The Channel, from the Lizard to Dover. Vasca took sightings and struck north to cover his tracks. He carries dispatches for a gunsmith in Amsterdam, so the tale is sound. The weather was against him. Storms that battered the coasts here were more violent at sea, and pushed him into Rothwell's guns. Vasca swears he signalled that he was on legitimate business, overtaken by the weather. He would have done so, there is no doubt. Rothwell did not care to see the signals, and opened fire. Six lads died.'

'Who were they?' Of a sudden Channon's appetite was gone.

Diaz's face was grave. 'One of them was the little *zambo*. Little Marcos. I am sorry.'

So was Channon. Marcos was part Spaniard, part Indian, part Portuguese — even he was unsure, since he was a bastard who had known only ships since he was born. He had been a gunner's mate. And another of Channon's friends was gone. He drew a tankard of cider toward him but had no taste for it. Mauricio frowned at him as he left the inglenook, and Diaz followed him outside.

The overcast had deepened and they heard the rumble of thunder in the north. To Channon it sounded like gunfire between big ships. He shivered, recalling the way a ship staggered in the water under the recoil of her own broadside, how a galleon pitched like a cork in a tub as she was pounded, dismasted, her canvas set ablaze by red-hot gravelling and chain shot.

Soon, it began. He closed his eyes to the placid village. Diaz waited patiently. He was a veteran of too many campaigns and knew Channon's wayward, soldier's heart.

At last Channon said, 'And what of Sir Charles Rothwell? My uncle has his suspicions as to who paid Copeland.'

'Mauricio is probably right, but I have no proof. Give me time.' Diaz touched Channon's arm. 'Sup with me. it will be stormy soon, you may be caught here overnight.'

The storm broke with a peal like cannonade. Channon stood at the door and watched the lightning in the north. Rothwell's estate of Halstead Hall lay there — won at cockfighting, the fat, breathless taverner swore as he swabbed the tables. Rothwell's bird fought like the devil in silver spurs. Channon listened without interest as the storm passed and the sky quickly brightened.

Mauricio drowsed by the hearth and Channon woke him with a soft word. 'If you want to stay the night at Whiddon Manor, we'd best be on our way. It's getting late.'

'Better there than here,' Diaz agreed. 'These inns are full of thieves. I nearly lost my purse last night.'

A boy ran for the horses, and Channon offered his hand. 'Look into the matter of Copeland, Tonio, with all speed,' he said quietly. 'I've a feeling, here.' He rubbed his belly thoughtfully. 'As if hell is about to begin, and soon. Accounts must be settled between Rothwell and myself, and we have little time. Call it a soldier's intuition.'

Perhaps Diaz shared the same throb of premonition. Channon wanted only to return to Blackstead, and to Robin. If little time remained, it was better spent busy at love than brooding. The death of an old friend, Marcos, came as a blow. Rothwell would pay for that, too.

Late afternoon was humid and warm as they rode up by Whiddon Manor. They had daylight left, and as Mauricio turned toward the tall gates Channon called him back. 'If we press on we can be at Blackstead in an hour. You can see the roof from the next hill.'

'Family duty,' Mauricio chided. 'Sir Henry knows I am at Blackstead. What will he think of me if I pass by without bidding him good day?'

Channon had no interest in meeting a distant cousin. He drew rein on the rise and gazed down on the Armaghs' private domain, unaware of Mauricio a pace behind. Robin's world stretched from hills to river to forest, sheltered, almost like a garden. Its beauty had moulded him into the gorgeous youth Channon had come to want so fiercely. There was a dreamy otherworldliness about Robin, a strange quiescence. A pagan purity, as if he was unsullied by any hand.

And I am to sully him? Channon thought ruefully. Or, complete him. Open his heart and mind, as well as his body, let loose his passions. A shiver prickled him as he turned back to Mauricio. His uncle regarded him strangely.

'What is it, Dermot?' A gloved hand smoothed white hair disordered by the breeze. 'Something troubles you.'

'I am preoccupied.' Channon forced a smile.

'With the death of your friend?'

'That too,' Channon admitted. Marcos's death preyed on him like a hawk. 'And other matters.'

'Affairs at Court?' Mauricio gathered his reins. 'Elizabeth is no lady, but her father's heir. There'll be trouble, mark me well, if the privateers slip the leash. English peers — the Queen herself! — invest in privateering, piracy, as if it is a legitimate enterprise.'

'But we ourselves looted the gold from the natives in the Americas, so we have no cause for malice,' Channon said indifferently, and urged his horse on along the rise.

The old man shook his head. 'You are no Spaniard.'

And Channon replied with a fond, insolent look. 'You may be right! I am an Irishman.'

They clattered into Whiddon Manor as sunset began to blaze. A groom led the horses into the lamplit stable and Sir Henry Leighton greeted Mauricio like a brother. The house was dark, dreary. No young people lived here. Henry was an elderly widower, his brood had long ago flown and even his servants creaked with age. The house smelt of beeswax and pepper; footsteps seemed intrusive.

They were ushered into the parlour, where servants brought wine and sweetmeats and Henry poked at the hearth. Channon stood at the window to watch the first stars wink over the hills. The thunder was gone, the moon shone like a lamp. Mauricio sat by the fire, pink-cheeked in the warmth. He would not stir before morning.

Sir Henry delivered a tirade on the wrongs of privateering and the inevitability of war, as the table was set for dinner. Every man had expected it for a decade. Spanish nobility answered Philip's call to arms, pledging their wealth as well as their sons. A fleet, an army. Channon should be there, not mouldering in this chill place till he was sure the damp seeped into his very bones. Despite the hearth, Whiddon Manor was dank, and he cradled a cup of wine as he held his hands to the fire.

The proposition of a night spent here inspired a shudder. He would be a mothball by morning. He took his place at the table, ate the dry, pungent flesh of the swan, basted in butter and stuffed with almonds and apricots. Sir Henry was deep in his cups already.

Channon watched Mauricio indulge in too much wine, and then the old men retired to the library to bicker amiably over the price of silver, and Spain's foolhardiness in basing her coinage on precious metals which were swiftly made off with, leaving poverty behind. He stood at the dining-room windows, gazing into the night.

'Sir?' An old woman bobbed a stiff-backed curtsy. 'There's a room for thee. Will I put the warming pan in now?'

Channon weighed his choices. Mauricio would sleep till noon, and Sir Henry would applaud the indulgence. A hunter's moon glared above the woods. What chance of making it over the hill without injuring an Armagh horse? Channon knew the path well, the moon was brilliant and the sky was clear. The ride to Blackstead was a scant two miles. He would be shirking his duty to Mauricio if he left, and his uncle would be angry; but where was the need of a soldier in this house?

'Sir?' The servant waited impatiently.

'I am returning to Blackstead on business,' he told her. 'Do not trouble Don Mauricio tonight, but tell him when he rises, I shall return at noon to escort him home.'

She bobbed another curtsy and withdrew into the shadows as Channon left the house. The groom was dozing over his work, mending tack by the light of a stuttering candle. Channon sent him to fetch up his horse.

Chapter Seven

Tara had run well that morning, but Robin knew Channon had let him escape. He fled like a coward and scolded himself the whole day. The lads who stabled Tara took his flush for exertion, but it was closer to terror. For one moment he had taken Channon's smile for mockery and hated it, for it brought a twist of fear, desire, envy. Fear, because lust was blazing. Envy, because Channon was so much the accomplished adventurer when Robin Armagh was nothing. The pounding of his heart betrayed him.

No girl had ever kissed him so, and he had kissed several maids, and a countess. None of them shamelessly plundered his mouth as Channon did. Robin hungered for more and feared the ferocious need. What did he know of the rites of love?

Even the fear was arousing. The notion of his possession, his complete humiliation before Channon. He must think, and when he was hurt, confused, he fled to the orchard. He lay in the grass among the old apple trees and gazed into the windblown canopy. He had wanted to lose the wager, and excitement thrilled him at the wickedness of what he had done.

Channon was temptation, darkly beautiful, overwhelming in this place where milk-and-water servants and his sisters were Robin's only company. Into the bland, lilac-scented nest came a bored, profane soldier, and in minutes animal lust speared Robin's loins.

Not only Channon hungered for release. Robin's own needs were accommodated in silence and solitude, with an open window to dispel the sinful, erotic odour of wantonness, lest someone know — *That I am a man, not a eunuch,* he thought. Channon would understand, would touch him with that sure, frightening knowledge. He savoured half-formed images as morning warmed. The groundsman's black cat climbed onto his chest and Robin stroked her silken fur. It reminded him of Channon's hair, and he heard the soldier's voice again. *I want you for my lover.* Robin's heart squeezed. Was it mockery? But Channon had spoken fiercely, gripped by the same lust — he, who had sampled all pleasures and knew wheat from chaff.

Bedding with a man was at odds with all Robin had ever dreamed. A comely maid at Court who loved him and lay with him as his wife, he had hoped. But the dream was improbable. He had never been invited to Court, nor would he have been permitted to go. William's fury ignited at a glimpse of Robin's face, and Richard was at Hampton. Sir Richard Armagh would be embarrassed by the chatter of courtiers seeking titillation to pass the time.

Robin savoured the dream and ruefully dismissed it. It was not to be, but Channon had already chosen. And if Robin declined he knew he would spend the rest of his life wondering — what if?

Time had flown when he went to find the Spaniard. His belly quivered in anticipation of the surrender, but hooves rang on the cobbles and he hurried his pace. He reached the stable only to see two of Blackstead's best horses departing.

Young Thomas was forking hay. Robin called his name. 'Do you know where the guests have gone?'

'To Colbridge, sir.' Thomas spoke with a thick Suffolk burr. 'Back by sundown, else they'll stay the night at Whiddon Manor and be back on the morrow, so I heard.'

The few curses Robin had learned from the stable lads sprang to his lips as he climbed to his bedchamber. Midday was warm and he cast off cape and doublet. Mistress Lovell fed him, frowned over him, but he barely noticed her. Time was when he had run to her with scraped knees or knuckles bruised by his tutor's cane. The woman's ample comfort filled the absence of his mother as she soothed his hurts, nursed his illnesses and was paid in smiles. But today Robin's mind was far away.

Only let them return tonight, he prayed, and saw the absurdity of praying for the opportunity to sin. Disappointment shortened his temper. He had no patience for his sisters' childish games and his father's taciturn lectures at dinner. He endured in restless silence and retired early.

Sprawled on his bed, fully dressed, he glared at the moon through the open casement. Had Channon wanted to go? Robin had fled like a frightened girl. Had Channon changed his mind, was it over before it began? *Faintheart!* he chided himself. *Fool, coward! When he returns, make amends for your rudeness.* He would cite his virginity. Bitterness contended with rueful humour at his own expense; humour won.

It was late, the moon was setting and he was dozing when he heard horseshoes in the yard. It was unusual for a rider to be out at night, and usually spelled trouble. Robin hurried to the window. The moonlight was bright enough for him to see the tall, arrogant figure striding across the yard. His cloak swirled, his pace betrayed his urgency.

Channon.

He had come back alone? Robin's first thought was for the frail old man, who might be taken ill, or worse. He stirred at the casement, about to call when Channon stopped in mid-stride and looked up. They froze as Robin leaned out over the trellis. Channon's face was white in the moonlight and his shadowed eyes commanded Robin.

At last the boy found his voice. 'Is there trouble?'

'None save our own,' Channon answered, too softly to be heard from the house.

He said no more, and disappeared about the corner. Still at the window, Robin heard the quiet closing of the door under the climbing roses, the creak of a stair. A measured tread covered the passage to the room at the end and Channon's door closed. Robin bit his lip.

He had expected Channon to come to him, had been braced for the Spaniard's anger after the morning's cowardice. Channon could easily take what he wanted by force. But Robin was still the earl's son, and Channon was a guest.

So I must go to him. Tension knotted his belly. The humbling of his pride stung, but Robin knew what he wanted, and his bare feet padded soundlessly along the passage.

Below, a steward moved from library to kitchen, a cat mewled, and he froze. This was a dangerous affair. His father was goaded to fury by his liaison with the woman, but for this he would be insane. Robin's eyes were wide open, but he was deterred only to caution. He wanted Channon with frightening urgency, and the time had come for Robin Armagh to act upon his own will, have what he had never been allowed.

The exhilaration of the ride had sharpened Channon's senses. The stars were bright and the path tolerably dry. He had planned to knock discreetly at Robin's door, announce his presence and retire. But the face of seduction looked down from the casement... Robin knew. Channon closed his door, lit a branch of candles and, waiting, hoping, prepared for bed without haste.

He was not disappointed. A tap of knuckles, and his pulse leapt. 'Aye, I am here.' The whisper brought Robin in. He stood in the candlelight, a fantasy in molten gold. Loose white linen gaped artlessly to display his chest. The rich russet of his hose revealed the shape of his legs. Channon held out his hands. 'I hoped you would come to me.'

The boy was silent. His eyes were wide, his hair stirred by the breeze from the open window which stuttered the candles. Haunting shadows wreathed his face.

'Come to me, Robin, I shan't hurt you.' Channon held out his arms, watched Robin hesitate a moment longer, then step forward.

The embrace was first tentative, soon fierce. Channon kissed him searchingly. Robin was hot, thin, hard in his arms; and he was shaking. Channon soothed him with caresses, tasted his skin and found it salt-sweet, smooth as velvet.

'Sir?' Robin whispered as he was drawn to the bed.

'I have a name,' Channon said softly.

'Dermot.' Robin took a breath. 'I won't deceive you. I shall be lacking as your lover, for I have no knowledge.'

'Your first night with a man?' Channon murmured fondly. 'Special, I would say.'

'My first night with anyone.' Robin ducked his head in a moment's intense shame.

Channon gentled. 'You give me your most precious gift, which can be given only once in all your life, and you apologise?' He kissed Robin's palms, his throat and breast. 'Let me love you a little. I'll teach you the game. It has its rule, points to score, prizes to be won.' He rubbed a fold of linen between his fingers, and as Robin drew out the laces he slid the shirt off. 'God's teeth, you're beautiful. Your skin is perfect.' He took Robin's mouth again, nibbled his full lower lip, then bent to suckle one rucked nipple.

Fingers clawed Channon's shoulders as Robin cried out. 'That makes me ache inside.' He was inarticulate as Channon's teeth bit gently, then transferred to the neglected pap and began again. Engrossed in unexpected pleasure, Robin accepted the stroking of his soft inner thigh. Deftly, Channon stripped him, bared each new area with a kiss, till Robin lay naked. His eyes were feverish with desire and his chest heaved. His long, slender cock arched over his belly, slick, gleaming in the candlelight.

Satisfied, Channon feasted his eyes from the modest pelt of down on his chest to the long, tapered legs. 'A prize worth winning!' He smiled into the stormy eyes. Robin was waiting, trusting. Channon stood in the light to disrobe for Robin's pleasure, and his knowledge. Channon was very big, and as his cock sprang free at last he heard a quiet French oath. 'Don't be afraid. I'll not hurt you, my word upon it.' He saw Robin swallow.

'But you must enter me, and — surely I am not large enough. I could not be.'

'Hush.' Channon sat on the counterpane beside him and cupped his chin. 'I'll take that from you when it is what you desire most, and fear is gone. There are ways, but you must trust me, even love me a little.' Robin tried to speak but Channon silenced him with a kiss. 'Hush, I said! I'll bugger you when you tell me you are in dire need of it, and not until! For now, let me show you how men make love.'

Despite Channon's experience he too was young, just a few years Robin's elder. His body was hard, round with muscle, his thighs roped with sinew. Robin whispered that he hungered to be touched not only by the gentle, sword-callused hands but by every part of the soldier's skin, and Channon smiled. The boy had seen his many scars too. Each told of a battle won.

Robin murmured in delight as he was pressed into the mattress. Channon's cock nestled against his own, caressed it in a hot, slick glide as the powerful hips began to hump. Robin cried out aloud but Channon's tongue in his mouth muffled him.

It was beyond bearing. A sudden gasp, a warm gush on Channon's belly, and it was over too soon. Frustrated and ashamed, Robin turned his face into the pillow as if to hide, but Channon's brow creased only for a moment. He smiled fondly at the boy. 'It is the way of things, my lad! Next time will be better. Fetch me pleasure with your hands. See my delight and stir your loins anew.'

He turned onto his side and tugged Robin with him. The slender right hand found him, cool fingers wrapped about his cock. Robin had obviously tended himself, for though the caresses were hesitant they were not clumsy. Pleasure racked Channon, and he writhed and bucked in the delight of Robin's grasp.

The lad learned quickly. The caresses grew bolder and brought Channon effortlessly to release. He spread his thighs and begged mutely for all Robin knew, but Robin needed no encouragement. Coming was savagely sweet. Channon clung to him, his teeth clenched in Robin's shoulder, and poured his seed over the hands that had loved him.

The room righted at last and he opened his eyes. Robin knelt beside him, aroused again, gleaming with perspiration. Channon smiled. 'You've a talent for that! Well practised?'

'You have my secret,' Robin confessed breathlessly.

Channon's laughter was not mocking. 'Lie down. Let me...'

Panting, Robin did as he was asked. Channon kissed breast and belly, sharp hip bones, the softness of inner thigh. Robin's hands clenched into the bedlinen and his face twisted. Channon watched him shiver as his cock was kissed. 'Not so quick this time!' A nod, and he bent his head to the boy's torture. His own body would soon stir again.

Muscles corded with effort, and Robin could bear little. The moment Channon sucked strongly, climax shattered him. Channon took every drop and parted from him with a kiss. 'See? Waiting makes it better. Loving is an art.' He lay down and covered Robin's mouth. 'Taste yourself.'

'Salt... bitter,' Robin murmured. His hands strayed across Channon's chest. 'I would taste you also, if I may.'

'I'd not coerce you.' Channon rubbed his cock on Robin's hip. 'Your mouth would be my joy, but the whim is your own.'

To his surprise Robin straddled his legs and studied him from brow to knees. 'All I see is beautiful, as I never knew a man could be. May I lie between your legs?'

Captivated by the cherub's face as Robin became intent on the blind thrust of his cock, Channon spread for him. A lick from root to crown dizzied him. Encouraged, Robin swallowed him deeply, hesitant but growing bolder. Channon surged up fast and his hands cupped Robin's face. 'Lift your head,' he warned, too late. He bucked once into Robin's throat and the boy gasped. For a moment cool air replaced the heat of his mouth before the swollen lips closed about him to take his seed.

Some unfamiliar feeling kindled in Channon's chest, unknown because it had never been there before. He stroked the soft, damp hair, caressed Robin's scalp as they sagged against the pillows. He folded the boy in arms that shook. Green eyes shone in the candlelight; the shame of failure was gone. Twice, Channon had responded to Robin's hands and mouth, he was confident now. He hunted for a kiss to share the seed that had filled his throat, salt, bitter but irresistible.

Channon held his head, licked clean his mouth and cheek and courted his tongue. Robin had never been kissed so thoroughly and was shaking when he was released. He clung tight, panting against the soldier's throat while Channon held him and murmured meaningless words until Robin was limp with sleep.

Still Channon held him, stroked his back and smiled. Nothing was more rewarding than liberating the senses of another. Robin was beginning to blossom. When the bloom was full he would be the kind of lover for whom men and women alike would contest, not merely handsome but skilled and gentle. Channon credited himself as the tutor.

But the picture of Robin in the arms of another, man or woman, pained him. Resentment surprised Channon. He had rarely felt such possessiveness. He tried to shrug it away as sleep thickened his thoughts, but the rational part of him knew the truth. There would be no escaping the velvet trap he had carefully spun about himself, and so deftly locked himself into.

❖ ❖ ❖

A flood of sunlight woke him. The casement stood wide, birds carolled, he smelt the earthy scents of woods and river. Dawn was an hour old when Channon stirred, and at once was aware of his cramped limbs. The cause of the discomfort made him smile, and he woke his bedmate with a kiss.

'Robin! You must return to your own bed soon, before the house stirs.'

Green eyes opened, soft and dark. Robin was as beautiful as only a young man could be, Channon thought. He kissed the upturned mouth as the lad stretched and moved away. The absence of his weight allowed Channon to breathe, but Robin had turned his back in shame. His body was proud with a morning erection he was trying to hide. The virgin's terrible innocence endured.

'Not so fast,' Channon purred. 'You cannot leave like that, and if you could, I would not allow it.'

'I am sorry,' Robin whispered. 'I often wake so.'

'Good.' Channon pinned him down and settled on him, shoulder to shoulder, hip to hip. 'Then, often we'll do this upon waking.' He moved strongly, slowly, certain of what he was doing. 'I would have shown you this last night, but we were both too eager.'

'Surely, I was.' Robin was gasping. 'What must I do?'

'Hold me,' Channon said against his mouth.

Beneath him, Robin bucked like a colt and was wild, and the rush to completion was helpless and ecstatic. Robin tried to drowse again, but Channon swiftly stroked the slender, sinewy body awake.

'You must go. Lie abed in your own chamber till your servants are unsuspecting. This room smells ripe but the wind will freshen it before they are in to change the linen. Come, Robin! Time to leave.'

He slid reluctantly out of bed and stood in the sun to gather his clothes. Channon feasted his eyes again on a tousled, sylvan creature whose face mirrored the night's pleasure and whose body moved with languid, sated elegance. The curve of buttocks drew Channon's palm, though the bed was still warm with the heat of Robin's body.

'We'll ride again this morning,' he offered. 'Meet me in the kitchen, breakfast with me. We can enjoy the sun before the rest of the world wakes.'

A blush warmed Robin's face and he stooped to kiss. 'I have much to thank you for.'

'Thank me?' Channon made scornful noses. 'It is I who should be thanking you.' He patted one hose-clad buttock, rubbed it affectionately. 'You were my joy, the only joy that can be given as a gift... now, go. I heard a maid a moment ago and we'll soon be at risk. Your father wouldn't relish the loving there has been in this bed.'

'For he would see no love,' Robin murmured, 'only sin. And since he is ignorant of the pleasures you showed me, he would assume I was buggered. I hardly feel that I have sinned. I feel free, and happy.'

'You haven't sinned,' Channon scolded. 'That nonsense exists in the minds of churchmen. Pay them no heed. Rather, heed the voice of your heart.' He paused, one brow arched lazily at his lover. 'What does it say?'

But before Robin could reply they heard footsteps in the hall below. The servants were about and it was foolish to tarry. Bemused, uncomplainingly bewitched, Channon watched his companion flee. The night had not despoiled Robin. Channon regretted nothing he had said or done. He pillowed his head on his folded arms, contemplating the day in better spirits than he had enjoyed for months.

Chapter Eight

Robin could have run. Delight thrummed in his limbs, yet he was afraid. The fear which chilled him had nothing to do with his father, nor the possibility of discovery. It was simpler, and infinitely worse.

He had dreamed of love often enough to know how it felt. For Margaret, Countess of Roebury he had suffered a boy's infatuation; the feeling he nursed for Channon was different, and his heart squeezed painfully. He was in love, and it hurt as keenly as any wound. Even in the first blind moments he knew it was to nothing. Channon would soon be gone, first to Court, later to Seville, then to sea, perhaps the Americas where a mercenary might seek a fortune in the midst of war.

There could be no chance of Robin following. In Spain he would be an enemy and, when the war began, a prisoner. In Panama or Vera Cruz he would be a corpse. He had never handled a sword, never brawled. Though Robin dreamed of glory he was no fool. Love was the dream from which one woke in pain.

He slid into bed and gazed at the low oak beams of the ceiling. Loving Channon was doomed to tragedy. It was wisest to say nothing, keep secret what he felt and accept what he was given until Channon was gone.

He kicked down the linen, studied his body and recalled what had been done to it. He thought of Channon's formidable physique, the dark threat of his risen shaft, and his loins quivered. Was the act of buggery pleasurable? Or did a man endure it, so as to give pleasure to his lover?

Robin shuddered. He would do it. For Channon, even if it hurt he would endure, give him the rapture he could have from any silly girl without a second thought. What a girl could give him, Robin would give him, and damn to pain. Channon would ensure that he suffered no more than he must, and Robin would draw his own pleasure from Channon's delight.

In an hour he rushed into fresh hose, linen, boots, leather jerkin and cape, garments suited to the chill of the early morning. Maids were polishing in the hall; a little scullion laboured with a scuttle of wood as big as herself. The kitchen wenches bickered over the bread and no one spared him a glance as he went to the pantry for quails' eggs and pork.

He discovered himself famished after the night's exercise and ate a lot. It was some time before he looked up from his place by the inglenook and found brown eyes regarding him amusedly from the door.

'Good morning, Master Armagh.' Channon stepped in. 'You are in good appetite. And fair spirits?'

'Fine spirits, sir.' Robin could disguise neither his blush nor his delight. 'Will you eat with me?'

Channon seated himself by the hearth and gave Mistress Lovell a smile. 'If this comely matron will feed me.'

She produced a platter heaped with pork, eggs and cheese, and Channon tackled the food as eagerly as Robin. He was famished, and Robin was deeply gratified. He absently admired the soldier's cheek, his mouth, his lashes. He was handsome as none other Robin had ever seen. Heir to good blood on both sides of his family. Channon looked up and winked, making Robin choke on the last bite of his breakfast.

He patted his lips. 'Why are you not a knight?' he asked, more boldly than he would have dared the day before.

'I am an Irishman, as much as a Spaniard. I was blooded at fourteen but my father fought against the English, as your ancestors did not. Your fathers became earls under the Normans, mine were killed. My father died well. I watched him fight as if he would cut himself a place in legend. His brothers died with him.'

'You fought?' Robin asked quietly.

'No. I was fourteen, and my mother was placed into my care. It was I who spirited her to a Spanish ship. Domenica ran home to her family, I had no option but to follow. Our lands were seized, I had no way back.'

'Tell me of Spain.' Robin leaned closer, intent on him.

Channon smiled. 'What shall I say? Heat and dust, the frippery of the Court, which swiftly bored me. Philip's palace is a nest of intrigue and avarice, and not for me. When Don Diego Valdez, whose brother, the vice-admiral, is governor of Havana, raised a mercenary army for Panama, I went with it.'

The brown eyes clouded and he would say no more. Robin had touched a nerve. Pain smouldered deep down, well-healed, but after all the years it hung on. Absurdly, Robin ached to soothe or avenge it. He could offer no more than a look, little knowing that his face mirrored his thoughts, and Channon saw everything. The mercenary smiled at him, though Robin could not know it was an expression of gratitude.

They left the house before they could be waylaid by Robin's taciturn father. 'I must ride to Whiddon Manor by noon,' Channon warned as they walked to the stable. 'I left Mauricio there.' The May sun was bright after the storm of the day before. 'Will you ride with me?'

I would go anywhere with you, Robin thought, but he said only, 'It is a fine day for riding. Sir Henry will feed us, too.' He took Tara from a groom and mounted up.

'He sets a good table.' Channon was in the saddle too, and urged his gelding into the meadow, after Tara.

They were silent for some time. The morning was already warm and Robin refused to entertain thoughts of the day he would watch Channon leave. His body was still languid, content after loving, yet his heart felt sore. He glanced at Channon to find the man watching him with an affectionate expression.

Under the scrutiny Robin faltered. He murmured Channon's name, stirring him. 'I am only thinking, how fair you are in the sun,' Channon told him. 'You have your mother's eyes, slanted and bewitching. Ah, I discomfit you!' He was teasing, and laughed at Robin's embarrassment. 'What else do you expect from me? If I were not beguiled, why should I want you? Why would I be planning what I'll do with you next?'

'You wish to bed with me again?' Robin whispered.

Channon's amusement did not mock. 'We'll lie together as often as we please. I'll show you all the ways men love.' He held out his gloved hand and Robin took it. 'My word upon it.'

Robin's fingers clasped his hand. He did not see Channon's brow crease, nor could he know of the needing that bedevilled Channon. Not a hunger for sex, since the night had sated him, but a yearning to be part of Robin, though not in any physical way. He could possess Robin's body without hurting him very much, he was sure, but not even that would suffice. It was not Robin's body Channon wanted now. It was his heart.

They drew rein by the willows and Robin slid down under the trailing branches. He wanted Channon's embrace, wanted to kiss. Channon plundered his mouth meticulously till he panted with laughter. They sprawled in the damp grass as the horses began to graze and Channon bared Robin's chest to nuzzle there.

At last he lifted his head and smiled into the face that was so very like Catherine Armagh's. 'Are your brothers this lovesome, you little wanton?' he teased.

'Wanton?' Robin echoed. He had not heard that accusation in three years. 'I suppose I am. Last night is the proof. I did things I never imagined before! My brothers? John is tall and handsome. He is at Court, but his health is poor. His pallor is no affectation. His doctors say he may not live.'

'I may have seen him,' Channon mused. 'He has your father's pale eyes, hair the colour of hay? He is a handsome lad, but not as handsome as this imp of mine!' Embarrassing Robin was easy and delightful. Channon laughed.

Robin was the picture of health. Channon nuzzled his chest as Robin continued, 'Hal is my favourite. A clever man who studies birds and animals. He is on a voyage to the Caribbean Sea. Lovesome?

71

Hal is a scholar, but not handsome like John and Richard.'

'Sir Richard? Now, him I know.' Several times, Channon had seen Mauricio passing letters to a man with cold blue eyes and pale skin. Those eyes were the same slanted shape as Catherine's but as icy as William Armagh's.

'Yes.' Robin stretched as his chest was petted. 'Shall I ever be Sir Robert? I doubt it! I'd call Richard the most handsome —'

'You would be wrong.'

'— but not lovesome,' Robin finished. 'He is as bleak as my father, which is why father loves him best. He would never have been seduced by Margaret of Roebury. Nor,' he chuckled, 'bedded by a Spanish soldier!'

'No?' Channon shared his amusement.

'He should have been a priest, I am certain.'

'Then, it's lucky I am,' Channon said against Robin's ear, 'that the sickly one, the pious one and the scholar flew the nest and left my delight for me to find.' He kissed Robin's nose, plundered his mouth again before he could protest. 'Tonight I'll show you how else to make love.'

The green eyes darkened. 'You'll couple to me since I trust you now?'

But Channon shrugged and disguised the rush of his pulse with bland words. 'You will know when it is time for that. You need not fear, but must be sure, and must want me fiercely.'

Robin frowned. 'You don't desire me in that way? Is my rump unsightly? I was never told so, even in jest.'

Channon laughed rudely. 'You have the most delicious arse I have ever seen! Coarse language raises your blush? I shall remember that, for I like to fetch roses to your cheeks! Ah Robin.' He held the boy. 'I've no wish to pain you, and in your virginity I can do you injury. You have courage, as last night proves. It is myself grown timid. I'll not be the one to hurt you, and it can go awry, sweeting. I've seen boys in straits you cannot imagine.'

'Where?' Robin propped his palms in the grass.

'At sea.' Channon chose his words carefully. 'I saw Don Julio Perez's bosun give a lad the choice between sixty lashes and two seamen who desired him. The boy was innocent. I saw a slender youth from the Indies, with skin like honey and eyes like dark velvet, sold over and over, for the sweetness of his body. Even I used him, weeks out from San Juan de Ulua, when I was desperate. He was ill in his vitals by then, which saved him at the last. Fearing his sickness, men spurned him.'

'What became of him?' Robin was hushed, troubled.

'Soft heart.' Channon tousled the auburn hair. 'He was baptised into the Catholic faith and went with the Franciscans as an interpreter. I hope he grew well. He was a rare beauty. Seamen can be sinners, and I was no angel. But my price is paid, the accounting is even.'

'Your price?' Robin echoed. 'There is no mark of a whip on you, only sword cuts about your right arm, and a scar on your back, from a heathen lance, I should say. What price, Dermot? Tell me!'

The questions snapped Channon out of the past. Robin's curiosity was aroused, and warranted. 'No secrets,' Channon whispered, rejecting the pride and honour of both the Irish ricon and the Spanish house that had nurtured him. His fingers cradled Robin's face tenderly, but the boy was impatient. 'Do not be shocked, nor disquieted. I am long recovered. But you have guessed by now. I was raped, like the boy from Panama. It was men of Leyerre's crew, on the *Santa Marguarita*, which sank my little ship. As a privateer we carried no flag. The gentlemen were ransomed without question but I was sixteen and taken for an ordinary seaman, perhaps a pressed man. Later, they realised they had bound the Cervallos' favourite nephew over a barrel and raped him bloody.'

Despite the sun Channon shivered. Memory cut like a knife. Sickness, pain, the terror that it would go on and on till he was dead and cast overboard with the refuse. The sound of his own voice, panting begged pleas for mercy which were unheeded. The sourness in his mouth as his belly emptied, the ache in his head as he hung over the barrel, quivering and ill.

The sky dimmed and Robin had murmured his name a third time before he returned to the present. Channon forced a smile and plucked a strand of grass from Robin's hair. 'I cannot bear to cause pain to one I adore.'

Robin's face had paled, then crimsoned. Channon had no objections to being held tightly, and lay with his face pressed to the boy's bare chest. Arms closed about him with surprising strength. He breathed the warm, woody scents of Robin's body and spoke against the hollow between the boy's lightly pelted breasts.'I would not violate you carelessly.'

'Never?' Robin whispered. 'Not even if I want it?'

'You know nothing of it.'

'Nor will I, unless you show me! Must a man hurt?'

Unwelcome scenes commanded Channon's mind. He shut them out with an effort and smiled. 'Who can say? A thick salve makes him slippery and loving fingers make him lax.' Robin's look of incomprehension made him laugh. 'You portrait of innocence! How have they sheltered you all these years?'

'My apologies,' Robin said, flustered. He was being teased, but could not think how. 'Dermot, please!'

The Spaniard relented. 'Loving fingers, deep inside. There is a place that ignites at a clever caress. Were I to enter you, I would touch you there, and give more pleasure than I stole.' He watched Robin's eyes widen and laughed again. Such glorious innocence was a joy. It was Robin's shield, but it could be a weapon against him. The thought taunted Channon.

'Tonight.' Robin's mouth gaped like a landed fish. 'Will you show me, tonight?'

'If you return the favour.' Channon kissed him.

They rode back to the house before noon, and Mistress Lovell took a message from Robin for his father. 'Tell him I have gone with Señor Channon to escort Don Mauricio home. We will not be needing luncheon.'

'Two less to feed,' she said cheerfully as the young men hurried up to change.

The horses were eager to race where, a day before, Mauricio had set a sedate pace. The ground was dry but the beck was much deeper and Robin took them a mile north, where a hump-back bridge crossed the stream. They doubled back along the rise to Whiddon Manor a little after noon.

Sir Henry's elderly groom took the nags. They smelt mutton and ale from the coachman's house, and Channon hoped for an invitation to dine. A maid was polishing at the door, and dropped a curtsy before them.

'Don Mauricio's escort,' Channon told her. 'Where shall I find him?'

'They are dining, sir. I'll show you in.'

'I know the way. Master Armagh?' Channon ushered Robin ahead of him and dropped his voice. 'You know Sir Henry?'

'A little.' Robin tugged his sleeves and finger combed his hair. 'Not socially. I have never been in this house.'

'Then follow me.' Channon showed him through the cherry wood doors. 'Mauricio, you look in better health today.'

Better health, and bad temper. A dismembered goose commanded the table and the two old men wore bleak faces.

'What became of you last night?' Mauricio asked tartly as he patted his lips with a napkin.

Sir Henry waved the young men to be seated and Channon pulled up a chair. He carved for himself and Robin. 'I rode to Blackstead on personal business. You had no need of me.'

'Personal business?'

It was some time since Channon had seen Mauricio so annoyed. He set down the knife. 'As I said.' He arched a brow at his kinsman. 'You were safe, and I — an ornament.'

'An ornament!' Mauricio snatched up his cup. 'Pleasant, Dermot, to know the value you place upon my life!'

Sir Henry cackled like a crow. 'Mauricio! He means a wench. He had a bed waiting, and you kept out of it. Let him be. He's young, and you've begun to forget what that means.'

'Personal business.' Channon regarded Mauricio over the messily butchered goose. 'I returned swiftly, the moment I was free.'

'Noon,' Mauricio grumbled. 'Had you returned before nine I should not even have missed you.'

Robin spoke up quietly. 'My fault, sir. I detained him, wanting stories of the Americas. I insisted and he was too polite to send me away. If I should apologise, I do.'

Surprise silenced Mauricio, and he relented. 'Young men! Well, I came to no harm.' He returned to his meal, slicing apricots with a knife like a razor.

'Young men,' Henry echoed wistfully, as if he longed to turn time back twenty years. And he was chuckling over Robin, so he recalled those three-year-old indiscretions. Channon saw Robin's dread, but Henry treated the matter with jocularity, as if the boy's amorous misadventures were an achievement. Not every youth could catch a countess's eye.

Robin kept his eyes on his plate and was silent until he was spoken to. Unless Henry mentioned his secrets, Mauricio would never know.

A Catholic knight would surely condemn him. He wondered how Mauricio viewed Channon's sensuality, but Channon was a man, a soldier, it was not the same. Robin was still a boy in his father's house. It was not the same at all.

'By God,' Henry was saying, 'I've a mind to have a hand in it myself. I'll not see another fight in my lifetime.'

'You, march to war?' Mauricio demanded, for Henry suffered the bone-ache, his hands were knobbled, his back stiff. 'Put on your armour and sharpen your sword?' Mauricio was disbelieving.

'Better to die gloriously than in bed, like Falstaff.' Henry made a face. 'No glory in that.'

'Better to live a long, happy life,' Mauricio argued. 'You have years yet. Watch your grandsons grow, wave from the shore as young hawks like my nephew spill their blood for glory.'

'Or not,' Channon added, 'if we can help it. There's no glory in bleeding. Nor in standing on a battlefield amid your dead friends and brothers. The joys of battle are for poets left at home, not for soldiers.'

Henry nodded sagely. 'He speaks truth, Mauricio. You were never a soldier, but I was.' He leaned toward Robin. 'You wanted stories, lad? I could tell you stories! I fought in Bloody Mary's day.'

Channon frowned. 'On which side?'

Another cackle of laugher. 'Both — but years apart. I was for the rightful Queen, King Henry's daughter. I was with the lads who went against Northumberland in '53.' His face darkened. 'Two years on, it was bitter, when the burnings began. My friends were to be martyred. I fought to win them free.'

'And could have been burned yourself,' Mauricio added.

'Mayhap. But I was young and daring.' He raised his cup to Channon. 'Grasp life in both hands, boy. Reach out and take what you would have, for time is a thief and soon you'll be like me. The spirit is steel but the flesh is broken.'

Channon lifted his cup but looked at Robin, who had heard the advice with a frown. He had tarried at Blackstead too long, and was chafing to be free before his tutor returned in autumn. Robin was a reluctant scholar, but a good one, and his education outstripped many of the ranked and titled. Not even Mauricio was as well read.

Pastries and sweetmeats followed the goose, while Henry told grim tales of battle. Channon took them for that they were, an old man's glory-mongering, but Robin hung on every word, as hungry for the stories as Channon was bored.

It was mid-afternoon when Mauricio stirred at last. 'I've presumed upon your hospitality too long, cousin.'

'Nonsense.' Henry offered his hand. 'I hope to see you again before you leave Blackstead. When will that be?'

'I wait each day for a dispatch from Hampton, recalling me to service — and bloody service is it! I am cut to tatters, no matter that it is not done with a sword. I have spoken against Frobisher and Drake, which few men can claim.'

'And lived to tell of it,' Channon added. 'Frobisher and Drake are at least honourable. Less can be said of Rothwell.'

'Rothwell,' Henry spat. 'God grant the cur shall answer for his evils.'

'Lady Catherine was very beautiful.' Channon frowned at Robin. 'If the portrait is true.'

Henry sighed heavily. 'She was fairer than the artist made her. An angel, with a voice like a lark and skin like white velvet. Even when time had its way with her — she was not young when Rothwell began to want her — she still had her beauty and charm. She was much like young Robin, I tell you.'

'So I see.' Channon studied Robin's profile against the window. 'And Rothwell struck her in anger, Mauricio told me.'

'She was made like a bird, her bones so fine,' Henry said sadly. 'Unlike Robin! Then, there was poor little Jane, the wench who saw the blow struck. She died soon after. Sickness, the physician swore. Jane had never known a day's illness, not even pox. Pretty girl, that one. The last in my bed.'

His lover? Channon was astonished but Henry's eyes brimmed as if the girl had died only a week ago. Abruptly, Robin got to his feet and left the room. The old men looked after him, as if his exit was rude. 'Forgive him,' Channon said quietly. 'It is his mother you discuss. Your leave.'

He was sitting on the side of the horse trough, watching the ripples as he drew his fingers through the water. He did not look up as Channon appeared, and was silent till Channon touched his cheek, not quite intimately. His eyes were stormy.

'What is it, Robin?' Channon would have held him, but they had no privacy.

'I was a child,' Robin told him. 'My brothers were still boys, my

77

sisters were babes. Rothwell came visiting. My father and brothers had gone to Ralston and I was playing in the hall. I heard the man ask my mother to go away with him, and did not know what he meant.'

'That was when he killed her?'

'No, it was much later, and in his own house.' Robin stood and hugged himself. They walked along from the manor and he let Channon lead him into the garden, where high hedges shut out the breeze, shut in the sun. There, he surrendered to Channon's embrace. 'I heard Rothwell call her a "doxy", and did not know what it meant. I asked Richard and he cuffed me, told me not to say such words. I was to be a priest, you see.'

'I know.' Channon drew his lips across Robin's forehead.

'Rothwell came again, several times. He and my father did business. Rothwell keeps a private army, all well-mounted. His stables are full of our horses. My father visited Halstead Hall, mother was invited and he insisted she go. She railed at my father. Rothwell had said, "Every women is a whore beneath her skirts, even the Queen." My father was half angry, half mocking. He said he would have words with Rothwell.'

'And did he?' Channon stroked Robin's shoulders.

'When it was too late. Then there were too many words.' Robin wrenched away and turned his back. 'I remember little of it. I was grieving and very young.'

'My poor boy.' Channon embraced him. 'I was almost a man when my family was butchered, and my mother lived. My sire died out of his own foolishness. No one forced him to stand and fight.' He kissed Robin's neck.

The tousled copper head rested on Channon's shoulder. Robin looked blindly at the sky. 'I heard the word "murder", but it was quickly silenced. Then Jane was dead too. My father was white with rage. One afternoon Rothwell visited with a company of men. I was at my widow. They drew swords but no blood was let. I heard everything.'

'Threats, promises,' Channon guessed. 'If Armagh spoke the word "murder" again it would be a matter of Rothwell's honour. He offered to fight?'

'A duel,' Robin turned into Channon's embrace, arms about his waist. 'Rothwell is a soldier. Ten years ago he was in his prime, while my father was never a fighting man. He withdrew and has been silent since, conniving in private.'

'Conniving?' Channon held him firmly.

'At Rothwell's downfall in business.' Robin sighed. 'It would have been simple to hire a murderer, but every finger would have pointed at the Armaghs. Rothwell's men would have razed Blackstead.'

'The man has the devil's own luck.' Channon's grip tightened on Robin for a moment, then released. 'I have a score to settle with him also.' Robin's brows arched. 'First, I shall not forgive him for grieving you. Then, he attacked the *Alcanzar* in heavy seas, and my good friend was killed.'

'Your good lover?' Robin hazarded.

'Once, long ago.' Channon smiled. 'Are you jealous?'

'No.' Robin looked away.

'You are, and it sits prettily on you!' Channon teased. 'Don't be jealous. The past is the past. I will settle Rothwell for you, and for Marcos. And there is more. You know Mauricio was poisoned. I killed the man who meddled with his cup, but who hired him? Tonio Diaz will be at Court by now. If Rothwell's hand is in it, he'll have the truth... and I will have Rothwell.' He made a neck-wringing gesture. 'There. Lady Catherine's vengeance, a decade late.'

Robin was dubious. 'Rothwell is a fine swordsman.'

'So am I, and I am younger, and lighter. If the duel is fair, legal, it must go my way. It is a very proper sport between gentlemen, Robin.'

For a moment Robin hovered between horror and approval, then threw up his hands. 'Christ, this maddens me! My mother is ten years dead. To have you crippled for ancient grievances —'

'And Marcos is newly dead.'

'Your good lover,' Robin said darkly.

Channon frowned. 'Jealousy is not so pretty on you now. It does you no credit. The past is gone.'

'So is my mother,' Robin hissed. 'I'll not have you maimed on her account.' He held out his hands and Channon grasped them. 'Marcos was killed in an act of war.'

'England and Spain are not at war,' Channon argued. 'He was killed, and five lads with him, by a pirate. Rothwell is a privateer, like Drake and the rest. But at least they do not molest ships in the Channel, almost within signalling distance of their own ports.'

'I heard Mauricio say the *Alcanzar* was on Philip's business, charting the coast,' Robin said curtly.

79

'You have sharp ears.' Channon's embrace crushed him. 'It is not your concern, Robin. You are a scholar and a lover. Leave intrigue and war to those who plan and fight it.'

Robin lifted his head. 'I am not yours to command.'

'Then, when you flee Blackstead you'll run to war?' Channon demanded as Robin tried to escape. Channon's arms held him fast. 'Answer me!'

'I don't know.' Robin's threshing stilled. 'I know only, if you are killed I shall die.' He leaned heavily on Channon's chest and his breath scudded moistly over the soldier's neck.

Annoyance was gone in an instant. Channon stroked his hair. 'Oh, Robin. If you were mine to order!'

'How would you command me?' Robin whispered.

'I would order you to stay safe.' Channon's lips explored his ear. 'To be happy. To be well bedded, often.'

'With you?' Robin looked searchingly at him.

'I must leave soon. You know that.'

'Take me.' Robin's fingers clenched in Channon's sleeves.

'Where would I take you, to Seville? You are an Englishman! They would lock you up. You speak the language but could never pass as a Spaniard.'

Robin bit his lip. 'Then, where do you go after the embassy is expelled?'

'Where I am sent. I know that no better than you.' Channon kissed his lips tenderly. 'Battle fascinates you?'

'As does anything of which I know little,' Robin admitted.

'Aye, *very* little.' Bitterness roughened Channon's voice. 'Don't be duped by old men's tales. There's a stink to a battlefield, and death is ugly. Pain is simply pain, mercy is scarce and glory is a myth. You yearn to flee?'

'You know I do.' Robin was confused now.

'Then run, but please God, not to war.'

Robin gave him a shrewd look. 'You have your own tales of glory.'

'Such as they are.' Channon shrugged. 'I ran away to war, I admit. But I was trained for it since I could walk.' Annoyance sharpened his voice. 'I was wounded time and again, had three ships sunk under me, was raped and ransomed before I was nineteen and I was a chieftain's son! I survived. Do you fancy you would? Or would you seek the protection of a gentleman, as many do, and whore for your survival?'

Now Robin wrenched away. 'You know little of me, but you know me better than that. Or am I dishonoured already, sinning in your bed? You said I had not sinned. Now you tell me differently. Shall I hurry and confess myself?'

'Oh, Robin!' Channon caught his shoulders and spun him about. 'It was not what I intended to say, and not how you understood it.' He took a breath. Robin waited, silent and defiant. 'You may run to war and discover your error too late. The only way back alive is with a man's protection, and you have but one way to earn it. Take care the mistake is never made. You might rue it.'

'Oh.' Robin's cheeks coloured. 'Forgive me. I snarled like a mongrel.'

'Forgiven.' Channon touched his burning cheek. 'I cannot bear thoughts of you in blood and chains. Run to London, not to sea, and not to war. I can help you. I know some men, a ship's chandler, a chart maker. Your skills with language, numbers and maps stand you in good stead. I can give you a letter of introduction. Keep safe, Robin. Let me leave Blackstead knowing you are safe.'

Robin searched his face. 'And what shall I know of you? That you have gone back to sea.'

'First, home to Seville,' Channon corrected. 'Then to Madrid, to watch Philip's peacock courtiers flirt, drink, dance and grow fat.' He signed resignedly. 'I am for Philip's service. I believe they sent me here to learn pretty manners before I am loosed among civilised men.'

'But Mauricio's life was at risk,' Robin added.

'There are a dozen at home who could have done this duty.'

'But you are the best of them.' Robin touched his face. 'The soldier who has seen all things and survived.'

'Flatterer.' Channon kissed his fingers. 'Perhaps I shall rot myself with drink, so bored in Madrid, or be implicated in some intrigue over a bastard child.'

At last Robin laughed, a sound Channon loved. 'Dermot, you are a madman.'

'No,' Channon corrected amiably, 'an Irishman.' He caught Robin's hands. 'Promise me. Run, but not in search of glory. Promise, or I'll know no rest.' The words escaped before he could stop them.

'Then, stay with me.' Robin was quick to pounce. 'Keep me safe!'

The proposition made Channon groan, for it was tragically impossible. 'Soon our countries will be brawling like common drunkards. Were I in England when it began, I should be imprisoned. Where you in Spain, the same.'

'There are other counties,' Robin suggested.

'Nowhere will be safe for strangers, Robin. People will see spies everywhere. We would fight every day to keep our liberty. I cannot take you into that.'

'Will not,' Robin argued.

'As you wish. I am as Spanish as you are English, and the pair of us are Irish to boot. That is a precarious position, no matter where we are.' Robin's face twisted. 'And you forget my duty to my family. We will survive only so long as we stand together. Mauricio will soon be expelled, and I must go with him. You know that.'

'I know.' Robin closed his eyes. 'There is no chance that Elizabeth and Philip will amicably resolve their differences?' Channon shook his head slowly, emphatically. 'Then all I heard is true. They are seeking men for army and navy, laying in powder and shot. I heard that Walsingham, almost on his deathbed, was marketing for armour.'

Walsingham, whose spy, Pompeo Pellegrini, had brought back the secrets of Spain's crippling debt to Genoa's powerful bankers. 'You heard correctly,' Channon said bleakly. 'This whole country is eager to fight. This business with Rothwell is proof of it.'

'I saw a letter from Dandrige,' Robin began.

'That fop?' Channon knew him as a parasite, listening at keyholes, surviving by stealth. 'What did he write?'

'That Elizabeth is Rothwell's investor.' Robin rubbed his ears as he remembered the price of his curiosity.

'She is,' Channon said acidly. 'She also invests with Drake and Hawkins. Pirates, the whole company of them. But not murderers,' he added thoughtfully. *El Draque* was many things, not all of them honourable, but he was not like Rothwell.

They were silent a long time before Robin said, 'Sleeping dogs are best left to lie. Catherine Armagh is a memory now. Keep safe, Dermot.' He took Channon's hand tightly.

The soldier smiled fondly at him. 'There's a bright side to this. No war lasts forever. Win or lose, it will be over before long. In Madrid I'll come to no harm, and at home you'll be safe. Perhaps I shall not be sent to sea, if it's over soon. I'll return, seek you at Blackstead or in

London. Farewell is not the same as goodbye, in any language.'

By tacit agreement they let it rest as voices shouted in the yard, and Robin stirred. 'Mauricio is ready to leave.' He had turned to go when Channon caught him, kissed him deeply for a moment while they had the privacy of the tall hedges.

The horses had been fed and curried. Sir Henry was out, stoop-shouldered but still spry. He issued invitations to return at their pleasure, but Channon had no intention of coming back if he could help it. He smiled politely as he helped Mauricio to mount, and bade the old man good day.

Chapter Nine

Afternoon was hot and woodsmoke curled on the still air over Blackstead. As Mauricio strolled toward the house the young men tarried in the yard. Channon sweated in the black velvet doublet and damned the convention that made him wear it.

'Do you swim?' Robin asked. 'The river is sluggish, well suited to swimming.'

And he swam like a fish. He easily outpaced Channon, who had spent little time in the water since his boyhood ended so abruptly. Hours later, exhausted and happy, they sprawled in the grass to dry. Their talk carefully avoided any mention of the morning's altercation.

Instead, Channon spoke of Seville, his mother and his appreciation of the finer things in life, of which Robin was one. The lad laughed, as Channon had intended, but it was not a jest. Robin was fine, laughing in the sun as his hair dried feathery and beads of water were trapped in the down on his chest.

Without warning desire exploded along Channon's nerves. He pounced, pinned Robin securely and humped against his damp skin till the slender frame trembled with passion. They were hidden by the willows, the knoll, and distance. Robin responded wildly, and as he came Channon recognised the strange, sweet pain in his chest. He was in love.

Startled, he lifted his head to look into Robin's face. The boy's features mirrored the frightening emotion which gripped Channon;

his eyes were dark with it, the hands stroking Channon's arms and the legs hugging his hips spoke it fluently. Channon closed his eyes and mourned. *Damn to honour, damn to duty and war. Christ Jesus, I love him!* And it hurt.

Shadows lengthened as they ambled in to change for dinner. They parted at the head of the stairs with a smile of conspiracy. Robin retired to his room and Channon dressed swiftly in black velvet, doublet, hose and trunk hose, white lace collar. The absence of colour suited his rank, heritage, and his mood of mourning.

Preoccupied as he left his room, he heard Robin's quiet movements behind his own door and passed on in search of a cup of wine. Or three, to calm the foolish churning of his belly. He had poured a rich madeira when he heard Mauricio and Armagh in the library, arguing in hushed but angry tones. Channon could not help but overhear.

'You are a fool, William, and will soon be a dead fool!' Mauricio was furious. 'You could lose your head for this!'

'If I am discovered,' Armagh argued. 'I shall not be. God's blood, if I cannot trust you, whom can I trust?'

'But I am not the whole embassy, and Hampton is infested with spies. I guard my words even in my own apartment. I trust Dermot, I trust Antonio Diaz, who has served my house all his life, and no one else. I cannot carry messages for you. The danger is horrifying. If it were discovered that the Spanish embassy is involved, under Elizabeth's very nose — by God, the war I am trying to avert would flame up tomorrow!'

A terse pause followed before Armagh snapped, 'Then I shall find another courier. Captain Vasca is still in York. If you trust Channon, send him with the dispatches. The *Alcanzar* is under repairs. She cannot sail until she can bear a storm, and the work will take another week. The Spaniards must oversee the hammering of every nail, since they suspect English shipwrights of villainy.'

'I suppose Dermot could carry letters to Vasca.' Mauricio sighed. 'I can tell you, Vasca is travelling by coach to London to state his case against Rothwell. He is persuasive and handsome, the Queen may be charmed. She is still a woman, despite the crown. Rothwell's fortunes may be in tatters and my own vengeance won with the same stroke as yours — the stroke that lops Rothwell's head! But this other matter could set your own head on the block, and for what?'

'For the lives of Catholic boys whose liberty may well lie in my hand,' Armagh said sharply. 'What should I confess, if I did nothing? I was never a soldier, but I can do this. And what I can do, I must. I thought you would understand, if not assist me.'

'I shall ask Dermot,' Mauricio mused. 'His will be the final word as to whether he runs your risks. I commend your motives, but a day arrives when one's own neck comes first. You have too much to lose if you are discovered.'

Curiosity prickled and Channon was waiting when Mauricio entered the dining room. The servants were not yet busy but he smelt pastries, rabbit and onions. A glance at Channon, and Mauricio knew he had been overheard.

'Risks?' Channon prompted. 'Will you tell me, or is it a secret from me also?'

'Risks,' Mauricio said acidly as he glared into the hearth. 'Will you carry letters for William?'

'That would depend on their content. They are for Vasca, I heard. What is this about Catholic boys?'

Mauricio rubbed his palms together. 'Our battles will be fought principally at sea. Our ships will try to land, but long before troops are ashore in Devon or Cornwall there will have been terrible fighting. Many ships will limp away. Damaged ships run with the wind, not against it, so you said. I know little of ships, but I believe I understood.'

'You did. Just as the *Alcanzar* could only make for the Humber, with the sea against her and rents at the waterline. So?' Channon waited.

'When damaged ships escape, they may limp to Ireland,' Mauricio murmured. Servants had gathered in the hall outside. 'Survivors will be hunted by Protestant loyalists, and if they are caught, will be sent to England for trial and execution. After surviving a sea battle they will be cut down by Protestants in a Catholic land.' He closed his eyes. 'William's intention is to give succour to whomever can reach his estates in the north. His cousin, the Earl of Armagh, will do this. But the details must be arranged.'

'Philip may supply a ship to take away fugitives, or arms for their defence while they are on Armagh lands,' Channon mused. 'Will Vasca take the letters to Madrid?'

'He should.' Mauricio massaged his eyes. 'His mission was one of intrigue to begin with! Diaz said he is travelling to London to speak against Rothwell. I ought to be there when he does. We should return to Hampton very soon.'

Channon's stomach knotted. Already? He mocked himself mercilessly. 'It will make an instructive foray for Robin.'

'For Robin?' Mauricio's brows rose.

'I promised him an outing,' Channon lied smoothly. 'I said I'd show him London. He has never seen the city, and I should like to be with him when he does. Such a comely lad could be eaten alive.'

'Or assaulted in the street,' Mauricio said bleakly. 'If you promised, so be it. But for God's sake keep your eye on him. I'll not know where to begin to explain to William that I took his son to London and brought back a mass of blood and bruises.'

'I'll take the greatest care,' Channon promised ruefully. Movement at the door caught his eye. William was making way for the kitchen maids. He helped himself to madeira and arched a brow at Channon, who smiled thinly. 'You appreciate what you ask of me?' Channon asked bluntly.

'You are a soldier and a Catholic, and must sympathise with my intention,' Armagh said guardedly.

'I do.' Channon looked into the fire. 'Mauricio cannot carry the dispatches. If they are found on me, it will be my neck, but what else would be expected of an Irishman?' The absurd danger inspired a wry chuckle. 'Aye, my Lord, I shall take good care of the letters. And of your son.'

'My son?' Armagh echoed.

'I promised him an outing.' Lies gained substance through repetition. 'He goes to London with me. I'll fetch him home none the worse for wear, and richer for the education.'

Armagh frowned deeply. 'You spend a good deal of time with Robert.'

More than you know, Channon thought ruefully. 'He is good company, near my own age. Trust him to me, he'll be safe.'

Standing quietly at the door, Robin heard those last words and wondered what Channon could mean — what his father knew. But the earl was not angry. Robin had chosen a doublet of burgundy red, hose to match, lace about neck and wrists. Channon looked tall and broad in his Spaniard's black, which suited him, emphasising that tangible aura of menace which demanded the respect of strangers. But Robin knew the other side of him, soft and smiling in the aftermath of lovemaking. That was the Dermot Channon he cherished. The earl was oblivious to him and Channon was beckoning him to the privacy of the window corner. Robin took a cup from him and sipped the rich wine.

'I have a surprise for you,' Channon whispered. 'You come to London with me shortly. Vasca is to speak against Rothwell, and Mauricio will attend to see the hearing is fair. I shall escort him, of course. And you also, my lad. I'll watch Hampton turn lovesick at sight of you. What, you do not want to go?'

Robin's mouth had slackened. 'Dermot! When do we leave, what must I take? Where shall I stay — what do I wear?'

Channon laughed. 'Like the most feather-headed maid of twelve with her first invitation!' Robin flushed and looked away, and Channon regretted the jest. He dropped his voice as the servants clattered about. 'Robin, I meant only that I cherish your innocence, and shall cosset you later.' Robin's cheeks burned but he managed a smile. 'You'll find Hampton jaded, tawdry and unspeakable. Jewels compare poorly to a boy's innocence.'

'Dermot,' Robin remonstrated with a skittish glance at his father. 'You must to tell me what to wear, do and say. Master Grey was to teach me manners this next year, but I... will be gone.'

'What he can teach, I can teach better.' Channon assured him. 'And I promise to rap your knuckles only when you deserve it. Or swat your bare rump, if you prefer.' Robin choked on his wine and Channon stifled his humour.

The daughters came down, squabbling like gulls. As Armagh and Mauricio seated themselves Channon took his own place, and spurned the grief that shadowed the future. Time to mourn when the day arrived. Robin was excited, ate hurriedly and said nothing; Armagh did not seem to even notice he was at the table.

Servants whisked the little girls to bed and the elders withdrew to the library. Channon made a show of yawning and bade them goodnight. Robin had retired twenty minutes before.

No light spilled under the boy's door. He had gone to Channon's chamber. A branch of candles was lit, and he sat at the casement, watching the moon. At the click of the door he jumped up from the window seat. Channon opened his arms and Robin came to him at once, his wilful body aroused without a caress.

'Wanton,' Channon teased affectionately.

'Am I?' Robin drew back. 'I know nothing of these games, I confessed last night. How should I behave? Am I wrong?'

'It was a jest!' Channon cuffed him gently. 'I wouldn't change you for the world. Save to have these clothes off you. I've not see your skin since we swam... too long ago.'

They disrobed eagerly, sprawled on the bed, and Channon produced a phial from the folds of his discarded clothes. 'A medicinal oil to guard you from harm when my fingers plunder you, as you desired.' He set it aside. 'Now, come to me.' Robin moulded to him, hot and shivering, and Channon smiled into his hair. 'Does the intimacy trouble you? Only speak, and we'll forget the oil.'

'I trust you,' Robin whispered. 'I would feel your own secret places, if you would allow it. Is it seemly for a man?'

'You also are a man,' Channon scolded.

'I am a boy! Each moment in your company reminds me.'

'A beautiful youth.' Channon kissed him. 'You shall have my secrets, all of them. You are my sweetheart, such secrets as I have are yours.' Small biting kisses covered Robin inch by inch until he begged for respite, and Channon let him rest. His legs were splayed, and the thatch between was as auburn as his head. His cock arched over his belly and his balls were swollen. Channon's eyes lingered on the parting of his thighs and a lick of painful lust seared him as he thought of fucking, his own pleasure torn from the body of another.

Robin regained his breath as Channon swallowed the furious lust and smiled. He helped the lad over and whispered an oath as he caressed the perfect buttocks. 'Christ, Robin, how can you trust me so? Another would rape you without regard for your hurts. Never trust yourself to strangers, do you hear? They may not love you, and if they hurt you there will be killing when I hear of it!'

The words were a fierce hiss which Robin heard through a haze of desire. 'Love?' He turned slightly to see Channon. 'Love me?'

'There it is,' Channon confessed. 'You have the truth. It was likely foolish to speak. But promise me you'll let no strangers use you. If you knelt for them you would be swiftly fucked, and it may not be so pleasant as you desire.'

'My word on it,' Robin whispered as lust shivered him. 'Dermot, do it to me.' He was looking at Channon's cock, which speared like a cudgel from its dark nest, powerful, arresting. 'Do it to me now, I don't care that it hurts, I want it.'

For a moment Channon closed his eyes. He saw the faces of lads who had been ravaged, memory taunted him and sweat prickled his sides. 'Tonight is not for buggery.' He took the phial in trembling fingers. '*El Draque* brought this from the Spice Islands. Little did Sir Francis imagine where it would find its way! Now, breathe deep, for it will be strange. Not hurting, but odd. Like this.'

Robin gasped, first at the caresses, then the slow, careful piercing as those fingers entered him. Channon watched him closely, and knew what he must feel. He was on the brink of some greater sensation, needed more to discover it, and lifted his lips. He cursed softly as one finger became two and he felt a sting of pain. Strange sensations, as Channon has promised.

Then pleasure wrenched through him as that place inside was touched at last. Channon knew to the second when pleasure began. What the place inside was, he did not know, nor did he care. Robin was alight now, and surrendered to desperate lust, no hope of holding back.

'Hush,' Channon soothed. 'It is like this to be fucked by one you love. When virginity is spent you'll accept me without distress. Sweet, to give pleasure and receive it at the same time.'

Robin was on his back when he returned to his senses. Every thought and emotion was written on his face. 'I love you,' he whispered hoarsely.

'I know.' Channon shifted uncomfortably and groaned as his neglected cock touched Robin's hip. Somehow Robin turned and took the big lance on his tongue. Channon had waited too long, it took little to finish him, plunge him into doped exhaustion. Robin swallowed his seed to the last drop, parted from him with a kiss and looked into Channon's face.

Pride flushed Robin now and Channon wondered what he saw as he studied his lover. Not for him to know the picture he presented — debauched, beautiful in the candlelight, or that Robin was proud that he could satisfy such a man. Channon lay with his head on Robin's lean thigh, nuzzling when the fancy took him. The air was redolent with the musky tang of sex.

Exhausted, they slept as the waning moon was framed in the open casement. Channon was sound till dawn and stirred when the birds began. Robin slept in the crook of his arm. Sunlight threaded copper through his hair, seducing the fingers. Channon loved the feel and smell of it, and kissed the warm crown of the boy's head. Still, he did not wake.

It was early and Channon let him rest. What skills would he teach next? Sensual games Robin could not envision. All his life, Channon had imagined love a myth, told to small girls to soften the blows life would bring. But love was real, captured here, curled beneath the counterpane and waking with a drowsy smile. Channon took his first kiss as the green eyes opened.

'Good morning... my love,' he whispered.

'My love,' Robin echoed. 'Daylight. Must I go?'

'It's early, lie with me a little longer. Will we swim again? I like to watch you. Like a seal! Have you ever seen seals? I have, and porpoise. When you dive and show your rump to the sun, I could eat you whole.'

'You did!' Robin stretched. 'My father would whip me for this. Oh yes, tied to the gate, with my back laid bare for the long cane. He has flogged the grooms for less.'

'And you fancy I'd allow it?' Channon demanded. 'You know better. But he'll never know, you are safe.'

'This bed betrays activity,' Robin observed. 'The servants will know.'

'Know what?' Channon smiled boyishly. 'That a Spanish mercenary of ill repute sleeps naked and enjoys lustful dreams. I'm young, it is expected of me. Your own linen tells the same story.'

But Robin shook his head. 'I am too careful, too wary of my father's ire. Soiled linen would make him think I had a girl with me, and I would have a rare set of stripes. I tend myself well clear of my sheets, and keep a rag to hand. My back is unmarked, as you've seen.'

'I've kissed it often enough. Turn.' A beautiful back, Channon decided as he tongued down Robin's spine, boyishly slender. Robin squirmed at the kisses, and Channon threw the counterpane down and kissed his buttocks too.

It was folly, and they knew it. They had no time to fan desire and spend it, and at last Channon sat up. 'Enough. You must go. Breakfast with me, and later I'll show you how to wrangle in the water.' He stretched till his joints crackled. 'I feel alive! I believed this stay in England would be drab. You changed that.'

'My pleasure.' Robin reached for his clothes. 'The talk of war is on every man's lips. We'll soon be apart.'

'But not for long.' Channon stroked his back as he wriggled into his hose. 'Spain needs a swift victory. The treasury is bare, Philip is in debt. If the war lasts long, bankruptcy will win for England where guns fail. Philip is no fool despite English jests. He has his reasons for wanting this island, not least being right of inheritance. Queen Mary bequeathed the right of succession to him.'

'Without right,' Robin argued. 'I was taught, succession is a question of pedigree, not favour. It is how the Armaghs came to be earls in England. A sixth cousin wed a French knight, whose son was made Earl of Blackstead, many years ago. Lancaster and York jousted, and the only heir was the Irish black sheep. Pedigree.'

Channon made a face. 'Bloodlines, politics. Give me a foe, a sword. I'm a soldier. Show me an honest fight.'

'I've never handled a sword,' Robin mused as he dressed. 'Teach me, Dermot. I must leave soon, and I'd rather have some means of defence.'

'You have the legs for it,' Channon observed, remembering those thighs gripped about him. 'You would learn quickly. Have you fought with your fists, like most boys?'

'Only once,' Robin confessed. 'Over a wager. My brothers broke it up. I was a child. I never wanted to fight — I have no wish to now, but I think I must learn.'

Warmth suffused Channon's chest. They had sheltered Robin completely. He was not the brawling kind, but the world was filled with men who would use him, break him, for his beauty and innocence. *And I cannot stay*, Channon thought. All the more reason for Robin to be adept with a sword when he left Blackstead. He took the boy in his arms for a final moment.

'Lessons will occupy us till we leave.'

Robin kissed him, still dreamy, half asleep.

Very much aware of his own nakedness against his lad's clothes, Channon palmed Robin's buttocks and dealt each a squeeze. 'Meet me later.'

They swam while the horses grazed, and dozed in the sun. On a cloak at Robin's side was an old rapier that had belonged to his brother, Hal. It had been in the attic for years and was blunt, mildewed, but it had been a gentleman's weapon. Channon recognised the swordsmith's mark. It was from Rizzoli of Cremona.

His praise for the sword pleased Robin, who swore to clean and whetstone it. For now, it would do as it was. He grasped the hilt and assumed the swordsman's stance through gifted mimicry. For years he had watched Richard and Hal practising. Channon took the game slowly. Robin was fit, strong, well able to keep pace, and lacked only knowledge.

He had natural balance and learned quickly where others toiled. Channon corrected his grip, the angle of his wrist and the position of his feet.

'On your toes. If you fight flat-footed they will cut you up. One thing to be flat-footed on the boards of a stage, with a make-believe sword! You'll feel the strain in your legs soon, and know which muscles need to be worked. Now, do as I tell you. Never watch the other man's sword. He'll dupe you with it.'

'Then what do I watch?' Robin was eager.

'His eyes,' Channon told him. Robin looked directly at him. 'Never take your eyes off his. In time you'll learn to see his limbs with the same look as holds his eyes. The blade is an extension of his arm, and yours. Never feel that the sword is a device in your hand. It is part of you. How does it feel?'

'Strange.' Robin moved the old rapier in the air. 'I'll grow accustomed to it. I shall practise, when you are gone. Sir Henry Leighton would watch me, keep me from bad habits. And John comes home sometimes.'

'But soon you'll be gone,' Channon reminded him. 'I am an assailant, now. I'll cut you up, you must stop me before I lop your head.' He made the cut slowly to give him time.

And so the lessons began. Robin was clumsy at first, but supple with youth and eager to learn till at last Channon called the lesson done.

'Enough, before you overtire and become clumsy again. Come and swim, cool off.'

They plunged into the river, naked and gasping at the sudden chill. Channon dunked him, and Robin came up spluttering.

'Did I do well enough?' he asked when he could breathe.

'You'll be a fair sword in a week, a good one in a month,' Channon told him. 'No flattery there, but the truth. Spurn arrogance, my lad. Know your worth but fight only when you must. I've seen men whose skills are blinding.'

'Better than you?' Robin was disbelieving.

Channon dunked him again. 'Much better! Men who could cut me to tatters. Though, the more skilled the swordsman, the less he picks foolish duels. Only fools fight for the sake of it.' He smiled as Robin shook water out of his eyes. 'You'll be good enough.'

Pride lifted Robin's chin. 'And I ride well,' he added. 'I shall be safe when I leave, Dermot.' He reached over with a bold, nipping kiss.

'And beware of strangers,' Channon insisted. 'Bed only with men you know and trust, or the consequences can be costly. Pox and pain! They make an obscenity of the word "bugger", and not by chance. To some it is more pleasurable to hear a lad scream and see the red of his blood than to please him.' He caught Robin's shoulders. 'You can die for pleasure, Robin. Know this, and beware.'

Smiles were gone. 'I'll keep safe. I would say you have completed my education.'

'Not by many a fathom.' Channon embraced him, spun them about in the water. 'The arts of love are not so easy to master, but your studies are progressing well.'

They left the water more exhausted than they entered it and stretched out to dry before hunger sent the home. Mauricio was sunning himself in the garden, and called Channon as he heard the young men on the path. Channon joined him, and the old eyes widened.

'You look like a vagabond gypsy!'

For the first time Channon took stock of his looks, and laughed. His doublet was off, his shirt open, his hose dusty, his hair tangled. 'Swimming, Mauricio. An excellent exercise.' No need to add that he had humped a boy in midwater, to Robin's delight as well as his own. 'You needed me?'

'Only to tell you, we leave for Hampton tomorrow. Vasca will be in London soon. Pack tonight, Dermot, we leave after breakfast. A few days at Hampton, till Vasca rejoins his ship, then home to this safe haven.'

The young men hurried inside but Channon sent Robin to change before Armagh could glimpse him, flushed, dishevelled and exhausted. Robin might be disciplined, which Channon would not permit. The scene could be devastating, and was best avoided by stealth.

Pigeon pie and ale awaited them, while Mistress Lovell argued with her daughter, Ellen Mary, whose husband was marketing for swords. 'They're recruiting,' she said in a broad, slurring Norfolk accent. 'My Danny's going to march with 'em.'

'Like a fool.' Mistress Lovell punched dough with both fists. 'He'll come 'ome bloody, and it'll be thee who picks up the pieces, my girl.'

Ellen Mary sighed. 'Master Rupert was boasting to the grooms, if the Dons set foot in England, 'e would take arms and kill such as 'e can find.'

'Mind your tongue,' the cook said sharply. 'Señor Channon has no wish to 'ear such gossip.'

Channon smiled at them. 'I'm a soldier first, an Irishman second. What remains is Spaniard.'

Forgiven, Ellen Mary bobbed a curtsy and hurried away.

But the depressing talk reminded Robin of the parting that must come. His father was reading the day's letters even then. Richard had written, as he often did. His letters were not for Robin, but if a ship returned from foreign parts it might bring one from Hal. These fascinated Robin, and he was allowed to study them with his tutor.

After envying his brothers all his life, he confessed to Channon in a scant whisper, only now did envy melt away. Channon gave him a soft, lover's smile as they sat to eat, and Robin flushed. Did he long for the night, like Channon? Was he still tingling after wrangling in the water?

'Pack,' Channon said as they finished eating and went upstairs. 'I'll choose for you. Wear your best, but not frippery. I don't want you strutting like a peacock. Show them the Robin Armagh I know, and they'll love you.'

They were on the stairs, and Robin turned back to look at him. 'What of my disgrace?'

For a moment Channon wondered what he meant, then recalled the Countess and swatted his rump. 'They'll see you and envy the lady! Unless I'm mistaken, you will find such invitations most common. Now, what shall you pack?'

He searched Robin's closet, selected the greens, russets, hose, trunk hose and doublets, capes, his best boots, the whitest linen and lace. The boots were set out for polishing overnight, then Channon buckled the valise and packed his own.

'Drab,' Robin accused as he saw so much black.

Channon chuckled. 'The height of propriety in Seville and Madrid. Black matches a man's vile heart. We are all depraved, you see, bound

94

for hell on one road or another.' He leaned over to kiss. 'Some roads are more pleasant than others, and since all lead to damnation, why not travel the good ones?'

Finished packing, they rode about Blackstead's boundary as far as the village of Ralston. There, Channon ordered ale and they drank beneath the tavern's creaking signboard. Coachmen in scarlet livery were working on a vehicle. The device on the door was a rampant lion, and as he saw it Channon's good humour ebbed.

'What is it?' Robin was too sensitive to his moods not to notice.

'You recognise the lion? That's Rothwell's coach, I know it well.' A woman sat within, and Channon studied her discreetly: a dark woman with hair bound severely beneath a lace cap, which made her delicate face look pointed, pixy. She wore a hooded cloak, and one white arm lay on the edge of the door. 'Who is she?' Channon murmured.

'Lady Melisande, a Frenchwoman, Rothwell's wife,' Robin told him. 'He married her not long after my mother...'

'Was murdered,' Channon drained his tankard and clattered it down. The woman's large amethyst eyes turned to him in startlement and he smiled. She was too far away to see the coldness of the expression, and answered with a stiff nod. 'A lovely woman,' Channon observed. 'Soon to be a widow. Is she blessed with children? Rothwell never mentioned his family in my hearing.'

'A son.' Robin looked away. 'The birth was difficult, they say she can bear no more babes, and was lucky to live. The boy must be seven years old.'

'Almost the age you were,' Channon said gravely, 'when your mother was murdered.' He looked into Robin's shuttered eyes, a hand's span below his own. 'I don't say it will be my hand that wreaks vengeance. Let Vasca and Mauricio address the Queen.'

The coach rolled out a moment later. Channon watched it out of sight down the lane, and shepherded Robin to the bench by the plastered wall, under the thatch. Hens scratched at their feet, they heard the ring of hammers from the stable, and the sun was warm.

'A fine life,' Channon said indolently. 'Were I wealthy, I should live like this. Idle and fat.'

'So you've not yet found your fortune,' Robin observed.

'Found and lost it,' Channon said offhandly. 'There's another, somewhere.' He chuckled. 'The Cervallos gave me a home, nothing more. I am a mercenary, a black ram! When I returned from Panama at nineteen my pockets were heavy, but they are empty now. Family debts, taxes and the Church. Popes and cardinals sup like princes and sire bastards, living richly on the wages of such as myself.' He gave Robin a mock bow. 'I bring you little, if you hoped for a dowry.'

Robin was silent for a moment, then spoke softly, lest they be overheard. 'Bring yourself, Dermot. I ask no more, and would take no more supposing you were a prince. I have my honour. My fortune will be won with these hands, as was yours.' He drained his tankard. 'I'll leave Blackstead when you go.'

'And I promised you a letter of introduction.' Channon stirred. 'I'll see to it directly... after we ride back through the woods and tarry a while. I want your mouth, and the night is too long away.'

The letter was carefully written before dinner. Robin read it twice before the indigo was dry on the white vellum. It was addressed to Master Edward Blythe, Cartographer, or Master Jacob Fitzjohn, Chandler. Robin knew both by reputation. Blythe supplied charts to the Admiralty, Fitzjohn victualled the ships of notorious privateers. Hawkins, and the Master Thief himself, Drake.

'Hide it,' Channon advised quietly, as the earl was within earshot. 'Both those men will recall favours they owe me. If your tutor taught you well, your services will be valued and you've no more need of my assistance.'

A restless unease haunted Robin now, as if his journey had already begun. It beset him in bed that night, though he was sated in Channon's arms, and not till Channon slapped his buttock sharply to still his wriggling did he apologise, and explain. Channon kissed his forehead.

'You are becoming a man, shedding your boyhood as snakes shed their skin.' He smiled in the darkness. 'When Spaniards are at liberty here again, and I return, I'll seek a boy in London and find an accomplished businessman! Would that I could stay and watch you bloom. But I'll puck the full-blown rose, that will suffice. Here, kiss me, then sleep. We are on the road early tomorrow.'

Robin licked the sensual pout of Channon's moth, showed him every skill he had been taught. 'I am accomplished at kisses, at least,' he teased, then yelped as Channon grabbed and pinned him down.

Chapter Ten

Miguel Vasca was Drake's age. His skin was swarthy after long years in the sun and wind, his eyes were nested in creases and his hair was as white as the lace at his throat. He was still handsome, Channon thought. He had good bones. Time would be kind.

Twice, Channon had sailed with him, once to the Guinea Coast, a second time to the Azores, to escort a fleet out of Rio de la Plata. The bullion fleet, Philip's salvation. Vasca took his wrist with a whispered reminiscence before he passed on to the business of the moment.

He had arrived that morning. Tonio Diaz greeted him on behalf of the embassy, and Vasca was with the spy when the Mauricio's coach entered Hampton. Guards stopped and searched it, and Mauricio held his tongue though he whitened with anger.

Sitting quietly at Channon's side, Robin was large-eyed. The Captain of the Guard inquired his name, and it was Mauricio who answered, 'Master Robert Armagh, son of the Earl of Blackstead. You may know his bother, Sir Richard.' Hauteur furled about him like a cloak.

Then the coach was in the regimented gardens and they heard music, gaiety. Hampton was entertaining, as it did almost every night. Elizabeth hungered for youth, beauty. As if she might poach some of it for herself, she surrounded herself with maidens and beautiful men. Essex, Hatton, and in his day, Robert Dudley. Dudley was aging now, and did not wear his years as elegantly as Vasca.

Standing back as the older men thrashed out their business, Channon studied Robin. He was in burgundy doublet and hose; his face was honey brown, his hands slender, one at his waist, the other curled about the rapier. Over breakfast he had stripped away the mildew and soon it would be like a razor.

He was saying nothing, seeing everything. What could he know of this world? Channon wondered what he had been taught. Did he dance, did he speak the double-edged courtly language that with the same statement flattered and demolished? Channon stepped closer.

'Stay near me,' he murmured as the old men moved off. 'We dine in our apartments tonight. Vasca speaks against Rothwell tomorrow.

You shall see the Queen, and your brothers. They often listen to the debating, and with Rothwell involved in this they'll certainly be there tomorrow.' He fell into step beside Robin. 'They will be surprised to see you.'

'Shocked,' Robin corrected. 'I'll not approach them. It would embarrass them.'

'Nonsense,' Channon retorted. 'Turn here...you sleep with me tonight. You are my guest, and I neglected to inform a soul that I would be fetching a guest back with me.' He dropped his voice. 'You shall be in my bed. To my pleasure.'

'Mine also.' Robin was intent on the women, while Channon studied him. Ornamented gowns, blinding hues, ropes of pearls and glittering gems drew his eyes.

'They are beautiful,' Channon prompted.

'They are like painted pictures,' Robin whispered. 'It is impossible to see the lady for the paint and the gown! One could paint a hen up as a peacock, but it would still be a hen.' He gave Channon an apologetic smile. 'I've only ever known our maids, my sisters and the wenches from Ralston. I have never seen anything like this.'

Channon was delighted. 'You've no liking for it?'

'I am unsure,' Robin admitted. 'Were I to kiss — say, that lady — as I kiss you, her paint would be all over me!'

'And she would slap you,' Channon added. Robin shot him a startled look. 'I taught you how men kiss, hard and deep. One kisses a lady lightly.' He laughed again at Robin's bemused face. 'This, Master Grey could not teach you! Ah — Stephen! Stephen Tanner!'

It was Bevan's page, who had brought the sleeping cup and been duped by Walter Copeland. The lad saw Channon and hurried toward him with a smile. 'You are returned, sir! And good to see you, sir.'

'And you.' Channon tugged the boy's cap straight. 'Do you know Sir Richard Armagh and his brother, John?' Stephen thought for a moment, then nodded. 'Take a message to them, that Don Mauricio has returned and is entertaining Capitan Vasca. If they wish the news at first hand before tomorrow's brawl, they may dine with us.'

Servants had lit the Ambassador's hearth. Maids ran in with fresh linen as Mauricio poured wine, and Channon drew Robin into the adjoining bedchamber.

'Is it to your liking? I sleep here, to be near Mauricio in the event that he's threatened in the night. If we are quiet he'll hear nothing.'

The bed was enormous, with green drapes embroidered in gold thread. The mattress was soft, the linen stiff and white. Robin gave Channon a rueful look. 'Dare we consort here?'

'If we don't,' Channon said drily, 'we'll be the only lovers left wanting! There are trysts and dalliances in every nook. Adultery and sodomy are everywhere, lamented and celebrated in sonnets that are penned by the volume, by young men whose passions would astonish you. Your family has shut you away too long. You are your own judge, and too harsh a master.' He drew Robin out of the chamber and closed the door. 'Time for folly later! For now, Tonio is waiting.'

The spy had delivered letters and carried information that could have him expelled or executed. Robin helped himself to wine and sat in the carved wooden chair by the hearth. Mauricio and Vasca were conversing softly in their native language. Rothwell's name was mentioned, and the *Alcanzar*. She was still on the Humber, and Vasca's papers remained hidden. If they were found the Captain was at risk. The ship had been searched twice already.

Across the hearth, Channon and the spy spoke in undertones too soft for Robin to overhear. Channon was taller than Diaz, younger and more handsome, he thought. The two were old associates and at ease together. Often they smiled, and once Channon touched Tonio's shoulder. Robin watched Channon open his doublet, remove a sheaf of letters, and Diaz's dark eyes widened. Channon gestured with the letters, smoothed the man's fretting. He sorted them and handed two into Diaz's care. The rest he kept.

They spoke intently until a knock announced servants with food and wine. Diaz left with a bow before Mauricio, as the air filled with the aromas of goose, veal and pork. Robin set down his empty cup and joined Channon.

'What news did he bring?'

'Mixed news,' Channon said thoughtfully as he lit the candles with a taper, the length of the walnut dining table. 'Trouble in Spain. Philip's fortunes are dubious, as a result of his obsession. Ships,' he added as Robin waited. 'A very great many ships. But for ourselves the news is good. We have a case against Rothwell. Tonio spoke to the man's loose-lipped servants. Copeland often visited — he had a doxy among Rothwell's women, sired a bastard that is soon to be born fatherless, thanks to my hand. It seems he bought hemlock and foxglove in an apothecary in Cheapside, at Jeremy Britton's behest. Copeland's doxy told this to Tonio for six pennies.'

'Britton?' Robin echoed. 'Not a name I know.'

'He is Rothwell's cousin and commands one of his vessels. See? Six pennies in the palm of Mistress Edith Pledge, and she will speak publicly. She must, since she is with child and Copeland is dead. Rothwell may yet find his neck sundered.'

Robin's eyes closed. 'Vengeance has been a long time coming. My father will rejoice.'

'I dare say.' Channon touched his cheek and gave Mauricio a speculative look. 'Do we wait for John and Sir Richard? I'm famished, and they may not come at all.'

'Sit,' Mauricio decided. 'If they come late, so be it.' He skewered a pigeon on his knife and turned to Vasca as he took his seat. 'Your mission was to chart the coast, against the day troops might land. What news have you for Philip?'

The brown, weather-beaten face was cynical. 'The English are vigilant, there'll be no surprise when the conflict begins, and it'll be fought at sea. I must tell His Majesty there is no chance of landing troops. Better to secure Ireland, if he would listen! But he will not. Were I in command of this shambles of a war, I would put men in Ireland and Scotland and nip England on so many flanks, she is like a dog with fleas. I would employ men like young Channon, born in the bogs and at home there, place under their command the best troops Spain has. Better men than went with Pizzaro, and by God, Francisco Pizzaro smashed an empire.'

Silence reigned until Mauricio said quietly, 'You counsel against launching the fleet?'

Vasca studied his plate as if it were a scrying glass. 'England is a fortress, so any battle must be fought at sea, and I have seen too many of them to be complacent. Do you recall the storm on the Azores in '84, Dermot? The French were on us before we saw them in the twilight, and we ate their shot for dinner. They hurt us, Mauricio. Then we won the day.'

'You won, after being surprised and assaulted?' Mauricio demanded. He looked along at Channon. 'How was this?'

Robin hung on every word, and Channon told the tale to him, not Mauricio. 'The wind is a fickle, capricious lover, one moment at your back, the next in your face. It drove the French upon us and we could not run. An hour later, when by some chance we had enough guns left to fight, it swung about and drove the French onto the Azores. We battered them to kindling against the coast. Not one ship was afloat when we were done. We anchored, rode out the gale, made repairs and took the Frenchmen home chained to our oars.'

'You see?' Vasca leaned toward Mauricio. 'Engage the English in the Channel and it will be like dogs fighting in a yard. With God's grace the wind might serve us well '

'Or serve the English,' Mauricio patted his lips with a napkin. 'Philip is no fool, Captain.'

'He is possessed,' Vasca murmured, 'and too beguiled by the dream to change his plan. Spain is impoverished for this passion of his. Your own household is quartered for sale, and but for Dermot's fortune, every ducat he brought back from Panama, your estates would have been forfeit years ago in taxes to the crown and Church.' He sighed deeply. 'Philip must go on, for the sake of Spanish pride.'

'Pride is a costly luxury.' Channon drained his cup and Robin silently refilled it. 'There is more, Captain, if you'll take further risks for survival, not pride.' He slid the letters from his doublet. 'Dispatches from Armagh, for Madrid. If you are found carrying them...'

'Heads would be lopped,' Vasca said shrewdly.

'And yours with them.' Channon looked into Robin's face, and arched a brow at Mauricio.

The Ambassador outlined Armagh's intention briefly. Channon's eyes remained on Robin's face, watching his thoughts artlessly displayed as he listened and weighed the danger. It was treason, a capital offence. At last Vasca accepted the letters and thrust them into his doublet.

'Hare-brained, yet brave,' he sighed, 'They will go along with the papers I already carry. I can be hanged but once! But Armagh knows the weight of this business, I hope.'

'He is no fool,' Mauricio said ruefully, 'and one commends courage... but this kind of courage can kill a man.' With the letters safely away they were dismissed, and Mauricio turned to Channon. 'What has Diaz heard of Rothwell?'

Channon told him tersely. 'Do nothing, Mauricio,' he finished. 'The whole sorry affair may end tomorrow, without our involvement. When Miguel speaks against the privateer the Queen *must* punish Rothwell. As he said, a man can be executed only once, despite the number of his crimes.'

The evening was still young when Vasca returned to his own apartments and servants removed the debris of dinner. Mauricio was drawn with fatigue after the journey and retired with a posset; a fire smouldered in Channon's own hearth, but it was too soon for young men to settle.

Instead, Channon shepherded Robin out, whispering so as not to disturb the old man. 'Come, see the court you have imagined for so long, all frippery and deception.' He kissed Robin's ear before they stepped into candle shadows and bright music.

Robin saw maids of his sisters' age in silk and pearls, courted by whey-faced young men. Old knights whose battles harked to King Henry's day, celebrated by boys whose battles were not yet fought. Drake and Frobisher, bickering with chandlers over the price of powder and shot; shipwrights with plans spread on the dining tables; minstrels singing for comely maids and comely boys alike. Young men whose hair curled on their shoulders, wooed for their beauty; figures embraced in the shadows. And when Channon drew his eyes to one such pair he saw two men, one blond, one red-headed, stealing kisses as they gathered up their scattered music.

Lilac and rose masked the earthy scents of people. Ale and wine flowed and dice rattled. Sonnets, madrigals and prayers were sung against coarse street verses. A draper slung his brocades and broadcloth over both shoulders as Hatton and Raleigh chose fabrics for new suits. Liveried servants rushed on errands; lovers trysted, and by midnight the passages were quiet as revellers withdrew to private entertainment.

Light-headed with wine and bewilderment, Robin was flushed and bright-eyed. Channon stood back as a boy sang to him, a French love song that embarrassed him. Channon's French was too poor for him to follow it, and Robin refused to translate. A dowager dropped her kerchief at his feet, and when he retrieved it, stroked his hand intimately, which flustered him again. Sultry eyes issued invitations, and Robin smiled shyly. The woman was a widow, old enough to be his mother. She passed on like a galleon under full sail, and turned back just for a moment to look at the new boy.

The wine had gone to his head, and Channon urged him back to their room as the watch called midnight. Mauricio was asleep, the hearths were burning low. With the doors bolted he stirred the embers with an iron. Robin sat on the bed, fumbling at his laces with fingers that defied him.

'This is Hampton Court,' Channon said softly as he bared Robin's chest and kissed it. 'Do you envy your brothers now?'

'I don't know.' Robin pulled the points of his hose, shrugged out of the doublet and bent forward to let Channon tug his shirt over his head. Then he sprawled on the bed. 'Nothing is what it seems, and — sin is everywhere! My father would never tolerate this.'

'Yet your brothers do,' Channon observed. He peeled Robin like an onion and pushed him into bed. Robin turned onto his belly, face lost among the lace pillows. 'You saw deceit and adultery?' Robin grunted. 'Beauty and grandeur?' Another grunt. 'Robin?' Channon peered down at him. 'Robin!'

But he was asleep, and Channon mocked himself with laughter. What plans he had made! There would have been coupling, cherishing fingers, a sweet salve, the dark rapture of mating between men. He shook his head, folded his clothes and slid into the bed. With the curtains drawn the world was darkness, cool linen, soft mattress, and Robin's warmth and steady breathing at his side.

His hands explored the slender young back, the roundness of buttocks, the moist, inviting place between. Channon kissed his nape and pulled up the counterpane.

Ministers and admirals took their places about the Queen. From the back of the vast hall Robin could see little and was disappointed. Taller men blocked his view, but he saw the Queen go by. She was as tiny as he had imagined her grand, just a little, frail bird of a woman with flame-coloured hair and a high, arching collar. She carried a fan and would gesture with it; the sharpness of its sword-like cuts indicated her annoyance.

He stood by Channon with the common petitioners. Most were on business, and some made notes. Far away, at the fore of the hall, Mauricio stood with Miguel Vasca at the left of the throne dais. Opposite were Drake, Rothwell and Rothwell's cousin, Jeremy Britton, the trustee who ran Rothwell's errands like a lackey and took his orders even as Walt Copeland had taken them. All evils led back to Rothwell. Robin held his breath.

Elizabeth's voice cracked like a whip over their heads. Robin did not envy Mauricio and Vasca. When it began, he was grateful to be far enough back to be unnoticed. Channon seemed content to watch. Beyond him stood Richard and John.

It was months since Robin had seen them. They had come to Mauricio's apartment in the morning to breakfast, and Robin heard their voices while still abed, wine-fuddled and drowsy. Channon's bed was a cocoon of warmth. He pulled the linen over his head and listened as Channon shaved and dressed. Mauricio's servants admitted the Armagh brothers and scurried to fetch the food.

Determined hands pulled down the linen and cold fingers made him yelp as Channon stroked him awake. He spoke in a bare whisper. 'Your brothers are here. Will you meet them, or is your head like a hornets' nest?'

He slid out of bed, shaved sketchily with Channon's razor and dressed while his head throbbed pitifully. Only then did he show his face to his brothers. Richard regarded him mutely, surprised, not pleased to see him. But John embraced him.

'Robin, you've grown, I hardly knew you! What are you doing here?'

Channon had followed him out of the bedchamber and made some remark that sufficed. Robin was too tongue-tied. John was pale, but no more frail than he remembered. Perhaps the physicians were wrong. Robin prayed so.

His head still throbbed a little as the whipcrack voice of the Queen cut across the assembly, silenced the muttering and invited the Ambassador to speak. Unable to see, Robin listened intently.

Mauricio's voice was soft. 'Majesty, I present Captain Miguel Vasca, who will state his grievance against Captain Rothwell, who attacked the *Alcanzar* in open waters some weeks ago.'

'In English coastal waters,' Rothwell argued, not giving Mauricio a chance to finish. 'Within sight of our defences.'

'Blown in by rough weather,' Mauricio retorted, 'and passing the English coast on King Philip's business. The *Alcanzar* was searched and only official documents were found. Business for a gunsmith in Amsterdam.'

After a moment's silence Robin heard Elizabeth's voice. 'Guns no doubt intended for the shooting of Englishmen.' Laughter rippled through the assembly.

'I cannot say, Ma'am,' Mauricio said patiently. 'Will you hear Captain Vasca?'

'Proceed.' She sounded bored, Robin thought. How often had she heard the same story? English privateers were infamous. In public they were criticised, in private, celebrated.

The Queen's bored tone curled Channon's lip. Richard Armagh muttered beneath his breath. 'Jesu, where is justice!' Channon glanced at him and saw the earl in every line of the young man's face. Little wonder Richard was the favourite, and Robin was resented. Richard was his father over again. How Robin had been born of such a sire, Channon could not guess. John was silent, one hand on his brown doublet. He was shadowed and unwell, and the veins in his hands were like blue threads. Channon thought of Robin's robust health and hard young body, and gave thanks.

The Spanish captain spoke well, in thickly accented but attractive English. He described his business with the gunsmith, Jan van der Zaalm, and the gale that beat his ship inshore. He swore Rothwell's *Rosamund* gave him no signal, but opened fire at first sight, which must constitute an act of war, if war existed — piracy if it did not.

All present expected Rothwell to refute Vasca's charges, and he did. 'I signalled,' he snapped. If Robin closed his eyes he saw the man's face, ten years younger, as he cornered a woman in her husband's absence:

'Faith, madam, every woman is a whore beneath her skirts, even the Queen. All I want is a night or three, favours as come naturally to women. Straddle me and you shall be rewarded for the fine, comely doxy that you are!'

That same voice was saying, 'The *Alcanzar* ignored my signal and I fired. She was a warship, just off our coast.'

'No state of war exists between England and Spain, sir,' Vasca said levelly. 'If you signalled, we saw nothing. The matter rests with Her Gracious Majesty. King Philip trusts my lady to see that justice is done.'

'Sweet words,' Channon whispered acidly. 'How sweet prevarication can sound, spoken by a gentleman.'

The pause was pregnant. At last the Queen began, a speech of outrage. Sir Charles Rothwell bore the punishment, such as it was. Words. She flayed him for minutes, invoked the lore and tradition of the sea, the brotherhood of seamen. When she was done, sentence was passed in clipped, barbed phrases, and Channon hissed curses Robin had never heard in any language.

Rothwell was to be fined, the funds paid to the yard on the Humber where Vasca's ship was under repairs. And what of the lads who had died in her? Channon's mouth compressed. The whole *Alcanzar* incident was resolved with a polite making of amends. Mauricio had a single bolt left to fire.

'Majesty, a moment more,' he said with an edge of steel in his voice that commanded attention. 'Information has reached me of the night I was poisoned. The page, Tanner, swore it was Walter Copeland who administered hemlock and foxglove —'

Again Rothwell interrupted. 'Master Copeland is dead.'

'Indeed.' Mauricio spoke mildly. 'But a woman overheard him dispatched on an errand to purchase the poisons. This woman, Copeland's woman, can tell us who sent him.'

'I don't —' Rothwell began.

'Be silent!' The Queen's whipcrack voice lashed him. 'Let Don Mauricio have his say or we shall be here till midnight!'

'To the point,' Mauricio agreed. 'Platitudes aside, Ma'am, it was Captain Rothwell's cousin, Captain Jeremy Britton, who sent Copeland for poison. I have never spoken to Captain Britton, let alone angered him, so I assume he acted upon Captain Rothwell's orders.'

In the silence which followed one could have heard a pin fall. When she spoke again Elizabeth's voice was deceptively silken. Robin wished he could have seen through the crush.

'How say you, Captain? You stand accused of murder now. Speak, man! The charge is a serious one.'

'I call this woman of Copeland's,' Rothwell said, too smoothly. 'Where is she, Don Mauricio — *who* is she?'

'She is Mistress Edith Pledge,' Mauricio said icily, 'a maid in your own service. If you wish her fetched, Captain Britton will surely send a message.'

'Captain?' Rothwell said, aside to his cousin. 'You had best fetch the wench, and have this settled.'

Muttering stirred among the gathering as Britton summoned a page. Channon's fists clenched and Robin stepped closer.

'Dermot —'

'It feels wrong, I know,' Channon agreed. They are too smooth. Best wait, Robin. Few moves remain in the game.'

Other matters occupied the time as the page scurried away. Nerves strummed as minutes became an hour, and they were still waiting. At last the little boy in Britton's blue livery ran into the back of the hall, waving a slip of paper.

It was taken from him, placed in the Queen's own hand, and the assembly fell silent as she read. To left and right of the hall, Mauricio, Vasca and Rothwell's party glared at one another.

'A death note,' Elizabeth said at last. "There is no future for me, alone and with child. Soon my shame will be seen plain at a glance... I must make mischief with myself, and gently meet my end, for honour's sake." ' She paused. 'The girl is dead. How very unfortunate.'

'How very *convenient*,' Channon growled. 'Damn!' Turning quickly, he left the hall, Robin on his heels. Richard and John stayed to listen, but what more could be said?

'Dermot!' Robin ran to catch up. 'Dermot, wait!'

But Channon kept pace until he reached an open door. No need to knock. It stood wide, and they heard weeping from within. A stout matron huddled by the hearth, a kerchief pressed to her nose, and as Channon and Robin watched a litter was carried out of the servants' rooms. A sheet draped the body of the girl. Channon stood back to make way. Behind the litter was the physician, John Glover, whose face was like a thundercloud.

'She made away with herself?' Channon asked tersely.

'Poor girl,' Glover said sadly. 'Few knew she was with child, but as she wrote, it would soon have been plain at a glance. It was hemlock. She had it in her rooms, somehow.'

'Copeland purchased it, to dose my uncle,' Channon said sourly. 'Damn! If she could have waited another day.'

'The poor child,' Glover repeated as he hurried after the litter.

'Poor child indeed,' Channon whispered. 'And I fancy myself responsible. Not so pleasant to bear, Robin.'

'You?' Robin echoed. 'Copeland was dead by your hand, I suppose, but —'

The matron dabbed her eyes and rose unsteadily. 'Did you know her? She had so many men friends. Any one might have been the baby's sire. Everyone loved little Edith! I just don't know why she would make such mischief.'

'Her honour,' Channon said softly. 'She was unwed.'

'But there's five lads I know who would have wed her for a smile.'

The matron scrubbed her red nose and left them.

At Captain Jeremy Britton's threshold, Channon and Robin lingered with a creeping suspicion that chilled the blood.

Chapter Eleven

The mercenaries closed ranks about Rothwell like a private army. Anger whitened Channon, and Robin was silent over luncheon as they watched Mauricio's fragile health shatter before their eyes. Defeat was bitter. Robin brought the old man a posset and a rug for his knees, and he slept in the afternoon, but Channon was restless, prowling like a cat, his knuckles white on the hilt of his sword.

The sounds of young people at play lured Robin into the sun. Shuttlecock and croquet, draughts and cards amused people his own age and younger. To Robin they seemed empty pursuits, and his eyes never left Channon. He could not be still, as if defeat choked him, Robin thought, and he remembered what Dermot had said, early one morning, in bed. Give him a foe, show him an honest fight. Channon was a soldier. Courtly guile irked him with its poisonous politeness and deceit.

They were walking from courtyard to courtyard. The sun was hot, and sweat prickled Robin's skin. Channon seemed not to notice. They had turned to walk back when the fall of booted feet brought Channon to a halt. Only Robin heard the Irish oath on his lips.

Rothwell was leaving. Behind him was Jeremy Britton, a small, dark man with tightly curled hair and a black goatee beard. He was flanked at left and right by men in Rothwell's livery, and all were armed. Channon stepped into their path.

'Leaving in the hour of victory?' The Irish was deliberately heavy in Channon's voice.

'I've tarried too long, to please your kinsman,' Rothwell said tartly. 'My ship has been in port a week longer than she should have been. The Queen has heard your bilgewater, Channon. Stand aside.'

Slowly and very deliberately, Channon lifted the black pigskin gloves from his belt. Unfolded, they struck Rothwell smartly across the left cheek, then the right. Rothwell's eyes widened and his face flushed. A pace behind him, Britton swore, one hand on his sword, but Rothwell barked crisply, 'Hold, Jeremy, the challenge is not yours!'

'But, Charles,' Britton protested.

'I said hold, damn you!' Rothwell squared his shoulders and searched Channon's face. 'Tell me why, before I cut out your liver, you Irish mongrel.'

'For Mauricio de Cervallo,' Channon said lazily. His accent thickened. 'For a friend on the *Alcanzar*, killed by your cannon. For Edith Pledge, poisoned with the same hemlock as almost murdered Mauricio... for Catherine Armagh, ten years ago, and Jane, the maid who saw the blow struck, and died for it. Enough?'

Rothwell took a deep breath. 'More than enough. Enough to have you hanged, save that you challenged me and it will be my pleasure to disarm you and flay you with your own sword.' He snatched off his cape. 'Where, and when?'

'There is,' Channon said with infuriating blandness, 'no time nor place like the here and now.' He glanced about the courtyard. 'We've witnesses aplenty. I see no cause to delay my flaying.'

'And your second?' Rothwell flung his cape at Britton.

'Master Robert Armagh.' Channon stood back, and for the first time Rothwell saw the young man. 'Surely you know him. A woman called Catherine beguiled you with that same face, ten years ago. Robin Armagh shall second me.'

A pulse pounded in Robin's temple as he stepped forward. Rothwell looked at him with eyes like ice. 'Well met, sir,' Robin said quietly.

'So this is the root of it.' Rothwell looked long at Robin, then refused to look at him again. He drew his sword, tested the whip of its steel, and followed Channon into the shadowed courtyard. Guardsmen muttered along the walls and footsteps hurried away as a boy ran for an officer. Rothwell smiled. 'It will be over before they can stop it. We have witnesses aplenty, as you said, to swear I was provoked and fought in self-defence.'

Channon smiled thinly, handed his cape to Robin and drew his own sword, It was one of Quiepo's, from a forge in Salamanca, and fitted his hand by design. He cut the air to find the balance and then swept it aside and offered his breast to Rothwell. 'You may have first blood, Captain. If you can draw it.'

Rothwell tried. Standing back, with Britton, Robin could not breathe as he watched the older man's sword twitch close enough to Channon's face to shave him. Steel rasped and chimed then as they began in earnest, and Robin knew at once, Channon was toying with him.

The Spanish-Irish mercenary was in command, Rothwell was his puppet. And Rothwell saw this in the same moment. His face whitened, in fear or fury, Robin would never know.

He fell back and began again more cautiously. His cuts were close to the body, defensive. Channon laughed in his face. 'You are too old for this, Captain. Would you prefer to let your lackey fight for you? I'll play him at your game, if you wish.' Rothwell did not answer; he was panting now, with scarlet cheeks.

His mercenaries stood at the door with the palace guards. Robin glanced at them, half afraid they would take Rothwell's part. They could make it murder, if they fell on Channon. A sword was half drawn and Robin took a breath to protest. Before he could speak a young guardsman thrust out his pike and a deep Cornish voice growled, 'Hold, sir. 'Tis a match between the gentlemen.'

The sword was sheathed again and Robin began to breathe. Ten paces down the courtyard, Channon's blows gained speed and weight. Rothwell retreated before him and the tip of the Salamanca rapier flicked his cheek. First blood trickled down Rothwell's face and soaked his lace. Channon mocked the man with chivalry. He drew back to get him gather wits and breath, for which Rothwell cursed him roundly.

Steel chimed again as the thick roots of the swords hammered together and locked. Robin's hands clenched into Channon's brown cloak, and then Channon flung Rothwell back and offered his breast once more. Again, Rothwell tried, but his blows were ineffectual. As if he was bored, Channon turned them aside with taunting ease.

Footsteps pounded in the passageways behind him, but Robin did not dare take his eyes away. As if time slowed, he watched the tip of Channon's sword flicker like an insect across Rothwell's face.

Blood blossomed where his right eye had been and he screamed. The cry echoed off the walls, and Robin took a breath as Rothwell sagged to his knees. Hands like talons clutched his face. Channon's boot gave him a gentle shove onto his back, and as he toppled the rapier's point tucked in beneath his jaw.

'Enough! That is enough!' The voice bawling across the courtyard belonged to Sir Christopher Hatton, once a solider, now the Captain of the Guard, grown rich from his investments in the voyages of men like Drake. He spoke with the Queen's authority, and even Channon responded.

Would he have killed Rothwell? Robin believed he would. The deed was performed in symbol even as Hatton stood, fists on his hips, in the doorway. The tip of the rapier barely broke he skin as it travelled from ear to ear below Rothwell's jaw. The scratch would heal without trace, but Rothwell would know the truth. His life had been forfeit.

Then Channon stood back and Britton shouted for John Glover. Rothwell rolled onto his side, hands clasped over the socket where the eye was gone. Channon cleaned his sword on the hem of his cloak, resheathed it and gave Hatton a wry smile.

'A challenge, with witnesses, sir. Ask your own guardsmen. Ask Master Armagh. Sir Charles offered to flay me with my own sword. I fear he was not quite equal to the task.'

Hatton was furious. Blue eyes blazed at Channon though he said nothing. Behind him women were tittering, and Glover's voice shouted for them to be gone. As the physician bustled into the courtyard Channon gave Hatton a stiff-necked bow and shouldered through the crowd. Robin followed, oblivious to their stares.

As they left the scene Channon slowed his pace. 'So, Robin, is honour satisfied? Rothwell lives, but will carry our mark to the grave. For Marcos, Catherine, and the rest. Did you wish him dead?'

'Did you?' Robin whispered.

'Until I saw him at my feet,' Channon confessed. 'There's something obscene about a man grovelling at your feet.'

'My father would have killed him.' Robin fell into step as they returned to the embassy apartments. 'He'll salute you when he hears of this. Dermot, will there be trouble for you?'

Channon's hand was on their door. 'Doubtless Britton will try to make a case, but we have too many witnesses. A dozen guards saw it, as did you. If Rothwell owns a shred of honour he'll silence Britton, lest his name be bandied about as a cur who offers to flay a man, then bemoans his own scratches.' He opened, and thrust Robin inside before him. 'Mauricio is gone,' he said a moment later as he looked into the bedchamber. 'He may be with your brothers, or Vasca. Come, change and dine with me. I've an appetite.'

Exhilarated and troubled, Robin changed hurriedly. He had never seen blows struck in anger before, nor blood spilled. He had never been permitted to stand up as a man, and be seen as one. Pride throbbed through him, and passion rose with it. As Channon dressed he touched the fair skin he loved, stroked the muscular back. Channon looked curiously over his shoulder.

'I love you.' Robin kissed down his spine. 'I was your second, they accepted it.'

'You are a man, and an Armagh.' Channon caught Robin against his bare chest, held him there. 'You'll learn your worth, and value your name. I was pleased to have you as my second.' Robin's arms went about his neck. 'Robin, what is this, grief?'

Love hurt like a bruise. Robin pressed his face to Channon's shoulder till he could trust his voice, then stepped back with a smile. 'No. Dine with me, then. Watching men try to maim each other arouses the appetite.'

And more appetites than one. Desire simmered as Robin sat with Channon at the long table in the common dining hall. Nobility, soldiers in favour, captains, merchants and ladies chattered about the match between Rothwell and the Spaniard. Rothwell's eye could not be saved; he was abed, doped, yet otherwise unscathed and fortunate to be alive. Hatton glared at Channon as he passed, but said nothing; Channon lifted his cup in mock salute. None of Rothwell's company was present.

Mauricio and Vasca came late and wore studiedly bland faces, but under the chatter Vasca leaned toward Channon and said, 'By God, the audacity of youth! Would you have killed him?'

'Had he shown me more of a challenge,' Channon said thoughtfully. 'As it was, it would have been murder. I am a soldier, Miguel, not a murderer. Rothwell is getting old. He was a fine swordsman in his day. Now, he is a fool.'

'Just so.' Vasca clasped his shoulder. 'It was well done. I should like to have seen it. I've had the tale at second and third hand a dozen times. Rothwell's men are furious. Dermot, take care. Hampton is not safe, you should leave.'

'And no safer for you,' Channon retorted.

'I leave on the *Nicodemo Ruez*, with tomorrow's dawn tide. The merchantman will return me to my ship. And you?'

'With Mauricio's approval,' Channon glanced at his uncle, 'we'll leave at first light for Blackstead. No more can be done here. This nest

112

of vipers tries my patience.'

Mauricio lifted his cup. Vasca seated himself, and Channon turned to Robin. The boy was flushed, his breathing deep. 'Robin!' Channon whispered, and leaned closer to tease, 'You look likely to rape me behind the privacy of a closed door!'

'Not I,' Robin murmured, 'but you'll certainly do that to me, tonight.'

Much later, Çhannon remembered those words. Mauricio and Vasca had left to meet Diaz, write dispatches and reports, since Vasca's next port was Santander. The contract for the gunsmith was delayed and Vasca was headed like a pigeon for Madrid. The embassy apartments were deserted.

A log burned in the hearth of his own chamber and Channon tied back the bedcurtains. Robin lay naked across the quilt, wreathed in heat and musk. He had already received every caress Channon knew, and his eyes glittered. His blood was up, his chest heaved. Channon was feverish with wanting. He had left the bed deliberately, distanced himself till he commanded his wits. He would not force Robin, no matter what the boy said.

Stretched on the rack of his own lust, Robin was dizzy though he had not been drinking. He buttocks were already slick with the oil stroked deeply into him, as Channon had done once before. Tonight it was not enough. He watched Channon, naked in the firelight, and moaned woundedly.

'Dermot.'

'You madden me,' Channon groaned, 'when I wish to be gentle. Hush, give me a moment.' The madness calmed into tension and he returned to feast on Robin. His mouth was everywhere, and soon it was Robin gasping as teeth branded the softness of his buttock. There, Channon stopped. Robin knelt, waiting, and if the moment had ever been right, it was now.

The oil was warm, sweet smelling, and Robin was open already. He would suffer only a little. He mewled, unable to rest. Words of love and lust were like caresses. Channon knelt behind him, let him feel the heat of his cock in his cleft. A wriggle, and Robin gasped. Channon lifted up his hips. A shove against oily muscle, a cry from Robin, and he was inside.

Nothing had prepared him for the magnificent anguish of entering Robin. Dreams and experience both dimmed. Robin was a hot, moist velvet glove; his muscles spasmed, he was hurting and Channon stilled, only half buried. Robin was tense, his skin gleamed, but slowly the spasms abated and Channon pushed a little harder, deeper, forcing in the last fraction.

A choked cry stopped him and he shook his head clear of its scarlet mist. 'I'm hurting you. Too much, Robin?'

'Like a lance in me,' Robin whispered. 'Ah, God, I'm so full of you, I cannot breathe.'

'Wait. Only wait a while.' Channon reached under his quivering belly and stroked his cock hard again. Being still was a sweet, terrible torture, when he wanted to thrust with all his strength. But at last Robin began to relax, and sighed. Now there would be pleasure. Channon stroked him constantly and chanced a gentle push.

He felt the jolt as Robin ignited and knew he was right. Robin gasped, squirmed with a thrill of delight. Channon pushed again, earning a cry as the slender hips humped back to meet him. It was pleasure, not pain, racking Robin now.

He had waited too long to have much discipline, but Robin was also too close to last. He came as Channon moved strongly in him, and fell onto the bed. Channon went down on his back for the final hunt for completion, and Robin groaned in his rhythm, little animal cries. He gasped as he felt Channon spend, deep inside.

For some time Channon rested dazedly on him before reality reasserted. Robin was a hot, sticky, trembling bundle of exhaustion in his arms, huge-eyed and bewildered. He gathered the boy up and rocked him.

'I tried to be gentle. How was it for you?'

'Terrible and wonderful, beautiful and frightening,' Robin whispered as he got his breath. 'I have never felt so besieged. Nor so loved. It hurt, but then hurt was gone, and...' He held on tight. 'You were sweet in me at the finish. Hot and big, so hard. You owned me.' He paused, wriggled. 'Am I injured? I feel—'

'Sore,' Channon guessed. He put Robin on his belly and spread him to see. 'One bright drop of blood only. I think you will live after all.' He sprawled on the quilt and pulled Robin against him. 'You are my heart.' He opened his mouth for Robin's tongue and his hands roamed over the boy's back and rump. 'I was as gentle as I could be, taking my pleasure.'

'My pleasure, rather. Cease this cooing!' Robin laughed wearily. 'I love you. There's no more than that, no more I want.' Then he yawned, making Channon chuckle.

'You are fatigued. Let me wash us both, then into bed, and I'll fetch a cup of wine.'

A wet cloth mopped Robin swiftly, then he held open the bed and settled the boy against the pillows. Robin caught his head to kiss, and Channon was pleased to oblige.

Yet pain cut through Channon's chest despite his smiles. Dalliance was one thing. Folly with a wench, forgotten in the morning; or a delicious wrangling in the arms of a mate at sea, the dark intimacy of fucking a willing boy. Love was not the same. Green eyes watched him, heavy with sleep. His own body trembled as he recalled Robin's liquid insides. He closed his eyes and struggled for sanity.

Separation loomed, months of emptiness, danger, battle, the very real possibility that Channon would not live to return. His farewells to Robin could be final. He put the bleakness from him, snatched up wine and cups and returned to the bed. Robin's slender arms tightened about him and Channon pressed his face into the soft, auburn hair to banish the futile grief.

Chapter Twelve

The bond was strong between Robin and his brother, John. Robin was as healthy as John was fragile, Channon observed as their coach left Hampton after an early breakfast. John was cloaked against the coolness, blue-shadowed but smiling. He coughed, held his chest, and his eyes often closed with some mortal weariness. Where Robin was boyishly slender, John was merely thin, his legs spindly, his face gaunt.

Yet John was in good spirits and he loved Robin. The two embraced before they stepped into the coach, and John laughed. 'You were quite the man, I hear! My little brother, seconding the Spaniard in Rothwell's duel.'

His 'little brother' stood taller than John, and Robin was heavier, much more muscular. He took care to settle John beside Mauricio, and fetched him a rug as the long whip stirred the horses. John would not live. His lungs were gone, if Channon was any judge. He had watched a mate die with the same malady on the voyage home from Panama. Did John know he was dying?

Some sadness beneath his smile said he did. He clasped Robin's hand. 'I'll tell father you honoured the Armaghs,' he promised as the coach rolled north toward Blackstead. And then he coughed harshly in the river wind, and Robin held him.

'John, won't your physician give you something?' he asked softly.

'They have.' Exhausted, eyes closed, John rested his fair head on Robin's. 'I get better every day, Robin. Soon I'll be as well as you. You'll see.'

It was a lie. In bed that night, Channon felt wetness on his shoulder and looked into Robin's face in the candlelight. 'Did I hurt you, little chuck?' They had coupled again at Robin's demand, gently but thoroughly, and Channon had clamped a hand over his mouth lest the whole house hear his cries.

'No.' Robin bit his shoulder in admonition. 'I am thinking of John. He won't live long, will he?' Channon said nothing, but tightened his embrace. 'I wish he could have what I have had since you came here.'

'John may not warm to men,' Channon said drowsily.

'I meant, I wish him this happiness,' Robin corrected. 'Someone to love him, a woman if he desires it... but I'd rather his love was a man.'

Channon lifted his head in surprise. 'Why?'

'He is frail, and needs a man's strength to support him. I saw the women at Court. Feather-headed, powdered — *doxies!*' Channon laughed quietly. 'You know what I mean. They were pretty, but it was all paint, powder and skirts.' He wriggled closer. 'I like men better. I love you.'

'And I you.' Channon kissed him. 'Go to sleep. It is later than you know.'

John did not ride or swim, but when he heard the clatter of swords in the afternoon he came to watch. Robin was growing adept, and John applauded delightedly. 'My little brother! You'll fight your own duels soon, Robin, and win them.'

He was twenty-two, a year younger than Channon, but in many ways he was more a boy than Robin. In Channon's arms, Robin was

116

strong, fiercely passionate, alive and eager. John was frail and beautiful, almost childlike in stature. Channon could not imagine him feeling passion, in the arms of man or woman.

The earl fussed over him and ignored Robin. He gave a grunt of acknowledgment when he heard of the duel, but Channon heard no praise for the boy. Robin had hoped uselessly and went away disappointed. Channon soothed the hurt later, and Robin was wild.

In the mornings, John and Mauricio sunned themselves and played chess while Channon and Robin fenced, rode and swam. In the afternoon the invalids slept, while the others escaped from Blackstead and rode as far as the horses could take them. Often they returned too late to sup with the household. Mistress Lovell would leave a cold platter in the pantry, and Robin was delighted to avoid his father.

It was warm, and a fortnight flew by like a martin beneath the eaves. Channon banished reality and cherished days spent at sport with Robin, nights surrendered to pleasure.

Mauricio's health and appetite improved and colour returned to his face, but he waited for each day's dispatches, and every day Channon's heart squeezed as he anticipated the recall. Though Robin was silent, he shared the torment. When the last dispatch was set aside, he would be pale with relief.

It was a week before Channon noticed the young maid, Grace, making eyes at him. She was pretty, soot-smudged in the morning, rumpled by evening, plump and comely in a girlish way. She was always near, watching him, and Channon gave her a smile, though no thought of abandoning Robin to share her pillow occurred to him.

The boy had more beauty and sensuality in one of his bones than Grace Hobson would ever command. Channon knew the girl was puzzled and annoyed. He gave her a penny to run his errands. She took the coin and kept out of his way till Channon began to forget her. He had time only for Robin.

Late in May the weather worsened. Rain fell constantly, confining them to the house. John and Mauricio played chess in the library, and with the earl busy Channon dared ambush Robin in his own bedchamber. They fanned and spent desire, with the servants just the other side of a locked door. Robin was outraged but the danger made for desperate lust. Often Channon had to smother him to keep him silent.

Rain was still falling when the courier arrived. His cloak was wet and sodden as Channon met him at the door, and Master Rupert fetched a fresh nag. Mauricio, John and Armagh were mulling toddies in the library when Channon took in the pannier. He was eager only to escape. Robin was in the solarium, whiling away the inclement weather with his books.

Mauricio pounced on the leather dispatch bag before it left Channon's rain-damp hands. His eyes lit upon the Queen's seal, pressed into scented wax. Channon held his breath as a dirk split it, for he knew what it must be. The old man grunted as he read the lines of elegant script.

'Trouble, Dermot,' Mauricio began.

The earl was behind him, listening intently. John drowsed by the chessboard with a pewter cup held loosely in his oddly feminine hands. Mauricio passed the dispatch to Armagh.

'Read this, William. I am summoned back with all speed.'

'Tomorrow?' Armagh sipped his hot wine, glanced at the paper and gestured at the window. 'This is poor travelling weather.'

Mauricio was agitated. 'Nevertheless, travel I must, and we've no time even to pack. The state of affairs is grave. I wish to God I could send some prevarication and remain here. Blackstead has been home to me. You have my gratitude, William.'

'Nonsense.' Armagh set down his cup and looked at Channon. 'Will you return?'

'For our baggage.' Mauricio read the dispatch again. It was signed in Elizabeth's looping hand, Channon knew that signature. 'This will be the end of it. They have sunk the *San Demetrio* and have the crew in chains. *San Demetrio* is said to have fired first, her officers are for ransom, and Capitan Fernandez was carrying certain documents from the port of Corunna.' He shook his head and folded the dispatch. 'Little is divulged here, which in itself bodes ill. We'll be expelled, then surely the fighting begins.' His eyes closed. 'Oh, God.' A sound of quiet resignation.

The same resignation churned in Channon's belly as he took his leave with a stiff half-bow. John frowned after him as the library door clicked shut, and Channon took the stairs to the solarium. He shut that door also, for privacy.

The tropical plants had been fetched home by Hal. Potted, nurtured in the glass prison, they were lush and green. The air smelt of rich, wet black soil, to Channon unpleasantly reminiscent of the forests of the Indies. Robin had curled up in the window seat with a book in his lap as rain sluiced over the leaded panes, shutting out the world. He had an unearthly look, Channon thought, a fey quality. The green eyes were dark. He knew.

'I saw the courier,' he said as he closed the book.

'Aye.' Channon sat beside him and held Robin's head to his shoulder. 'We must go at once.'

'Then this is the last.' Robin's arms circled Channon, too tight for comfort.

'Not quite the last. The embassy will be expelled and we'll return for our baggage on our way to some ship. There will be a night for us, Robin, I'll make it so. We'll arrive at last light, too late to go on before morning. Then we'll retire, you and I, and make merry. Loving to remember through the months till the foolishness is over and we are together.'

Robin nodded mutely. His eyes covered Channon's face as if he must commit it to memory. 'You'll not forget me,' he said with a quiet dignity beyond his years and experience. 'No matter how long.'

'You made certain of that,' Channon confessed. 'Were I given my pick of the consorts and concubines of Europe, none would seduce me. Christ Jesus, I love you.' He savaged Robin's mouth until he tasted blood. 'There is no time, but listen for news. Each tale of outrage brings me nearer.'

'And nearer a ship for Spain,' Robin added bitterly. His mouth was swollen. Channon traced his lips with one fingertip. 'I'll listen.' He was not too proud to show Channon brimming eyes. 'One day we will clasp and never part. Promise me.'

Tenderness overwhelmed Channon, and his smile was a mask. Robin knew. They kissed gently now. 'My word, on whatever honour I own.' Rash and impulsive, he slid the signet from his right hand and pressed it into Robin's palm. 'It is the sum of my father's inheritance, the seal of a *tuatha* that no longer exists. One day I'll return to claim it, and you with it.'

Then Channon fled. He packed lightly and hurried out with Mauricio. The rain was cold in his face, chilling him to the bone in moments. John was already in the coach, rugged and cloaked. The stay at home had enlivened him, but duty called him back to Hampton also.

The journey was less arduous than simply bitter. Channon wore a bleak face as the coachman whipped up the four matching bays. He left behind his heart, the best of him, and the wound might have been physical. The coach turned south, but the lush farm country passed unnoticed as his mind lingered behind, caught in a snare of his own making.

From the solarium Robin watched the vehicle leave with a chill in his belly that reached every extremity.

It was still raining next morning. The sky was an unbroken pall, as if it too mourned. He sat in his room and looked across the grey-green hills. The sodden woods seemed drear now, impressing on him the emptiness that had engulfed him before Channon came. He had been unaware of it then, having nothing to compare it with. Now, he knew. The time had almost come for him to leave.

Almost. There must be one last night, when Channon returned. Then, no more. Master Grey would find him gone. No books, no knees bruised at prayer, no knuckles bruised by the rapping that fetched his mind back from daydreams. *London*, Robin thought, chin cupped in his palm on the window-ledge. *London, and my fortune.*

The letter Channon had written was hidden with the sword. He had learned swiftly, being young and limber. He knew his own worth now, and Channon had taught him other lessons, perhaps more valuable. To beware of men who would use him, to choose his lovers carefully. The notion of other lovers was unwelcome and Robin resolved to wait. The war could surely last no more than a year, and a deft right hand would comfort him that long.

He closed his eyes to the rain-veiled landscape, intent on the daydream. Channon, naked and aroused, the flush of desire on his cheeks, a diamond glitter of lust in his eyes. Dermot, sated and at peace, propped on pillows while his fingers played in the light pelt of hair between his lover's nipples. Robin shivered at the now familiar thrill of wanting.

Such dreams would warm his nights while he waited. Spain and England could not fight forever. Channon would soon be in London; he would find a young cartographer, or a chandler's clerk haggling over the price of grain. Then there would be fever, Robin thought, a frenzy spent in lust, gentled into love. He would greet Channon as a man, an equal, without fear of his father or discovery. Many men at Court desired their own sex, he had seen them, and Master Grey mentioned young rascals who were easily satisfied. They need only be discreet.

In two days the weather warmed, and he swam and rode alone. None of it was the same without Channon. Blackstead had briefly come alive, and with his absence the life extinguished as if it had never been.

Stories abounded of the militia, recruitment and soliciting for arms. Tales of shipbuilding, of signal stations in Devon and Cornwall, where Spanish warships would first be sighted. The whole country was committed to war, it was on every man's lips. Naval agents were in Blackstead's woods, axe-marking the straightest trees for the shipyards.

England was rich in that treasure. Channon valued highly the natural wealth that was taken for granted. A ship might cost twenty ducats a ton to build in England, since timber was free for the felling. In Spain the price was much higher, since foreign timber was purchased and transported at great cost. Spain was too dry to grow oak, elm, pine which were necessary to build fine ships. Vessels built of Spanish timber were by comparison poor. The fleet had emptied Philip's treasury, and still he was in debt to bankers in Genoa and elsewhere.

Let it be over soon, Robin thought. *Let bankruptcy end it if guns will not!* The prayer was repeated often as days passed and stories of Hampton's tension were repeated in the shires. Channon must be in the thick of it, kicking his heels while Mauricio grew frail under the assault of men like Frobisher, Drake and Hatton.

Almost a week after Channon's departure, news came that Rothwell was at Halstead Hall. He wore a patch over his eye and a sour face. His ship, the twenty-two gun *Rosamund*, which had so nearly sunk the *Alcanzar*, was victualling, at the Admiralty's disposal.

The same day as brought this news, Robin first noticed the maid, Grace Hobson, flirting. She fluttered her eyelashes at him over breakfast, touched his arm, not quite innocently showed him a shapely ankle when she could manage it. He smiled, but Channon preoccupied him and he barely noticed her coy invitations.

Nor did he notice when her mood turned to resentment. Spite. He never knew where the scurrilous gossip began, but of a sudden the grooms were sniggering, the servants disapproving. Even Mistress Lovell sighed over him, and Robin knew something was wrong. The sniggers could hardly escape his father's attention, and Robin was not surprised when he was called to give account.

The earl was white to the lips with rage, but to Robin the scene was oddly unreal. He felt distanced, as if he were a spectator at a play as he knocked and entered the study.

'You have heard the gossip, no doubt.' Armagh stood with his palms on the desk. His voice was terse, brittle.

'Gossip, sir?' Robin echoed.

'You're deaf, as well as an immoral wastrel!' Armagh stroked his doublet. The lace at his throat fluttered, betraying angry breathing. 'The grooms are prattling about your dishonour, but I would hear it from you. Tell me the truth. I shall know if you compound your sins by lying. Did you bed with the Irishman?'

'Bed with him?' Robin's heart skipped. A pulse raced in his head as his blood first heated, then chilled.

'Did you lie with him?' Armagh elaborated brutally. 'Did you invite buggery? Speak! Did you share the sodomite's bed?'

Lies would have been easy, but the old man already knew what he believed, without any need for proof. And lies would betray Channon, betray everything they had felt, said, done. Robin took a harsh breath.

'I shared his bed in love. I was cherished, not abused.'

Armagh's face flushed. Robin saw the blow coming but ducked too late and took the full force of the roundhouse slap. Stunned, he plunged over the desk and into the wall. It was late; a last glimmer of daylight limned the terrace windows. He pulled himself halfway up and did not see the second blow at all. His eyes lost focus, the bloody sunset sky coloured his mind for a moment before all was darkness. As he went down all he felt was the surge of his father's hate.

He woke in the chapel where the Armaghs were christened, married and buried. His ancestors were entombed beneath the stone slabs flanking the altar. Candles stuttered in the cold night air as he sat up on the smooth polished floor and rubbed his head. His mouth tasted of blood. Father Thomas mumbled the old prayers without pause, but Robin saw a second priest. Benedict. He looked dizzily into the bleak, dispassionate face. Nausea churned as he fought to clear his head. His brains were too rattled for him to understand the Latin or the outrage, but he saw the scourge and his mouth dried.

The linen shirt tore from his back as he knelt on the flagstones. Rebellion warred with bewilderment, and the sickness of concussion fettered his limbs. Father Thomas prayed on, intoning for his soul. Robin struggled vainly to find his feet before Father Benedict could begin the penance.

A dozen cuts opened across his back and he slid down, crucified on the stone. His mind dimmed as agony replaced rebellion. He had not the strength to escape. The priest's arm swung in a slow, steady beat, delivering every measure of the penance without stint. Robin bit into his lips and tongue, waiting for it to end. When at last it did, darkness fell once more.

He woke again to fever and thirst. The tang of vinegar stung his nose, the pain of a compress tormented his back. It was daylight, the compress was almost dry. Whoever had applied it had left a jug of water by his bed. The sheets were drenched, his body still ran with sweat. The need for water stirred him, but movement aroused a sharp cry, hastily stifled. He bit into his arm until the anguish of lacerated skin dwindled, leaving him weak and ill. He drank the pitcher dry, great gulps that hurt, before he fell back onto the sheets, into a fitful sleep.

It was dark when he woke again. An old steward who had played with him a decade before was watching him. He spread on a salve and clucked over the mass of swollen, blackened welts as if he considered the penance too great for the sin. Robin was silent, turned his face away and sat up as he was urged.

He took a bowl of onion soup from the gnarled old hands. The fever was gone, his head was clear though it ached. The thick brown comfrey salve soothed his back until the pain was a dull, nagging heat. He was shaking, defiant now. And angry.

The fury was not directed at priests who were merely observing time-worn tradition, but at his father, a vengeful, pious old bastard who must have a man's fancied wrongs set right in the eyes of God. Anger dizzied Robin as the servant left him.

He stood, swaying, and paced the room, naked, hurting, nursing a rage beyond his years. He would leave this house, never to return as long as he lived, as soon as Channon had collected his baggage and gone. Nothing bound him to this estate save the necessity to heal his back and the need to be here when Channon returned. Thereafter, no chain would be strong enough to hold Robin inside these walls.

Chapter Thirteen

London was a shambles, Hampton a furore. Mauricio's efforts were futile and hollow in the face of half-substantiated rumours that a Spanish fleet had sailed almost a week before, from Lisbon, only to be torn apart by storms. Channon cautioned him, but he fretted himself into sickness with each day's fresh bickering.

Until accurate dispatches arrived they were all poised on the knife's edge, but Drake would soon be on his way to Plymouth. Channon would trust *El Draque* before any other man at Hampton, and Drake judged the rumours reliable: the Armada had already shipped out of Lisbon, northbound into the teeth of a devastating Atlantic gale, and as May became June that fleet was said to lie at Corunna, under repairs.

The lines etched deeply into Mauricio's face. The good of his stay at Blackstead was swiftly undone. In the evenings, Channon stoked his hearth and pressed a sleeping cup on him.

'A letter came from Enriquez,' Mauricio said as he began to drowse. It was midnight. Hampton's revels had not paused, but Mauricio was spent. Enriquez was a Spanish knight whom Channon had met once and liked, though the man was too remote to be called a friend. 'There have been desperate orders for timber and tar and rope, to be hurried to Corunna.'

Channon laughed bitterly. 'What are we doing, Mauricio? The King bids you publicly deny that the fleet exists, yet Enriquez tells you it is there. The English have seen it! Captain Robert Keble swore he saw all of five hundred ships at Le Havre, days ago.'

'I say what I am told to say,' Mauricio said tiredly. 'Keble knows he saw a fleet. You and I know it exists. But we suffer through the formalities.'

'As if it were chess,' Channon said acidly. 'Like the ritual of a duel. Where is the point, when five minutes later a man will be dead, which is the purpose of the match!'

A faint smile lifted Mauricio's lips. 'You've no taste for the rules of the game.'

'I'm a soldier,' Channon retorted. 'Rest. I half-carried you to bed and fetched that cup myself, then stood here and made you drink it.

So, sleep!'

The sharpness of old bones had troubled him. Mauricio was losing flesh and would not live long if this game went on. Channon would never understand why men pretended it was a sport, like a hunt. No enjoyment was derived from it. Only hunters relished the hunt. Where was the sport, for the stag?

The old man sank deeply into the bed. Channon was about to close the curtains and summon the page who, these nights, slept at Mauricio's feet, but a hand on his arm held him back.

'What will become of us?' Mauricio whispered.

'Sleep,' Channon repeated. 'I'll be near. You'll come to no harm in the night, I promise you.'

He could promise little else, he thought bleakly as Mauricio turned onto his side and closed his eyes, as if consigning himself to the hand of God.

The Cervallos had not been rich since their two ships were sunk, laden, in the Antilles. Their fortunes were thin even then, the voyage should have bolstered them. A gale sprang up from the east, one of the great storms that often boiled out of the mid-Atlantic and wreaked such havoc. The *Marianna* and the *Rosa de Marbella* were lost with few survivors. Four lads made their way home aboard a Dutch flying-boat two years later. The Cervallos were doomed to deception.

Their public face was proud, their manner grand. Only the family and close friends knew the truth. Mauricio carried off his public office with flair, and no one guessed that his family was no more wealthy than a London tradesman.

The silver was sold to pay Crown taxes, which went to Genoa to pay for the fleet. The jewellery was sold to pay Church tithes, which went to Rome, where cardinals lived like princes. Channon's pockets were bare again. At nineteen he was wealthy in his own right, just back from Panama with a whole skin. It was all gone, for family pride. From his years abroad he had received several suits of clothes and a good horse. Not much to show for the risk of his life. Embittered but resigned, in a few months he had returned to sea.

The Cervallo fortunes would worsen with the war. The Crown demanded investors. Resentment soured Channon. He would be in jeopardy again soon, on some stinking, rat-infested ship, parted from everything he had come to want. Robin.

Fretful, he settled to rest. The page would call if Mauricio needed him before morning, but sleep eluded him, and as always his thoughts turned to Robin.

The page shook him awake an hour after dawn. An early audience had been called, which Mauricio must attend. Lord Admiral Howard and Drake would be present, and in the night John Hawkins's ship had come up the river.

As he shaved and dressed, Channon remembered that Hal Armagh had sailed with Hawkins. Then Hal was back, God willing. What would he make of his brother's sins? Not, Channon thought wryly, that he would ever discover them.

The assembly was impressive. Channon stood at the back, watching his uncle as Mauricio bowed gracefully and stood aside. The room was filled with faces he knew. Lord Admiral Burghley; Walsingham, still pale and sick; Raleigh, and Martin Frobisher, talking in undertones. *El Draque* himself, rotund, bearded and commanding. Drake regarded Mauricio scornfully, but spoke civilly. It was not Mauricio as a gentleman whom he scorned, but the Empire he represented. No personal insult was intended, none taken.

And Captain Robert Keble had come to bear witness to what he had seen in Le Havre. 'I say, it was a fleet,' he began, reiterating the news of the evening before. 'Four, even five hundred ships.'

Drake puffed out his cheeks. His beard, like his hair, was almost entirely silver now. Once it had been the same copper as Robin's hair. Channon was drawn to the man, whose eyes were Robin's shade of green, too, his cheeks of the same slight rosiness.

'I cannot believe this.' Drake regarded Keble with the same scorn Mauricio received. 'Vastly overstated, Ma'am,' he said to the throne dais.

The Queen fanned herself with peacock feathers. A scarlet gown favoured her frail body, with a high collar about her pearl-roped head. She looked hawkishly at Keble. 'Captain?'

'Ma'am, I saw what I saw,' Keble insisted. 'I have my officers' testimony, also, written down last night after Lord Admiral Howard spoke against me. There is no mistake.'

A paper was handed up to the dais. Elizabeth read it swiftly and passed it to Drake. At the back of the hall Channon was merely an observer as she arched one plucked brow at her admirals and the bickering began again.

Channon had heard it all before, and closed his ears. Mauricio could say only what he had been instructed, while Drake and Howard reported every new atrocity at sea. Mauricio would counter with accounts of Spanish ships boarded, sunk, until the axe fell at last: if the fleet had lain at Corunna since the end of May, five days now, a scrupulous, factual report must be at hand, which would mark the end to this impotent performance, and the beginning of war.

Folly, Channon decided. A waste of lives, to decide who sat on an elaborate chair and wore an absurd hat. He watched impatiently as Drake and Hawkins took the floor. Elizabeth called for Sir Christopher Hatton, whose ships roamed at will, with the Queen's sanction.

The Captain of the Guard was her favourite, and in every way Drake's opposite. Where Drake was broad, strong and below average height, with a thick Devon accent, Hatton was tall, slender and elegant. He was still beautiful though the first bloom of youth had gone. Channon was not blind to his looks, but despite Drake's girth and bluff manner, he preferred the candour of the soldier.

Drake was aggressive; Hatton had a velvet tongue. Mauricio was a pawn between them, a mouse between two cats who took turns to maul him. He wore Spain's official face until it was time for battle-lines to be drawn and guns loaded. Channon found it preposterous.

He knew many of the privateers personally, through his service with the embassy. Some were charming rogues, like Drake. Some, like Hatton, were rich, powerful, courted by ladies of good family, and lads too. Morality here was easy. Sonnets were addressed to young men and the trysting was delicious. The astrologers, Dee and Kelly, diverted gentlemen who had grown bored with politics. Intrigue relieved the monotony, but the routine was punishing. Channon longed for Robin and was torn in opposite directions.

If war was joined soon, then just as soon Philip's creditors would howl for blood and finish it. But with the embassy expelled, the reality of separation began. At Hampton, Channon was taunted by the knowledge that a day's ride would put Robin in his arms. He was not free to go, but it was possible. Once war began only a treaty of peace would bring him back. And it could take so long.

The dismissal came at last as a relief. Mauricio was haggard as he spoke in weary tones with Robin's brothers. They were at the Ambassador's hearth, drinking mulled cider. Summer had begun but the great building never really warmed. Channon was packing in the bedchamber where he had made love to Robin just once. He buckled his valise and looked through the open door at the Armagh brothers.

John was ill. His temples were blue-veined and often he paused between words to draw breath. Sir Richard, William's heir in every way, appeared not to notice. Channon's lip curled. How had old Armagh sired a son like Robin?

Mauricio refilled his cup and moved nearer the hearth, where a portrait of the Queen gazed stonily from the chimney corner. Channon dumped his bags on the stained oak table, perched beside them and watched Mauricio's shoulders droop. The old hands trembled now. He was worn to rags, ailing, and relieved to be expelled. Seville, and home, beckoned.

An armada lay at Corunna: more or less, one hundred and thirty warships, a force of galleons and *galleasses*, storm damaged but by now well under repair. Several ships of the Biscay squadron had sighted them and run for home, hampered by the same capricious weather which had frustrated the Spanish fleet. There could be no mistake this time; Drake was already on the road for Plymouth, and Howard had been ordered to join him there.

'Were I Philip,' Mauricio said wearily, 'I would see the great hand of God in that storm, and cancel this preposterous scheme.' He sighed. 'Philip, doubtless, perceives God's will in different ways.'

No more remained to be said, and the silence was leaden. The Armagh brothers wished him a good journey and clasped his wrist, then the chamber was empty and Channon packed for him while he rested, for his bones would protest the roll of the coach.

For Channon the journey north was a bittersweet ordeal. His loins ached for Robin's touch and taste, a consuming desire to have him in every way possible. The ache persisted until the coach rumbled through familiar gates and the driver reined back the tired nags. Channon stepped down first and gave the house a searching look.

Had Robin seen them arrive? Where was he? Old Edward greeted them, and as Mauricio went ahead Channon beckoned the servant. 'Is Master Armagh at home?'

'The earl —'

'Robin. Is Master Robin at home?' Channon corrected.

Blue eyes looked piercingly at him from beneath bushy silver brows. 'Aye, sir.' Edward seemed to begrudge the words. 'The earl is on business in Plymouth.'

'Oh?' Channon might have sounded indifferent, but the news was welcome. With Armagh gone, Robin would be at ease. Nothing would mar their last night.

Two weeks days without him had been a drought. As he saw Robin on the stairs it was all Channon could do to keep his distance. His heart quickened to match his loins, and he knew he was silent too long. They were at the foot of the stairs, oblivious to Mauricio and the servants bustling in the hall.

At last Channon found his voice. 'We leave tomorrow for Plymouth, and Santander. Tonight —'

'Tonight we pack,' Mauricio said over his shoulder as he sent for a meal. 'And the weather will betray us, no doubt!'

It was mid-evening but Channon had not appetite. He took a step closer to Robin and murmured, 'Your father is away.'

'Victualling his ship.' Robin's voice was hushed with anguish.

'Upstairs,' Channon urged, 'while the servants are fussing and we can escape.'

Robin led him up to the room they had shared so often. A closed door, and they were clinging, too desperate even to kiss at first. Channon caught the boy's face between his palms, eager for his tongue. They fell across the bed in a tangle of limbs and he drew the laces from Robin's shirt.

As he slid his hands inside he felt a coarseness and heard Robin gasp. Channon sat up to see his face. His eyes were downcast, his cheeks bright with shame. Silently and very gently, Channon removed the shirt and put him on his belly. He lay still, eyes squeezed shut, and Channon's mouth dried.

Twenty stripes patterned his back, livid and scabbed though the swollen bruises had yellowed. The flogging was a week old. Tears scalded Channon's eyes as he bent to kiss what skin was unbroken, and stroked his hair.

'Your father did this?'

'Priests prayed for my soul and scourged me.'

'You let them?' Channon could not contain his revulsion.

'My father had struck me already. I was unconscious when they began, too sick thereafter to escape.' He turned over carefully and lay on the scabs. 'I waited only for you. When you leave, so do I. There's nothing for me here. My father cannot bear the sight of me, nor I him. I stayed only for you.' He caught Channon's hand.

'Christ Jesus.' Channon picked him up, held him against his chest.

'I cannot leave you.'

'Don't,' Robin begged. 'No promises made tonight and broken tomorrow. You go where I cannot follow — but not forever. Please God, let it be over soon.' He lifted his head with a faint smile. 'Everyone knows I bedded with you. They'll know I am with you again, and I don't care. I am your lover without deceit tonight, for tomorrow I leave. Love me, Dermot. Do everything to me.'

'Everything?" Channon explored his chest with light fingers.

Robin drew him down. 'I want everything. Fuck me.'

'Gently,' Channon murmured. 'Time for wildness when — oh, when you are my guest, in my home. In my house, outside Seville, I have a vast bed with red drapes and a goose-feather mattress that will swallow you whole. For now?' He stood to remove doublet, collar and linen. 'For now, let me see how to ravish my love without opening his back. You are not in pain?'

'Sore,' Robin admitted. 'Sometimes I bleed on my sheets. I'll bleed on yours and betray my presence here.'

'And what of it?' Channon pulled him up, stripped him with careful hands and knelt at his feet. 'I'm proud to be your lover,' he said fiercely. 'I have the most lovesome bedmate in this country, and how I'll live without him I cannot guess.' Kisses fell from Robin's sharp hip bone to the crown of his cock as he spoke. Fingers clenched into Channon's shoulders as he took the shaft into his throat and urged Robin to possess his mouth.

As Channon's hands clenched into his buttocks Robin surrendered and bucked like a colt, unable to stop. Channon urged him, clever fingers incited him to frenzy till he froze, and Channon swallowed his smooth, salt semen. Robin buckled at the knees.

'Be still,' Channon whispered, unaware that he spoke in Spanish. 'Lie on your side, spare your back.' He settled Robin and struggled for his wits and breath. 'What will you have from me, Robin? I'd give you the world. Only tell me.'

'Couple me,' Robin slurred. 'Fuck me. Let me repay pleasure with pleasure.'

Channon's senses swam as he put Robin on his belly. 'Have you a salve? This — an ointment for your wounds?' His hands shook as he unstoppered the pot. Robin struggled to his knees without prompting, and opened for Channon's fingers like the heart of a rose.

He cried out as he was pierced, and Channon let him. It was not a cry of pain. He went down on Robin's back, mouthed the scars as Robin began to rouse once more and was wild. He muffled his own cries in Robin's neck as the young body gripped his cock and drew him in. For sublime moments he struggled to keep the coming at bay, before Robin's climax finished him.

'Dermot?' Robin's voice was distant and Channon fought back to awareness to find his weight pillowed on the boy's lax body. He held himself on palms and knees, and slowly withdrew. Bites branded Robin's shoulders, his buttocks were oily with the salve and his back was bleeding, but Robin was doped with contentment.

'Christ,' Channon whispered. 'Without you I shall wither.'

From somewhere Robin found a smile. 'At night, close your eyes, pretend your hands are mine. You will know you have been with me, for I'll have done the same.' His eyes glittered.

Kissing them, Channon tasted salt. 'Let me see to your wounds... the price was too high. To be flogged for love.'

'My father saw only fornication and buggery,' Robin said as Channon traced the pattern of the welts and his buttocks were gently bitten. 'It is no matter.'

'Yet you're bleeding,' Channon said regretfully. 'Let me bathe us both and see to your back.' He brought ewer and basin to the bed, and the wet cloth pressed Robin's back until the sluggish flow stopped. The linen was stained, but he barely noticed. Robin murmured in relief. 'Better now,' Channon guessed. 'Here, up with you and hold me.'

Lush kisses stirred them again. Robin's eyes sparkled as they parted. 'You can teach me little about kissing,' he teased as he surveyed Channon's swollen mouth.

To his surprise the brown eyes widened and Channon's brows rose. 'You think not?' He patted Robin's hip. 'Spread for me, and I'll give you a kiss you've never known, one that will make you mine.' He put Robin on his knees, spread the long legs, palmed his buttocks and for a moment let him wonder what would be done.

The stripes were ugly. Channon's heart squeezed as if Robin had grasped him there and his grip on the uplifted buttocks gentled. Robin was panting, aroused again with boyish swiftness.

'A kiss,' Channon promised, 'to make you mine.' He put his head down and delivered it with a probing tongue. Robin gasped, and Channon had only to kiss the yielding muscle a second time for him to come helplessly. Channon lifted his head, astonished by the quicksilver response. Robin quivered, eyes wide as Channon pushed him flat on his belly and swabbed his scars again.

Breathless and ecstatic, Robin struggled onto his side, reached for Channon and mumbled against his neck. Channon's cock was hot against his belly and he took Robin's hand to it. 'What will you give me?'

'I would kiss you that way.' Robin panted.

Channon gave a start of surprise. 'You desire that?'

'I would do anything for you,' Robin confessed.

Before he would kneel Channon devoured him, and then Robin approached this cautiously, for it was strange. The last light of sunset coloured Channon's skin as Robin learned his final secrets. He bent to the task, and took the soldier's surrender with a rush of heat. Channon was as helpless as Robin had been. It was not the actual kiss, but the notion of what Robin was doing that destroyed him. Surely, the most intimate of all acts. He swore and shouted Robin's name as he came. If the household heard, so be it.

Robin had forgotten his back as he crawled into Channon's arms. Spent, Dermot looked only a boy himself. Robin buried his face in his lover's chest and they were silent for a long time. When they spoke at last it was not of the war but of the future, hopes and dreams. Channon held him and wished never to see the dawn, nor to feel the burden of duty on his shoulders.

Impossible dreams taunted him and were dismissed. When Robin stirred to lust again at midnight, Channon loved him gently; and again at dawn. They had not slept, but it was not fatigue that pinched Channon's features as they heard the servants. A mortal weariness dragged at him.

The sky had brightened, the sun shone strongly across the river. Downstairs the maids were busy and hearthsmoke prickled Channon's nose as he lay still, not a muscle moving. Robin sat, elbows on his knees, his eyes on the window. His back was sore and would be rubbed painfully by his clothes, but he seemed not care as he turned to kiss.

There was a terrible finality about it. Channon ate at him until they could not breathe, and when he released the boy Robin slipped away completely. He stood in the sun, gathered his clothes but did not dress. Heavy eyes lingered on Channon, as if committing him to memory. Then Robin nodded, satisfied, and turned away.

'I shall see you like this when I dream,' he whispered. 'Time to go.'

They dressed in silence. At the door Channon caught him, reluctant to make an end. Robin trembled with some bitter resolve. 'No grief,' Channon remonstrated. 'Look to the future.' He breathed deeply the scents of Robin's body. 'You'll be mine, for good and all,' he said in a fierce whisper, before Robin fled.

Mauricio was shouting for servants and Channon realised belated that he had not yet packed. An evening's work was completed in an hour as he slammed his belongings into valises as if every blow struck William Armagh. Mauricio watched shrewdly but held his tongue, for his nephew's temper was vile.

The rumble of wheels made Channon swear beneath his breath as his bags were carried down. He had no stomach for food. As the coach drew up he searched for Robin, but his room was deserted, as were kitchen and library. He had gone already, running from everything he had ever known.

Because of me, Channon thought bitterly. Guilt flayed him, though he knew it was needless. Robin was becoming a man, it was past time for him to forge his own life where he would be respected for his learning, loved for himself.

Fury exhausted Channon and he fought to rein his temper as he mounted the coach. Mauricio's face was disapproving, as if he knew an affair of the heart was at the root of his kinsman's foul mood. If he had known Channon was already pining for the love of a young man his Catholic heart would become a turnip. Channon seethed with anger that would not be quelled. Mauricio must never know; he would surely never forgive.

The coach rattled to the gateway and there, mounted on an old grey gelding, an animal of no value, was a figure in brown leathers and green cloak, clad for the road. The wind whipped his hair, the sun gleamed on the sword at his left hip.

He had waited. Channon's heart twisted as the coach pulled out. He raised his hand as if to touch, then the moment was gone and he was alone, despite Mauricio's presence. He had never felt so completely alone, and though Mauricio frowned at him he would not speak. He wished he knew how to pray, and believed in something to pray to.

God speed an English victory, if that is what it takes, any end to this folly! Eyes closed, he summoned Robin to mind and clung to his dreams as the coach hurried him to Plymouth, and exile.

BOOK TWO

The Privateer
February — August, 1595

O, never say that I was false of heart
Though absence seem'd my flame to qualify!
As easy might I from my self depart
As from my soul, which in thy breast doth lie:

That is my home of love. If I have rang'd,
Like him that travels, I return again.
Just to the time, not with the time exchang'd,
So that my self bring water for my stain.

Never believe, though in my nature reign'd
All frailties that besiege all kinds of blood,
That it could so preposterously be stain'd
To leave for nothing all thy sum of good;

For nothing this wide universe I call,
Save thou, my rose; in it thou art my all.

Shakespeare, *Sonnet 109*

Chapter Fourteen

Indigo, parchments and vellum were scattered on the desk in scholarly confusion, but the cartographer knew to a hand's breadth where any item lay and rarely glanced up from his work. The vellum was bleached almost white, the finest stock for a master craftsman. The reefs and islands of the Caribbean formed a delicate web, like gossamer, each strand lovingly copied from the most scrupulous charts in a folio captured seven years before, the property of the captain of a Spanish man-o'-war. Those charts, worth more than their weight in gold, fell into the hands of the Queen, passed into the care of Hawkins, and then into the possession of the man infamously known as The Master Thief of The Unknown World. Drake.

It was cold. A brazier burned by the desk, but each time the door opened the draught made the whole shop little warmer than the street. The old man had had his fill of climate and customers, though it was still just three o'clock. He had gone home to his wife and hearth, leaving his young associate to attend to his affairs.

The young man had proved himself capable, and in any event they were his affairs also. He had been a financial partner in old Ned Blythe's business for several years.

The bell at the door tinkled, announcing the lad from the port office. A gust of February air ruffled the vellum and the flames stuttered in the black iron brazier. The door slammed swiftly and the lad stamped his feet as he hurried to warm his hands.

''Tis cold enough to freeze the water in a man's very kidneys,' he exaggerated in his thick Cornish accent, and twisted his neck to see the cartographer's meticulous, beautiful work. The artist did not look up. 'Ho there, Master Armagh, are thy ears deaf of a sudden?'

'My ears are in fine vigour.' A green-eyed glare over the vellum stilled the portmaster's lad. 'What brings you here, Jim?' He returned to the detailing of a coastline in the Spanish Americas.

'A letter for thee.' Jim opened his coat and rummaged through his pockets. 'A ship's 'ome from the Indies, the *Roebuck*. Just dropped anchor this mornin'. God's blood, what 'ave I done wi' that thing? I 'ad it a moment ago. I know I 'ad it when I stopped at yon butcher's — '

With a resigned sigh the quill and indigo were set aside. The chair creaked under the artist's weight as he sat back to wait for the boy to finish his monologue. He would get no more done till he had quiet, and the work was too important for him to risk error. Flaws in a pilot's reef chart could sink a ship and cost lives. Much more was at risk than the chartmaker's reputation. Jim was at a loss to know where the letter had gone, but it could have come from only one place.

Hal was still in the Americas, in Panama or Provincia del Darien, pursuing his fascination. Birds, butterflies, insects. The work was incomprehensible to Robin Armagh, but Hal was happy flirting with butterflies. In the scheme of things a man's happiness mattered most, so Robin approved.

Once, it seemed he had but one friend and kinsman in the world, and it was Hal. He had returned on Hawkins' ship and was with friends in London, recovering from the illness of the voyage, when Robin left Blackstead.

Seven years on, Robin could still flinch in remembered pain, as if the lash bit into his back again with each unwanted memory of the day. But keener pains were to come and now, today, his father's ire seemed little to fret over. His back would always bear the scars but they meant nothing to Robin. Other, deeper wounds were more telling.

Hal had found him a fortnight after the Cervallos were expelled. Robin closed his eyes to the dim little shop and for the thousandth time wished his memory was less mercilessly sharp. The June day was warm as he left Blackstead. London bemused him with her sights and sounds, her barrage of smells. In his doublet was a letter of introduction, kept safe, treasured since it was written in Channon's own hand.

He found his way to Ned Blythe's late in the evening and the shop was closed. He owned a few shillings, and that night bedded in a chamber over a noisy taproom. He was at Blythe's door when the old man arrived next morning, holding out the letter and hoping to God he would enjoy a moment's charity. His back was sore. The welts were open again after the ride, and his heart was like a stone.

Channon was gone. Now, Robin must keep safe and wait out the months. The fighting must soon begin. Already the taverns were filled with false alarms of Spanish ships seen on the Cornish coast. Blythe read the letter with difficulty. He held it to his nose and turned it to the light. His sight had failed, Robin realised at once. Aside from the favour Blythe owed Channon, this alone was good enough reason for the old man to hire a young apprentice with keen eyes.

The work began as simple copying, and Robin showed his skill with pen and ink; soon he was entrusted with detailed work. In a fortnight his back had almost healed and he was too absorbed in his craft to notice who had entered the shop.

It was Hal, bright-eyed with tears. From the earl, he had heard the story of Robin's new disgrace, and Robin was afeard that Hal had come to fetch him back, or chastise him anew. But after work, when he was free to go, flexing his aching hands after the long hours of copying and study, he found himself in Hal's arms, petted as he had not been since childhood. Hal was grieving.

How many years had he spent at sea? Enough to be no stranger to the love between men. He had said nothing to the earl, nor would he, since William was immovable, furious. Instead, Hal had asked everywhere for a boy called Robin, and found him at last in Blythe's shop.

Robin could still feel the cool, careful fingers that examined his back, the first time it had been seen since Channon left. He had never dared show anyone the marks of a new flogging, lest the scars brand him a criminal. Hal wept over him and gave him money, but by then Robin had received his first wages and was in decent rooms. Soon Hal was gone again. He was rarely in England but never forgot to write. Robin always listened for news of a ship that might bring a letter.

Opening his eyes, he watched Jim going steadily from pocket to pocket. He would not have lost it — he was too careful, despite his jackdaw chatter. He was eighteen, newly employed in the port office. The whole Port of London had become his province when the world of ships, mariners and adventure had beckoned him from a Cornish farm.

Smiling, Robin recalled himself at eighteen. Had he been so raw and eager, like a puppy, anxious to please? He knew he had, and it was luck alone that Blythe gave the pup a home. Robin had discovered the thrill of the sea trade, of being the first to hear stories from the New World, as if there was some connection between the riverside warrens and the exotic lands across the sea.

The Port of London was simply a port, chaotic, noisy and aromatic, filled with men who went home at night to wives and children. The mariners who were the real adventurers merely passed through, unknown, unremembered.

Robin glanced idly at the brass timepiece on the shelf by his desk. Soon he too would be home, and well done with the day's work. His hands were cramped and even his young eyes protested the hours of concentration.

A bright hearth awaited him; mulled ale, pigeon pie and Jenny, all white lace and pink cheeks, with her arms full of little Robin and Bess. A kiss for each of his twins, and their nurse would bundle them into the nursery. Then Jenny would want to talk, sing and play the mandolin. Later, perhaps, to lie with him.

He would never forget Jenny's voice as she argued with her father. Blythe wanted his prettiest daughter to marry well, and who had she chosen? The copyist. Robin could not tell her his heart belonged to another, though she knew he was pining. She would sit with him in the afternoons, so quiet he began to forget she was there, and thus forgot to mask the old pain. She saw him aching for someone he had lost, but Jenny Blythe could wait. She had patience, Robin granted. How long had she waited for him? Too long.

'Ah, 'ere it is!' Jim exclaimed, and pulled the letter from the bottom of one capacious pocket. 'Now, 'ow did it get there?' He handed it with a flourish to the man who made maps for Drake, Frobisher and Howard. 'From the Americas?'

'From my brother.' Robin could not mistake Hal's looped scrawl. The back of the letter was affixed with plain wax, the Armagh device stamped into it with Hal's signet. He had reached for a knife when the bell at the door tinkled again and called him back to business.

With a sigh he pocketed the letter. He would find time to savour it at length. A glance at the door brought him to his feet in surprise. Even Jim recognised the burly visitor, and withdrew to a discreet distance.

Few men on the docks would not have recognised the man. Robin was pleased to call him an acquaintance, since he had done the admiral service many times. Drake appreciated fine work and did not stint in his praise. Blythe's shop had a good reputation, and Master Armagh did the old man credit.

Robin had not expected the admiral to call but the charts were well progressed, and he turned them on the desk for Drake to see them. 'Good day, sir. You look prosperous,' he said by way of greeting. 'Your charts will be ready, my word upon it.'

Eyes as green and slanted as Robin's own appraised him, twinkled with some mischief, and Drake nodded. 'They're almost done now, I see. Fine work, young Robin, as I have come to expect.' He plucked at his beard. 'And if I told you the sailing date is advanced?'

'To when, sir?' Robin frowned at the charts as he calculated how long he must have to complete them.

'Friday's morning tide,' Drake told him. 'There's dissent at Court.' His lip curled. 'Delay longer, and the milk-sops may call an end to the scheme. What say you, Robin?'

'They will be ready,' Robin judged. 'I can work by night to finish them. Send a lad, or I can bring them to your dock.' He stood aside as the Master Thief held the charts to the light and studied their detail. Robin took pride in the work. Some men were troubled beneath Drake's cat-like glare, but Robin knew the value of his skills.

At length Drake set down the vellum and warmed his hands at the brazier. 'Hawkins sails with us, have you heard?' He shook his head. 'Too old. The trip will kill him, mark me well.' His tone was cutting. 'Too old, aye, and too cautious.' He rubbed his hands together, held them to the blaze again. 'And we sail not a day too soon. The Spaniards have had fair warning of our plans. We'll have no element of surprise.'

Robin's brows rose. 'I've heard a little myself sir. You are bound for the Spanish Americas, I know, and —'

Drake shot him a glare that would have withered another. 'There is free talk of this?'

'Not free talk, sir,' Robin said quickly. 'But I overheard a Hollander who had been at Court. They whisper, as if of great secrets. And then...' He gestured at the charts. 'I know what coasts I am drawing!'

'Aye.' Drake returned to the fire. 'Ah, 'tis too late, in any event. His Catholic Majesty knows. And so be it. If there's to be a fight, then let us fight!'

'I have a brother in the Americas,' Robin mused. 'A letter just arrived on the *Roebuck*. I've yet to read it.' He watched the burly figure in brown doublet and cape move stiffly about the shop as Drake examined this and that chart. Some depicted the sky, astronomer's maps. These were Robin's favourites, for the sky was filled with mystery and magic.

'Your work?' Drake asked shrewdly as he held a map of the northern stars to the window. 'I know your hand. With your knowledge of sky and ocean you could be a ship's pilot, and a good one. What keeps you here? Are you such a landsman?'

'I merely look to my affairs,' Robin said smoothly. 'This is my business too, sir. Ned Blythe paid me well when I began here, seven years ago. And paid me better when I wed his daughter! I have a wife and babes, and am not so anxious to see the world that I'll set all this into another's hands... yet. I am still young,' he added ruefully, 'and time can lie heavily on a young man. One day, perhaps.'

For some time Drake frowned at him, before he stirred. His square, callused fingers plucked at the hem of his cloak. 'I came to tell you I sail sooner than expected,' he said bluffly. 'I'll expect the charts no later than Thursday eve, young Robin.'

Robin nodded deeply, a half bow. 'I shall fetch them to you personally, sir.'

The bell rang again as the Master Thief left, and Jim came to warm his hands. 'Thee could've been a pilot, and thee stays 'ere instead?' he demanded. 'In God's name, why?'

There was no simple answer. Robin returned to his chair and inked his pen to make the best of the last of the poor daylight. Soon he would be working by candle, which strained the eyes. Ned's sight had ruined early. Robin had received offers of work at sea — pilot, navigator. Once, he would have accepted with a boy's foolish innocence, but Robin counted himself fortunate, his education was properly completed.

Pain kindled in his belly as he recalled the tutor who ushered him to manhood. The old, sweet ache was not dulled by time. Channon's face haunted him whenever he allowed himself to dream. Many nights, he woke with Jenny beside him, listening to the reassuring sounds of his house by the river, yet his body was raw. His heart ached for days which could never return.

Channon was dead.

How long had Jenny watched him pining for that lost love? Months became years while Robin waited. The great Spanish fleet came soon after the Cervallos left. Working with Blythe, Robin had every tale at once, every whispered rumour of the war that began as a roar and then, though it dwindled, refused to die.

Seven years later it still simmered. The tale of Sir Richard Grenville's last battle fast became a legend. He challenged a Spanish fleet with one ship, Drake's old *Revenge*, and battled it out though he had twelve feet of water in the hold. *Revenge* was razed to the waterline and capsized by a full Atlantic gale, Grenville died of his wounds and his crew were dispersed to the galleys. The war went on.

A year after the great battles in the Channel, hope burned in Robin. Channon was his life, and Jenny watched him retire into some private realm where he was unreachable. There, he lived. Jenny did not know the name, much less the gender of his lover, but she knew that lover lived in his private world with him and she grieved, for his pain and her own. While Robin belonged to the other, she had no hope.

An end to hostilities never seemed at hand. Two autumns after the great armada was smashed, Robin began to wake to the truth. He sat in a riverside tavern where he often listened to mariners' tales. Four lads bragged of battles between English and Spanish vessels, tales of glory in which English ships were invincible. Robin heard of the Spanish nobles captured for ransom. The names of Channon and Cervallo were never mentioned.

The war could endure indefinitely, he realised as he sat in the dim drinking-house among the rattle of coins and dice and the rank, yeasty smell of old ale. It could go on forever. Despair gnawed him. As he drank the last cup and left the tavern unsteady on his legs, he knew he must not look for Channon's return, but for a letter.

A message, passed from hand to hand, brought in by a Hollander, a merchant, and delivered to Blythe's. Channon would be aware of the state of affairs. He must write.

But no letter arrived, and as winter set in, bleak and hard, Robin began to guess the truth. He would sit at the window in Ned's study, gazing through the tiny glass panes at the yew and elm, picked out in crystals of frost. Ned had brought him out of his lodgings when Robin began to cough with the damp. The Blythe house was almost empty, since Ned's large family was grown and gone. Only Jenny was still at home.

Winter was bleak for Robin in many ways. He was ill, though not seriously, and Ned's stout, matronly wife nursed him. The bleakness was in his heart, as he guessed the truth and grieved. For Channon to be so silent, so absent as months became years, he must be dead. Were he alive he would have sent a letter, something, anything to make separation bearable. No storm of grief purged Robin's pain, for realisation crept insidiously into his bones. Had Channon died at sea? Had he fought in the Americas?

With spring Robin listened for seamen's tales again, but he found no pleasure in them. Instead he wondered bitterly which of the braggarts had been aboard the ship that sank Channon. Which of the gunners drinking ale in the smoky taproom had put the final shot into a Spanish warship.

He could not deceive Jenny. She knew he was tormented. They shared quiet hours in which she was simply near, fetching some item he needed without being asked. Robin grew accustomed to her voice and ways until, when they were apart he noticed her absence more than her presence. She was a fine girl, two years younger than himself, the last fledgling from the nest.

He did not love her, and Jenny knew that also. She did not ask him to love her. It was enough that she cared for him, and they shared gentleness, friendship, trust. Robin never spoke of his grief and he treasured Jenny because she never asked. For this, he was grateful. How could he have explained that he ached for a lover who was not merely a Spaniard, which was close to treason, but also a man? Blythe was a good friend and a forgiving father, but Robin doubted he would have been forgiving enough. Silence was his only option, and to his surprise he found Jenny supportive.

She pardoned his moods and his taciturn temper, teased him gently, first with words, later with kisses. Pretty and plump, she was everything Channon was *not*, which may have been the reason Robin was at peace with her. Nothing about her made him think of Channon. Jenny could have found husbands by the score to love her as Robin knew he never could, no matter the fondness they shared, but her decision was made.

It would be Robin Armagh or no man. Robin thought the words a jest but realised the truth later, when she rejected Sir Jocelyn Hardy, who served at Court. Furious, Hardy railed at Blythe to prevail upon his daughter. By chance Robin was in the library nearby and heard every word.

Ned promised he would do what he could, and as the knight left he summoned Jenny. She spoke up boldly. 'I've told you countless times, why do you not listen? I'll have Robin or I'll take no one!' Ned raised his voice under his own roof for the first time since Robin had known him. Sir Jocelyn was a knight, he said, and Robin had hardly a penny to his name. He was pretty, but Jen was not the only lass with eyes for a comely youth — if he chose another, what then? Robin knew the look she would have worn as she said, 'Then I'll have no one. I may not be the only lass to see Robin, but I'm the only unwed daughter in his master's house, and the lass who spends each evening and Sunday in his company!'

Astonishment overtook Robin. Jenny had waited for so long, patient and gentle. From Channon he heard only the silence of the grave.

Spring was bright. Warm days lured the couple onto the river, punting, courting with Blythe's approval, and in summer they married. Robin thrashed through one hellish night with Channon's ring in his hands, aching and praying. Dermot was surely dead, and had he been alive, he would have castigated Robin for the years of self-imposed loneliness. At dawn Robin smiled at the signet and imagined how Channon would scold. His eyes would glitter, part teasing, part irked, and that sensual mouth would be stern. He would counsel selfishness and indulgence.

Still Jenny waited, young, pink and pretty, and Robin surrendered. The wedding was for kin and friends, but no Armagh attended. Even Hal was abroad again, and John was too ill to travel. His physicians were helpless.

Of that day Robin recalled resignation, tiredness and lingering sadness. Of the night to follow he remembered more. Jenny was shy, ticklish, and knew nothing of love. She liked to kiss, but when he tried to take off her nightgown she stopped his hand. He only lifted the hem, and that in the concealing warmth of the bed. She had always trusted him, and still trusted, though he hurt her a little. She had heard that virgins must hurt, and gritted her teeth, wanting it to be over soon. She desired only his embrace, his kiss. Lovemaking held no joy for either of them. Jenny wanted to know nothing of the rapture of coupling, and her grim resignation to the act of consummation stole Robin's pleasure.

It never mattered that he did not love her. Love had died with

147

Channon. It was a place in his heart, a warm, sweet ache he could never share, nor find again. What Jenny offered was enough, and though he did not love her he treasured her.

Their wedding was early in the summer of '92, and by Christmas she was round, ripe with the twins. She only laughed over her condition as she toiled about the house, but Robin was aghast. All at once, with dizzying suddenness, he was wed with a son and daughter, and modestly wealthy as Ned embraced him as a partner.

Robin was twenty-three when his children were christened. John attended, sickly and pale, thinner then even. Sir Richard was absent, but Hal was briefly in London, publishing a set of documents while he waited for a ship. Marriage and business made Robin respectable, and Hal teased that the Armaghs' black sheep had been tamed. But Robin was already chafing at captivity.

The sea lured him. In the portside taverns he listened to mariners' talk as he lingered over a cup in the evening. When the sailing master of a merchantman offered him the position of pilot, he was tempted. But the man looked at him with hot, hooded eyes that roamed over his body, and Robin knew lust when he saw it. Four weeks at sea, beyond reach of any port, it would be a struggle. A young man beaten to his knees and buggered, by one if he was fortunate, by many if he was not. He never forgot Channon's counsel.

If Channon had told him the truth, he was beautiful. Robin had scant regard for his own looks, but he was still slimly made and knew his slender limbs would lure men who desired youths in the absence of women. The fascination of the sea remained but he was not ready to pay that price. To give his body in love to one he adored was one thing. To give it in lust for the privilege of being one man's catamite rather than the plaything of a dozen, was another. It could end badly. He never forgot Channon, whose story had appalled him.

Thoughts of the Spanish-Irish soldier commanded him for wasted, cherished minutes as daylight faded and the February twilight gathered. At last Robin saw the hour, discarded his pens and decided to call the day done. He doused the brazier with a scuttle of ashes, snuffed the candles and locked the door behind him with a thick iron key.

The street led down to the river but he turned right, past the tavern, and held his cloak about him as he hurried to the livery, where he would enjoy mulled ale while a boy saddled his horse. Enough twilight remained to see him home.

The cold was striking and Channon was on his mind as he hurried in out of the stinging wind. Master Possnet waved and whistled for his sons. Robin warmed himself at the saddler's hearth and gratefully took the hot cup.

The observations Drake had made troubled him. Marriage and business were swiftly becoming no better than a prison, and Robin longed to escape. The yearning for freedom was almost as keen as it had been while he languished at Blackstead. He had made his share of mistakes, he admitted as he drank the hot ale and then mounted up. Marriage had seemed the best course; it pleased him to make Jenny smile, and Ned boasted happily that his grandchildren had noble blood in their veins. Their grandfather was an earl.

But as Robin turned the horse into the chilly night he wondered wryly how far his forbearance would stretch. Before him was the promise of a long, uneventful life as he watched his wife grow fat, sired a tribe of children and amassed a small fortune.

Once, Blackstead had been his prison and Channon was his salvation. Who would liberate him now? Who would pluck him from the satin prison of his own making? He hurried the chestnut mare through the cold river wind.

Yet he had the best of luck. John would not live long. He coughed, his breathing laboured and lines of pain etched about his eyes. Richard, the old earl's favourite, was in good health but ill spirits. He was trying to father sons upon a new wife, as was his duty, but no children came. His bride was a lovely Frenchwoman with two daughters from a previous marriage, so the fault was not hers. Was Richard impotent or sterile as a mule? Robin had his suspicions. His brother was so like his father, pious and loveless.

And the Earl of Blackstead's health and sight were poor. Richard's wife led him about while he railed at his servants, so John reported. Hal visited when he could, but his visits were taxing and grew more rare. Robin never visited, nor asked after his father. Across his back the faint lines had silvered with age but still persisted, reminding him of shame and fury. And of Channon.

His dreams were as fresh as ever, untouched by time. Robin had forgotten nothing. Channon's face was unaged, unchanged, smouldering with sensuality. Brown eyes roved over him, aroused him without a touch from Channon's hands. Robin's own hands did the touching even now, seven years after they parted.

How long had Channon been dead? Robin had no means to know until hostilities ceased and he was free to travel to Seville. As he urged the chestnut mare homeward he wondered if peace would ever fall again. He let the horse pick her own way through the gloom. She knew the road well, and his mind was too consumed by the past for him to notice the riverside streets.

Chapter Fifteen

The house stood by the river, a gentleman's residence with elegant gardens, yet Robin was restless. The dream of love was as taunting as the longing for freedom. Hal's letter crackled in his pocket as he swayed to the mare's gait, and he admitted his envy. Would Hal accept the offer of a good companion on his next voyage? Surely two brothers travelling together could see each other safe.

The ring of horseshoes returned him to the present as the mare ambled into her own stableyard. Yellow light spilled from the windows as a drape moved aside, and as he swung down a door squealed on unoiled hinges. Tom, the steward, peered out and called over his shoulder, 'Aye, 'tis the master, home safe.'

Then Jenny's voice called for firewood and wine, and Robin put the memory of Channon back into the private place where he kept his dreams. A lad rushed to take his horse and he hurried in out of the cold.

As he threw off his cloak he smelt spiced wine. Mistress Mallory, the housekeeper, had a hot cup for him and he drank it to the lees. Its warmth restored life to his bones before he turned to his wife.

Winter suited Jenny Armagh. Her skin became pale as porcelain, which made her hair seem darker, her eyes brighter. Robin swept her up, kissed her cheeks. She was so small that, plump as she was, she weighed little. Nothing about her brought Channon to mind.

'And how's my pretty lass this cold day?' he teased.

'Glad to have you home!' Her arms wound about his neck, her blue eyes danced. She had crushed his collar, and straightened the lace again. 'Little Robin has a sniffle, but the physician says 'tis but a cold.

150

Father has the same cold, but you and I shall escape.'

'With luck.' He hugged her and set her down again. 'What do I smell cooking? I could eat a nag!'

'Rabbits,' she told him, and tugged him to the parlour where a fire blazed and the room was cheerful with brass lamps. 'Let me look at you, husband. You're pale, Robin. Are you sure you're not catching father's sniffle?'

'Quite sure.' He sat and propped his feet in the hearth. 'It is chilly tonight, m'dear, if you notice!' He rubbed his hands together. The gesture reminded him of Drake at the brazier, and he recalled Hal's letter. 'Oh, see here, I've a letter from my brother.'

'Hal, of the birds and beetles.' Jenny kissed his hair.

He smiled. 'The very same.' The sealing wax tore raggedly and he brought a lamp closer as he opened the letter. Hal's hand was bold, clear. Robin expected some fascinating account of life in the Americas, stories from one scholar to another. Hal always remembered that Robin had been allowed to read his letters as a boy.

What he saw took the smile from his face at once. The lamplight shadowed his features, and Jenny watched him frown. 'Whatever is it, Robin?'

He finished the letter before he would share it, then went back and read it aloud in a hushed, disbelieving tone.

'My dearest Robin, I send his letter with a Hollander whose *zabra* lies anchored below me in the cove of Puerto del Miel, and I pray it reaches England before winter. But Captain van Nekk sails first for Vera Cruz to victual, so I may only hope.

'I write, dearest brother, in direst need of aid. I know my pleas would fall on barren ground were I to beg support of father or Richard. Poor John would come to my aid, but when last I saw him he was ill unto death.

'Well might you ask how I am in Puerto del Miel, which is a Spanish anchorage. With regret, I write that I am the prisoner of Don Julio Recalde, an officer of King Philip; and I am accused of spying. I shall die unless a ransom is paid in the amount of five hundred guineas, whereupon I may be released, on pain of exile from the Spanish Americas.

'Father would refuse me. The price is high, the fault of capture my own. But I pray, Robin, do not forsake me. Upon my return I shall certainly repay you. Don Julio will wait for this letter to reach England, and will tarry as long as '97 before I am condemned to the sword.

'I am presently in good health and fair spirits, but eagerly do I await the arrival of your agent, and I remain, as always,
your brother Hal.'

The letter fell to Robin's lap and he was silent for some time. He studied the fire, unaware of Jenny's frowns. She had inherited her father's intellect, and had absorbed every word. When he looked up at last he saw her working slowly through some plan, and arched a brow at her.

'You'd waste your breath, speaking to the earl.' She sat on his right knee, one hand on his shoulder. 'Your father is an old fool who cares nothing for his sons. Richard is a younger fool who cares only for his career. John is so ill... you're alone in this, Robin.'

'I am. I have the money, Jen. We can afford it even if Hal could not repay us. It is the price of his life! Is a man's life not worth that sum? But could I trust the ransom to an agent? What man do I know who would have my interests at heart, and not make off with the money and seek his own fortune?' His eyes closed. 'God help me.' Before his mind's eye was a face, beautiful and dear to him. 'There was a man, once.' He stood, brought Jenny up with him and embraced her. 'You know what I must do.'

'You'll go,' she guessed bitterly. 'Oh, Robin, no. There are such dangers! Such things I have heard!'

'As have I,' he said drily. 'And more than you, I fancy. Oh, Jen, it is just a journey. A quick passage out, find Hal and return on a merchantman, a tobacco ship, perhaps a Hollander. I'd be back in a year, two at longest, even if I must wait the winter out for a ship. Recalde will safeguard us once the ransom is paid, I've heard his name praised by the men who buy charts from me. We might even come home aboard a Spaniard.'

The woman's face was bleak. 'You believe this?'

'That we'll return aboard a Spanish warship?' He forced a smile. 'No. But Recalde is an honourable man. Some Spaniards reckon honour above life. I knew a man before the war... honour was all he possessed.' His eyes clouded and he stirred. 'And I know another man who'll get me safely to the Americas, if I can leave by Friday's dawn tide. Drake sails on the Queen's orders and with my own charts to steer by. He would take me aboard, for he knows me, and under his flag I shall be safe. Ah, smile, Jen. What harm can I come to, sailing with Sir Francis?'

'He sails on Friday next? So soon?'

'It is best done swiftly,' Robin mused. 'How is Ned? If I am to be gone for a year or two we must make arrangements.'

The old man had taken to his bed. He lay on a mound of pillows, a tincture in his hand, a book in his lap. Robin read the letter aloud and outlined his thoughts; Blythe was no fool. Eyes as bright as a rook's appraised the young man as he fluffed the pillows, and gnarled, blue-veined hands reached for the letter. He read it for himself while Robin sat on the bed, studied his clasped hands and waited for a verdict that could not change what he must do.

'You'll go,' Ned said at last. He smoothed the white linen at his breast.

Robin nodded mutely.

'And you sail with Drake, if he'll have you?'

'He will have me,' Robin said softly. 'He respects my work, and my mission is on behalf of an earl's son. I told Jen, you've no cause to fret. What can befall me, travelling with Drake and dealing with a Spanish gentleman? I'll be home soon, aboard a tobacco ship, mark my words, richer for the experience and with Hal safe.' He took the letter back and read it slowly. 'I must go. What kind of fool would entrust such a fortune to an agent?'

Blythe made a face but nodded. 'Aye, there's sense in it. But what of your work? These eyes of mine are too old to do your work all year! I'll need to hire another.'

'Stephen Craddy studied with the Queen's master cartographer,' Robin suggested. 'He brought me a letter of recommendation last week. Employ him, I'd trust him.' He smiled wryly. 'He has that kind of face.'

'You've an answer to everything.' Ned leaned into the pillows. 'All right, Robin. Talk to Drake on the morrow, and if he agrees, send Craddy in the afternoon. A year?'

'Or two,' Robin added. 'And I return with a brother, Ned. I care nothing for the money when it is the price of a man's life... and when that man is Hal Armagh.'

Sleep was impossible that night. Dinner was sumptuous, rabbits broiled in ale, but Robin forced himself to eat while his belly churned and his heart sped. Jenny left him to himself and brought the twins to him only for a moment before they were whisked away by their nurse. Robin held them, preoccupied as he made plans, broke them and made others.

Much later, when they were alone and he was pulling on his white linen nightshirt, Jenny hit him with a pillow to win his attention. 'Ah, now you notice me!'

His eyes were dark in the light of a single tallow candle.

'Oh, Robbie, if you're to leave so soon, at least be a husband to me till you go. You're a stranger of a sudden, looking through me. I miss you already, and you are still here!'

He gave a guilty chuckle and opened his arms. 'Forgive me. It is a shock, Jen. I never imagined this could happen.'

'What, with the war lingering on? The Americas are Spanish property,' she argued. 'Hal always saw the danger.'

'He travels with neutral Hollanders and keeps to himself.' Robin slid into bed. Jenny pressed close, wanting his affections for a little.

The nightshirt twisted about him and he thought, how he hated the garment. Did a nightshirt preserve lovers' modesty, or keep them apart? He wore it for her. Jenny was shy, for so forthright a girl. She was the first lover he permitted himself after Channon. His first and only woman.

She never knew. He was adept, and she assumed he had enjoyed many ladies' favours. Jenny would never dream that what Robin knew of love he had been taught by a single master in the art, who was anything but a lady. His kiss was sure, his hands gentle but firm, his body a tool he used so adeptly.

Many kisses and caresses, and Jenny was alive in his arms, comfortably familiar, a buffer against the trials to come. She wanted gentle loving, and Robin gave her all he had. He knew how to please her, and it was ironic that long dead Channon was due a lady's gratitude, though she would never know it.

He kissed her to sleep in the crook of his arm and watched the candle burn down as the night wore away. He did not sleep, but the hours were not wasted. With Jenny safe and satisfied his mind was at liberty to wander. If he thought of another's love, where was the sin in dreaming?

They were boyish dreams of swimming, fencing, coupling in the grass while the horses grazed. Channon had brought a light to Blackstead which had not burned there since Catherine Armagh's death. Robin's memories of his mother were not as sharp as those of Channon. She was beautiful, not much bigger than himself, and he was but eight years old. Her voice was light, with the Dublin accent of her girlhood. Robin remembered milky skin, rosy cheeks, copper hair, green eyes like a cat's. And grief.

Mass was said for her soul by Father Doughty, in the chapel where she was buried. William was like a statue, his face a mask through which no feeling showed. Richard and Hal were young men and kept their grief private while John, then twelve, held Robin and wept with him. It was difficult to recall details now, but Robin could still see the motes of dust in the shafts of sunlight below the windows, still hear Doughty's voice droning Latin while the liquid voices of castrated little boys sang praise to the God who had allowed Charles Rothwell to strike down a woman with a single blow.

The child rebelled. Robin's faith was gone in the blink of an eye. He prayed to please the priests, confessed his sins and undertook penance mechanically. When Channon arrived he was ripe for picking. Channon had only to issue an invitation for Robin to fall into lust, and love.

Lust was spent, love endured. As Robin saw out the cold February night, sleepless but content, the old, well-polished memories were his delight. Channon, drowsing after making love; cutting Rothwell with the rapier in the courtyard at Hampton; floundering in the river while Robin swam like a fish. Dermot, bright-eyed with desire, wanting him. Once the memories had been painful, but not now. They were all he had.

Warmth suffused him. Channon had left his mark indelibly on the world — Ned remembered him well. Dermot had caught a thief in his shop, a Portuguese who came in to browse and would have stolen a valuable chart. Blythe had owed him a favour since then. Channon supped with him, charmed his wife and daughters, and when Robin brought his letter of introduction Ned was pleased to read Channon's name. He had looked forward as eagerly as Robin to the end of hostilities, the possibility of Channon's return.

As years passed it seemed Ned simply forgot him. Robin might have been his own son, while the Spanish-Irish soldier was so long gone, he might never have been at all. But Robin forgot nothing, not the dark, silken hair which Channon wore close cropped, nor the taut, boyish skin, the muscles like steel, hard after an hour's fencing.

He kept up his fencing when he could find a gentleman to practise with him. Being Blythe's son-in-law he was welcome in many houses and partners were plentiful. The rapier with which Channon had taught him was like a razor. He often wore it but had used it in anger only once. Rothwell's men were drunk in the Normandy tavern, four river rats with ill manners and long memories. They had watched while Channon took the sight from their master's eye, and thought to even the score. The blade slid from its scabbard, light and cool in Robin's hand. Everything he had learned came together in a superb moment. Then, the bark of a pistol, and it was over. The taverner was furious. 'Not in my house, Jack Fitzroy! Get out in the street to brawl! Don't you know Master Armagh, Drake's mapmaker?' Did Drake's name end the scene? The river rats left sullenly.

They would run to Rothwell. *Rosamund* lay anchored on the river, Robin had seen her as he rode by. She came through the bloody, hectic months of July and August '88, dismasted but otherwise sound, and was soon repaired. She went out again to fight and plunder, and had been to the Indies twice. Rothwell was rich on the spoils, and bragged that *Rosamund* had sunk eight Spaniards.

The boast soured Robin's belly. Had Rothwell sunk Channon's ship? If he had, Dermot had surely perished in the wreck, for had he lived as Rothwell's captive, Rothwell would have made sure all London knew his vengeance was in hand at last. He wore a patch over the ruined eye, and Robin could imagine the malice he nursed for Channon.

Now *Rosamund* was victualling again, to sail with Drake. Robin knew little of Drake's business. It was no concern of the chartmaker, but loose-lipped couriers said Elizabeth had given him the duty of seizing the Spanish gold ports. This would curtail Philip's wealth, and with Spain finally bankrupt the war must end. The plan was sound, Robin mused, and a strong fleet could do it. From his work, he knew every inlet and headland along the Isthmus, and every Spanish anchorage. They were strong, and Drake would enjoy no easy victory. Perhaps Rothwell would pay his price on this voyage. It was long overdue.

An hour before dawn Robin drowsed with fretful dreams, as even in sleep his mind began to accommodate to the voyage.

Chapter Sixteen

Morning was bleak and blustery. Fair sailing weather, Robin thought as he rode not to the shop but to the dock, a mile down river, where the little fleet lay anchored. They were victualling even then, and he drew rein to watch as a powder-hulk warped out to discharge its load of gunpowder and shot. Mist still curled on the surface of the grey, sluggish river and the wind had an edge like a dirk.

He pulled his cloak tighter and hailed the lad in charge of the victualling. The admiral, he was told, was ashore, breakfasting at the King's Head, and Robin hurried into the inn's humid warmth. He was blind for a moment in the sudden dimness. The tavern smelt of mutton, onions, ale and hearth smoke.

Drake was arguing with a foppish, well-mannered and very pretty young man. Documents lay on the table, pinned down by a tankard. Sir Francis was annoyed, and Robin stood back, listening to the verbal broadside. The young man withdrew, suitably chastened, and the tavern was quiet once more. *El Draque* in a righteous temper was best avoided.

The green cat's eyes still glittered angrily, but surprise quelled a measure of his temper as Drake saw Robin's face. 'What brings you here?' He beckoned for another cup of ale. 'Not trouble with the charts?'

'No, sir.' Robin seated himself and accepted the ale. 'But still, trouble.' He set out his business in a few brief, acerbic words, knowing Drake would not appreciate passionate speeches. Then he spread his elegant artist's hands. 'There you have it. I must be in Puerto del Miel without delay, or it is my brother's life.'

The unexpected petition diverted Drake from his anger with the Queen's courier. He sat back and plucked at his beard. 'Julio Recalde has an excellent reputation, this I know.' His accent thickened. 'If he has your brother, I'd wager you'll not be duped. And you would sail with me, no doubt?'

'That is why I am here, at an ungodly hour on an icy morning,' Robin said drily, 'when I should be warm at home, finishing your charts! I'll pay my passage, Admiral, and still be in your debt. I know what a favour it is.'

'Favour?' Drake snorted. 'You sign aboard a warship, Master Armagh! This fleet does not embark on a jaunt down the river, we go to fight, and will taste of Spanish guns along the way. You share our risks and if we sink, you drown with us.' He leaned on the scarred, pitted table. 'Sea, wind and Spaniards. Consider all three before you wager your fortune or your life.'

'I have considered everything,' Robin admitted. 'I lay awake all last night, weighing odds! It is not my life, but my brother's. If I cannot sail with you, then I go with someone
else, for go I must. I'd rather it was with you.'

'Would you?' Drake frowned. His face was tanned brown by the elements, his eyes deeply lined. 'Why?'

'They say you are a fair and decent sailing master,' Robin told him candidly, 'God-fearing and strict as a father with his sons. Little escapes your eye, and those who sail with you trust you implicitly.' He chose his words carefully. 'I've never been to sea but I can read charts as well as draw them, I speak several languages and have studied navigation. I might turn my hand to useful employment if you've need of me, or be a passenger if not.'

The silvering curly head nodded. 'Aye, well spoken. You know the risks, and the rewards. I've no room on my own ship, mind. You'll travel with Downing, on the *Swan*. He has a spare corner to stow you in.' He offered his hand with a faint smile. 'Welcome aboard.'

Robin found the admiral's hand callused, leathery — the hand of a man who had worked and fought all his life. 'I wish,' he confessed, 'I could say I was pleased to be aboard. However — ' he chuckled. 'Necessity, sir. And I thank you. I shall see you on Thursday eve, with your charts and my bags.' He withdrew his hand and stood. 'How long before we see the Isthmus?'

'That's in the hand of God,' Drake said indifferently. 'With good winds and no Spanish intervention, we may enjoy a quick crossing. Then,' he added with definite glee, 'there's a game to be played with His Majesty's lackeys.' He appraised Robin closely. 'I'll put you ashore as close by Puerto del Miel as may be, then you're on your own. You speak the language, which is something... till Thursday eve, then.'

'Good day, sir,' Robin said quietly, and left the admiral to his business.

He hurried the horse through the chill February drizzle. The cartographer's shop was icy, and he lit the brazier, warmed his hands enough to use his materials. First, he wrote a letter to summon Stephen Craddy before the day was out.

Drake's charts were the only commission he had to finish now. He had not noticed the morning pass by when Jenny arrived with his dinner in a covered basket. A look at his face, and she knew.

'Sir Francis will take you,' she said bitterly, as if she had hoped Robin would be refused.

He merely nodded as he attacked the cheese and onions with relish.

She watched him eat in silence and studied the meticulous charts, which were almost complete. The names of exotic ports taunted her, reminded her of the danger. Robin sailed upon a warship, not a lumbering merchantman. But his mind was set, he had that stubborn look she had seen often before. It would be useless to cajole, so she kissed his cheek instead as he finished his meal.

'Little Robin is much recovered today,' she offered. It seemed Robin barely heard. He made a cursory acknowledgment and returned to the work at once. Jenny dumped the scraps into the basket with a noisy sigh and was at the door before he looked up.

His mind milled in confusion but he knew he was neglecting her, and gave her a guilty smile. 'Forgive me, Jen, I am poor company. I'll have to work late to finish, too. I'll leave you on Thursday afternoon. Drake hopes for a quick, uneventful crossing. I'll bring you an Inca trinket to remember this adventure.'

'Bring me back yourself,' she said tartly, 'whole and sound. Nothing else will do! Good day, sir. I shall see you some time tonight, I imagine.'

With that she was gone, and Robin sighed, at a loss to know what to do or say. Even then, Ned was gathering the ransom. The price of a man's life in gold coins would fill a small chest. It was a fair price, Robin judged, one they could afford, and since Hal was an earl's son it was not so high. Each gold coin was an admiral's pay for a day's work, or more than a month's pay for an ordinary seaman. If there was justice in the scale of payment, Robin could not see it. He returned to the charts, eager to have them finished.

Jenny was less resolved. By evening she was angry and had begun to weigh Robin's life against Hal's. No matter that he sailed with

Drake, the dangers were dreadful. Not wanting to spend his last hours at home fighting with her, Robin chose silence over argument and kept his own company.

Ned came to him early on Thursday morning, when Robin was working in the study at home. The charts were finished, he was merely checking every number and angle, and adding embellishments as the artist in him desired. He looked up, mutely asking, and Blythe nodded.

'The chest is full. I called in every debt owed to us with explanations to the gentlemen who've come to our aid. One and all wish you well, and so do I. We'll have a tight year, but we'll manage. Craddy is a nice lad, well-mannered with customers and clever with inks. But, best hope your brother will honour his word and repay us!'

'You may count on it,' Robin assured him. 'And Drake agrees, Recalde is a fair man. Hal will not be ill used in his care, and we'll not be cheated.' He threw down his pen and rubbed his tired eyes, 'I must leave soon. Where's Jen, will she see me off?'

But Ned shook his head. He stood at the window, watching the labourers trimming the yews and weeding the knot garden. The clouds parted and a pale blue sky appeared. A harbinger of good weather? Drake's eyes would be on the sky too.

'Jen went out in a fine temper and won't return till late,' Ned sighed. 'Hal's life is not worth the trade of your own, she said... and forgive me, but I agree. She loves you. And you're like my son, Robin.' He came to the desk and offered his hand. 'I know! For a man it is a matter of family pride, but see Jen's thinking. Without you, what is she?'

'A widow,' Robin said drily, 'young and pretty, and not wanting for money! She'd be wed to a knight of your acquaintance before a year was out. All right, I make too light of it. But fret less for Jen. If I die, it was always in the cards. I came to you as a runaway, I was a shady risk then, and now.'

A rude snort answered that, but Ned smiled. As he left, Robin consulted his cumbersome brass timepiece with a sigh. Drake would not take kindly to delays.

The charts were done, dried and rolled before dusk. Robin had packed, a few cases containing a minimum of belongings. The ransom chest sat atop them, and on the lid of that, an old but cherished sword that had not tasted blood in years. It was polished brightly, its harness refurbished...

The weapon brought Channon to mind. It was sweetly painful to draw the blade, feel its balance. Caring for it was a mix of punishment and pleasure. A thousand times it called Robin back to the meadow at Blackstead, where the summer sun gleamed on the river and the soldier mocked him for his mistakes before tumbling him in the grass. Love-making rewarded him for his best efforts so that he would try harder next time.

He buckled on the harness and swung a heavy blue cloak about his shoulders. Hooves were ringing on the cobbles already. He was to have an escort to the dock, lest he be robbed before he even made it to sea.

Ned came down, still pale and unwell, with little Robin in the crook of one arm, Bess in the other. He and Robin lingered at the door, and farewell was difficult.

'I wish Jen were here,' Robin admitted as he kissed his children and touched the old man's shoulder. 'Tell her I care for her, Ned, and will hurry home. Tell her I have no choice in this.'

'I shall,' Ned said bluffly. 'Fare you well, Robin. Our prayers go with you, if not Jen's well wishes.'

Twilight was early, the sky deep and stormy. The wind was chill as the party clattered down to the dock where Drake's ships yawed on the rising tide which swelled the river. Drake was wrapped in a green cloak, his unmistakable voice booming out to the victualling crew. He turned to greet his young cartographer with a preoccupied frown, and Robin presented the charts.

'I've brought a few items of baggage, and my brother's ransom. May I go aboard and make safe?'

'The *Swan*,' Drake pointed. 'Yonder frigate. Michael Downing is her master. He'll stow the ransom in his own cabin. I told him your business. A boat'll be along shortly.' He thrust out his hand, 'Good fortune, lad. I'll give you a smooth passage, God willing.'

Robin grasped Drake's callused hand and smiled. As his escort withdrew he found himself attended by a brawny seaman who threw his bags into a longboat for the slow pull out to the frigate. The *Swan* was a neat little ship of twenty-two guns, low in the water, laden with the provisions for an Atlantic crossing.

His insides clenched as he thought of the months to come, but Robin had no time to fret. Captain Downing had seen the longboat from his weather deck, and it was he who hoisted the passenger aboard. He was a small, stout man with silver whiskers, pale blue eyes and a genial, friendly smile. Robin took charge of the chest as the seaman shouldered his baggage, and Downing conducted him aft.

The sterncastle was cramped, already occupied by the ship's full complement. Downing apologised as he showed Robin the corner where he would sleep.

'It will suffice, Captain.' Robin did not need to feign a smile as he felt a growing exhilaration. For years he had longed to escape. 'I'll be comfortable. If I can be of some service, you have but to ask.'

Downing knew he was Drake's master cartographer, and appreciated the offer. He left Robin to stow his gear and took charge of the ransom.

The tide was still rising. The deck beneath Robin's feet heaved gently and he knew at once he was about to sicken. It was said almost everyone sickened for a time, so he bore the nausea lightly. The captain's table was well set that night, but though he was invited to dine he refused food and took a cup of wine instead. Downing guessed his trouble.

'Are you sickened, Master Armagh?'

'I am,' Robin confessed ruefully. 'A storm in my belly.'

'Salts,' Downing said, and sent his cabin lad for medicinals. 'Then stand on deck, fix your eyes upon the horizon and breathe deep. The sickness will soon pass. 'Tis more a malady of the ear than the belly, though you might not credit it!'

It was dark by then and the advice was impractical. The horizon was lost in the pall of river mist. Still, Robin stood on deck and turned his face to the wind till well past midnight, despite the cold. A boy was singing, playing a battered lute. His songs shifted from shanties to madrigals and back at whim. At last, tired and with the hope of sleeping, Robin retired to his corner and put his head down on a pillow that seemed hard as a brick.

His cabin mate was already asleep. He did not meet the man formally until morning, when the roll of the hull woke him. He knew at once they were moving, as he felt the slight vibration through the ship's wooden skeleton as she butted through the river chop, eastward to the sea. He had not bothered to undress and was on deck in moments, hoping for a grand sight as the fleet shipped out.

Only the silver-grey swirl of mist greeted him, and he stood by the helm to make the acquaintance of the men who would be his companions for so long. The gentlemen — few among them without title and estate — were breakfasting on salt pork and ale. One offered his hand to Robin without preamble. His face was young, smooth-shaven, his fair hair combed neatly about a shapely skull. Grey eyes smiled at Robin.

'David Beaufort,' he said as he clasped Robin's wrist. 'Your cabin mate. I was asleep when you retired, and gone when you woke, or I'd have introduced myself sooner.'

'Robin Armagh.' He smiled as the young man stooped to pick up a little dog, a ratter he called Peg. The Yorkshire bitch was tame and eager to make friends. Robin let her lick his hand, and stroked her ears. 'You've been to sea before?' he asked Beaufort.

'No,' Beaufort admitted. 'Never beyond the Lizard.'

'Then this is your great adventure,' Robin observed. The other man played fondly with his dog. How old was he, twenty-one? Younger than Robin by several years, slender and boyishly handsome. He was fortunate to sail with Drake. In another fleet, David Beaufort could have been easy prey. Robin's mind returned to Channon's tales and he looked away, intent on the overcast sky.

The wind scattered the mist, and Robin eagerly counted the ships of Drake's fleet. Beyond the sands, in open sea, the squadrons massed: six warships and twenty-one armed merchantmen, strung out in line astern, often barely in sight of one another as they tacked toward the mountainous waters of the Atlantic.

This was Beaufort's dream and he was filled with enthusiasm for his first venture. Robin watched his boyish exuberance with a wry smile while thoughts of Channon damped his own spirits. Young David had scarcely heard of the cruel games men sometimes played, long at sea. *And God grant he never learns of them*, Robin prayed silently. Beaufort had a pretty face and graceful body, very like Robin's own. And he was cursed with the handicap of innocence. Or ignorance.

But Drake was strong on the Protestant faith. Divine service was held twice daily on each vessel and the officers kept a strict watch, rooting out such evils as gambling. And fornication, Robin thought ruefully. He wondered how effective the admiral's orders would be when the fleet was months from home.

He did as Downing suggested, stood with his back to the foremast, eyes on the tilting horizon, till his ears found their balance and his gut ceased to churn. For several days he was unwell, but before the strung-out fleet had passed the Lizard his appetite was back and he accepted Downing's invitation to dine.

The gentlemen were tiresome, living conditions were cramped, and he was soon grateful for Beaufort's terrier. Brown ship rats the size of rabbits inhabited the holds, and by night found their way as high as the sterncastle, hunting for food. Peg proved worth her weight in gold and was quickly adopted by Downing and the privileged few who bunked on the upper decks.

The weather worsened before England was over the horizon, and Robin watched the sky resignedly. The sea was violent and the crossing would be vile, but with a gale astern the warships would fly. *A fast crossing*, he prayed to the old sailors' gods, *and a safe one!*

Chapter Seventeen

The Atlantic had a personality — capricious, fickle, devious. Seamen spoke of her as if she were a lover, adored but not trusted, and Robin learned the truth of this in the first week of the voyage.

With England six weeks astern and the islands of the Antilles far behind, Drake's fleet had already probed deep into the Caribbean, a sea which Spain had made her own; but Robin was not duped by the brilliant blue of the sky. Davey Beaufort was sunning himself in the waist as if he had not a trouble in the world, but the old mariners were splicing and battening. A glance at the water, rather than the sky, was their warning. If Robin had learned anything from these past weeks, it was to keep silent and watch. The common sailor had much to teach his betters.

The sea was running at odds with the wind, and the *Swan* made little headway despite her billowed sails. To west and south were acres of blue sky, halcyon and calm. But Robin glanced aft into the north-east, and saw the gradual darkening of the horizon. A storm was gathering, like a great beast let loose. The look of it dried his mouth and his suspicions were confirmed by the bleakness of Michael Downing's pink, plump face.

'Trouble, Captain?' Robin asked quietly as Downing paced between the weather-deck's guns.

'Aye.' Downing turned away, his blue eyes slit against the brightness as he squinted into the rigging. The *Swan* was running under almost every rag she had. 'We must catch up the fleet. We are lagging, as you know. Ho there! Hoist me a topsheet!' he bawled at the lads scrambling in the nets by the ballooning mains. But he shook his head as his men set to work. 'When yonder blow hits us we'll take in those sails or lose a mast.' He was angry. 'Then, what chance of us catching the fleet!'

Robin gazed into the north. 'The storm should hold off till noon,' he judged. 'By how much are we lagging?'

'Too far.' Disgusted by the turn of events, Downing spat over the side. 'God's blood, this is fair fortune.'

'So we ride out the storm and rendezvous with Drake when they take on fresh water at Guadeloupe,' Robin suggested. He knew the charts as well as Downing did.

The older man merely grunted as he returned to his work and left the passenger to watch the sky. Robin stood in the stern, his clothes dampened with spray as the wind rose and cut the crests off the waves. Whitecaps loomed from horizon to horizon, and soon the wind screamed like a banshee in the rigging. This was an Atlantic storm which swept into the Caribbean, likely wreaking havoc in the islands, and might rampage on, right across the Isthmus.

The *Swan* had weathered other storms as she came across the Atlantic, but this was the worst, and it was terrifying. Robin clung to the lines and gazed into the teeth of it. Like a live animal, he thought, and pitied the lads sent aloft to trim sail. Snatches of prayer carried on the wind. Death was a hand's span away. With sails furled the frigate wallowed like a pig, but it was this or be dismasted, and the coasts of the Americas still lay a week or more away. Not, Robin knew, that there was a friendly port where an English ship might undertake repairs. She would more likely be blasted out of the water by the first *gallizabra* to come upon her.

The *gallizabra* was relatively small and as fast as the *zabra*, or frigate, long in the keel and low in the water, but with the insurance of oars and twenty guns or more. The design was very new, from the Havana shipyards of the naval constructor Pero Menendez Marques, and it was the first Spanish warship to command the respect of the English privateers.

Lightning forked around the mastheads as the riggers took in the last of the canvas before the gale could tear it away. To Robin, who clung to the sternlines, it was as exhilarating as terrifying, and he was determined not to miss a moment. In the long, tedious weeks of the voyage little had stirred him or fed his imagination, and nothing was worthy of memory save the sea, and her capricious lover, the wind. He knew he would remember this storm as long as he lived.

If he lived — if any of them lived. For the space of a few incredible hours he thought they would not. The *Swan* heaved and pitched like a cork in a bucket, at the mercy of wind and white water. Was this what men came to sea for — to feel this hellish intoxication? Robin wondered at the height of the storm as his blood raced and his heart pounded his ribs. An instant from death, he had never felt more alive.

Channon ruled his mind and heart so strongly, it seemed his lover was beside him. He felt as if he shared some part of Channon's world, and understood a fraction of what had made Dermot who and what he was.

Near the end he was certain they were done for. Lightning struck, thunder rolled all about and a tangle of mizzen plummeted to the deck, where it was caught in the netting and held by squealing hawsers. Heart in his mouth, Robin crossed himself instinctively and waited for the lightning to strike again and finish them.

The ship staggered, the lines to main and foremasts snapped like lengths of twine and the *Swan* listed dangerously before she rolled upright, crippled but afloat.

And then, with startling suddenness, the storm passed over, the sky brightened and the wind dropped. Soaked, frozen and shaking, Robin cut the line that had tethered him and made his way forward into the chaos of fallen rigging.

Many were injured, some were dead. The ship carried no surgeon and the lads were trying to tend one another. Friends and lovers supported each other as Downing clambered through the mess of timber and hemp to assess the damage. He was cursing as Robin fell into step beside him.

'We'll limp,' he said darkly, 'but we can tack up a few sheets. The yards are splintered, see?' His face was drawn with fatigue. 'I wonder, how sound are our masts?'

Robin said nothing. Even Downing's officers avoided him in this mood. Lads went up to cut away the ruined lines and hoist tackle up to what crosstrees remained usable. Robin took a cup of wine, sat against the side as the sun grew warmer and watched the seamen work. He had no skills to help.

By evening two topsails were up, and one mainsheet. Not much to take them to the Isthmus, where they must seek some cove unknown to the Spaniards who commanded those shores. The fleet had gone over the horizon. Now, the night sea was totally dark.

With the navigator injured, more duties than he could manage tied Downing's hands, and he summoned Robin to his cabin a little after midnight. 'You once offered me your aid, Master Armagh, and I've need of it now. Admiral Drake informed me that you know the sky as well as the sea.'

'I do,' Robin affirmed. 'You wish me to affix our position?'

'As closely as you can,' Downing said tiredly. He opened an iron-bound chest and showed Robin his most precious timepiece, a fine clockwork device from Amsterdam. 'Thank Christ, it was not damaged. I hope I can trust you to make the calculations correctly. Do your best work, for our lives surely depend on it.'

The task was not difficult, merely complex and time consuming, and one needed an excellent knowledge of the sky. Robin called Beaufort to his aid, took the timepiece on deck by lantern-light and turned his attention to the stars. As the constellations rose he marked the time of their appearance and consulted a chart of his own making.

Long before dawn, he had set the ship's westward position. Beaufort watched over his shoulder as he worked and marvelled at the intricacies of navigation. To him, they were a mystery.

'You were well taught, Rob,' he said. 'Will you teach me?'

'If time permits,' Robin agreed. He looked up into the other's face in the flickering light. 'Remember, I leave you when we are near Puerto del Miel.'

'Your brother,' Beaufort said soberly. 'You walk into awful danger for him.'

'He's my friend as well as my brother.' Robin rolled the precious charts, for rain was about to begin and they must not get damp. He was frowning as he led the way below. Though he took great pride in his work, the results of his calculations were dire. Downing waited in his cramped little cabin, and at Robin's face he prepared for the worst.

'We were blown far south-west, Captain,' Robin told him. 'Into the lanes between Hispaniola and Cartagena.' Hispaniola was the most ancient settlement in the Caribbean, and the most populous. 'A fleet of Spanish warships lies at Santo Domingo,' Robin added very quietly, though Downing knew this well enough.

'Oh, God.' Downing rubbed his face hard. 'Dangerous waters, these. King Philip's warships haunt them.'

Robin had heard every story, most of them from Channon himself. Hulks laden with gold looted from Inca mines lumbered eastward from the Isthmus, and the bullion ships were guarded by Spanish men-o'war in great convoys bound for Seville. One crippled English frigate would be easy game. Robin carefully locked away Downing's beautiful clock. 'There's no mistake, sir. To be quite certain I checked each figure twice.'

'I trust you.' Downing had watched the way Robin handled the charts and timepiece, and recognised the hand of a master.

'So, our course?' Robin asked as he helped himself to wine.

The captain slammed a half-empty tankard onto the table and mopped his lips with a kerchief. 'Bear south-west with all speed — which will not be much, I grant you! — and we might slip into the coves west of Cartagena, if we don't hang ourselves on a reef or run under the guns of a Spaniard. Christ Jesus, this may be the end of us, Robin.' Few men did Downing address informally, and Robin was touched. Downing had reached out for friendship or support, and in return he made the gift of intimacy. Robin answered with a faint, regretful smile.

'If I may, Michael, I'll search the charts, find us an anchorage. I drew them myself, I know them almost by heart.'

The older man accepted readily. It was a task he should have done himself but his hands were occupied and he was weary. He passed the folio into Robin's care. 'You should have been a ship's pilot, lad.'

'Should I?' Robin asked softly. 'Perhaps. I —'

Knuckles rapped at Downing's door. The captain was wanted on deck, and Robin settled to work at his table.

He worked the whole night through, unaware that he had fallen asleep over the charts until a hand on his shoulder shook him. It was Davey Beaufort, with a cup of mulled ale. Daylight streamed through the sternports as the ship ran almost due west... Dawn. Robin jerked awake, took the cup and looked into Beaufort's worried face.

'What is it, Davey?'

'You,' Beaufort said softly. 'You look like a ghost, Rob. Are you sickening?'

'I'm tired,' Robin admitted. How long was it since he had slept properly, eaten, or been warm and dry? 'I'll rest later,' he promised.

'Hot food and wine,' Beaufort counselled. 'Downing won't return for an hour yet. Use this cabin. I'll strop a blade for you, if you like.'

Robin smiled his thanks, only then realising that he wore several days' growth of beard. The last week had been too fraught with danger to even think of bathing. He dined well on pickled pork, oranges, pigeons' eggs and black bread, then indulged in the luxury of a pail of hot water, a keen razor. Beaufort sat on Downing's unmade bunk to watch. In an hour Robin felt restored, and had Davey to thank for it.

He earned a shy smile from the younger man, and felt a start of surprise as he saw the expression in Davey's eyes. Friendship, respect and affection were growing swiftly, as feelings do in rough times. Young blood ran hot. Lust would bloom soon. Was this how a man met the love of his life, far from home and in need?

Pain assaulted Robin, but he patted Davey's shoulder as he went out to breathe the fresh morning air. If only it had been Channon, he would have had something to give. If only. He scolded himself for the sentimentality. Davey was no more responsible for his feelings than Robin could be blamed for his own. Yet as he well knew, there was no part of him that could love. Not Davey, not Jenny. Love was a dream that belonged seven years in the past.

Limping under her meagre rigging, the frigate lumbered on. The reefs and shoals of the Isthmus were still days away when the dead were buried. Downing spoke the old litany over them, empty words made hollow by repetition.

Hammers rang on all decks as the shipwrights made what running repairs they could. Only six out of twenty-two guns were in firing order. The rest had upturned and must be remounted. But they had powder and shot aplenty. Enough to make a fight of it when the lookout high on the splintered foremast sighted a Spanish sail on the horizon.

Robin's heart leapt. He hoisted himself into the lines and his shaded eyes found the speck of ivory-white almost at once. A good-sized vessel under full sail, making fast headway with the aid of her oars. A long, low hull, quick to turn, part galley, part frigate, typical of the new Spanish men-o'-war. Philip's shipwrights had been quick to learn the bitter lessons of the Armada tragedy. Seven years had changed everything at sea. This was a *gallizabra*.

She came up fast, oars augmenting the wind, and the *Swan* swung broadside to show her four guns. Robin's chest vibrated with the recoil that kicked through the hull as shot pierced the Spaniard's sails. Another round slammed into the water just before her bow. Downing's gunners were undershooting and overshooting to get their range. The captain stood in the waist, eyes skinned for a sight of the Spanish commander.

The *Swan* was too storm-ravaged to outgun or outmanoeuvre the *gallizabra*, so it would be fighting, hand to hand, when she was boarded. Robin glimpsed the men along the Spaniard's rails, and saw the sun gleam on upheld swordsteel.

His old rapier had never been used in anger, but he was sure of his skills. May afternoons by the river taunted him as he buckled on the harness. Summer days filled with laughter and love, so different from the desperate struggle here.

Death was in the wind. He smelt blood already and his nostrils flared like the stag scenting the hounds. His marrow chilled as he climbed on deck. He had two options now: die or surrender. With surrender he might be ransomed, like Hal. But who would come for him? Not Richard, nor his father. John was too ill, and Ned too old. Channon's tales of anguish haunted him and he bit his lip till he tasted blood as the *gallizabra* loomed closer.

The impact as the ships collided was stunning. The main mast, already weakened, shattered loose and plunged into the deck. Robin's heart squeezed. Captivity aboard a Spanish ship could mean delivery into the hands of the Holy Inquisition, conversion to Catholicism so as to serve a life sentence at the oar of a galley. The alternative was the gallows. Or his captivity could mean the abject life of a catamite, made sport of, vengefully, for past ills done to his Spanish owner's mates.

The hilt of the sword was cold, hard in Robin's palm as he pressed to the wall of the forecastle. The *gallizabra* turned with difficulty at close quarters. Her sails spilled the wind and flapped loosely, but the frigate was dead in the water, a hulk waiting to be raped. With her masts down she had already begun to list heavily, and Robin guessed that her holds were filling fast. Planking must have ripped away in the collision. She would not be afloat in another hour.

The *gallizabra* was bigger, stouter, barely touched by the *Swan's* poor gunfire. Her larboard oars withdrew, grappling irons thudded over the side timbers and a chorus of voices was raised, some praying, some cursing as battle erupted.

Eager for blood, the Spanish crew made an admirable foe, but Robin saw little of the fighting. It was as much as he could do to safeguard his own skin. The animal instinct to survive drove him now. Three men were dead at his feet in as many minutes, their blood spattered his hands and clothes. Downing's company fought like madmen, but they were far outnumbered.

Robin feverishly weighed death over capture, and he handled the sword with the speed and agility of desperation. From the corner of his eye he saw Davey Beaufort go down, little Peg at his heels even then.

On the foredeck, Downing was dead already, cut to pieces by fragments of shot before the boarding. Robin shifted his grip on the sword. If he was to die, so be it.

He would always recall that hour as the finest of his life and take pride in the spirit that looked upon death unflinchingly. Four Spaniards lay dead about him before a cutlass, nearer axe than sword, sliced into his left side. Winded, he fell to his knees in a haze of red.

Vision dimmed, he expected to feel the final blow at any instant, but the man who would have dealt it was down himself a moment later, sprawled over Robin's legs with a dirk in his back.

Consciousness was fading and Robin fought now as never before, simply to stay awake, gripped by the terror that he would be left for dead on a sinking ship. But the darkness, like treacle, swallowed him up.

Chapter Eighteen

The sun was full in his face when he woke, and his senses reeled. The deck was steeply canted as the *Swan* listed, sinking by the stern. The dead Spaniard lay heavily over his legs, but as Robin's eyes blinked open the body was dragged off him. He moaned, tried to speak, and someone heard, for he was lifted by hands from behind.

The wound in his side burned like a brand. His thoughts dimmed again, though he knew the cut was not deep enough to be the death of him. He was half aware as he was jolted across the crazy tilt of the deck. The gunwales were already under. Spanish voices called out but he could not follow the words as his mind wandered. He knew only that he was passed from hand to hand, onto another deck that was sure and level.

They left him there, winded and gasping, and he swam in warm honey, oblivious to the struggles of his fellows. He heard the iron clatter of manacles, but in his delirium it seemed the bell at the door of Ned Blythe's shop.

He swam up again in time to see the grappling hooks retrieved as the frigate was cut loose to sink. Downing, Beaufort and many good men went with her, but Robin was incapable of grief. Half conscious, he watched her masthead slide out of sight.

He woke properly as the irons closed about his legs, but now he was in the dimness of a hold that reeked of damp timber, tar and old canvas. A face peered at him in the light of a stuttering lamp and he kept still as his ruined clothes were cut away. They were soaked in his blood, and that of others. The breath tore from his throat as the wound was dashed with vinegar. Weakness and sickness overwhelmed him and he retched, turning onto his side lest he choke himself.

His ears rang but the sickness abated when his belly had emptied. A pitcher of tepid, brackish water was held to his mouth by the old man who tended the wounded. There was no physician. Robin drank and murmured his thanks in the man's language. As he struggled to sit against the timbers a linen shirt and breeches were pressed into his hands. The man was a peasant, uneducated but not unkind.

'I threw away your clothes,' he told the Englishman. 'Too bloody to be cleaned. These will have to do. I told the *capitan* you are a gentleman, an officer. You are the only gentleman surviving. The *capitan* will come to see the prisoners by and by.'

'Thank you.' Robin moved cautiously, dressed with difficulty and pressed a hand to his side as the wound protested. The vinegar still burned, but it was the best treatment. A physician would have done the same. The leg irons were removed to allow him to put on the breeches, then refastened.

In no condition to fight, he slid down the curved timbers and sat very still. Had he been an ordinary seaman he might have been shackled by the wrists also. Only his fine clothing and sword saved him rougher treatment.

Weakness overcame him and his limbs shook. He closed his eyes, fought off the darkness as long as he could, but at last surrendered. He slept, oblivious to the crush of English captives in the hold, the roll of the ship as she got underway and the passage of time.

It must have been several hours before voices stirred him, and he blinked awake with an effort. The hold was almost dark and the sudden light of a lantern dazzled him. It bobbed closer as he squinted toward the sound of approaching feet.

The lantern stopped every yard or so along the hold as each prisoner in turn was examined. The captain would be assessing the value of his capture. None of the common seamen was worth a ransom. The frigate's gentlemen, bound by honour, would have fought to the death, as Robin himself had intended.

Then the lantern was poised over him, hurting his eyes. He looked away, tried to hold up one hand to shield his face, but his arm was snatched aside. Fingers gripped his chin to force his face back to the light. He held his breath and waited.

The figure behind the lantern had frozen. The hand cradling his jaw was cold and unsteady. No one spoke for the space of a dozen heartbeats, then Robin heard a sharp intake of breath, a Spanish oath, a deep, soft voice like dark velvet, speaking his name.

'Robin? Robin Armagh? It cannot... Christ Jesus, *Robin!*'

Dizziness stormed in his head. Robin fought his spinning senses, tried to sort phantasm from reality, but his eyes had grown accustomed to the light now and he would see. Behind the lantern was a face, fair-skinned, with sleek, cropped brown hair. The features were changed only by maturity that afforded them a greater beauty.

Disbelief stupefied Robin and he shook his head, mute, afraid for his sanity. Then the fingers that had turned his face to the light traced his nose and mouth, and he knew them as surely as he knew that voice.

'I am mad,' Robin whispered. 'I must be. You are dead! Am I dead also, then? Is this hell?'

'Alive, Robin. I am alive again in this instant.' The lantern clattered down as the Spaniard knelt. Cool hands cupped Robin's flushed face. 'I have been dead, or the heart of me has... ah, Robin, what were you doing on a warship? You've not been a seaman all these years?' But without waiting for an answer he called over his shoulder, 'Valdez, strike the irons and put him in my cabin. This is the son of an earl, not some common cur!' Shadowed eyes returned to Robin and he shifted into English. 'I must look to my duties, but they'll take you out of here. Be patient.'

Too dazed to respond, Robin gazed bewildered after him. The young man called Valdez took up a mallet, hammered the iron pins from the manacles, and strong hands lifted him to his feet. The wound stabbed him and he bit his lip as his belly heaved again.

'Slowly,' Valdez said softly. His English was heavy with a soft Castilian accent. 'The old man said the wound is not dire.'

'I am merely sickened,' Robin gasped as he clutched dizzily at Valdez's arm. 'And I am grateful. Who are you, sir? The captain's friend?'

'And the mate of this vessel,' Valdez added. 'Can you walk? Let me help you.'

Robin had his wits back but leaned on Valdez as he was propelled toward the stairway leading up out of the darkness and reek of the hold. He looked back, tried to make out the faces of the captives, but he knew no one by name.

The climb taxed him and he saw little as he stumbled in Valdez's wake. A door slammed, jarred him from his daze, and he found himself blinking at a small but richly appointed cabin. Furious yapping greeted him. On the divan, which stood against a bulkhead, was the Yorkshire ratter, Peg. The little bitch flung herself at him, and as Robin sank onto the bed he took the dog under his good arm.

'Two survivors, eh?' He fought to grasp his sanity.

He saw a chart table, littered with rolled and unrolled maps, two stout tub chairs, the divan itself, a seaman's chest and an ottoman matching the divan, both Turkish. The stern-ports were open and he turned his face into the cool sea wind to clear his head. The terrors of battle and madness tormented him and he struggled to make sense of the scene.

Channon? Alive, and in command of this vessel? Channon had survived? Helpless euphoria circumfused him.

Only later, as he waited and his mind and belly settled, did he begin to think clearly, and very different emotions awoke. Resentment replaced the euphoria as he sat holding the ratter. Seven years had passed, in which Channon had not troubled himself to send a letter, nor even a verbal message, as if Robin did not merit the effort.

Then it seemed to him that his life had been taken and sundered, thrown aside as worthless. That he had been discarded when he'd outlived his usefulness to a bored soldier who had desired entertainment and, afterward, could not even find time to send a word to ease the bitterness of separation.

Resentment swiftly became anger, ice in his chest. He had been used. He saw now what a fool he had been to play Channon's games, and a fist squeezed his heart. There had been less pain when he believed Channon dead and never doubted that he had been loved. Tears stung but he refused to weep. He nurtured the ice, the anger, as a shield against self-pity and self-mockery. He had been duped as a young innocent, and seven years of dreams mocked him as he waited for the master of the *gallizabra* to come and take possession of him. He was Channon's property.

'God help me,' he whispered, eyes closed, 'for no one else will.'

Captive, hostage, oarsman aboard a galley, catamite in the bed of whoever bought him. The choice was Channon's and Robin shivered as he wondered how far he had been duped as a boy. Had Channon borne him any genuine affection, or simply mocked him with the many sins he had committed? And even if Channon had felt some fondness then, how could it have endured? His years would have been filled with beautiful, skilful lovers. Why should he remember? Robin bit his lip until he tasted blood.

Shouts from the deck signalled Channon's approach, and he put down the terrier. Peg hid, cowered under the chart table, and Robin stood with his hands clasped behind him, chin held proudly, teeth clenched till his jaw ached.

Daylight silhouetted Channon as the door opened. He was broader than he had been, more muscular. His physique was daunting now, his stance arrogant. Then he was inside and the door slammed. Full daylight from the stern-ports displayed the industries of time and Robin caught his breath.

Before him was a mature man, richly handsome with smouldering sensuality. His body was powerful, lithe as a big cat, in a working-man's snug linen breeches and white lace-collared shirt. Polished brown boots buckled about his knees and cupped his thighs, and the shirt was open in the heat, displaying his broad, smooth chest.

Nothing had changed. The foolish churning of Robin's insides began again, and the softening of his heart, like a pleasurable sickness. He rebuked himself, drew his shoulders back and ignored the wound. His eyes were icy as they met Channon's, and he saw the lust in the Spaniard's face. Not even that had changed. Robin cleared his throat.

'Well met, Captain. The years have been kind to you.'

They spoke in English, and Channon's soft accent was a curious mix of Castile and Ireland. He looked long at Robin and seemed to hunt for words. 'Time has been as kind to you. You're more beautiful than I remember. Your hair is redder, your eyes more green.'

He stepped forward, both hands on Robin's shoulders. His fingers closed on thinly muscled bone and his breath was warm on Robin's neck. The closeness was tormenting. Robin wrenched away. If they kissed he would forfeit the game, for his body was as wilful as ever. He tore Channon's hands from his shoulders and turned away.

'Is this how it will be?' He levelled his voice with an effort. 'Set out the terms before it begins, so that I know who I am, and what. I would not like to cause you displeasure. Am I your hostage against Drake's fleet? Am I your captive, will you ransom me? Am I for the Inquisition, the galleys? Or for your bed?' Fury shook his voice, and the rage was as much at his own helpless lust as at Channon's betrayal of youth and innocence. 'I shall be an adept catamite, Captain. I was well taught. I know how to pleasure a man, where to stroke, what to kiss.' He lifted his chin as Channon gaped at him. 'The terms, so that I know my place and may remain in it!'

'Terms?' Channon lifted one hand to touch but withdrew it as if he believe Robin would bite. 'What do you ask? You are a captive under Spanish law, I suppose, but I'll set you ashore in any neutral place if you desire that. Robin, what is it? There are daggers in your eyes.'

Irony curled Robin's lip. 'And I am to believe you? As I believed you last time? I gave you everything I had, and for what? To be discarded like a worn-down shoe!' He glared into the perplexed brown eyes and squared his shoulders. The flare of heat from the wound only fanned his anger. 'Will I whore for you? Aye, I see lust in your face. Is this the price of my life?' He choked off a bitter chuckle. 'A fair price.'

'Price?' Channon echoed. 'Robin —'

'Spare me sweetness,' Robin spat. 'I am a man, if you care to notice. The pill needs no honey. If it is my body you want, say so. I am —' he gave the Spaniard a mock bow — 'your captive, your servant, most probably your slave, since God has seen fit to deliver me into your hands.'

Channon stepped back. His fists clenched, unclenched, knuckles white. 'You hate me. You'd kill me, had you a dirk to hand.'

But Robin shook his head. 'I've no death wish as yet. Were I to kill you, your crew would sport with me till I also was dead. I think I have a card or two left to play. My family would buy me from you. What says your mercenary heart now? A chest of gold coins, for my freedom. Am I worth that much?'

Channon's face was hardening. 'I must remind you, Master Armagh —' the formality was leaden '— you are alive and above decks at my pleasure. Why you hate me I know not, but I advise you, look to your welfare and guard your tongue. You begin to anger me.'

At once Robin lowered his eyes and folded his hands. 'My apologies. What does the captain desire? How shall I serve?' Seven years' foolish, loving dreams taunted him mercilessly and sharpened his words till they bit like a sword. 'No doubt you desire to purge your lust in me. So be it. Your whore, sir.' He turned his back, leaned both forearms on the chart table and presented himself shamelessly.

The mockery and provocation were savage, and Robin knew he had goaded Channon past endurance. He shivered as he heard guttural expressions of unleashed anger and closed his eyes. Now, it began. Channon's hands closed on his shoulders, bruising as they shoved him toward the divan.

'You little bastard,' he hissed in Castilian. 'You were a harlot then! For how many have you whored since? I thought you were so innocent. How many have had you, *sweeting*? For how many have you lifted this pretty arse? Ah, Christ, how was I duped to believe you loved me! Little English mongrel — you wouldn't know the meaning of the word!'

As the savage hands threw Robin onto the divan his wound opened. Pain and nausea coursed through him. His head spun again and his thoughts dimmed as his shirt tore. His belly gave a dry, painful heave before darkness engulfed him, mercifully sparing him the ordeal of rape, and he embraced unconsciousness with gratitude.

Chapter Nineteen

Blood laved Channon's hands as he tore the shirt, and surprise quelled a measure of his anger. Robin had collapsed, his skin was grey, waxen, sheened with sweat, and the wound in his side gushed. Channon hissed an oath through his teeth and lifted Robin from divan to deck before the bed-linen was ruined.

For a time he glared at the body at his feet, caught between rage and pity. In sleep, Robin looked so much like the boy he had known that Channon's wilful heart pained. But fury seethed in him, aroused by a stranger who wore Robin's face and mocked him like a harlot.

Seven years had melted away as if they had never been, and for one moment Channon believed in his father's saints. The pulse had hammered in his head, he could neither speak nor think. He hurried back to the cabin, and how long did it take this creature to smash his dreams? Five minutes? Less.

He threw open the door and barked at a lad to run for old Geraldo, who tended the wounded, and tell him to fetch an iron. The wound must be cauterised, swiftly. Alive, Robin was a prize, worth a decent ransom, as he claimed. And until the time came for his return he could be put to some useful service, Channon thought bitterly. If he had whored until he was so adept, let him do it again. Channon's bed had been empty too long.

Geraldo knocked discreetly. He had brought a poker which was set to heat in the brazier, a salve and a tangle of ragged bandages. The iron glowed cherry red before he was satisfied. Channon lifted Robin's inert body and held him while the iron scorched, sealed and black-ened the wound. The reek of burning filled the cabin and he turned his head away, but Robin was unconscious and felt nothing.

The old man stepped back. 'Will I take him to the hold, *Capitan*?'

Channon considered it, but shook his head. 'By and by. There are matters to be reckoned first. A score to settle. I'll send for you if he worsens.' He swept up the frightened terrier, which had been cowering behind the chart table. 'Take the dog and feed her.' Geraldo left with the ratter squirming under his arm, and Channon lifted Robin's dead weight back onto the divan.

He would wake soon. He had not bled enough to imperil his life, and would be sufficiently lucid to give account of himself. Channon poured a cup of madeira, looted from an English merchantman off the Azores, and sat down to wait.

In half an hour Robin stirred fretfully and half woke, but his mind was wandering. He murmured disjointed words in Latin and English, verses and prayers, as he if conversed with some Master Grey. His tutor, Channon recalled, disquieted as memory ushered him back to another world. He searched his heart, relived his lost dreams until Robin's voice rose quite clearly.

'Dermot! Ah... Dermot.' He was still wandering. Channon watched and resented the intrusion into his thoughts. Robin threshed, twisted away from his pain. 'Dermot.' A whimper. 'Love, ah, love, come back to me. Please, I cannot — Dermot! Dead. He is dead.'

Tears leaked from beneath his lashes, and Channon held his breath. The words were spoken unwittingly in his fever, there could be no deception. And they were not words of hate.

Almost reluctantly he clasped one of the fine, artist's hands. 'I am here, Robin. I've come back,' he said softly. 'What troubles you?'

Whether Robin was speaking to him, Channon would never know. 'My love is dead,' he slurred. His hands clutched Channon's. 'He left me and he is dead. I can't — never!' Harsh sobs shook Robin, and the words cut Channon to the bone. He understood no more than he had an hour before, but of one thing was he certain.

Once, seven years before, a young man had loved him. What became of that love he could not begin to guess, but Robin had not duped him. At once he reproached himself for the things he had said, the way he threw Robin onto the divan and tore his clothes, in that moment fully intending buggery. Rape.

As Robin shifted painfully in his delirium, Channon slid down onto the cushions and cradled him, lest he reopen the wound. Slowly Robin stilled.

Holding him was as terrible as wonderful. Channon smelt that scent, which he had never forgotten, and his limbs weakened with delight. His fingers longed to stroke. Robin's breast was downed more luxuriously. His bones remained close beneath the surface, his nipples invited kisses. His belly tensed as he fought through the painful delirium. His legs were still slender, long and lean.

And his back still bore the scars of the flogging. Channon swore as he felt them out. Twenty stripes, testimony to what love there had been, and the price a boy paid for it.

And you were whipped on my account, he thought bitterly, recalling all too well how it had ended. He brushed back the damp copper hair and set his lips to Robin's hot forehead. 'Shh, be still. Rest, then rail at me, let out all this anger, this hate. Then give me the truth.' He closed his eyes, pressed his face to the tangled hair and waited.

He had already given orders to abandon the wreck of the frigate and make port. Home was a safe anchorage in the mouth of the Rio de San Francisco, five days' voyage, given a fair sailing wind. The English gunners had cost the *gallizabra* only a little, but it would be wise to make repairs before venturing out in search of new plunder.

For an hour Robin alternated between sleep and delirium and Channon held him until he slowly regained his wits. A pitcher of water was to hand and he held a cup to the parched lips. Robin gulped noisily.

'Slowly, or you'll sicken,' Channon cautioned. He held the cup until Robin had taken all he wanted and was limp against him. 'Now.' Channon shifted on the cushions and took Robin's dead weight against him. 'Now you'll tell me what that outrageous performance was about. No more furious lies. You confessed everything in your fever. You wept for me and begged me to return. I am no longer prey to the folly of your anger, and I'll have the truth.'

Silence answered him as Robin tried to struggle away, but at last he surrendered. He gave a harsh sob and his words were indistinct. 'I waited,' he said hoarsely. 'Waited, and waited. You did not even send a letter. Not even a word from the tongue of a free merchant. I waited for you until I *knew* you must be dead, and then I mourned till I thought grief would kill me.' His hands clenched into Channon's sleeves. 'Sweet Jesu, forgive me, but I thought you cared for me.'

'And believed me dead until we met in the hold,' Channon whispered. 'Robin, you are as silly as you're beautiful. Or thrice so. I loved you every moment, save for one or two just now, when you mocked me.'

'But, why?' Robin struggled to sit. Channon allowed it and propped him with cushions. The wound was black but the cauterising held. 'Never a letter, Dermot, never a word!'

'I had no means.' Channon leaned into the cushions and looked his fill. It was difficult to credit how time had taken a beautiful youth and made a more gorgeous man. Even pale and overwrought, still in pain, his eyes were luminous, his mouth invited kisses.

'Tell me,' Robin whispered. 'Must I beg to know what became of us? I will if I must.'

He was waiting for the truth. Channon rubbed his palms together and chose his words carefully. Everything hung on them. If they were to be friends, much less lovers, the matter lay in his own hands now. He guessed rightly that Robin's thoughts were still muddled, and spoke in English. There must be no misunderstanding.

'A ship took me from Plymouth to Santander and soon Mauricio and I were before Philip at The Escorial. I never before knew the King so consumed by rage. While I stood by, listening and horrified, he gave orders for the fleet to sail from Corunna, where it was making repairs. Four weeks later it did put to sea a second time, and the rest of that episode, you know. Doom, death and glory... not much glory for Spain.

'I didn't sail with the fleet, though many of my fellows did. I would have gone, with the King's orders, but in fact I was ordered otherwise.

'Soon after we arrived, Mauricio collapsed. Philip had railed at him for his inferior services, which was unjust. It was too much for him and he fell ill. His face brightened with colour while his eyes were dull. He clutched his chest as if he were wounded. Philip's surgeons examined him and sent him home to rest.

'Or, to die in Seville, far from Philip! I saw out my duty as his keeper. It was a bitter homecoming, and more bitter yet when we saw what was left of our home. My cousins, Ramon and Luis, had sold almost everything. Even the drapes were gone. They hung calico in their place, dyed burgundy — a decent deception for the sake of pride. The farm, the horses, everything was sold to pay taxes to the crown. To build more warships, I imagine.

'Then the Church required its tithe. Cardinal Casserati visited to collect, not long after I secured Mauricio at home. The old man was abed and sick. The servants had been dismissed. My cousins' wives and daughters managed as best they could, work they were neither bred nor trained for. They wore brave faces for Casserati. Too brave, I think, for the cardinal rendered accounts to be paid, our duty to Rome.

'I told him, nothing would be paid. He was angry, there was shouting. God knows what I said to him, I don't remember, but he stalked from our house with a look that might have turned us all to salt. He didn't return, but the shame was the end of Mauricio.

'He cried out in his sleep that night and I held him while he threshed through his death. By dawn he was at peace. He was buried in the crypt beneath the family chapel. The funeral was sombre, late in July, yet the sun shone and larks sang as if they celebrated the freedom of a man's soul.

'Our grief was as nothing against Spain's. The Armada. So many boys died. More than one hundred and thirty ships sailed from Corunna, and sixty-three were lost. Some half-wrecked hulks limped to Ireland, where most of the lads who dragged themselves ashore were seized by the English garrisons and executed. No Spanish family was without a son, a brother, a father, who went to his death aboard Philip's ships. And then bloody Philip, God curse him, paupered us to fight on.

'Most of us begged for peace in August, when the tale of Calais was told. A fleet lay anchored there, victualled and manned, ready to sail, when *El Draque* sent the fireships. They say the powder and shot exploding aboard the devil ships could be heard for miles. It seemed hell had erupted in the harbour. The panic was appalling.

'Ships cut loose their lines and anchors and tried to flee but they had only minutes. *San Lorenzo* was disabled and ran aground on the sands. *San Martin*, the flagship, escaped but the fleet scattered before a south-east wind. *El Draque*'s own ship, *Revenge*, and other ships of Frobisher's squadron destroyed the *San Martin*, the *San Mateo*, the *San Felipe*.

'Philip beggared the country to fight on — too proud, too stubborn or too stupid to admit defeat. We sold the house in Seville to a merchant. Everything was lost save the Cervallo title, which passed to the eldest, Luis. The women banded together in a cottage on the old estate. We men divided to try our fortunes in foreign parts. We would seek wealth, return and set the family to rights, we said. What else could we do?

'Capitan Orlando Martinez had salvaged a ship and planned a voyage to the Americas as a privateer. I knew him, and signed with him, in command of a company of soldiers who would fight overland, run the gauntlet of the Indians. It was the third time I'd signed for such duty and my belly was like hot lead at the prospect.

'We sailed direct for Tierra del Fuego and by some blind chance the wind favoured us. We stood off for just a fortnight before Martinez committed to the hazards of the strait. He took us through, and we sailed as far north as Coronado Bay before we met ill fortune...

'It was Christmas of that bloody year, '88, when we left Cadiz upon this great gamble. Martinez skulked through the Atlantic. We would cram on all sail and run like whipped dogs at the mere glimpse of a ship on the horizon! Honour was second to survival. We ran like thieves and went thirsty, but Martinez got us to the Americas without incident. We anchored in Catholic ports on the Atlantic coast, and there we had our first taste of fighting.

'English privateers attacked San Julian, where we were taking on water. Martinez had us out and running before we could be sunk, and we stood off with several warships, emptying every gun we had into them. Our small victory was a good portent. When we sailed south the wind, as I said, was with us.

'We slunk by Tierra del Fuego not long before Christmas of '89, and it was an easy passage. By then even I believed we commanded luck and would return home in another year or two with our fortunes rebuilt. Martinez skulked up the Pacific coast as he had scuttled through the Atlantic. He was a shrewd man and I admired his courage and foresight. When ill fortune beset us at last it was not the English but, so they said, the hand of God.

'The seas were mountainous. The storm raged out of the west like a dragon and drove us aground in Coronado Bay, on the Pacific shore of the Isthmus. It was March or April when we struck. The ship staggered like a drunkard and the wind pushed us over, broadside, till the sea was over the decks. She swamped like a river barge. The lads took what they could and swam for their lives.

'Some fools carried too much away and drowned in the surf. Others, I among them, took just a pistol, powder and shot, in oilskins. We stood on the beach and watched the ship smashed to timbers. The storm scattered her bones, debris drifted in with the tide, and we salvaged what we could. A little food, a barrel of wine, water. There was little... and oh, there was panic.

'Capitan Martinez had drowned. We found his body, half eaten by fish, and buried him decently. Sixty of us survived from the crew of seamen and soldiers. The nearest Spanish port on that coast is Old Panama, but we'd passed it a week or more before the storm ran us aground, we had no chance of covering that distance to get back there on foot. Before us was the whole Pacific Ocean, behind us the jungle. The only ships we could hope to see were privateers — if we waited a year or more to sight a sail! We had no clean water, no food. Aye, there was panic.

'The soldiers took charge, as often they must. We scouted inland for a stream, shot monkeys and cats to eat. It was the boy, Pablo, who set our feet on the road out. He'd never been taught the art of navigation but he watched over Martinez's shoulder for months while he served as his cabin lad. He had a notion of where we were, how far north we'd sailed.

'And then, a little luck. The fossickers were hunting for shellfish and instead they came upon Martinez's chest, still closed, in the rocks. The water had got in but the charts were still legible. I could read them well enough, any number of us had the skill.

'We celebrated Christmas on the beach, then consigned ourselves to God and marched eastward toward Bahia da Almirantes. The following months were a nightmare of fighting and disease. We were in the swamps and jungles, and the savages were never far away. Soon we ran out of powder and shot for the few pistols we owned, and fought with lances and clubs stolen from the bodies of the Indians who attacked us.

'Thirty of us were alive when we came across the Isthmus, and half of us were dying. I was nearly dead. I have my scars to show for it. My legs. I had ulcers that would have taken your fist, filled with suppuration. I was raving with fevers when they carried me into a crevice in the coast called Santa Catalina, one of the gold ports, kept so secret that its position is not recorded on any map I know.

'I knew nothing for months more. I drifted with delirium and frenzy... and I was one of the fortunate ones, for I survived. Of Martinez's crew, only twelve of us did.

'A young Jesuit tended me in a monkish little cell. I would lie awake, when I was sane for an hour, and look at the tortured figure on the cross hanging over my bed. When I rambled in my fevers I talked to it. Christ and I had long, intimate conversations. Every riddle of the heavens was explained to me, but I forgot everything when I woke. But the young priest heard me speak to Christ in my delirium and believed me a true son of the Church. He heard my confession, gave me absolution and communion.

'What faith I ever owned was purged from me forever, but I said nothing, for I owe that priest a debt I can never repay. With his own hands he held me up in the first days when I regained my feet. It was almost Christmas again when I was walking well. In the November I spoke to Don Ricardo Vallejo, who commanded the garrison at Santa Catalina. I wanted a ship to take me home. Back to Spain.

'He told me to wait and watch the sea, I'd see a ship when one arrived. So I waited, I and the dozen survivors from Martinez's doomed expedition. And next summer the *Esmerelda* appeared. I'd never seen a ship like her. She was like no ship that ever launched from a Spanish yard... a *gallizabra*, of course, part *galleasse*, part frigate, long and low, nimble and quick, built by Menendez in Havana, designed to carry gold to Spain without need of an escort of warships. We learned a little from our defeat at English hands in '88.

'She was under the command of a fool, Capitan Alonzo Corco, an animal with regard for neither his own men nor his enemies. But I was so desperate to leave, I signed with him. I was well by then, and old Corco knew my family in Seville. We rode out with the evening tide, but there was flat calm. The slaves took us out.

'Below decks they lived in their filth and died in droves. They were Englishmen, French, Spanish criminals, whoever bore the brunt of Philip's wrath. Above decks the Spanish sailors were ill used. Never a day passed when the lash did not tear a man to tatters. I sealed my mouth and hoped for a quick passage home.

'Two weeks out, I learned the truth. Corco was under the King's orders, bound for Tierra del Fuego and the Pacific coast. He would never have got a crew without pressing men, had these orders been public.

'I was bound for the same hell I had almost killed myself to escape. I hoped then for an English privateer to sink the *Esmerelda* and ransom me back to my family!

'It was not to be. This time we stood off Tierra del Fuego for three months, waiting for the sky to clear. The passage is so narrow and twisted, so filled with hazard, not even a *gallizabra* dare enter it with a gale on her bow and thunderheads boiling about the masts. The weather was against us every day but Corco refused to turn back. At last we limped through Magellan's strait and were in the Pacific once more.

'By then we had sickness aboard. The men were ill and before us was a hellish voyage. Corco tightened his grip upon his crew... I heard the first rumour of mutiny before we put Tierra del Fuego astern.

'I was in command of a company of soldiers, and when I heard the whispers I should have gone to Corco. He would have flogged and hanged any man for a breath of mutiny. I was silent.

'My soldiers would have taken my orders, would have cut down the mutineers till the decks ran red, had I give the word. But my men had taken much of Corco's punishment. On that ship the pious old bastard enforced the letter of state and Church law. Sodomy is a crime as well as a sin. Four of my men were hanged. No matter that Paolo and Julian and the others had been bedmates and kin for many years.

'I might have tried to stop the executions, but it was too early. I myself would have hanged in their place. I watched their bodies twist in the wind and cut them down later, poor devils who had done nothing save fall in love.

'When the crew arose, we soldiers took their part and seized the ship for our own. Corco's officers played out the game to the last, and none of them lived — though we'd have set them ashore had they surrendered their swords. We threw their bodies overboard. The last I saw of the flogger and the hangman, they were being ripped by sharks and the lads were cheering.

'We scuttled back through Magellan's passage — the return is always easy. The wind is at your back, out of the west. And we made our plans. Who was to say the *Esmerelda* did not swamp in a storm, as Martinez's ship died? Or that Frobisher or *El Draque* did not sink her, or plague destroy the crew? Spain would know no better.

'Some men wanted to hurry home to wives and families, others wished to be free, to love their mates as they always had. It was voted upon: to remain at liberty in the Americas, or return to Spain? I was one of those who voted to return. I had an *amante* waiting, and he'd already waited much too long. And so it was agreed, but we knew we must be cautious.

'Our plan was sound. We would take back a story that plague

broke out aboard. It is very common and will be believed, especially as the *Esmerelda* will return laden with plunder for Philip's hungry treasury. When that day comes, each man in her crew will have salted away enough to make him rich for the rest of his days. Only he will know where it lies buried. He'll return to the Americas on a merchantman, claim his fortune, no one the wiser to as to how it was won, and go home to Madrid or Seville, free. None of us will be fugitives, at odds with the law.

'We needed a safe anchorage where the hunting was richest, and we slunk into the Caribbean, unseen. We began to hunt as privateers, and pickings have been good. As a privateer, we changed the name of the ship. She couldn't be the *Esmerelda*. It was left to me to name her, for command of her lay in my hands. I called her for a black sheep I knew once, who took his courage in both hands and made life give him what he wanted.'

Channon fell silent at last. Robin was rapt. His eyes had never strayed from Channon's face for half an hour as he digested every word. Now he gaped mutely, his mouth slack, and Channon laughed quietly.

'Aye, you are aboard the privateer *Roberto*. And welcome, Robin. As my guest, passenger. Companion. My master, if you choose. As you have always been.' He offered his hands, and Robin took them. 'I sent no letter, my heart, for I was never able. I was gone from Spain a few months after the firestorm in Calais, expecting to be home in a year or two, with my fortunes repaired. And with enough personal wealth to keep you richly.

'There were times, many of them, when only the dream of you kept me sane.' He smiled sheepishly. 'But for you, I'd have been dead or mad.'

Slowly, almost reluctantly, Robin's fingers turned in Channon's palms and he clasped the soldier's wrists. 'The years have been savage for you,' he said thickly. 'For me they were kind. Forgive me.' His head bent, one beard-rough cheek pressed Channon's hand. 'Forgive me what I said. I thought...'

'That I used a boy, duped and discarded him after I disgraced him with sin.' Channon frowned at Robin's pale face, 'I never thought how it must seem to you. I've been a selfish boor.'

'No,' Robin protested. 'Fear made me foolish, just then. I thought I had been such an idiot, these years, and now would be used again, discarded again.' His voice was so soft, Channon strained to hear. His lips touched the Spaniard's knuckles. 'I don't think an hour would pass without a thought of you, nor a night without a dream.' His tongue traced a pattern on the back of Channon's hand.

Channon cupped his chin and lifted his head. 'You may not believe me, but I adore you.' Robin's eyes brimmed, and Channon tugged him into his arms. 'What business have you at sea? Surely, after all my advice, you did not become a mariner!'

'No.' Still weak, Robin settled again.

'You are shaking,' Channon fretted.

'With delight,' Robin said quickly. 'To be in your arms is heaven. And no, I am at sea for the first time. The *Swan* was one of Drake's ships, bound for the Isthmus to seize the gold ports and throttle Philip's wealth. That gold alone is what has kept Spain at war. And us apart.' He found a comfortable way to sit and relaxed. 'Do you recall my brother, Hal?'

'The butterfly huntsman?'

'Aye. He stands accused of spying in Puerto del Miel. Julio Recalde has him. I had his ransom in gold coin. I dare say it sank with the frigate.'

'A little chest of coins?' Channon laced his fingers into Robin's hair. 'It was brought aboard with the plunder. Don Julio Recalde, you say? I don't know him personally, but know of him. He is a gentleman.'

'So Drake said.' Robin lifted his head from Channon's shoulder. 'Hal will die unless the ransom is paid. I know it's part of your spoils, but — Dermot, please. I'll repay you somehow.'

'Hush.' Channon swept the damp hair from his face. 'Only one item of plunder do I desire from the wreck of the *Swan*, and I have him, I think. Are you mine, Robin?' A nod and downcast eyes assured him. 'Then Hal is another matter. I have all I could possibly want. The coin may as well be put to some good use.' He closed his arms about the slowly enlivening body. 'May I kiss you? Are you well enough?'

Robin slid his good arm about Channon's neck and pulled the dark head down. Channon's heart skipped as Robin's mouth opened invitingly, and he moaned as he felt the caress of Robin's tongue. The seven years might never have been. For a long time they were still, breathless, charting half-forgotten territory. Tongues duelled, but at last Robin lifted his head to gasp for air. The wound pained him, and Channon set him down flat on the divan.

Humour brightened Robin, and though his cheeks flushed as Channon examined the wound he was up to teasing. 'We should take care. If one of your men walks through that door —'

'Robin.' Channon's fingers combed through the light pelt on Robin's chest. 'You are aboard a privateer. We've been at sea for a long time. No man in this crew has seen a woman in two years or more! The only women I've seen since I left Cadiz are Indians, riddled with pox, thick with sallow fat. It's over six years since I've spoken to a girl.'

Robin recoiled. 'Then, aboard this vessel?'

'We know the ways to pleasure. Sailors and soldiers have always known, as have you and I. It's unwise to touch the Indians, even if you find a pretty one. Pretty or not, they're all poxy. But there are winsome lads on this ship, and they are clean.'

'And you?' Robin murmured. 'You've had lads often.' He stroked Channon's breast. 'I am grateful to them for pleasuring you.'

'Robin!' Channon hugged him carefully. 'It was over a year before I was so pent up that I sought a companion for a night. In Madrid they thought me peculiar, or incapable, for I could not be seduced. Martinez turned a blind eye to companions, as good commanders do. That's the sum of my transgressions, an hour shared with a warm body, and seldom. I preferred my own hands.

'When we were wrecked, all was danger and later, sickness. Then I was with Corco and dared touch no one. Those who did were hanged. Since we seized this ship I've bedded with one boy several times, and made believe it was you. Not much, Robin, to fill the years.' He kissed Robin's stubbled cheek. 'You've had my confession. Give me yours, we'll absolve each other and begin afresh.'

'Oh, Christ.' Robin turned his face to Channon's chest. 'There's no absolution for me. I had only one lover after you. Ned Blythe's daughter.' The words were muffled. 'She's my wife.'

A jolt of shock raced through Channon like a blow. He held Robin's head against his chest, kept silent and waited for more.

'I thought you were dead. I mourned for four years and at last I gave you up.'

For some time Channon said nothing, but his grip on Robin did not slacken. 'Do you love her?' He held his breath.

'No.' Robin's tone was scornful. 'How could I? And she knew I never did. It was convenient, comfortable and nice. I... have two children and Ned is my partner in business. My family is safe.' His fingers clenched into Channon's arms. 'I have no need to return, and shan't go back. They'll hear how the *Swan* sank in a storm. Drake knows no more. Next year, or the year after, they'll cry a little, then Jen will remarry. Sir Jocelyn has flirted with her all along.' He kissed Channon's smooth chest and as the shirt pulled wide, worried one nipple with his teeth. 'I chafed for years at my confinement, longing to escape. Jen cares for me, but...'

He lifted his head and Channon saw his anguish. 'Robin?'

'Must I choose?' Robin whispered. 'Wound her, or you? Poison myself with heartache? Christ! What manner of husband will I be if I return, knowing you're alive, wanting me, and all I want is you? I'd make her life a misery with my vile temper, and leave you just as miserable. Three lives ravaged.' Eyes fever-bright, he shook his head. 'Let her weep a little, wed Jocelyn Hardy and be happy.'

'And your children? I didn't think.' Channon shook himself. 'Surely you cherish them.'

'Yes.' Robin's mouth compressed. 'The break is cruel for me. I'll see none of them again, and it hurts. But I must choose. You, freedom and love; or family, confinement, and Jen's sorrow as I turn sour as old milk. I knew in a year it was a mistake to wed, but I had no reason to speak of it. Jen was good to me. I was an adequate husband. It was... not what I wanted.'

Channon weighed every word and did not underestimate his sacrifice. 'You forfeit kin and business for me?'

'For me, selfishly,' Robin corrected, 'and for Jen. I don't love her but I am so fond of her. I want happiness for her, and she'll have none with me after this, when my heart is with you. My children are babies. In a year, when Jen expects me home and instead receives news of the *Swan*, those babies will have forgotten me. I'll think of them with affection, it will be enough. Let them call Hardy their father. Jen will be rich and adored, Ned will have a knight for his son-in-law, and Sir Richard Armagh will share my father's relief. The black sheep is dead and gone.' He propped himself on his elbow. 'You're troubled, Dermot? You asked, am I yours. You don't relish the answer?'

'It affrights me,' Channon admitted. 'I was never offered so much.' He knew he must sound absurdly self-effacing, but Robin had shaken him. 'I shall spend my years trying to honour what you give me — aye, I am afraid!' But warmth flooded him as he kissed Robin's mouth. 'However, I adore you and I undertake the effort with good graces.'

'Three lives made content.' Robin sat and tugged off the torn, bloody shirt. 'Jen should not have to contend with a fiend who sports my face and every day pines for another.'

As the shirt came off Channon saw the wound. It was black, but sealed. 'Damn, what have I done to you? I threw you down, I was so angry. I didn't know you were injured.' The scene shamed him now. 'I would have raped you.'

'I richly deserved it,' Robin added. 'I behaved brazenly, as if I've been a rake. In fact, you and Jen are the only lovers I've ever known.' He caught Channon's sinewy wrists. 'Don't hate Jen, or be jealous. When I was grieving she comforted me and asked nothing in return.'

'Hate her?' Channon tousled his hair. 'I am grateful that a gentle woman gave you good company. And children,' he added, discomfited by the idea. It was a man who sat before him, plucking at bloodied breeches. Robin was twenty-five years old, no longer a lad, but mature. And the more beautiful for it. 'I have clean clothing,' he offered, 'though my things may be large, since you're as slender as ever.'

He slid off the divan, threw open the ottoman and selected not hose but a pair of brown linen breeches. When he turned back Robin had stripped. In the patch of afternoon sun below the stern-ports he moved carefully to spare his side, and Channon whispered an oath.

'God's teeth, you are a man indeed. The years have been your proving.'

Naked, Robin straightened. He was still lean but Channon saw new muscles. His tapered legs wore a light dusting of down that flared about his groin, the same copper as his head and breast. His cock, though still as fine, was stronger, thicker. He stood quite still for Channon to see his prize.

Channon went to him, stroked every part of him as if only his hands could convince him Robin was his. At last he embraced the smaller body, mindful of the wound.

'Will you lie with me tonight?'

'And every night,' Robin said quietly. 'I am not at my best with this gash, but I am quick to heal. A week or two, and I'll be mended. Then I'll give better account of myself.' He drew back with a smile. 'So much do I want from you, and want to give you. In the end my own dreams taunted me. Now, I have you.' The last was spoken fiercely.

Channon shuddered, painfully aroused by Robin's closeness and his words. Even through the linen of his breeches, his erection could hardly go unnoticed. 'Should I apologise?' he began. And then Robin's hand cupped him, pressed and rubbed in a steady rhythm that eased the ache in his balls. He groaned, unbuckled and dropped the breeches. Cherishing hands grasped him, urged, admonished and urged again, till Channon must spend himself. Coming was a little painful, he yelped into Robin's mouth and felt himself held captive.

If this was captivity, he decided as his cream filled Robin's hand, then freedom be damned. His legs weakened and he sat on the ottoman, tugged Robin closer and embraced the slender body. Robin was unaroused, too unwell to stir. He held the soldier's head to his belly as Channon breathed deeply the warm, heavy scents he had long identified with love. Robin and love were one.

Chapter Twenty

He had changed, yet not changed. Nothing about Dermot Channon was boyish now. His body had broadened with muscle, his face fined down to planes that were smooth, beautiful. His eyes smouldered, whether in anger or lust. His fury had been frightening, and Robin knew how close to violence he had been.

It was his own doing. Channon would not have been at fault if he had gone through with the act of retribution. It would have been a fitting penance for what Robin had said, and the dead faint was sheer good fortune.

As he dressed he checked discreetly between his legs, but found no blood or semen, no soreness. His body burned feverishly but it was the wound paining him, and he felt a pang of shame. The Channon he had known for so long would not punish a man who was already fainting and sick; but for those moments they had been strangers.

The horrifying story of death and struggle purged the resentment from them both, and the love offered freely moments later was precious. He had forgotten Jen. 'Are you mine?' Channon had asked, and Robin had made his commitment without realising what he had done.

There was no way back to the cartographer's shop, nor to Jenny's bed; no choice to be made. Did he betray her? In his heart he suspected he did, but nothing weakened his conviction that her happiness came first. Robin Armagh would madden her as he pined — not for an impossible dream but for a lover who was just beyond his reach.

Or would be become the adulterer? His mind's eye glimpsed secret meetings by moonlight on a remote beach where a ship waited, fetching a fugitive to England. Clandestine lovemaking in a tavern on the moors, pleasure seized out of guilt and hardship, till he was discovered... a man betraying his wife with the crime of sodomy. A Spaniard would be accused of seducing the son of an earl, perhaps of spying. Channon would be hanged, and possibly Robin with him. Jenny would never live down the disgrace.

The future loomed like thunderheads. He saw no way back without Channon, and none with him. *So I choose*, Robin thought as he dressed. *The half life of the adulterer, till I am mad and curdled? Or freedom, at what price? Jen's grief, before my children call that whey-faced knight their father!* He had no choice, yet still it hurt. Home called with a siren song, but he saw the doom in answering it.

Channon swiftly dispelled his misgivings, though one real fear lingered in Robin's mind — that Dermot would find the body of a grown man less appealing than the youth he had desired. Then, the blaze of Channon's lust was consuming. Robin was sure Dermot would swallow him alive, and was prepared to be fucked at once if he needed it, though he was himself too feverish to respond.

But Channon was too close, just at the sight of him, and needed only a helping hand. His coming was violent, probably painful. *Tonight*, Robin thought, *when I am rested I'll be a lover to you*. The taste of semen lingered on his lips. He had lapped Channon's cream like a cat at milk. Channon shivered visibly, and had kissed him to share the salt-sweetness. *Tonight, I'll stir for you*, Robin told himself, and was lost in his thoughts when Channon spoke.

'We're running for home. We must make repairs, patch a few torn sails, repair a little planking. Then we'll look to the matter of Hal.' Arms closed about Robin from behind and he sagged against the muscular chest as Channon said, 'We have a quack at our anchorage. If you are still feeling the wound when we are home, he'll salve it.'

'I am burned,' Robin said dismissively. 'Branded by the iron. It's no more than that, Dermot. Call it your brand of ownership, if you will! I would wear your mark proudly. It is merely a burn, and I have lost blood. I am dizzy!'

'Sit.' Channon kissed the back of his neck. 'Wine and meat will put blood back into you. Then sleep in my bed and grow strong. Tonight I must have every inch of you, Robin. I fear I cannot wait.'

'Nor can I.' Robin sat at the chart table and watched him move about the cabin, lithe as a cat as he swayed with the roll of the deck. He sent for food, and a young boy brought it. The lad's head was tousled and he smiled at Channon. Too young to be Dermot's lover, Robin guessed. Channon did not prey, but waited for the plum to ripen and plucked it the moment before it fell.

From the oar deck came the rhythmic stroke of a hammer, and Robin frowned as he ate the pork and wine. 'You keep slaves aboard a privateer?'

Channon gave him an appalled look. 'We took this ship easily, cut loose the slaves and bade them avenge themselves upon any man who had mistreated them. Oh, there was blood! When rage was spent all of us had the same choice. Freedom, a stake in the voyage. The slaves chose to fight with us and keep silent in years to come about their privateering, since the truth will hang them as well as us! Many are Protestant English sentenced by the Inquisition. The same choice will be offered to the lads off the *Swan*.'

'Dangerous,' Robin mused. 'They could betray you. When you take this ship back to Spain a noose could await you.'

'It could.' Channon sat and studied Robin's face so intently, Robin flushed and looked away. Love and lust were naked in Channon's eyes. 'But they'll not betray us,' he went on. 'Your countrymen have a saying, God helps those who help themselves. The *Swan*'s survivors will stay on for a fortune. We loot the French and Portuguese and leave alone Hollanders and Spaniards and, as a rule, the English also.'

'Yet you attacked the *Swan*.'

'She was damaged, low in the water, leaking like a hulk, with masts down. We thought she was dead, or in the hands of privateers. We were almost upon you when we saw your gunners rigging four cannon. Thereafter we defended ourselves. Or should we have turned tail and run from a sinking hulk? Do you complain, Robin? If we'd let the *Swan* limp by she would have been seized as carrion by Guillaume's corsairs, or Mateo Alvarez's cut-throats. We are not the only privateers in these seas, but I tell you, we're the most honourable.'

He leaned over the table and his hand closed on Robin's. 'Had you fallen to Guillaume, he would have used you badly so long as you could stay alive. And you were drifting into his waters without hope of defending yourselves. Christ! We sink Hubert Guillaume's vessels as eagerly as we sink French bullion ships!'

'Oh.' Robin patted his mouth with a lace kerchief. He drank wine from a silver cup, and the platter was porcelain. 'Forgive me. Perhaps I wrong you with these questions.'

Channon laughed, a sound which thrilled Robin. 'You were always a clever boy. I never knew another so well read. Mauricio merely dabbled in learning by comparison.' Then he leaned closer and his fingers traced Robin's features. 'How beautiful you've become. Or were you always so, and memory failed me?'

'It is in your eye,' Robin said softly. 'I see nothing comely in my face. It is your own that bewitches me. Will you kiss me?'

A lush silence followed. Channon was clearly aroused again, though he made no move to satisfy desire, and smiled instead. 'I could tell you of nights in the jungle, fevers and nightmares. You were my sanity. It was you I turned to, not God or saints. It was as if you never left me. I tried to keep faith with you.'

'Dermot, it doesn't matter,' Robin remonstrated. His hands rested on Channon's chest. 'I kept faith for years and I wed in grief.' He flushed. 'When I thought you dead, I wouldn't have noticed doomsday.' They kissed before Channon put the knife back into his hand and bade him eat. 'Upon your order,' Robin said in a Cornish brogue, making Channon laugh.

Soon he fatigued and Channon sent him back to the divan. He slept at once, unaware of the soldier's quiet presence as Channon sat watching him in the shifting patterns of light from the stern-ports.

The *gallizabra* butted into the south-west, and the sun had painted the sea the colour of blood and gold when Robin woke again. He opened his arms and Channon lay down with him, aroused in a moment, humping slowly at his hip. Clothes marred the pleasure and at last Robin stopped him.

'Against me,' he whispered.

Channon stripped them both, and Robin cried out as he felt the weight of a man, heavy upon him for the first time in so long. Swiftly, Channon took his weight on his palms.

'Have I hurt you? The wound?'

'No.' Robin pulled him down as Channon tried to sit. 'The wound is a brand, of course it hurts. Love me. Love me!' His legs spread, scissored Channon's hips and pulled him down. Channon gasped a savage oath from the bogs of Ireland and was on him again.

Somehow he was gentle out of respect for Robin's hurts, but the blaze of lust would have tested a saint. Soon Robin was too tired to respond, and let Channon move as he must. It was a long time since either had made love properly, and coming was not without a thrill of pain. The sharp discomfort soon subsided, replaced by the delight of shared pleasure. Robin closed his eyes, recalling the nights when he shared a soldier's bed, exhausted and enraptured. Nothing had changed. Channon still whispered against his ear, the same tender words of reassurance, while his heart beat at his ribs.

He caught his breath and opened his eyes. Channon was weeping silently, unaware of the tears, and Robin embraced him. 'Are you at odds with me? The things I said! I was no man's whore, I swear. The years have made me virginal again. Touch me and be sure. I only taunted you, for spite.'

He took Channon's brown, callused hand between his thighs. For a time Channon caressed his balls and delicious shivers echoed his deep contractions. He was sure Channon would scorn to examine him, but then the long, gentle fingers slid further back, rimmed him, slick with his own seed, entered him and stroked.

He moaned as he thought of how Dermot would kiss his risen cock, and cried out again as the heat of Channon's mouth engulfed the crown of him. The buried fingers continued to stroke and though Robin would have believed it impossible, he hardened once more. In three years of marriage Jen had never seen his naked body, never touched his cock with her hands, much less her mouth. Robin had not realised how he had starved for this.

Then Channon's mouth was gone and hands pressed his chest. 'Take care, you'll open the wound. Robin!' Channon held him down and Robin clawed the cushions. 'Be still,' Channon insisted.

Robin steeled himself. Channon's eyes glittered like a wolf hunting for a mate. Robin could not breathe. He spread his legs till his tendons pulled, an enticement to fuck, but Channon would not be seduced.

'Not while you are half mended,' he said hoarsely.

The fingers inside Robin stroked again, he felt the heavy pulse of veins in the tight flesh of his arse as Channon returned to his task. He clawed for release as if he had never come before, and panted as

Channon sucked, greedy for his seed. Pain and pleasure peaked into exhaustion, and Robin dragged air into his lungs.

He would have served Channon in any way he desired, but when he struggled back to his wits he found a doped look of contentment on his companion's face. Channon lay with his head on Robin's belly, quite spent.

'Dermot?' He tugged the cropped brown hair, wanting an embrace. Channon grunted with effort as he obeyed. 'I didn't touch you!' Robin whispered.

'No need of that,' Channon slurred against his mouth. 'Christ, you're like no other I ever knew. You spread and give me all you have, crying love aloud. Such trust affrights me.'

'You'll grow accustomed to it,' Robin guessed. 'I'll pleasure you, any way you wish.'

It was dark outside the stern-ports now. The night watch sang, incongruously, ballads of war which lulled them just the same. They did not stir until a light tap at the door intruded, much later. Robin started awake, disoriented, struggling, but Channon merely tossed a Turkish quilt over their legs and called in reply.

Robin's whole body stiffened as the door opened. He pressed his face into the cushions and mortification flushed his cheeks. He did not see the man who had come in, but heard a softly spoken, well-educated Spanish voice.

'We measure two *varas* of water in the hold, Dermot. We're pumping, but cannot lower the levels.'

'And the weather?' Channon yawned. One hand rubbed Robin's back, lazy soothing circles from shoulders to buttocks.

'Fair, but there's a wind, high up. We may not reach Rio de San Francisco before the storm is on us.'

'Then one of the islands,' Channon decided. 'How long, Pasco, to reach Isla Verde? Could we anchor before the weather worsens?'

The other man considered for a moment. 'I'd say so. I've set all the sail we can carry but we're heavy in the water. The oars are working without pause.' He chuckled. 'We are low in the water not merely with bilge! The weight of goods from the frigate is considerable. And on that score, how fares your guest? Geraldo said he set an iron to his side. He thought you might return him to the hold but from what I see, I doubt it!'

Channon's voice warmed with gratitude for Pasco's concern. 'He's well, and needs only rest now. His name is Robin... Roberto. Aye, he is as much a black sheep now as ever.'

'Roberto? Then this is the lover for whom this ship — ?' Pasco laughed quietly. 'When he's well I shall make his acquaintance! For now, we steer for Isla Verde.' At the door he paused, his voice husky with affectionate humour. 'Sleep well, Dermot.'

'Roberto?' Channon teased as the door closed.

Robin lifted his head to display a furious blush.

'That was the pilot, an old, old comrade,' Channon admonished. 'He marched over the Isthmus with me, kept me alive. I cried out to you in my fevers, he heard your name too often for me to deny it. So I spoke of you, how I missed you and dreamed of returning to you when the war ended. I'm sorry, Robin. He knew of us long ago. But we have many couples aboard. No one would care if you kissed me in full daylight on the weather-deck.'

The blush was fading and Robin smiled sheepishly. 'It is I who should apologise. I am not ashamed to be your lover. But it is strange.' He caressed Channon's chest. 'Give me time.'

'All the time in the world,' Channon offered. 'We'll anchor to make repairs soon. We've close to a fathom of water in the bilges, and Pasco sees rough weather on the horizon. We'll wallow if we're caught at sea, and be at the mercy of Guillaume's scavengers, and others. The privateers can be savage. From Isla Verde we sail for home — the Rio de San Francisco. Then we'll speak of your brother. Julio Recalde will stand by his bargain, and we'll see Hal on a ship bound for a Dutch port. He can make his way from there.'

'And then?' Robin was exploring the hot, dry wound.

'Then we'll idle in the sun, love and play, till every man in this company is rich and the hold is filled again for Philip. And then, sweeting... Spain.'

Robin sat against the cushions. 'I am an Englishman. They would have me before the Inquisition, a prisoner of war.'

But Channon shook his head. 'Call yourself Chantry, Doyle or Keohane. I'll say you are my companion in adventure, a Catholic, as I pretend when I am in Spain, a deception for the sake of liberty. If you're the black sheep I told Pasco, you'll stoop to it at once!' He kissed Robin lightly. 'I'll present you at The Escorial as a Catholic hero who helped win His Majesty's treasure. He may even knight us both. Don Roberto — it has a fair sound.'

The idea amused Robin, and laughter pulled his side. Channon held him till the pains eased.

'Now, sleep,' Dermot insisted quietly. 'I must speak to the pumping crews and check the pilot's work. I'll be gone for some time, so sleep sound, all night if you can. If you need some service before I return, shout for my steward, Rodrigo. He'll do your bidding as my own. You are my *amante*, they all know it.' He kissed Robin's lips in parting and reached for his clothes.

But Robin lay awake for a long time. The lamps burned out, plunging the cabin into darkness. His mind spun as he tried to chart the chaos of the day's events. Where had he been at dawn? He had woken with Davey Beaufort's hand on his shoulder and his back aching after a night spent cramped over Downing's charts, which he had searched for an anchorage where the *Swan* might make repairs.

It seemed a year ago, a decade. He was sure he would not sleep for the tumult of his thoughts, but his body was exhausted. The wound was hot and nagging, but it was Channon's love that had spent him.

He heard Dermot's voice often, calling to men aloft, and at the oars and pumps. To some he spoke in English, to others in Spanish dialects. At last, Robin surrendered to sleep.

Chapter Twenty-One

Channon perched on the edge of the table, a cup of wine halfway to his lips as he watched Robin work with the ocean charts, meticulously marking the position of Drake's fleet, his destinations, the anchorages where he would take on water. This information would keep the *gallizabra* out of trouble. If she ran into the teeth of the fleet, though she was fast and nimble, five surviving warships would pound her to tinder.

But Channon's eyes were not on the charts. He studied Robin instead. So his beard grew ginger, like his hair, as red as Drake's. In Madrid they would readily believe him an Irish soldier of fortune, for they must surely see the look of *El Draque* about him.

The helm shouted up to the riggers to set every sheet they could tack up. Isla Verde lay a day's run ahead and the wind was already rising. The levels of bilge in the holds were no higher but the pumping crews were exhausted. Channon had considered setting the *Swan's* survivors to work, but it was too soon. They had not heard the terms of their situation, and until they did any work asked of them would be taken as forced labour, which made for a poor beginning.

It was mid-morning. Robin had slept late and eaten a great deal before he asked for the charts. He was bathed but not yet barbered. The safety of the ship was his priority, not his looks. Channon revelled in his masculinity. His beard was quite heavy and his skin once again a healthy tan since his fever had gone. Asleep, he wore the face of a painted saint, serene and unearthly. Now, he wore a scholar's face as he worked.

It was hot already and he was bare-chested, unshod. Channon mourned that he had even pulled on the white linen breeches. The cabin was private but Robin clung stubbornly to modesty.

Just after dawn Channon had returned, moving about silently to let him rest, but had he dared one liberty. He lifted off the quilt to bare him. How much had he forgotten of Robin! The sleeper did not stir for a long time and he was intent on the long legs and quiescent genitals when Robin said amusedly, 'When I fell asleep I was decently covered. What happened to my quilt?'

Channon recalled his guilty start with a smile. 'I took it from you,' he had said. 'Beauty is not to be hidden. You'll wear less clothes in future, none of this swathing yourself to the chin.'

And Robin managed a shaky laugh. He was better, though the wound still hurt. His bladder was urgent, so Channon searched out the trousers and supported him as he stood, swaying. He enlivened before Channon's eyes and ate as if he had been starved for weeks. The ratter, Peg, sat at his feet, begging titbits, before Robin walked twice about the deck while his head cleared.

He stood in the bow to breathe the fresh wind, and at last Channon insisted on making introductions. Robin had already met Geraldo, who had doctored him. Pasco, the pilot, smiled at him teasingly. He met the mate, Valdez; Miguel, the master mariner in charge of the riggers; Orlando, a steersman with one good eye keener than another man's two; and Rodrigo, who was Dermot's steward.

The little lad who had brought the food was Nicolas. Then came the mercenary soldiers. Spinola, Delgadillo, Calderon, Bras de Fer — men whom life had deeply scarred. And the Englishmen who had laboured at the *gallizabra*'s oars when she had been the *Esmerelda*. Thomas Ticker, John Smyth, Jeffrey Farr, and too many others for Robin to remember.

He was discomfited at first, Channon knew, stiff with disquiet. Every man knew he was the captain's *amante*, his lover, and Robin fretted that he would be taken for a catamite rather than a bedmate. Channon set that right at once. He deferred to Robin constantly, let him walk ahead when they explored the ship, asked his advice, showed him every respect. His slightest whim was answered as a command.

By mid-morning Robin was more exasperated than discomfited, but it was the crewmen who set him completely at ease when he watched them sit down to sup together. They paired off, old couples embraced comfortably and casual lovers flirted for the amusement of it. Slowly Robin relaxed, though Channon saw him blush at the sight of lads openly kissing. Pasco gave him he charts at once when he asked for them.

'He was *El Draque*'s master cartographer,' Channon said pridefully. 'He'll chart us their course and anchorages, so we can stay well clear of the English fleet.'

It took an hour, while Channon sat by and watched the work. Absorbed, Robin did not notice when Dermot began to watch him instead. At last he set down his pen and sat back in the carved wood chair. The charts were left opened out and weighted for the notations to dry.

'There, *capitan*, that's the sum of what I know.'

Channon's hands cupped Robin's nape, absently stroking as he examined the work. Fingernails rasped through the wiry beard, reminding Robin of his looks, and he leaned his head into Channon's bare chest.

'It is well done,' Channon told him. 'Pasco will study these thoroughly while we make repairs. With luck we'll not even sight their sails.'

'But what of the privateers?' Robin stood and stretched both arms over his head.

'They know our flag and we'll fire on them, on sight.' The charts had dried and Channon rerolled them. 'Guillaume tests us now and then. He's battle-mad as even the Irish never were. But no one knows our home anchorage.'

'The Rio de San Francisco,' Robin mused. 'Have you a blade? I must look like a bear!'

'Like a man,' Channon corrected, but handed him a stropped razor and sat on the ottoman to watch him use it. The whiskers were shorn away, leaving his skin boyishly smooth, inviting kisses. Channon teased him into laughter, then picked up the charts. 'Show Pasco the fine points of your work. Our lives could depend on it.'

Emilio Pasco was a small, wind-tanned Spaniard from Madrid. He was not of good family, but as an orphan had been taught to read by the Carmelites who found him on the street. He was an intelligent man, and well read. If there was a single scholar on the ship before Robin's arrival, it was Pasco. Channon left them to talk and they worked well together. Robin's Spanish was excellent and Pasco admired him for it.

By afternoon they were satisfied. Pasco rolled the heavy vellum sheets as the first patter of rain began. The sky had darkened and the sea rolled, pitching the ship like a toy. Robin withdrew to the cabin to watch through the stern-ports. This was a cousin to the wild beast of a storm that had crippled the *Swan*, but not so fierce.

Riggers furled canvas on Channon's order and the oars were shipped. She rode out the wind and white water with a stability the Spanish warships of past years had never commanded. The hull was based on the *zabra* design, long and low.

The storm fled over the horizon and the pumping crews rested. Channon went below to measure the levels of bilge, but they were no deeper. Robin held a lamp for him as he and Valdez waded knee-deep in the oily, black water.

'A day or two to make repairs,' Valdez mused. 'I would not care to weather another storm in this condition. The wind is still screaming out of the north-west, it could bring the devil himself with it.'

'And when do we reach Isla Verde?' Channon dried his hands on a bundle of rags.

Valdez was not a navigator, and Robin answered. 'If the helm holds to his course with one sheet up before the gale, we'll anchor at your island before midnight.' Captain and mate looked up at him, and Robin smiled. 'Forgive me, Valdez. I drew the very charts Pasco navigates by. I believe you took them from a French ship?'

'Aye, we did.' Channon threw away the rags and waded out of the water. He hung on a handhold, a little below Robin on the stepway.

'We took them from the *Charlotte*, when we sank her a year ago.'

'I thought so.' Robin nodded. 'It was Captain Lapierre's commission. I worked six weeks on them — I'd know my own charts anywhere. So, forgive me, I know these waters well, though I've never sailed them.'

Channon laughed. 'By God, my *amante* does me credit!' He reached up to caress Robin's face. For just a moment Robin stiffened at the display of affection before Valdez and the pumping crew, and then relaxed.

On deck, couples were settling for the night. Many stood by the rails to watch the stormy sunset, others embraced in the lee of the deckhouse and enjoyed sensual sports, music and laughter. A boy danced, got up as a gypsy while his lover strummed a lute and his admirers clapped. Men were coupling in the shadows while dice rattled and a barrel of wine was broached.

Bemused, Robin blushed at their antics and Channon laughed quietly as they embraced. 'We are a privateer, a long time at sea. Until we return to Spain we are free.'

They stood in the shadows aft of the helm, and since the sun had gone it was cold. Channon kissed Robin's mouth, his face, and Robin was hungry for more. They had come up fast on Isla Verde, and before Channon released him the lookout called from the masthead.

The island was on the larboard bow. The wind had whipped away the overcast and the moonlight was bright enough to pass them safely through the heads, into concealment.

With quiet promises of his return, Channon released Robin. The riggers took in every patch of sail and the *gallizabra* went into Isla Verde under oars. Her anchors cut into the water as she pulled out of sight of the open sea. About them now, Robin saw a sheltered nook within high headlands. The body of the island lay between the ship and the wind, and of a sudden it was calm.

Satisfied, no longer worried now that the ship was sheltered, Channon arranged the rostering of pumping crews. Repairs could wait till morning, but the labourers were tired and sore, and Channon broke out the *Swan's* stores of wine. They were happy, then, and Robin heard their revels as he and Channon retired.

Little Nicolas brought food, lit the lamps and set out fresh linen. 'Sheets from a lady's bed,' Channon said amusedly as he displayed the embroidery and lace. 'From a Portuguese pirate. God knows where they were looted first, but when the bastard fired on us we sank him and took his chattels. He tousled Nicolas's long black hair. 'This boy was among them, eh, Nic?' The child smiled at him. Channon cuffed him gently and gave him a push toward the door. 'Until our blue flag is seen, we look like a Spanish warship and are fair game. Privateers prey on one another also.'

The door closed and Robin said softly, 'The boy loves you, and not as a father.'

'Perhaps.' Channon turned to the food. 'He was a catamite at ten, but he's not been touched since. Time for him to be a child before he begins to play men's games.' He poured the wine and held a cup for Robin. The green eyes were dark, hot, and Channon's pulse quickened. 'Eat with me, then...'

He held a chair out at the table. Robin sat, and Channon kissed his ear, both hands inside his loose white shirt to explore his breast. Breathless already, Robin leaned back, head tilted, hunting for Channon's mouth. Channon indulged him and chuckled.

'You're an avid lover. I'd half forgotten.'

'You shall be reminded!' Robin examined the food. 'The wound is only stiff now. If I don't bend sideways it gives no trouble.'

'Still, Channon mused as he refilled their cups and chose a squab, 'you'd do well to take care.'

'Bending sideways,' Robin said, amused, 'was never necessary.'

'Necessary?' Channon took a draught of wine. 'For what?'

'For you to fuck me,' Robin elaborated.

The suggestion warmed Channon's face. He put down the wine, wiped his mouth and sat back. 'No, that is not required,' he admitted. Robin have him a beguiling look. 'You are determined to seduce me?'

Robin nodded. He drank and left a drop of wine on his lip, maddening. Channon leaned over to lick it away, only to find Robin's tongue in his mouth. Its rhythmic thrust suggested another act and Channon surrendered. He caught Robin's head in both hands.

'What shall I do with you, Robert Armagh?'

'Fuck me,' Robin whispered. 'How do I seduce you? My skills are rusted. Marriage and bedsports are strangers! God-fearing women will not play! Loving is rushed between bed-linen and nightdresses. I never saw my Jen's body, nor she mine.'

Channon heard a cutting edge in his voice. Frustration had tormented him for so long, he had ceased even to notice when he was

204

tense, aching. Pity gentled Channon. The trouble was in part his fault, for he had taught Robin the intense pleasure of lovemaking. Not the guilty coupling of the pious, but the lush sensuality of the sinner. But for him, Robin would never have known what he was forbidden, and might never have yearned for it.

'I am seduced.' He clasped Robin's hand. 'Your skills are not so rusty! To bed?'

They doused all but one lamp as the wind sang in the lines, and Robin shivered. Channon ignored the sound of the ship. From the ottoman he produced a phial of oil, and presented it to Robin as a gift. It smelt faintly of almonds. Robin set it aside, and Channon stripped him slowly.

He kissed the brand, worried Robin's nipples with his teeth and knelt before him. His hands and mouth dizzied Robin and they sank onto the divan. They pressed tight, now frenzied, now passive, slowly, thoroughly rediscovering each other.

It was a night Channon would always remember. When Robin turned onto his belly to offer his buttocks he could have been the virgin boy again. He was tight, his neglected body hurt as Channon's thick cock pierced him and he bit into his arm to muffle his cries. Channon waited, stroked him till pain was supplanted by pleasure, allowing them to make love.

Years before, the deed had been boyishly swift. Now they were slow and sure, and it lasted much longer than that first ravenous coupling in an apartment at Hampton. Robin was exhausted, Channon no better, and they mocked one another with rueful laughter.

'Terrible and wonderful, beautiful and frightening,' you said once,' Channon whispered as they embraced.

'And you were sweet in me, at the last,' Robin added. 'Hot, and so hard.' He paused, wriggled. 'Give me a rag, keep this fine linen spotless.'

'Christ.' Channon had turned him onto his belly to tend him and saw a drop of blood, a little oil. He swabbed both away. 'I hurt you.'

'Nonsense,' Robin retorted. 'You imagine I've never seen my own blood, and my skin has never smarted with abuse?'

Channon's eyes devoured the thinly muscled back. The twenty stripes were a web of silver lines. The priest had shown him no mercy, he would carry them for life. 'You suffered unduly,' he said quietly. 'I'll cause you no more pain.' He kissed the soft, sore place he had

pierced like a lance. 'Will you have a salve?' The balm produced a'
luxurious sigh, before Channon embraced him, careful of the wound.
His heart squeezed as Robin set down his head. 'You grew up nicely.'

'Nicely!' Robin was slurred with sleep. 'I am glad,' he confessed. 'I
worried that your taste was for boys, and I had grown too old to stir
you.'

Channon's fingers ceased their massage of Robin's buttocks as the
confession astonished him. He dealt a stinging slap to one soft cheek,
then rubbed the little smart with the same hand and had Robin's
mouth. 'You were a pretty lad, but you've grown to beauty. I am in a
constant fit of lust for you!' He paused as Robin stroked his face. 'Will
you ever want me to fuck you again?'

Now Robin looked up, amused and affectionate. 'I won't lie. It hurt
and was most uncomfortable, and now I am sore! But there was more.
You moved in me and I was alight. I think I might hate being fucked
if it was not done with love or at least care. But I might also crave the
little pains and great pleasure that blossom inside when you move
there and are delighted in me.' He cuffed Channon's head fondly. 'So
long as it is done with love I am —' he chuckled — 'at your disposal,
my *amante*. My dearest love.' The last was hushed, sincere, and Robin
set his mouth on the Spaniard's.

They slept then, replete and exhausted. Channon held him and let
the roll of the *gallizabra* lull them to peace.

Chapter Twenty-Two

Before dawn hammers were ringing below decks as sprung planks
were patched, and sailmakers mended canvas that was already
well repaired. On close inspection, Robin saw that this ship was
deeply scarred from many encounters. He offered his help where he
could, while Channon was called to duty.

He had woken late, stiff and aware of a lingering tenderness,
testimony to Channon's pleasure. And his own. Channon waited for
him with a kiss, a stropped razor, fine garments, and a salve if he
wanted it. In an hour Robin was bathed, well fed and clad in looted
Italian silk. Channon's fussing charmed him and seemed to delight

Dermot also. Robin allowed anything Channon wished, and wore a blush gracefully.

The clothes he received had been made for a prince. Silk and velvet moulded about Robin's limbs, his belt and boots were of engraved red leather, the shirt was light as gossamer. The rings on both his hands were set with emeralds and rubies. He had never seen such wealth.

At noon the *Swan's* survivors limped out of the hold. They had sickened in the rough weather but it had been safest to keep them below. They were clean, and a cask of wine was split on deck as Channon confronted them. He spoke in English, and offered them the same terms as any captive crew.

To begin with, they were free men. Would they be set ashore in the Americas and make their way alone, or would they fight with the privateers, for a share in the voyage? Channon spoke then of the corsair, Hubert Guillaume.

'Remember, this is not the only ship hunting in these waters, and some privateers would use you ill. We saw a hulk limping into Guillaume's path, and it was your good fortune to be sunk by the *Roberto*. The Frenchman would have sold you on an auction block in some Spanish port, and you would have ended your days as pack mules, in irons. Aye, we sank you, but you fired on us. What should we have done? Let you sink us? Or flee, and let you blunder into Guillaume?'

The survivors were surly but avarice persuaded them. By afternoon they were working alongside the *gallizabra's* crew and expected to be rich out of the venture, which was more than their contract with Drake's fleet had offered. Channon strode among them, little Peg at his heels. He learned their names and faces, clasped their wrists as comrades.

The wind fell in the evening. Pasco and Valdez called Channon with the news that the planking and canvas were patched and they might navigate the headlands, out of Isla Verde, while there was still a little daylight.

'Then we ship out,' Channon agreed. 'We have the wind with us, for a swift voyage home. And we have Robin's knowledge of Drake's plans to our advantage.'

In minutes the ship was out and running before a stiff south-easterly. Her yellowed sails filled and the oars lay idle. Channon bade Pasco fetch the charts to his cabin, and he, Robin and the pilot studied them by lamplight. Through the stern-ports the stars were brilliant. 'Drake is in these same waters,' Channon mused. 'Where would he be? It is April, early in the month. Are we at risk?'

'We may be.' Robin leaned on his palms and frowned over the maps. 'But I'd say, not yet. Drake's first priority is fresh water, and he'll forage north toward Hispaniola.'

'If he holds to plan,' Pasco added.

'Yes.' Robin looked up at Channon. 'Remember, the storm could have scattered the fleet. The *Swan* may not be the only one swept away. Several old ships were in that company. One was the *Rosamund*.'

For a moment Channon searched his memory, then his brows arched. 'She remains the property of Sir Charles Rothwell? So Rothwell survived the war.'

'The *Rosamund* was battered, and rebuilt on the river. I would ride past her to Ned Blythe's shop twice a day,' Robin told Pasco. 'I came to know her well.' The pilot cocked his head at him, and Robin sighed. 'An old score lies unsettled between Captain Rothwell and my family.'

'I remember,' Pasco said softly. 'Dermot told me a story, that he fought a duel in the courtyard at Hampton! I was not sure if I should believe it or not.'

'Believe it!' Robin looked at Channon over the charts. 'Now, to work. The Caribbean is full of Spanish warships. Drake is as much at risk from them as we are from him. Worse, we are a privateer and might be assaulted by anyone. English, Spanish, French, Portuguese, and the likes of Guillaume.'

'*El Draque* will be occupied with the Spanish shipping,' Pasco judged, 'and unaware of us. And our anchorage is safe.'

Channon poured wine, handed the cups about and sat on the edge of the table. 'So, Robin, where should Drake be at this time?'

One forefinger traced across the vellum. 'Here, just short of Santo Domingo. We might come across more victims of the fleet like the *Swan*, but every ship will need water. Drake and Hawkins must secure stores before making war.'

'Hawkins?' Channon echoed. 'The man is mad — he's too old for these adventures.'

'So Drake would agree.' Robin rolled the charts and nodded goodnight to Pasco as the pilot left. 'But it was thought Hawkins would moderate Drake, supply a cool, sage head.'

'Or a cold, dead body,' Channon added as he closed up the cabin.

He turned down the lamps and Robin watched shadows play about his lover's face. 'You're very beautiful, Dermot.'

'Are you are quite blind,' Channon said affably.

'Love is said to be blind.' Robin's eyes lingered on Channon's body until he shivered.

'Forgive me.' Channon mocked himself with a chuckle. 'I'm remembering how it was to be within you. I can think of nought else since you allowed it.' He gave Robin his hands. 'In three days we'll be home. Then you'll possess me.'

Heat flushed Robin's face. It was hard to imagine, now, the flustered hours a boy had wasted, wondering if he had the courage to take up the soldier's invitation. It was so long ago. His thoughts turned briefly to Jenny. The pain of parting had already dulled and would hurt less with the months. He set the past aside with an effort.

'It may be wrong for a captain to submit,' he cautioned. 'I'd never ask it of you.'

'Yet I offer it,' Channon argued. 'What troubles you? Your face is grave. No secrets, Robin.'

'I am thinking of old days, old ways. Has the past never haunted you?'

'Constantly.' Channon's mouth compressed. 'You know my scars. I have others you cannot see, but they're no less real. You'll heal them for me.'

And Robin recalled how Channon had been abused. 'You would let me fuck you, after you were used so badly? I'll not do it, Dermot. It would only arouse old shades.'

To his surprise Channon laughed. 'I know the difference between loving and ravishment! What did you tell me last night? Easy, you said, to crave the little pains and great pleasures!'

Robin shivered. 'I was molten fire. I thought I'd madden and wanted you to stop, but never stop. I was besieged yet wanted never to be released, I couldn't bear it but wanted it to go on. Confusion, contradiction, but this is what I felt.'

'And what I want,' Channon whispered. 'You, big in me till I fear for my mind. Robin! If you could see your face!' Robin's brows rose and Channon laughed. 'Lust and terrible innocence. Let nothing ever change you.' He held Robin against him. 'So Drake hunts up toward Hispaniola, and we sail for home. Puerto del Miel is westward of our anchorage. It would be safest not to take this ship into Recalde's harbour. *Gallizabras* are still rare and we'd not be forgotten — we might even be recognised as the *Esmerelda*. Better, we'll land by night, east of Puerto del Miel by Bahia Zarzurro and ride up. We have a few good nags at our safe haven. I'll speak to Recalde on your behalf and Hal's, and pay him. We can take Hal to Guadeloupe, by the precious fresh streams where Drake must find him when he takes on water for the voyage home. We've no hurry, since Recalde will tarry a year or two longer.'

Pleasantly tired after the long day, they bedded, and it seemed nothing Channon did could sate Robin's hunger. Channon indulged him carefully, beguiled by his wanton innocence.

Afterward, Robin confessed he had not realised how he had starved for the comfort of intimacy. Jen wore so many garments and thought it unseemly if he disrobed. They shared no closeness. A kiss, fumbling between the sheets as he sought the hem of her nightgown; her arms about his neck as he covered her, barely able to feel her through the robes they wore to bed. He saw her breast once by chance. Her belly was a mystery, known by touch. He knew she was moist, nothing like a man, tender in some way a man was not. Channon listened with passing interest to all this, and Robin realised he simply had no curiosity for women.

Of the voyage from Isla Verde to the Rio de San Francisco, Robin would remember a tableau of images that revolved about Channon. The captain in command of a warship; Spaniard, Irishman, soldier; the *amante* who looked upon him with unabashed lust, unashamed love. They wrangled when they pleased, which was often, and even the weather was fair.

They came upon the river at dawn, five days after the *Swan* went down.

Valdez called from the door, rousing Channon, and they were on deck in moments. Robin pulled on breeches and a shirt that gaped to his waist, unconcerned about its laces, without stockings or shoes. The morning was already hot. His skin was growing brown as he forgot the customs of modesty. To dress in this manner in England would be called a disgrace, but here was customary.

He stood at the rail, eyes shaded against the sun as the pilot took her in. To left and right were swamps. Before the *gallizabra* a narrow channel opened out, and the oarsmen rowed her in to keep her clear of the mudbanks. From the sea the river outlet looked impassable, but once through, the brown, turbid river opened wide, and Robin saw the safe haven.

The forest along the lush bank had been logged and the timbers built a series of cabins and a massive slipway. At Channon's shout the anchors dropped and oars trailed to brake the ship in midwater. She hove to a yard from her berth, a creaking, ant-eaten jetty on which stood a motley company of men. Spaniards, English, French, Portuguese, the survivors of ships liberated by the privateer. Robin watched old friends, old lovers, greet one another before many hands began to unload cargo.

The spoils of piracy were carried into a storehouse, where Robin was astonished to see powder, shot, canvas, barrels of tar, carpenter's tools, pine planking, ship nails.

'The makings of a ship,' Channon said with quiet pride. 'My good friend Leon Strozzi was a shipwright before debt consigned him to the galleys. He has made plans from our own vessel, and I swear we could construct another if the *Roberto* were sunk. But see here.'

He ushered Robin inside and opened a brass-bound chest. Gold and gems glittered within, emeralds, diamonds, silver ingots, gold chains and ropes of pearls.

'Choose any trinket,' Channon invited. 'Anything that takes your fancy. Here, this.' He looped a thick gold chain about Robin's neck. It was heavy with a weight of emeralds, and Channon smiled. 'These stones look fine on you.'

'It must be worth a queen's ransom,' Robin protested. 'This alone would make me rich for the rest of my years!'

'Then you're rich,' Channon said offhandedly, 'since it is yours. Come and see my house now... our house. Months pass, in these waters, when it is unwise to challenge the sea or the wind. We've made a cosy nest here. We are one ship, Robin, and can look to no one for aid, no matter the crisis.' He took Robin's hand and tugged him out of the cool, dim storehouse.

Bewildered by the wealth in gold and gems about his neck, Robin let Channon urge him along the river, and found himself in a spacious cabin. The walls were white plastered, the floor was thick with rugs looted from a merchantman. He saw fine chairs, pewter and utensils on a rosewood table, gilt-framed portraits of ladies and gentlemen; and an enormous bed, four-posted, with velvet drapes. Robin complimented Channon's taste with a smile.

'You enjoy fine things, Dermot.'

'I always did.' Channon poured a cup of wine and sampled the food left covered on the rosewood piece. 'I saw you in the garden one evening, and knew I must have you at all costs.' He chuckled. 'I cannot resist you when your cheeks blush pink.' He kicked shut the door and dumped Robin onto the gorgeous bed. 'I love you more now than years ago.'

No more than Robin loved him. But it was later, when they were taut with need, glistening with sweat as they wrestled in the heat of the afternoon, when he woke to what Channon most desired. Robin hesitated, but Dermot was sure.

'I am not afeard,' he chided as he pressed a phial of oil into Robin's hand. 'I've wanted this all along.'

Then speaking was impossible, for Robin's fingers were in him and Channon was captive. Robin had often stroked him within on the voyage home, opening him gently. He was very virginal after years of abstinence and his pains were quite sharp. But the liquid grip of him was maddening, and it was Robin who cried out, dizzy and overwhelmed.

This was nothing like loving Jen. A man's strength was yielded to him, a man's musk stung his nostrils as Channon moaned and heaved beneath him. It was too much. Coming thundered through Robin as Channon's seed filled his hand, and he went down, pressing him into the mattress.

Half-formed thoughts and endearments roused him at last and he smiled. Dermot was exhausted, still impaled, deeply satisfied. He protested as Robin withdrew, but allowed himself to be gathered up and panted against the younger man's breast as Robin said, 'I was quick and clumsy. Was it very bad? I'll do better, if ever you want this again. I love you.'

To his astonishment Channon chuckled. They parted to look at each other and Robin saw he was not being mocked. Channon's fingers knotted into his hair and tugged sharply. 'If I had a complaint, it is that the deed was too swift by half! It was wonderful, and I would relish your possession of me for half an hour.' He pulled Robin's head down to kiss.

'I'll strive to do better,' Robin promised when he was released. 'I know I hurt you.'

'A little.' Channon yawned. 'What of it? Terrible, beautiful, frightening, as you said. I've been fucked many times, but never with love, Robin, until now. It if hurt a little, so be it! I love you like this, guilty and repentant, though there's no need for it. Salve and kiss me, if you want to do penance. I'll enjoy the fussing.'

So Robin kissed him, and the clench of Channon's fingers in his buttocks told him better than words that he belonged. Channon stretched like a cat and knelt to be pampered. 'Where are your salves?' Robin asked.

'In the cabinet. I attend to my own scratches. I cannot bear the touch of a physician.' His face shadowed as Robin fetched a pot of thick, pungent golden-seal and comfrey ointment. 'I suffered greatly at the hands of army quacks in Santa Catalina. Pasco and Valdez carried me out of the swamps with ulcers on my legs, and the skin peeled off me in sheets. It was ugly, diseased, I smelt like rotted fruit.' He turned his face away. 'The surgeon cut me. They said once, it might be best to cut the very legs off me, but Valdez wouldn't allow it. Let him die a whole man, he told them, don't make him live as a cripple. I knew none of this — the drugs made me mad.'

'Yet they healed you.' Robin sat beside him. His hands lightly stroked the scars he knew so well. One was the size of his palm, puckered and still discoloured, dusky red-brown.

'But the days are gone when I could bear a surgeon's touch. Knives and drugs sicken me. I'd sooner die than submit. If I am sick or injured, I have you.'

Robin kissed the scars and slid into Channon's arms with deep misgivings. 'If I treated you I might kill you.'

Channon refused to comment.

The cabin was hot, airless. Drowsiness soon overtook them and they slept fitfully, half woken by the sounds of the camp. Hammers battered and artisans shouted as they worked on the ship. Laughter erupted, singing, noisy gossip as Valdez listed and tallied the goods taken from the *Swan*. Some were set aside for bloody Philip, against the day the *Roberto* would become the *Esmerelda* again. The King would be wooed, but the greater part of the cargo was divided among the men. They were already rich.

Knocking brought Channon awake with a start. He rolled over, one arm flung across Robin's back, and did not even open his eyes as he called, 'Aye, what is it?'

The door opened and Valdez's face appeared. He smiled at the bed. The captain and his *amante* were naked, Robin groggy in the humid heat of early evening, his face in the pillows as he muttered English obscenities. Channon's large, brown hand palmed his pale peach of a rump. Valdez sketched a fond, insolent salute.

'The ship is unloaded, the tally is done and we're to be feasted. Will you dine with the men, Dermot?'

A yawn delayed Channon's reply. 'Half an hour,' he told the mate. 'Let us bathe. Have the tally sheet to hand, I want to see it.' The door closed and he stirred his companion with a pat on the behind. But Robin's face was troubled. 'What distresses you?' Channon wondered quietly.

'Once, I was a modest creature with an inkling of morality! Now, it matters less and less when they find me... like this.'

Amusement and affection gentled Channon. 'Time for modesty when we return. Here? Relish your freedom. Most of the men have paired off. We are reconciled with God, one way and another.' He stood and stretched till Robin heard his joints crackle. 'Now, let me find clothes that will do you justice, so that when they see the Captain's *amante* they behold him as I do.'

He threw open an ottoman and seemed to have already chosen the garments before he began to rummage. Soft, snug breeches, the old Armagh green, and knee-stockings in the French style; a white shirt with lace at cuffs and collar. The gold and emeralds about his neck, white leather shoes, rings for half his fingers. The quality was superb.

'Looted from a French warship,' Channon told him. 'Their officers strut like peacocks. You approve of these rags?'

'I do! But let me bathe,' Robin said ruefully. 'I smell a little ripe.'

'You smell like a man,' Channon argued. 'I've no quarrel with that. Still, here.' Water slopped from ewer to basin and he produced a tiny cake of soap. 'It smells of violets, a lady's trifle. It shouldn't offend you.'

They bathed one another and Channon lingered over Robin's back, tracing every pale stripe. Robin squirmed but allowed him a lover's liberties till Channon rinsed him and stood aside.

'Are you clean enough now, you fastidious imp? You're violets,

214

head to foot!'

They were late for the feasting. The men had not waited and the food was well picked over. Robin saw pork, poultry, fish, all caught along the river. Dried fruit, oranges, limes, looted from ships from the east; chocolate, strawberries, potatoes from the Americas. He sampled a little of everything and took a lot of wine while Channon divided his attention between his platter and the accounting sheet. He and Valdez read through the lists together, and checked the figures.

'A year,' Pasco judged shrewdly. 'Less, if fortune smiles on us, and we can sail for Spain. We'll be so low in the water with treasure, the King will likely knight the whole crew. What say you, Dermot, if some of us stood together afterward? We might buy a ship, or build one, and come back to freedom.'

Channon looked along at the men. 'Some of us would choose that, but look at them.' He nodded toward the lads who were making merry at the far end of the table. They had a boy dressed up as a girl, and he was beautiful, painted, powdered, flirting. 'They want to go home.' He looked at Robin then. 'For some of us there is no way home.'

'Then, keep back enough to buy a ship,' Robin whispered. 'And those of us who are at odds with the law and the Church will return to freedom. We have no way home, as you say, but Pasco is right. You have found liberty here. I wonder if this kind of freedom is why Hal is so seldom in England?'

The evening grew cool. The tables stood along the quay where the ship had tied up. Other boats, built of rainforest timber by Spanish and English craftsmen, bobbed at their moorings. On the slipway, the skeletal keel and ribs of a half-built carrack waited for the flesh of its hull. These men had not been idle. Mules and horses grazed along the riverbank, and Robin heard the roar of a forge, cockfights, gambling, and the cries of lads netting for fish beyond the torchlight.

From the cabins came the sounds of love being made. The survivors of a dozen wrecks and mutinies lived well. The only missing comfort was women, and sailors had always known they were a luxury one learned to live without. What woman was such a sinner that she deserved to live among privateers? The life was hard enough on men. A woman would fare poorly and be old before her time.

The lads who were unable to pair off with their fellows for affection and release were resigned to solitude. But most of the men were easier to pease. Mariners learned the practicalities of life at sea before they were long out of their home port.

Night was like blue velvet and the moon was a lamp over the canopy of the forest. Monkeys screamed in the trees and enormous beetles droned through the heavy, humid air. Hal had taken home specimens pickled in jars of brine, huge black things with devils' horns. Robin ducked the live, flying creatures as he and Channon walked back along the river.

These lands were appropriately called the Unknown World, and he could only puzzle at the quirks of chance that had brought him here.

Chapter Twenty-Three

Two weeks later the *gallizabra* went out again, in fighting trim, and hunting. Channon charted a course well clear of the waters where Drake's fleet should be. His quarry was French and Portuguese merchantmen, which would be boarded, looted and then released, or the privateers who preyed on anything afloat and so were fair game themselves.

Robin had learned the names of Hubert Guillaume, Mateo Alvarez, and a rogue Englishman, Wilfred Southby. Often their ships roamed in packs, and often the sea ran red. The *Roberto*'s watch looked out as vigilantly for them as for Drake's feet, or for quarry.

'The whole Caribbean is their hunting ground,' Channon said over a dawn breakfast as they rode the tide out of the river. 'But we know much they do not. Guillaume and Alvarez may run under Drake's guns, and if they do —' he made a throat-cutting gesture '— it would be deserved.'

The wind was fair but the sky was heavy with cloud. Rain sliced the horizon and Pasco's course took the ship north, away from the threat of violent seas. Robin was anxious though he kept silent. The fleet was somewhere northward. If Drake's lookouts saw a *gallizabra*, he would surely fire.

Pasco was philosophical. Their quarry was in Drake's waters also and they were hunting, not skulking. The crew placed their trust in Channon and in God, in that order.

It was from Pasco that Robin heard stories of the mutiny on the *Esmerelda*. The crew knew they must fight Channon's soldiers for control of the ship, and if Channon had backed Capitan Corco, the mutineers would be hung. But Orlando, Miguel and others had diced and drunk with Channon in Santa Catalina and knew him well enough to approach him privately before the rising.

Their plans were unsound, though their intentions were sincere. Channon supported them but, Pasco swore, it was Dermot who planned the mutiny for them.

'Who better than an Irishman to plan an insurrection?' Channon said, laughing, when Robin mentioned Pasco's stories, much later. 'They'd have been killed. They're sailors, not soldiers. The soldiers followed me, not them. Why, Robin? Are you disillusioned with me?'

'Quite the contrary,' Robin corrected. 'I admire you.'

'So long,' Channon said quietly, 'as you love me.'

They had been at sea, making slow headway north on the fringe of the bad weather for five days when Valdez's cries from the masthead roused the whole ship.

'Sails on the horizon! I see two sails!' His eyes were sharp, and as Channon slid out of bed, pulled on his breeches and hurried on deck there was more. 'I see a red flag, Dermot,' Valdez bawled. 'Aye, 'tis Guillaume, and the other ship is a cripple.'

'Do you see her flag?' Channon shouted, hands cupped about his mouth.

'No, but she's English,' Valdez judged. 'A little galleon, riding low — taking water, I think. They have a mast down, which means they fought.'

Robin joined Channon as Valdez spoke. 'It could be one of Drake's ships. A straggler, caught in the very weather we've been dodging.' His shaded eyes were intent on the still distant ships. One was an obese French *galleasse*, the other little more than a hulk now. 'What will become of the English crew?'

'Guillaume will sell the lads as slaves and ransom the officers, when he's had his fill of amusement with them. There are never enough hands to work the mines and plantations. The Indians are worked to extinction and they're shipping blacks from the Guinea Coast of Africa now, did you know? Sir John Hawkins made the first slaving forays.'

'Hal told me. He sailed with Hawkins, though not on those particular voyages.' Robin climbed into the larboard lines, the better to see the ships ahead. 'Spaniards would buy captive Englishmen? Aye, a man is a man, where's the difference?'

'*Protestant* Englishmen,' Channon corrected acidly. 'Better Godless than witless, I've always said.'

But Robin did not hear. 'Dermot, I know that ship.'

'The privateer?'

'No, the galleon. I'm sure I know it.'

'One of Drake's?' Channon hoisted himself into the lines beside Robin. 'Or has Guillaume caught *El Draque* himself?' The jest was barbed.

'Not Drake. But if that cripple is not the *Rosamund*, I am blind.' Robin looked back into Channon's face. 'Charles Rothwell's vessel.'

Surprise quickened Channon's heart. 'Are you sure?'

'Almost. I will be if we draw closer. Remember, she's half sunk now.'

For a moment Channon gazed, slit eyed, at the distant ships, then he dropped down to the deck and his voice was a whipcrack of command. 'Gun crews, stand by your cannon. Riggers aloft and armed. *Move!* We're going alongside.' As the men scrambled he spoke quietly to Robin. 'We trust Guillaume as much as a viper. He'd fire on us if he thought he had half a chance of taking us in one piece. He's wanted a *gallizabra* for years.'

'You've run under his guns before?' Robin asked as little Nicolas fetched them pistols and powder.

Channon took two guns, loaded both and thrust them into his belt as he spoke. The ship cracked on good speed, a few degrees off the wind. 'We ran Guillaume's gauntlet just once, and sank his carrack. The French *galleasse* he commands now was a gift from the gods. She grounded on the coast and was easily seized. Guillaume looted the carcass and sold the crew, before high tides lifted her off the sands. She's the *Pandora*. Forty- eight guns, sixty oars pulled by slaves. The *Rosamund*'s crew could end chained on Guillaume's own deck if he has need of fresh slaves.'

The wind was almost dead astern and the *gallizabra* came up fast on the French privateer. 'They see us!' Valdez shouted. 'Gunners are loading but they'll be slow. They have the hulk moored alongside to rape her... ah. They're cutting her loose, Dermot.'

'Then there's no one left alive on her and nothing worth taking,' Robin hazarded. The wind whipped his hair about his face.

A scant few miles off the larboard bow, the *Pandora* began to come about. Oars cut into the water to manoeuvre her since her sails spilled the wind. The *gallizabra* was much faster, more nimble and unencumbered by the lumbering wreck.

'Surely they'll not challenge us?' Robin demanded. 'We could level her to the waterline, she'll never get clear of the wreck in time to show us her guns.'

'But Guillaume will try,' Channon said drily. 'Let him fluff his feathers. He's arrogant, but not a fool.' He cupped his hands to his mouth again. 'Lads, let him see you!'

Each man aloft was armed with a long-barrelled matchlock. A good marksman could drop a man on the deck of an enemy ship from a considerable distance.

The *Pandora* was still hindered and lumbering when Channon brought the *gallizabra* about to show Guillaume the broadside of his guns. They could sink the *galleasse* upon a whim, and Robin began to breathe again.

Watching from the masthead, Valdez shouted, 'They're dismissing the gunners, Dermot.'

And raising oars, Robin saw moments later. Men along the rails waved. Their voices carried on the wind, a mangling of French, English, Spanish, Dutch. Channon touched his arm. 'See the white hat on the weatherdeck? That's Hubert Guillaume.' He looked up at Robin, who hung by one hand, above him in the lines. 'Get out of the line of fire and stay out of Guillaume's way if you're able.' Then, shouting, 'Come starboard! Cut sail!'

The oars trailed to brake the *gallizabra* as Robin followed Channon forward. 'Why must I stay out of Guillaume's way?'

For just a moment Channon was irked at being questioned, before he remembered. Robin was neither sailor nor soldier, and unaccustomed at taking orders. He was a scholar, a gentleman, and a captain's lover.

'One of Guillaume's pleasures is goading me,' he said tersely. 'If he realises you are mine, he'll use you.' Robin's brows arched. 'Insult you, taunt you to madden me,' Channon elaborated, 'until I call him out. Do you want to see me fight over you, Robin? I will, if you like.

And Guillaume could well kill me.'

Robin recoiled. 'Best you, hand to hand? I don't believe it!'

'Believe.' Channon looked away. 'I am not as fast as I was, nor have I been since we marched across the Isthmus. I didn't walk for four months after we reached Santa Catalina. I am strong, but not fast, and Guillaume is... well, you'll soon see for yourself.'

The ships drew broadside, oars withdrew and grappling irons tethered them before lads aboard the *Pandora* ran out a wide plank. Channon stood at the end of it to wait. His hands remained close to his pistols, and as Robin watched from a discreet distance Nicolas fetched his sword.

He buckled on its harness, settled the weight deliberately and stood with his feet spread wide as the ships rolled. Off the stern, the crippled English galleon groaned woundedly as she died.

Little of her was visible, but Robin knew her by the bow, which was carved in serried, upthrust jags, like fangs. No other ship of her type and age had that decoration. It was the *Rosamund*. He tore his eyes away as she began to go under.

At the head of the boarding plank, Hubert Guillaume called Channon's name. His French accent was thick and his Spanish so bad that he shifted gratefully into almost equally barbarous English.

'Channon! Where did you come from, like a vulture around dead meat?'

'We were hunting, like yourself.' Channon ignored the taunt. 'You've sunk one of *El Draque*'s ships. You know his fleet is at hand?'

'*Oui*, but they are westward, attacking Spanish forts. This one was just a little draggletail, begging to be raped.'

From his place a few paces behind Channon, Robin studied the corsair. He was younger than Robin himself, and taller than Channon, with long blond hair worn like a cape over his shoulders and a broad-brimmed, white leather hat with three peacock's feathers. His body was lean, brown, long-legged and strong. He dressed in looted frippery, yet at once Robin saw the menace of the man.

Two pistols rode to left and right of his belt, and he carried both cutlass and rapier, as well as a dirk at his right hand. His face was clean shaven, strikingly handsome, with pale blue eyes, hawkish nose, wide, sensual mouth and high cheekbones. But it was not a kind face. Guillaume was a predator, an eagle, and proud of it.

A few careful steps brought him over the plank and he dropped to the deck before Channon. Marksmen in the rigging of both ships held the two captains in their sights. The truce was uneasy. Channon did not smile, but offered his wrist, and Guillaume clasped it.

'What you want, Channon? There is nothing here for you.'

Channon looked aft, toward the sinking ship. 'What becomes of the crew? If you're selling slaves, I might be buying.'

The pale blue eyes narrowed. 'Again? You have put the last I sold you in their graves already?'

'Twenty lived,' Channon said levelly. 'The rest were diseased, as you knew when you sold them. How many did you reap from the *Rosamund*?'

'Eighteen men and the captain. The gentlemen fought and died. I sell the lads in Nombre de Dios and ransom the captain.'

'If the lads live long enough,' Channon whispered. 'The sport your men relish would kill a horse.' Guillaume only chuckled. 'Are they for sale? They're worth more at market than killed for amusement.'

'Mayhap,' the Frenchman mused, 'if the price was right.'

'Then set a price.' Channon's hands cupped his pistols. 'I'll meet it, if it is fair.'

'And if 'tis not?' Guillaume taunted, eyes glittering.

'Then we might reach some other arrangement.' Channon gave the *Pandora* a hard look. 'This time I did not molest you. I could have sunk you twice over. Next time, I shall.'

'Or I sink you.' Guillaume was greatly amused.

Channon shook his head slowly. 'The *Pandora* wallows like a pig. We outrun, outgun and outturn you. We can cut loose even now and pound you to driftwood.' Guillaume's face hardened, his mouth compressed. 'So, Hubert. Set a fair price.'

For a full minute the two stood like statues and Robin held his breath. The Frenchman seemed to weigh anger against folly. Would he fight, or turn English prisoners into wealth? Channon's knuckles were white about the pistols. In the rigging above a matchlock rasped as it was cocked.

Then the corsair tossed back his long, yellow hair and laughed. 'You are a godless, black Irish rogue! And you have your bargain. Three hundred ducats for the seamen. Captain Rothwell is mine.'

'Two hundred.' Channon offered. 'Rothwell is overripe for your tastes, Hubert. Why do you want him?'

'Ransom. And a rich price he will bring.' Guillaume rubbed his hands together. 'He is of good family.'

'I want him.' Channon looked back at Robin, who stood with Pasco, silent and wary. 'Quote me his price.'

'You want Rothwell?' Guillaume was genuinely surprised. 'Why is this?'

'Old scores,' Channon said indifferently. 'None of your concern. Honour and vengeance for the dead. A little *zambo*, wantonly killed. An old man poisoned. Two maidservants, dead at his hand, and a beautiful woman whose neck was broken when she refused his courting. Rothwell has much to answer for, and aye, I'll pay his ransom.'

The Frenchman stood with fists on hips and regarded Channon rudely. 'Since when did you fret for women? As long as I have known you, it's been the same, You should have been a monk. I heard it from Luc. You remember Luc?'

'I remember a little whore you sent to seduce me,' Channon snarled. 'He painted his face like a woman and squirmed into my bed, on your command.'

'And you threw him out again. He told me you are a eunuch. You have no women, but will not be seduced by a boy. I wonder if your taste is for a man to show you his mastery, teach you how to grovel and serve.'

Channon's voice was icy with suppressed fury. 'And you would like to try.'

Guillaume smiled, showing almost perfect teeth. Robin held his breath once more, almost able to feel the tension in Channon's spine. He knew intuitively Channon was about to challenge as his fury peaked. And he knew just as surely that Guillaume had him outmatched. He was much younger, faster without a doubt, and he was not consumed by the fury that drove Dermot.

Against Channon's wishes Robin stepped forward and spoke in French, surprising himself with his fluency after so long. 'Captain Guillaume, your pardon. I am Robert Armagh, my father is the Earl of Blackstead.' The pale blue eyes examined him and Robin drew back his shoulders. 'The woman of whom Captain Channon spoke is my mother. Rothwell murdered her when I was a child. If you would sell the man, vengeance is more mine than Channon's, I —'

'Robin!' Channon barked, and then in Spanish, 'Be silent!'

'It is as much my affair,' Robin hissed angrily. Did Guillaume follow the rapid-fire Spanish? He hoped not.

'Get out of this, I said. The man has taunted me enough.'

'Only words,' Robin argued. 'Foolish words, at that. Let it be, for God's sake, Dermot. You want him to kill you?'

Channon glared at him but more pain than anger burned behind his eyes. 'Is it so obvious? I am not the man I was. Once, I'd have cut him limb from limb and you would have expected it. Now, you look at this French bastard and bid me let him flay me with words, and smile.'

'Oh, Dermot!' Robin dragged both hands through his hair, exasperated and angry. 'I said nothing of the sort. But you'll run no risks for a folly of honour. You're not sane, or you'd laugh in his face. A eunuch, a monk? Christ, a poor jest!'

A little of the hurt and anger quelled and Channon looked back at the coorsair. Guillaume had followed enough. 'Who is this Robert Armagh,' he asked slowly in his thick-tongued English, 'who orders you as if he you are his cabin boy? He is your master, *oui*?'

Channon took a deep breath. 'The master of my heart, I admit. My *amante*, which he has been these seven years. I was never a monk, Hubert, but I was faithful to this lad, and wise to be.'

The pale blue eyes stripped Robin naked and Channon's voice was a hiss. 'Take your eyes off him and banish such thoughts. I'll not fight for my honour today, but *his* is another matter. By God, I'll kill you if you lay one finger on him.'

Silence followed as Guillaume weighed folly and fortune once more. At last the promise of money won. He swept off the elegant white leather hat and bowed theatrically. 'Very well. Today. Two hundred ducats for the English captives. For Rothwell, I expect to be well paid. You won't short change me, Channon, vengeance or no.'

Robin stepped forward. 'Would you take this?' He ducked his head and took off the gold chain, with its weight of emeralds. One was the size of a pigeon's egg. It was warmed by his skin and he offered it reluctantly. It had been Channon's gift, which made it priceless. But the Frenchman's eyes glittered at the sight of it, and Robin placed it in his hand. 'It is worth Rothwell's life, I am sure.'

'Worth rather more,' Channon said quietly. 'Don't haggle, Hubert. The bargain favours you already.'

'I take it.' Guillaume turned the necklace over and over in his fine, slender hands, and thrust it into his shirt. 'And the three hundred ducats?'

'Two hundred was my offer,' Channon snapped. 'Pasco! Fetch the sum out in coin while the prisoners come aboard.'

The exchange was quickly made. Eighteen Englishmen came over the plank, bewildered, bleeding and witless with fear. They knew they were being traded between corsairs, for what duties, they could not guess. Robin's heart went out to them as he recalled his own dread when he lay on the deck of the *Swan*. Sir Charles Rothwell shuffled over last, manacled by wrists and ankles, with a length of chain between his feet and an iron collar about his neck. He was blindfolded, gagged, and staggered between two of Guillaume's men.

'He struggled and cursed, threatened to cut his own throat,' Guillaume explained. 'I told him I would bind him for his own good. I keep my promise, eh?' He watched Pasco come on deck with two heavy pigskin purses, took them and weighed them shrewdly between his hands. 'They feel right. If you have short changed me there shall be a reckoning, Channon.'

'You have the whole sum in Spanish coin,' Channon said icily. 'Be satisfied, you've done good business today.'

'Better than you.' The Frenchman taunted him with a bow. 'We shall meet again, my old enemy. I look forward to making better acquaintance of the man who mastered you. Such pretty eyes he has.'

'Get off my ship.' Channon's hands gripped both pistols and half drew them. 'I pray you will run under Drake's guns before the day is out, and he'll feed your bones to the fish.'

Guillaume laughed, but returned across the boarding plank, and it withdrew. The grappling hooks loosed and stout punts shoved the ships apart as sails began to billow. As they separated Channon barked, loudly enough to be heard on the *Pandora*, 'Gunners, stand to! If they load, fire at will!'

But the corsair's gunners remained idle and Robin began to relax as the wind and sea plucked the two ships apart. Pasco and Valdez held the blind, shackled Rothwell, and Channon gave him a sour look.

'Put him in the hold. I'll settle with him shortly. Leave on his irons, or he'll make away with himself as he promised that bastard. Strike the irons from the captives, feed them and tell them where they are.'

With that he turned his back on the company and retired directly to the cabin. Robin frowned after him but Valdez caught his arm and

224

said softly, 'He's angry and hurt. Speak gently to him. He is often unwise when his temper is up, or he's bruised. Don't anger him.'

'He wouldn't hurt me.' Robin refused to believe it. 'He could not. I know him better.'

The cabin was cool with the breeze from the stern-ports. Channon sat on the side of the still rumpled divan, a half-empty cup of wine in his hands, and did not look up as Robin entered and latched the door. For a long time they were silent, and when Robin touched his knuckles to Channon's cheek he turned his head away. Robin sighed.

'What is it, Dermot? I disobeyed a captain's order. Should I be disciplined? Then do it, but don't shut me away from you. I could bear a whip across my back easier than this. It would not be the first time!' He saw Channon flinch visibly at the suggestion. 'Dermot?'

'I've been taunted enough for one day, Robin. I still have a few scraps of honour left. Or would you sunder those too?'

Robin sat on the divan, splayed his hands across Channon's back and felt the tension there. 'Tell me what I've done to offend you.'

'Nothing.' Channon drained the wine and tossed the cup aside. 'You've done nothing, it was I who did it all. Guillaume looked once at us and saw you as my master. I am at your feet like a dog. A lame dog with broken fangs, whose master forbids him the dignity of his own defence.'

Mute in astonishment, Robin gaped. 'I stopped you challenging that bastard Frenchman, this is the sum of it?' Channon looked away. Robin's fingers clenched into the cropped brown hair and turned his head back. 'Don't shut me out! Have I bruised your honour? The puppy came between the wolves and spoiled their sport!'

A swipe of Channon's hand broke Robin's grip in his hair. 'I am a man, for Christ's sake. You'd let Guillaume say what he pleases to me?'

'I also am a man.' Robin's voice rose. 'I am as ready to fight for your honour as you are for mine. Or have you made me your catamite? Where is *my* honour?'

Channon's brow creased. 'Have I done that? You were a boy before, it hardly mattered. This time you came to me as a man. Have I made you feel less?'

'No.' Robin gentled his voice. 'You make me feel safe and loved, and I want no more than this. But if you imagine I'll stand aside and let you take on the likes of Guillaume over a few taunts, you're mistaken. Words are not worth fighting for.'

'You see?' Channon looked away again. 'You assume at once I would be killed. Once you'd have *known* I would win for you.'

All at once Robin understood, and felt a surge of both pity and futile, impotent anger. 'This is how you weigh a man's worth? In his ability to destroy other men. You've changed, Dermot. Once, you scorned to judge a man so.' Channon looked up, brooding, questioning. 'Once, you set compassion over killing. The march across the Isthmus changed you more than you know.' Robin turned away and was silent.

For a long time neither of them moved, and at last it was Channon who made the peace offering. He touched Robin's back. 'Am I not shamed? You think no less of me, knowing Guillaume is the better man?'

'The better — ?' Robin echoed in disbelief. He turned quickly and had Channon pinned to the divan beneath him before he could react. 'Guillaume is a savage. The better man? Because he's younger, and his legs were never butchered by surgeons after they rotted half away in the jungle? Good Christ, has your brain addled too? Is Guillaume the better man because he could cut you up with a sword? By that token, I'd be best if I took a pistol and shot you both dead!'

'Robin,' Channon yelped urgently as he began to bruise where Robin's fingers had clenched like claws into his shoulders. They released and Robin rubbed the bruises as Channon looked bemusedly at him. 'Perhaps Guillaume is right, and you are my master.'

'Bilge water,' Robin said tartly.

'Is it?' Channon shook his head. 'If I must have a master, better you than any man. I'll have no other man's dominion.' Robin looked at him, troubled. 'What, love?'

'You've accepted dominion under me?'

'Many times.' Channon closed his eyes. 'When you fucked me. And I'll accept it many more times, I hope. Guillaume knew at once.'

A pulse beat in Robin's temple and his hands stilled on Channon's bruised shoulders. 'I dishonoured you? A gentleman, a soldier?'

At last Channon smiled ruefully. 'Guillaume would say that. I would not.' He struggled up into an embrace. 'Treat your slave gently and he'll survive. Muzzle him when he blunders into danger. He's not the man he was, but he loves you.'

'Dermot, you fool.' Robin held him. 'You'll come to your senses by

226

and by. You, a chattel? Never in your life! Unless it is beneath my love, which is not the same. But speaking of chattels, what of Rothwell?'

'He's yours, you bought him.' Channon lifted Robin's collar, where the necklace had been. 'Will you kill him?'

'For years I wanted to,' Robin admitted. 'Now it seems like murder. Little blood stains my hands, and I want no more.'

'You'd free him?' Channon demanded disbelievingly. 'Ransom him home? Perhaps you would, but not I! A gallon of blood stains my hands, Rothwell's will make no difference. I am going to hell, there's no saving me, and as for sparing Rothwell — no, Robin.'

'Revenge,' Robin mused. 'A bad business.'

'Execution.' Channon stretched his legs out on the divan. 'Legal execution.'

'Then try him.' Robin curled up, cross-legged on the foot of the bed. 'He's a soldier. Every lad on this ship was once a king's or queen's man, soldier or sailor. Rothwell could have no better judges, and there's no better gallows than the yard of a ship at sea.'

Channon's brows arched. 'You are right, as always. Let Rothwell be tried by his countrymen, before God, and consigned legally to the gallows.' He leaned over to have Robin's mouth. 'My master is a clever lad, and I'll bow to his wishes.'

'Your *amante* is a puppy,' Robin retorted, 'affrighted at the prospect of confronting the man.' He got ruefully to his feet. 'Better now than later.'

They went to the hold together. The smells of tar, damp timbers and sacking reminded Robin painfully of his capture as the lantern bobbed ahead of him in Channon's hand. Only Rothwell was imprisoned. His dazed crewmen were at liberty.

The manacles and chains hampered him but his blindfold and gag had been removed. He stood, rolling with the movement of the deck, as the lantern approached. Channon set it on a barrel and he and Robin stood in the light.

The seven years had aged Rothwell. He wore a black patch over the empty eye-socket, his hair was grey, his belly fat, his face flabby. But he remained arrogant and gave his captors glare for glare.

At last Robin said quietly, 'Do you know me, sir?'

'I do not,' Rothwell growled.

'You should.' Robin stepped closer. 'Once, you desired a woman who wore my face. She refused and you struck her. Ah, so you know

227

me after all.'

'Robert Armagh.' Rothwell peered at him. 'The last I saw of you, you were a whelp, trotting at the heels of a black Irish mongrel.'

The blow carried the full weight of a man's arm and Rothwell staggered to his knees at Robin's feet. Robin's palm was numb. 'Hold your tongue! And when you address the captain of this ship, do so politely or I'll surely knock you down again!' Rothwell lurched back to his feet. 'You are my property, sir. I bought you from the corsair, did he inform you?' Rothwell nodded mutely as he licked at bloody lips. 'What shall I do with you?' Robin growled.

'No doubt you'll kill me.' Rothwell cuffed his mouth. 'I'd expect no more of cut-throat privateers.'

The taunt made Robin laugh. 'Being a cut-throat privateer yourself, I imagine you would think so.' He returned to Channon's side. 'You have charges to answer. Captain?'

Channon stirred lazily by the lantern. 'Your kinsman, Jeremy Britton, paid a man called Copeland to buy hemlock and other poisons, and tamper with a sleeping cup so as to murder Don Mauricio de Cervallo. Our witness, the girl, Edith Pledge, was poisoned with the same drugs before she could speak. You fired upon the warship *Alcanzar* in heavy seas, without provocation, before the declaration of war and killed six lads, one of them my friend. You killed, or ordered killed, Sir Henry Leighton's lover, a maid called Jane, who saw you strike the blow that murdered Lady Catherine Armagh.

'You'll answer these charges before God and your countrymen. I guarantee you'll be found guilty, and a noose awaits you. I shall tie it with my own hands.' He slipped his arm about Robin's waist. 'You face the charges tonight. You may state your case, if you have one. Good day, sir.'

The hatch slammed and locked, and Robin hurried out into the air. The hold was stifling with hate. Rothwell was at war with the world. Robin stood at the rails, looking eastward while murmurs rushed among the crew. Talk of Rothwell's trial was on every man's lips.

Pasco and Valdez commanded the *gallizabra* and watched Channon as if to divine his mood. For their sake as well as his own, Robin hunted for Channon's affections as the pilot steered west, away from Guillaume's waters. Drake could not be far away. The danger was real, but they saw no more sails.

228

In the evening space was cleared on deck, torches were lit and the crew gathered. Rothwell's liberated crew sat together, a little apart, as their captain was marched up, and Valdez bound him with his back against the mast.

When the charges were spoken publicly a gunner who had survived the wreck of the *Rosamund* spoke up for Rothwell and asked for evidence. Channon stepped into the torchlight.

'You must accept the word of gentlemen since we are far from home and these crimes are long in the past. I put it to you, Master Jago. Captain Rothwell was purchased at great cost and would fetch a fine ransom. We could have murdered him, yet he'll be tried before God. Why should we lie when, murdered, he'd be just as dead and, ransomed, this company would be richer!'

Each point was set out and debated. Crewmen bickered on into the night, but at the last it was reduced to a matter of honour. The gunner, Jon Jago, asked his old captain to speak, but Rothwell refused. He was looking at the stars as sentence was passed. Valdez had the rope over his shoulder.

It was passed to Channon, and Robin watched him slowly, carefully tie up a hangman's noose. How often had he seen this, on this very deck, when the *Roberto* was the *Esmerelda*, a hellship where lovers perished.

'Will you say nothing before you die?' Robin asked as Valdez and Pasco unbound the prisoner.

Rothwell looked at him, then at Channon. In the torchlight he seemed merely resigned. 'God will judge me now.'

'Then you're bound for hell,' Channon said softly. 'If you believe your own faith you'll have judged yourself tonight and saved God the trouble.' He looked into Rothwell's face for the last time and nodded to his crewmen. 'Do it.'

His death was likely the finest moment of Rothwell's life, Robin thought as he watched the noose pulled tight, the barrel kicked out from beneath him, and suddenly he was turning in the wind. He watched for a moment before the spectacle of death soured his belly and he went silently to the cabin.

He lay belly down on the bed, and minutes later became aware that Channon was with him. The hard, soldier's hands caressed him. Loving hands.

'How does it feel,' Channon asked, 'to be avenged?'

'I feel nothing much,' Robin murmured against the pillow. 'It is so long in the past, as if I dreamed it all. This is the reality. This ship, the sea. Us.' He turned over and pulled Channon down to lie with him. 'I don't want to go back. You could trust Valdez and Pasco to take the ship to Spain. Most of this crew would band together and return on another ship inside of a year.'

'But my family has waited a long time for me, and they're paupered.' Channon pillowed his head on his arms. 'I have duties to them as well as to my master.'

'Dermot, stop that!' Channon lifted a brow at him. 'The bark of command?' Robin punched his shoulder. 'Discipline too? There's a French riding quirt in the chest, if I must be beaten.'

Exasperated, Robin flopped down. 'Don't taunt me. Never in your life have you been switched. You know nothing of it.'

'While you were flogged bloody.' Channon pulled Robin against him. 'You'll never forget that.'

'Go to sleep,' Robin told him. 'The day has been an ordeal, and is well finished. They'll throw his body over, so Pasco said. We hunt for a month —'

'Then turn for home.' Channon cocked an ear to the wind. 'The lads will be up to shorten sail soon.'

Robin had grown so accustomed to the ship, he knew what duties the men must tackle at any time, in any weather. He was half asleep when he heard Pasco calling to one of the gunners to fetch a sword. Did he imagine the splash as a body hit the water? He closed his eyes and pressed close to Channon's side to share the heat of his body.

Chapter Twenty-Four

The Rio de San Francisco was rich with wildlife. Hal would have been enthralled, but he could never be allowed to see this place. Robin would lie in the bow of a longboat, trailing his fingers in the water as he drifted with the current and glimpsed the porcupines, jaguar, tiny deer and massive pigs, creatures which astonished him.

By candlelight he drew them. Paper and indigo had been taken from a French carrack, part of her liberty price. Channon sat for hours, watching the sketches emerge. Robin had a fine hand, a considerable talent.

'For Hal,' he said absently as he finished a study of an anteater the size of a large dog. 'He was no artist, but these will be my gift, when we buy him from Recalde.'

The journey meant no more than a week at sea. They would land with a pair of decent horses, in the safety of an obscuring headland. Then, a brief ride to Puerto del Miel, and Recalde would never know how they had arrived. Channon had planned it long before, but Hal was safe for another year at least, and they lingered in the river anchorage, which Robin swiftly came to think of as home.

The *gallizabra* went out briefly to hunt and returned laden, though Valdez suffered a pistol ball in the shoulder. Pasco had cut out the ball, sealed the wound with the hot iron and bandaged it while the Portuguese cargo was loaded aboard.

This bounty was for Philip, since enough to make every man rich already lay in the storehouse. Spain would soon beckon, and Channon idly dreamed aloud in the hot June nights. He would take Robin home to Seville, Madrid would welcome him and the Cervallo fortunes would flourish. Robin let him talk. They would buy a ship in Seville, the powerful river port from which sailed the great treasure fleets; and they would return to the Americas for their own, hidden fortune. Then, Channon promised gracious living in Tuscany, Rome, Venice. He never mentioned England or Ireland. There was no way back.

But for the moment Robin was intent upon Hal. The safest course was to set him ashore in the Antilles, where Drake's fleet must stop to take on water for the voyage home. The *gallizabra* could scuttle through the reefs by night; their charts were good enough, copied from the best Dutch maps.

Unrolled and weighted on the breakfast table, they were studied at length. The sky was clear, the wind fair, but Channon was wary of the weather. A swathe cut through the Caribbean where great winds would batter a ship to driftwood. The Indians called the winds *hurucan*, after their god of storms.

'But they should not whip up at this time of year,' Channon mused as he studied the wide vellum sheets. 'I think I shall greet Recalde as a Spaniard. And you, a Catholic Irish soldier in search of a fortune. We'll say we rode from Vera Cruz, a long and dangerous ride, but plausible. Then, he'll not look for a ship.'

231

'I might say I was Hal's cousin,' Robin suggested. 'He may see the family likeness.'

Channon looked up at him over the breakfast. Robin was eating fruit and eggs. His fingers were sticky, his chest bare, his hair grown very long. 'And you must be barbered! I'll grieve for that, but your hair will grow again soon enough. You know how I like to knot my fingers in it.'

'I do!' Robin gave him an amused look and sat back. 'I am Patrick Chantry, then, soldier of fortune, and the Armaghs are my cousins. A black ram, Captain.'

'Good enough.' Channon laughed. 'Wear a crucifix and swear by every saint you can remember. They'll believe. Religion is as good a disguise as a mask. We might leave in a day or two.' He smiled. 'I have fond memories of bedding you at sea.'

Once Robin would have blushed, but now he smiled and savoured the same memories. Hammers clattered on the ship even then as continual maintenance was done. Channon threw open the chest in the corner of the bedchamber and searched for suitable clothes. They could wear nothing new, if they had been on the road for weeks.

He set out well-worn leathers, linen that had seen better days, garments that were still presentable but suggested many months of living rough.

In two days, horses and harness were put aboard just before the peak of the dawn tide. Pasco took the ship out into the broad, sluggish river and a strong crew at the oars pulled her into the wind. Double rowing crews were aboard, as Channon was suspicious of that wind. If they met a *hurucan*, a powerful crew at the oars might be the price of survival.

A mile offshore the sea air cooled and the biting insects were left behind. Standing below the mizzen mast, Channon watched the coast drop away. The sense of freedom was consuming. Robin was even then within arm's reach. Their return to the city would come as imprisonment. Channon cherished the liberty to embrace Robin, kiss his mouth and release him before he could protest. They would enjoy no such liberty in Seville. Here, Robin only laughed. His tanned face made his eyes seem oddly light, and Channon thought he had never looked so beautiful.

Yet many of the men longed to return to wives and children. Others yearned for the gaiety of Madrid and Florence, or for the blessing of the Church. What would they confess of their years of freedom? For Channon, the world was in his arms as he held Robin. He wanted no more and would accept no less. In Spain they would pretend close friendship, the kinship of soldiers, and in the confessional, the priests would be deceived.

The *gallizabra* ran with the wind full in her sails and made good time while the oars lay idle. Robin's pleasure was to stand his watch as her navigator. He had great pride in his ability to work well, and Channon learned a new respect as he shared those watches. Robin was in high spirits, he revelled in the sea, in his duties, and in love. He wanted Channon often, needing to take as well as to give. Channon indulged him unstintingly.

Three days out, the wind swung westerly and brought a storm. It had been born in the Pacific and roared across the Isthmus like a dragon. The crew battened down and furled sail to ride it out, while the men at the oars sweated to hold the bow into the wind, lest the gale strike the ship broadside and overturn her.

At noon the sky was midnight black. By night no stars could be seen, and Robin rolled the charts. 'We must wait for clear skies,' he told Channon. 'I'll know where we are soon enough.'

Clear skies were days coming. When the wind tore away the overcast and Robin could work again, he pinpointed their position far north-east of their planned course, and gave the steersman instructions as Valdez held a stuttering torch for light.

'See here, Puerto Escorces. It's not marked but I know these waters. I copied from charts captured from a Spaniard, sunk in '88.' He pointed westward. 'A battle was fought there years ago, I read of it in the Spanish captain's journal. He fought an English warship, and sank her.' He rubbed his arms, for it was chill in the aftermath of the storm. 'Were I in command, I'd hold to open water till we have gone some distance by Puerto del Miel.'

Channon agreed. 'There's a tiny cove here, by Bahia Zarzurro. We'll go ashore there and arrive at Recalde's establishment a little after dark.'

'Safe,' Robin decided. He rolled the precious charts with a nod of thanks to Valdez before Channon led him back to their cabin.

The timekeeper's hammer rang through the whole ship and the oars kept its rhythm. The *gallizabra* could not remain in the cove after they landed, for fear of discovery. She must sail east, lose herself in the tangle of reefs until high tide, days later. Julio Recalde would be hospitable, especially since he would be handsomely paid in English coin.

They prepared for the deception cautiously. Channon had set out the clothes of a mercenary in the field. The boots were scuffed, the lace and trunk hose mended. A black doublet was slightly threadbare, the points clean but discoloured. To this he added harness, swords, dirks and pistols, and shared Robin's amusement as they waited for the watch to call the sighting of land from the masthead.

'Diego de Soto, your servant,' he said drily. 'Your true and loyal companion, Master Chantry.' The remark made Robin laugh, but they were tense. 'Our story will be accepted,' Channon said more soberly. 'If we are not waiting at Bahia Zarzurro when Valdez returns for us, this ship will steal into Puerto del Miel by night. Pasco and Valdez will be after us.'

'Too dangerous,' Robin argued.

'A necessary risk,' Channon argues. 'Privateers know the value of risks. Valdez will gut Recalde's stronghold like a fish to bring us out — and Don Julio with us, if he has tried to dupe us. But Recalde is a gentleman, and will not.'

'I pray you're right,' Robin sighed as he sorted clothes on the divan.

'You're an Irishman to the soles of your feet,' Channon mused. 'There's no concealing it. Here, wear this.' He delved into the ottoman for a big, black crucifix on a heavy gold chain, and a rosary made of ebony and rosewood. He looped the crucifix about Robin's neck and wound the rosary about his left hand. 'Count the beads and mutter, no one will listen, we all know the mummery.'

The crucified Christ warmed on Robin's bare breast. He was naked save for it and the rosary, and growing aroused. Channon swore softly. The adornments of religion made him seem nearer demon than angel, wicked. The personification of temptation, dressed in Catholic iconry.

'Mother of God,' Channon whispered. 'In Madrid they would burn you.'

'Dermot?' Innocent of his looks, Robin did not follow.

'*Hermoso*,' Channon elaborated. '*Malvado*.'

'*Mal* — ? But I've done nothing!' Robin protested.

'You need only be yourself! God's blood, man, dress before you rob me of what few wits I have left!'

Robin frowned and plucked at the clothes.

'*Hermoso*,' Channon added softly. '*Mi querido.*'

At last Robin smiled. He gave Channon a sultry glace and turned his attention to the soldier's clothes. Stirrup-scuffed boots, threadbare green doublet, a brown leather cape, harness stitched with Celtic ribbonwork, his own sword, a jewel-hilted dagger from a French forge. Dressed, he presented himself for Channon's criticism.

'Good enough?'

'It'll do.' Channon swung a cloak about his shoulders and fastened it. 'And I?' In the years he had spent at liberty even his fair skin had darkened a little. He would easily pass for a Spaniard of good family. Only peasants were vulgarly darkened by the sun.

'A soldier of fortune,' Robin observed, as a lad called down from the mast. Land was in sight. 'I think we've arrived. If my arithmetic is correct, and I judged the wind rightly, he has sighted Bahia Zarzurro.' He glanced through the stern- ports. 'The sun will set in an hour. The hunt is up, Dermot.'

On deck, two hardy ponies were already saddled. Their harness was soiled and scuffed, and Channon was satisfied. The ransom was in panniers, across the bow of his own saddle, and he stood aside as the horses were coaxed into a longboat. They were skittish but Robin was with them, and he had lost nothing of his way with horses. Channon remembered his handling of Tara, the jewel of the Armagh stable. The ponies calmed as the ship ran inshore and the oars trailed to stop her.

Bahia Zarzurro was a mere crevice in the coast. Behind it rose tropical hillsides, thickly forested and filled with animals. The entrance to the cove was just a hundred yards wide, its basin twice that in diameter. The ship slid ponderously through the water but Robin was still concerned.

'How deep is the channel?'

'Ten fathoms for most of its length,' Channon told him, 'shallowing to seven by the mud banks. We'll put the boat in the water no more than a dozen yards from ground. Can you hold the horses that long?'

Robin stroked their bony faces, spoke softly to them. 'They trust me.'

'When is high tide?' Channon asked of Pasco.

'Eight. An hour before moonrise.' He did not take his eyes from the cliffs ahead. 'We'll be away before then, Dermot.'

'Come starboard,' Channon said quietly. 'More. More. You see the mud?' Banks of black silt appeared out of the clear water. 'You know the channel.'

'Where is the landing?' Robin watched the mudbanks shrewdly.

'Between the boulder that resembles a lion's head and the tree that has been split by falling rocks.' Channon pointed. 'And aye, we have used this cove before. Trail oars! We'll ground in a moment!'

The oars stopped her a scant yard from the mud and the *gallizabra* rolled gently with the rising tide. If she had bitten into the silt the tide would have floated her off in an hour.

Hawsers squealed through their blocks as the boat went over the side. The ponies cried out but Robin held them firmly, and with just ten yards to row they were soon threshing through the mud. Channon and Robin went ashore barefoot. If they had ostensibly ridden from Vera Cruz, nothing would betray them faster than boots sodden with seawater, and scuffed old leather would take a day to dry out.

They rubbed their hose half dry and tugged on the boots, laced trunk hose to doublets and mounted up. As they settled into the saddle Channon turned back to call over his shoulder.

'Valdez! Keep safe and be here for us!'

The mate waved. 'We will. Take care on the road and trust no one, not even Recalde.' He spat over the side. 'Who can trust nobility?'

'I think,' Robin said as the horses began to toil up the trail, 'we've both just been insulted.'

'We have,' Channon affirmed. 'Ricardo Valdez was with me long before the mutiny. He suffered when a gentleman was offended by his manners. Perhaps he did not bow deeply enough. Have you seen his back? Fifty lashes never sweetened a man's temper. This way, Robin. Hold tight to my heels and let the nags pick their own way. The trail is steep, but I've ridden it several times. We hid here once to make repairs.'

The path wound up the hillside. Pebbles scattered from the ponies' hooves and Robin's heart was in his mouth before they crested the crag above the cove. There, the view stole his breath. The whole world seemed to be ocean, red under the bloated setting sun. The last storm was still on the horizon and the sun was a great golden egg, like the eye of a god.

Robin made that observation, and Channon nodded. 'The Indians worship the sun as their father. There is a tribe in Peru — I was there briefly, once. Pizzaro cut out the heart out of those people long before we were born. I have a copy of his journal in my library, unless my cousins sold even that to keep their children fed. When Pizzaro found that tribe they bent their knees before the Inca, the son of the sun, a god on earth. Atahualpa.'

'What became of the god?' Robin asked as he tried the strange name on his tongue.

'Pizzaro had him strangled.' Channon urged his pony west, toward Puerto del Miel. 'Pizzaro was a peasant, a mercenary, vulgar, godless, probably sodded.' He glanced back at Robin, well aware of his bitter tone. 'He made no claim to piety or purity, and was a fine one to slaughter a people and murder their god.'

'You believe?' Robin touched his heels to his pony's flanks. 'You believe this Atahualpa was a god?'

A smile lifted Channon's wide mouth. 'If I doubt God Almighty, why should I give my allegiance to an Inca god?' He looked speculatively at the setting sun. 'But their faith was as staunch as that of the priests who laid a whip across your back to force the price of salvation from you.' He sighed. 'You know where my faith lies, Robin. In friendship, loyalty, love. If there's more, I'll be astonished on Judgement Day. But if there is only love, at the last, it will be enough.'

Robin mirrored his smile and they rode in companionable silence as night closed down. The stars were brilliant and Robin was intent on the constellations in the south, which never rose over England. These, he knew from mariner's charts. Channon watched his absorption with pride. Hal could be no more of a scholar than Robin, and no more of an adventurer. Robin was thriving on the life of a privateer. The sketches he had made of the animals along the river were rolled with his pack, and Hal should be enthralled.

Two hours' ride took them from the cove to Puerto del Miel, and some uncanny sense of time told Channon the ship was long gone on the tide. The moon was a white lamp over the sea, and bathed the fortified settlement in cold silver light. They approached stealthily, circuited the walls half a mile out so as to come in from the north-west, where Vera Cruz lay, far away.

Spaniards believed the danger of attack from English vessels or privateers was slight along these coasts. Rumours about Drake's venture to seize the gold ports had been bandied about in England,

and probably in Madrid, before the fleet sailed, but *El Draque* had outrun the news. Recalde could know nothing. Channon wondered fleetingly if he should share what information he had, since Drake might well assault Puerto del Miel. But Recalde would demand to know how two weary soldiers of fortune came by knowledge of Drake's plans. Silence was safest.

Puerto del Miel was a tiny clutter of hovels and fortifications. One elegant house stood on the cliff above the cove. They saw no signs of life as they rode in. Moonlight, almost as bright as day, gleamed on the shingles of a few dozen roofs but they heard no singing, no revelry, and Channon frowned. Were they so pious that with benediction read they closed up and slept? That was not the way of soldiers. His left hand rode the hilt of his sword and he spoke softly to Robin before they were in earshot of the defences.

'I hear nothing from the port. What chance Drake has been here already and left nothing alive?'

'Possible,' Robin whispered. 'But he would have turned his guns on the fortress... I see no damage.'

'A light,' Channon warned. 'So someone is awake. Keep your pistols to hand. My belly is crawling.' He slackened the rapier in its scabbard and peered at the guardsmen who blocked the path before them. 'Is there hospitality in town for two travellers?'

Moonlight glittered coldly on polished casques and a pitch torch stuttered in the brisk sea wind. As the guardsmen drew closer Channon saw their pistols. Suspicion of strangers was prudent in a small anchorage that was likely filled with Inca gold waiting for a ship. He held his hands in plain sight and swung out of the saddle. Robin slid down, a pace to his left, and they stepped close together. The guards were thin, with gaunt, rat-like faces and feral eyes. They had done rough service lately.

'Hospitality,' Channon repeated. 'We have business with Don Julio Recalde.'

The guards said nothing, but came closer. Channon stiffened with anger but allowed his pistols to be confiscated along with Robin's.

'What is the meaning of this?' he demanded. 'Are you under orders?' Close to, these men seemed withered. Where had they been? 'What is wrong?' Channon's voice rose. 'Have you lost your tongues as well as brains and manners?'

For the first time he saw a glimmer of life in the lean, rodent face of the elder of the pair. 'You've come here to prey, perhaps?' The accent spoke of the gutters of Cadiz. 'Buzzards always hover to pick a man's bones clean before he is dead.'

'Buzzards?' Robin echoed. His Spanish was by now without any trace of accent. 'What does he mean?'

'I've no idea,' Channon said angrily. 'Come, man, speak plainly. I am Diego de Soto, my business is with Don Julio. Obstruct me in your master's affairs and he'll likely take the skin off your back when I have had words with him! Stand aside and let us pass.'

The guardsmen glared but at last moved back and motioned the intruders down the path which led into the clutter of buildings. 'You will see Recalde,' the rat-faced elder allowed. 'God willing.'

God willing? Channon gave Robin a puzzled look but held his silence. They heard cursing behind them as the horses were led up, and Channon glanced back to see the muzzle of his own pistol levelled on them. Anger flared and he chided himself. He had commanded a privateer too long and had come to expect proper manners. Soldiers rarely respected strangers.

The fortress, built of local stone, could be no more than thirty or forty years old. This anchorage had been used for longer than that, but only when Philip began to plan for war in earnest had there been a need for so many forts to guard the enormous cargoes of the gold, which was mined in Peru and hauled across the Isthmus to the Atlantic ports.

Wooden shutters locked in the house lights. Muted voices murmured but they heard no revels, nothing to suggest cheer as Channon and Robin were marched toward Recalde's elegant house. It stood apart from the clutter, inside high adobe walls above the town. Below, a galleon lay at rest with only a single lamp to mark its position. No sound issued from it. Puerto Del Miel seemed dead asleep.

Night-blooming plants filled the air with heady perfumes. The guards took them in through the garden and a pistol barrel rapped on the iron-bound ebony door. Channon heard footsteps and the door squealed open, spilling a draught of camphor, pepper, cooking food. A wizened old steward peered accusingly at the intruders.

'They wish to see Don Julio.' The soldier strode arrogantly into the house. 'What says the quack — and the priest?'

The old servant shrugged indifferently. 'The same story, too often told.' He glared at the strangers in the candlelight. 'You are fools to be

239

here. Pah! Had I the means, I'd be a league away, and running!'

Puzzlement became anger and Channon's voice was sharp. 'We know nothing and these dolts won't speak! What do you know, old man?'

'What do I know?' The servant rounded on the lounging soldiers. 'You brought them in without telling them? They'll likely take a bludgeon to your brains when they've had the truth!' He turned bright, angry eyes on Channon. 'Yellow fever has rampaged through the town like the wrath of God these past three weeks. No ship will anchor here, not even for water, nor to take out of this purgatory souls like myself, who have survived. 'Tis a sentence of death. These fools have brought you into the pit.'

The cold sweat of dread bathed Channon's skin and he recoiled, an involuntary flinch that brought him up against Robin. He felt Robin's hand on his arm as the world overturned in an instant. Disease was the goblin haunting Channon's sleep after his hell at the hands of surgeons in Santa Catalina. In one moment he relived the torment of knives, sickness, tasted the vileness of tinctures, smelt the rotten-fruit reek of his own wounds. He wanted only to get out, get away, run and keep running.

Robin's voice was very quiet. 'Don Julio is ill?' he asked the old steward. The man looked him over suspiciously. 'I am an Irishman, Patrick Chantry, a son of your Church,' he lied smoothly, 'in the pay of Master Robert Armagh. We have brought Hal Armagh's ransom.'

'Master Armagh,' the servant murmured, and shook his head. 'He died two weeks ago of the fever.'

The blow jolted through Robin as if he had been struck physically. Channon felt him jerk, and set a hand on his shoulder. He was shaking, but only Channon knew it, and he fixed the old man with a hard look.

'Your master is ill?'

'Unto death. They've given him till morning, but I doubt he'll live that long.'

'Is he lucid?' Robin whispered.

'He comes and goes with fever.' The servant shrugged. 'You want to speak to him?'

'About Master Armagh's possessions,' Robin said quietly.

'Then, bathe and eat while you wait. I'll call you when he is worth talking to. It may be some time.' The servant was indifferent. 'And as for you fools,' he snapped at the soldiers, 'if you live past morning you'll be more fortunate than Don Julio. If I were these men I'd part you from your breath!'

He disappeared into the house and Channon stirred. An outstretched hand demanded the return of their weapons and he said curtly, 'Our horses are tethered outside? Then guard them! If we find Armagh's ransom gone, we know whose throats to slit.'

Naked threat produced a reluctant salute from the younger of the soldiers. 'I shall attend to it... and Marcelo is right, we should have warned you. We thought you came to prey. It's happened before. We are wary of robbers of the dead.'

'Aye,' Channon allowed. 'Then make amends by guarding those panniers.'

In his shock, Robin seemed to have forgotten them. He had followed the servant blindly and his face was a stiff mask as they were shown into a chamber lit by cheap tallow candles. It was spartan, with only an unmade bed, a chest and an enormous crucified Christ on the wall opposite. Open windows overlooked the cove. As the steward left them Robin sat on the side of the bed and stared sightlessly at his boots.

'Dead?' His voice was hoarse. 'He cannot be. Not Hal.'

'Yellow fever takes any race — slave, master, heathen and priest,' Channon said quietly. He sat beside Robin and pulled him into his side. 'How long, since you saw Hal?'

'Three years. I stood on the dock till his ship was out of sight and longed to go with him. Freedom, liberty... death.'

'You loved him,' Channon observed.'

'Very much.' Robin rested heavily on him. 'After I left Blackstead he came to find me. He salved my back, gave me money. Gave me absolution, without saying a word, for the love my father condemned. He wrote to me every month and half of the letters reached me. Time was, he was my only friend. Christ! What have I done? I've killed him!'

'Robin,' Channon protested sharply. But Robin did not seem to hear. 'I should have been here months ago, and instead I idled with you, making love, playing foolish games.' His face twisted. 'My pleasure was his death. God forgive me, what have I done?' He wrenched away, hugged himself and rocked in a blind attempt to ease an agony of guilt.

241

Worse, Channon could not contradict him. They had lost weeks at home, lazy, beautiful weeks, the best of their lives. The last weeks of Hal's life, which had been spent in this living hell. The terror of disease had assaulted Channon, squeezed the breath from him, and Robin's anguish flayed him too.

'Listen to me.' He pulled Robin against him. Robin seemed unaware of him. 'Listen!' His fingers dug, hurting him to return him to reality. 'If Hal is dead, blame us both. I made the decision to delay, and it was innocently made.'

'Selfishly,' Robin hissed. 'And I let you make it.'

'Selfish?' Channon demanded. 'After we'd been apart seven years and found each other, and safety? If God had not desired us to lie together till we had our hearts in order, that storm would never have crippled the *Swan*. It was the storm that killed Hal, an act of God. Have you faith left, Robin? Answer me! Do you believe?' He took Robin's face between his hands and turned it to the crucified figure over the bed. 'Do you believe in *that*?'

'I don't know,' Robin whispered. 'I want to believe in life everlasting, so Hal is not lost... but I have seen too much. Death smothered me on the *Swan*, as if I drowned in blood.' He shuddered. 'I've had no faith in any gentle God since my mother died. To me, they are only words.'

Channon's arms tightened. 'When I was a child, wandering people came to our *tuatha*. Men cast out for their faith, an older belief than Christ, a clan of gods with strange names and powers, lost in time. Christians shunned them, killed them if they could, but I was young, wild. I went to their camp to listen. Theirs is an older faith, as deep and binding as the cross.' He frowned at the crucifix. 'I don't say I believe in them any more than in heaven or hell, but many paths lead to salvation, Robin. I've no faith in heaven, after what I have seen, but I believe in a life after this.'

At last Robin stirred. Channon touched his face and went on, 'The wanderers were the last of the druidkind, from Arran, Inisheer, Inishmaan.' He traced Robin's mouth with one finger. 'They told of an Otherworld called Magh Mar, the home of the Sidhe, and the faith of our fathers, eons before Christ was a worry in Mary's poor heart. Their faith was strong.'

'They'd be burned for it.' Robin took a breath. 'Just as well you never betrayed them. It changes nothing, Dermot. I killed Hal.'

'The storm killed him,' Channon argued, 'if there's any such thing as the hand of God. You wish to shoulder God's blame? Your courage does you credit! If you and I killed Hal, it was done innocently and God let us do it. He sent both the storm and the yellow fever, and we were puppets. Robin, the absence of malice is not absolution, but it is a beginning.'

'Absence of malice,' Robin echoed, eyes closed, clutching each word desperately. It was not absolution but it was enough. His face relaxed muscle by muscle and when his eyes opened they were sane. 'It's been a fool's errand. I brought you into danger for nothing. Forgive me.'

'Little fool.' Channon cuffed his head gently as they heard footsteps outside.

He opened the door to find Marcelo with a tray of food. He took it, and rebolted the door. The room was hot and he wrenched at collar and doublet, threw off both and pulled Robin to his feet.

'Eat. It is only goat meat, but the wine smells fair. And strip, before you boil like a sand crab in a helmet of water.'

Fumbling with his laces, Robin leaned on the window and gazed into the cove. The anchored galleon was lifeless. The crew was probably dead. No one would touch a victim of Yellow Jack for fear of the sickness. The skin sallowed, a man retched helplessly and spewed up blood while his body burned. Channon put it from his mind as he sampled the wine and stood behind Robin to enjoy the slight breeze. Robin's skin was clammy after confinement of clothes. His body smelt musky, male, familiar. Channon nuzzled the back of his neck.

'Have your ghosts gone?'

'A few remain,' Robin confessed. 'I've only ever read of Yellow Jack. Few survive.' He turned from the window as Channon handed him a cup. Channon sat on the sill with a stormy expression. 'Dermot?'

Confusion churned Channon's belly while Robin was peaceful now. He felt an absurd pang of lust which passed in the same moment, dispelled by the spectre of disease. Robin repeated his name several times before he could speak.

'I am merely thinking,' he said at last. 'I'd follow you anywhere, against all good sense. I must love you more than life, for if I'd known the plague was here, I would still have followed you. Foolish, but there it is.' He offered his hands, and when Robin took them he kissed his lover's palms.

They only picked at the food, then lay down and spoke in whispers as the night dragged through. Just before dawn, knuckles rapped again and Channon went to the door. Marcelo's face was grave.

'If you have business with Recalde, come now and be brief. They bled him again but nothing will save him short of a miracle. He's had the last rites.'

Channon shuddered. In his mind's eye was the bright steel of a surgeon's knife. His legs weakened with remembered agony and sweat sprang from his pores. Robin knew, but said nothing as they dressed hurriedly. Then at the door a hand held Channon back.

'You'd best stay away. I'll have a few words with Recalde and then return.'

'I am not a child,' Channon snapped. 'Credit me with courage to match your own.'

'My apologies.' Thoroughly rebuked, Robin withdrew his hand and turned away.

'Robin!' Channon whispered. 'I am near distracted. I meant no grievance.' He caught Robin's stubbled chin to turn his face back. 'When we are far from here I'll make amends.'

'I'll hold you to it,' Robin murmured, and stepped into the dim passage.

The smell of sickness hung about Don Julio Recalde's bedchamber. Marcelo admitted them, and they stood quietly in a corner, shocked by what they saw. Recalde was darkly jaundiced, thin, his veins like blue strings. His eyes were vacant, glassy, and his mouth gaped like a fish.

A thousand memories punished Channon. He clenched his teeth on a wave of dread as his belly ravelled. A surgeon hung over the bed at Recalde's left, and at his right was a priest. Prayers streamed from his lips as a rosary worked endlessly through his fingers. Channon stood back as Robin moved closer.

At the foot of the bed he crossed himself and kissed his crucifix. He knelt before the priest and only then addressed the dying man. Channon followed his example. The gestures spoke more eloquently than words. Robin cleared his throat and spoke slowly in his accentless Spanish. Recalde was lucid enough to understand.

'Master Robert Armagh sent me, but I know I am too late. Is Hal Armagh buried near here, sir? If I may, I'll visit his grave and pay his brother's respects.'

The Spanish knight seemed a century old as he struggled to speak. 'On the hill above the cove. He was buried a Catholic, though he was an Englishman.' One feeble hand pointed to the priest.

'It was well done.' Robin frowned at the priest. 'I thank you, Father. A Catholic burial would please the Armaghs. Is the service owed for?'

The priest paused in his litany for long enough to shake his head, then the rosary advanced with endless pleas to the Mother of God to intercede at the hour of a sinner's death. Robin looked back at Channon, who shrugged minutely.

Recalde coughed harshly. 'Take his belongings, for his brother. The time for friction is long past. He was good company. Tell them he was well treated under my protection. We played chess. I would not have killed him. I swear to God, I would not have! Take his things, get out before this place is the end of you also!'

He was rambling, and slid into delirium as they watched. His eyes rolled up and a river of sweat soaked his linen. Robin was immobile at the foot of the bed and Channon took his shoulders to move him.

The door latched behind them and Channon forced in a breath. The stench of death was pervasive. Robin stirred and knuckled his eyes.

'We leave at first light, when I've paid Hal my respects. Where are his things? Marcelo?'

Candle shadows announced the servant and a gnarled hand beckoned them to the chamber where Hal had slept. It was bare now, stripped, shutters locked, rugs taken up, tapestries gone, leaving pale patches on the walls. A single chest stood in the middle of the room. Robin unbuckled its straps and inside Channon saw a rare collection. Hal's treasure.

Butterflies. Hundreds, dried, hand-painted and mounted between sheets of vellum, their colours brilliant, each named and dated in Hal's unmistakable writing. Robin passed them to Channon and picked up his brother's pistol, his dirk, a signet with the Armagh device, a kerchief, a red-leather tobacco pouch, his pipe.

'He had no son to love them,' Robin whispered. 'I wonder if my own boy would like them, when he is big enough. There are no Armagh heirs, you know. Richard is childless through no fault of his wife's. John is likely dead by now. He never wed, nor did Hal. And I can never go back.' He wrapped Hal's things in a linen sheet, tied the bundle carefully and tucked it under his arm. 'A traveller could leave these at the shop for Ned Blythe. He need know only that they were Hal's.'

As Channon closed up the room it was almost dawn. Their chamber faced east and the fragile dawn light was at odds with the funereal atmosphere of the house. He snuffed the candles and collected their weapons from the bed. They must get out, quickly, as Recalde advised. It would be safest to camp at Bahia Zarzurro.

An Indian woman, grotesquely fat and squeezed into a Spanish gown, laboured at the kitchen hearth. She gave them breakfast, which they ate hurriedly, without sitting. The ponies and their guard dozed in the morning cool, and as the sun crossed the horizon Channon put boot to stirrup and gratefully turned his back on Puerto del Miel.

The cemetery was a plot of grass by one of the fortified gun emplacements. They let the nags graze along the steep incline, where the cannon nestled in a stone cradle, a big, black instrument of destruction. Powder and shot were kept under a thatch nearby and the gunners leaned lazily on it. They rammed the barrel with fresh ragging to clean it as the strangers passed. Channon spared them a glance.

By daylight the port looked dead. The town sprawled down the seaward slope under the guns. Below it was the anchorage, behind it the curve of the river, choked by flood debris, infested with mosquitoes. The air was thick with them and Channon slapped them from his face and neck as he followed Robin up to the cemetery.

A wooden cross marked Hal's grave. Channon read his name, the date, two weeks old, and the old seaman's prayer, *Santa Clara, ora pro nobis*. A generous thought, kindly meant. Recalde and his priest were fair men. Robin knelt, studying the grave for minutes. Channon would have sworn he was praying until he heard the curses. He was damning the Spanish, the English, the fever, the war, the Americas, thrashing through his grief and guilt, buttressed by rage.

The men working on the cannon blinked at the tirade as it rose steadily in volume. Channon let him spend himself, until he had cursed everything and everyone. Then Robin took off the crucifix and rosary, looped them over the cross and stood. His eyes were stormy, but sane.

'There's no more for me here. I think we must leave this place. Much longer here, and —'

Where the shot that destroyed the gun emplacement came from,

Channon did not know, but one moment the peace of the grave lay over Puerto del Miel and the next the air reeked with gunpowder, and the thunder of a broadside hammered about the cove. Shot screamed in the air, punched into the settlement, and Channon whirled, his slitted eyes hunting for the billows of white sail canvas.

Three English galleons were butting into the bay, three broadsides punished the ears as the best gunners in the fleet ranged their weapons. A second round impacted dead on target, knocked the cannon out of its stone cradle and threw the men away like dolls. Shards of stone and shot fragments filled the air.

Somehow, over the roar of triple broadsides, Channon heard the gasp of surprise and pain. He was already diving, his arms up to shield his head. The horses had bolted.

Beside him, sprawled in a tangle of limbs, Robin lay ominously still, and Channon's mouth dried. He flung his own body over Robin's as the gunners fired again. There was no time to think or see, but his fingers searched Robin's head and were wet with blood where a wound creased his scalp.

As the tumult began to diminish he dared lift his head and bit his lip as he saw the gash. Blood was warm, slick on his hands, but it was a shallow cut. A good surgeon would treat it in moments. Channon pushed up to his knees to survey the tumbled ruin of the town.

Puerto del Miel was gone, and Recalde's elegant Spanish house was a pile of rubble. The cannonade was over, he dared stand now, and looked down on the incoming warships. At his feet, Robin was deeply unconscious. Blood sullied his face.

A surgeon, Channon thought feverishly as he slapped the mosquitoes from his skin. They swarmed in clouds off the stagnant river. Did *El Draque* carry a surgeon?

Then he considered his clothing and swore. Everything about him would identify him as a Spaniard, he would be a prisoner in the same instant Drake accepted Robert Armagh as his guest.

With swift, savage jerks, Channon tore off his doublet and collar. He flung away anything that marked him as Spanish. 'I am an Irishman,' he said to Robin's sleeping body, 'like yourself. I'll be Patrick Chantry, soldier of fortune, shipwrecked in this forsaken place.' He turned his eyes to the sky, praying to gods in whom he had never believed.

Boats were already away. English lads pulled them in toward the beach below the cliff and Channon waved. A figure in the first craft saw him and a pistol was drawn, but the seamen took minutes to climb up by the steep path. Channon sat cradling Robin in his lap, and his temper was past snapping point when voices, thick with the accents of Devon and Cornwall, began to shout at him.

He set Robin into the grass and passed his hands across his face, unwittingly leaving a bright smear of blood. A pistol levelled on him but he smiled at the burly red-haired lad in charge.

'Good day to you, sir.' His accent was deliberate. 'Just a poor soldier, your servant, and in need of your assistance. My comrade is Master Robin Armagh, of Admiral Drake's acquaintance. Is Sir Francis aboard one of yon warships?'

If he was, Channon's anonymity was done for, and he would be arguing for his liberty, if not his life, for Drake must surely remember him as Don Mauricio de Cervallo's personal guard, a Spanish mercenary.

Chapter Twenty-Five

The ropes bit into Channon's wrists but he mustered his patience. He was at least confined in a gentleman's cabin, when he had expected to be thrust into the hold. Robin had been taken away by the admiral's own surgeon, and Channon was grateful. The wound did not look dire, but head wounds could be peculiar. A little nick, and a man might be mad, or childlike, for life. Robin was in the best hands now and Channon could only wait.

It had been hours already. The ships had anchored in the bay but would not stay long. *El Draque* had gone ashore to sift the rubble for documents, or an informant, and to open the bullion stores. Channon hoped he would find what he wanted and quit this open grave soon.

Tied by the wrists, he had been brought aboard, bound to a chair in this cabin and then abandoned. He was stiff, cramped, and the cabin was hot. His heart quickened as he heard footsteps and voices. One was deep, with a thick Devon burr. Drake.

He strode into the tiny cabin a moment later, stood at the door and glared at the captive. Channon held his breath. Seven years was a long time. Perhaps the admiral would not recall his face, his family.

But Drake's memory was sharper than that. 'I know you,' he said bluntly as he beckoned a gentleman into the cabin to second him and shut the door. 'Channon, is it not? By God!'

'Just a soldier of fortune now,' Channon said quietly.

'A Spanish mercenary,' Drake argued, 'in King Philip's service.'

Channon shook his head. 'Not in years, since the war cut the heart out of my family, and the Crown and Church between them paupered us. In the king's service?' He gave an ironic, bitter chuckle. '*El Draque* desires truth of me? I'd not give Philip a mug of water to douse himself if he were alight.'

His voice was filled with anger, resentment. Drake was an astute man who knew sincerity when he heard it, even if he might not at once understand. He pulled up a chair and called the gentleman closer.

'Unbind him. And you, Channon, tell me what you are. Know that you speak for your life, man. How do you come to be in young Armagh's company?'

Only lies would serve, but they could be founded on truth. Channon drew a deep breath. 'I cut loose from Spain years ago. Before the Armada sailed, in fact. Don Mauricio died, Crown and Church taxes ruined us, our women live like peasants in a hut and the Cervallo men are abroad in places like this, seeking a new fortune. I owe Spain nothing. I am my own man, Sir Francis, and an Irishman! Ask Robin.'

'I shall,' Drake assured him. 'Go on.'

'I am in his employment,' Cannon said offhandly. 'If you walk up on the cliff by the guns, you'll find a new grave, a cross bearing his brother's name. Hal Armagh was Recalde's hostage. Robin came with the ransom and hired me, a week's march along the coast, for protection.'

'And where is the *Swan*?' Drake leaned forward intently. 'Young Armagh was on Downing's frigate. She was separated from the fleet in a storm and we never saw a sail of her again.'

'Nor will you,' Channon said flatly. 'She was crippled in the storm and blundered into privateers' waters. There's a corsair by the name of Hubert Guillaume —'

'I've exchanged fire with him twice, this voyage.' Drake frowned. 'The *Swan* fell prey to privateers?'

That at least was the truth. 'She did.' No need to tell which privateers. 'I've known Guillaume for years and I don't quarrel with him. I value my neck! But I've known Robin even longer. We were like brothers in England, before the war.'

'I saw you together.' Drake pulled at his beard. 'Were there no survivors from the *Swan*, then?'

'Many, sir.' Channon stuck to truth as far as he could. 'But little could be done for them. One day, with God's grace, they'll find their way to freedom.' He took a breath. 'I diced for Robin and won him from Guillaume. Then I diced for the ransom and won it fairly, but we reached Puerto del Miel too late. The Yellow Jack has been in the town for weeks, Hal died two weeks ago.' He shrugged eloquently. 'Go ashore with caution. The town is a cluster of charnel houses, Recalde's body is yellow as mustard and Hal's grave is yonder. You'll find our nags, loose on the cliff, with the ransom. I imagine Robin would be grateful if you caught them. The ransom was rich.'

For some time Drake was silent, before he stood and moved to the door. 'I believe you, Channon. If you've gulled me, you'll die for it, but the tale is easier verified than you think. Your employer is just awake. Come with me.'

He led Channon to another, still smaller cabin high in the stern. It was darkened and he smelt vinegar and liniment as he peered in the dimness, just able to make out Robin, who lay on a bunk against the bulkhead. He was awake, a hand to his head. Ill and groggy, Channon guessed.

'So your head is wooden, as I've long suspected,' Channon said lightly. 'Are you well enough to speak? I am arguing for my life. Am I a Spanish spy, or an Irish soldier of fortune? The admiral is unsure!'

'Hold your tongue,' Drake said bluffly. 'I'll not have you tell him what to say. So, Robin. Tell me how you came into his company.'

Robin sat up, cradling his aching head. His voice was slurred. 'The last we saw of the fleet, you were headed over the horizon. The storm crippled up, we limped on and stumbled into privateers' waters. The *Swan* sank.' He took a deep breath. 'I was lucky. But for Channon, I'd be dead or in the hands of a man called Guillaume. What more can I say?'

It was just enough. If Drake questioned further, Robin's lies would surely differ from Channon's, and they could both pay the price. It was in the lap of the gods and Channon closed his eyes to wait. Drake said nothing for some moments, then gave a grunt of acceptance. 'You're fortunate, Robin. Do you know what became of your shipmates?'

The green eyes flickered to Channon's face. Channon chanced a minute shake of his head. Only Robin saw it. 'I was half drowned, Admiral, separated from them. I never saw them after the ship went down.'

Drake sighed heavily. 'A bad business. And this is not the worst of it.' He leaned on the close door and folded his arms on his barrel chest. 'A few days short of Dominica the fleet split up into a brace of squadrons, the better to hunt and fight. We lost the *Francis* there, sunk. Not much later, Hawkins died. Aye, John Hawkins is dead. I swore this voyage would be the end of him! He was sixty-two, and too old for young men's adventures. His heath was poor before we sailed.'

'I shall grieve, Admiral,' Robin said dutifully. 'Sir John Hawkins was a great man. My brother sailed with him twice. Hal also is dead, of the fever, and buried on the cliff here.'

'So Channon tells me.' Drake stirred. 'And you, lad, how is your skull? 'Tis unfortunate you were in harm's way.'

'Just a gash,' Robin said quietly. 'How it aches! Your surgeon gave me four stitches of fine catgut, but said it was a chip of stone rather than a fragment of shot that did the damage. I'll soon heal.'

'See that you do.' Drake opened the door. 'You may bunk here, the pair of you. We lost several gentlemen and have the space to spare.' He looked broodingly at Channon. 'If we come upon the ransom it'll be returned, and then we're for England, directly. I can deliver you home in a few months, God willing. I imagine you are eager to return, Robin. Your babes will be half grown by the time you are back.'

'Indeed, sir,' Robin whispered.

'We've had a hard run, these past months,' Drake growled. 'We are weakened and the weather is threatening. Aye, we are for home. We must take on water, but there's no Yellow Jack in Guadeloupe. Our holds are not as filled as they might be, but better take home half a fleet than none!'

With that he left them. In the dimness, Channon sat on the side of the bunk and pressed Robin into the pillows. He leaned over to open the shuttered port, admitting a crack of blue daylight. Robin swore and covered his eyes. He pressed his face to Channon's shoulder, and Channon held him. They were safe. Drake believed the story. After the death of Hawkins he seemed resigned to ill fortune.

'So,' Channon said at last. 'This is how it is to be. Strange, the way fortune has of making a man's life, then sundering it again. How is your head?'

'Easing. I had a tincture, vile but potent.' Robin drew back to study Channon's sombre face as his eyes grew accustomed to the light.

'Your wife will meet you gladly,' Channon guessed. 'I'll greet her and your children, and pass on, don't fret. England is not my home.'

'Hold me,' Robin whispered. 'I need it sorely.'

Channon crushed his ribs, and when Robin hunted for kisses, bruised his lips too. 'Robin, you must go home. Things will be as they are,' he said with spurious blandness.

'But you are free to be in England. Drake would speak for you, tell how you won an Englishman's freedom. You would find gratitude, not danger, in London. People will love you. A beautiful man is always cherished, for his looks if nothing else.'

'Beautiful?' Channon smiled reluctantly.

'A beautiful man whom I love too deeply to bear.'

The confession finished Channon. He turned away to hide hot, useless tears. Despair bruised him. 'You are wed! What will I be? A lackey, putting down roots on dry land while I wait patiently for your favours? A house by the docks, if I can earn enough at labouring, and now and then your wife allows you time to come to me! How long before people notice my midnight caller is a man, and I am stoned for it, or arrested?'

'Christ.' Robin's eyes closed and he took Channon with him as he fell onto the bunk. Channon's weight pinned him. 'I know, it is not what we desired. But wait, and think. We can leave again. A ship, our safe haven, the fortune you leave behind. Pasco and Valdez will secure the *gallizabra*, your trust in them is well founded. We'll be free, I swear it.'

'And your wife?' Channon was far from optimistic.

Robin sighed. 'She'll rail at me for these adventures. Jen will forget me in a year and wed Jocelyn Hardly. She may have forgotten me already. We parted bitterly months ago, and Hardly will be whispering to her, tales of Court, Queen and wealth.' He looked into Channon's face. 'We'll tarry in England only long enough to find a westbound ship.' He offered his hand, and Channon took it. 'Don't ever doubt me.'

Channon's mouth compressed. He withdrew his hand and took off his shirt. The cabin was hot. He mopped his chest with the sodden linen and turned his face to the breeze from the open port.

'I know you mean what you say, but it'll not be so simple. The Armaghs will want an account of Hal's death. The Queen will want a report on of Spanish fortifications here. Blythe's family will wine and feast you as a hero. Against all that you'll find escape difficult. You mean your promises here, but when your pretty wife cherishes you after you've charmed Hampton... better make a clean break. Part in love, take good memories with us and recall them often. Either that, or we'll limp on as guilty lovers, adulterers, sinners in every way.'

'Maggots have got into your brain,' Robin snapped. 'You're mine, Dermot. Christ! That bastard, Guillaume, looked once at us and saw it. You belong to me, and I keep what's mine.'

'Anger?' Channon smiled at him. 'Your head is mended.'

The tincture had eased it, and Robin's senses were clear. By the sky it was afternoon, and he had slept off most of the ill effects of both the blow and the drug. 'I am furious to be doubted,' he said sharply. 'Are you mine, or was Guillaume wrong, about you if not me?'

'You know my heart,' Channon remonstrated. 'I've wanted none other since you were just a boy. No other man has fucked me since I was a lad myself. I submit to you — only to you, and only because I love you.'

'Then why can you not believe what I say?' Robin was on his feet, fists clenched. 'I'll return to my family and forget you, will I, after I spent seven years waiting and grieving for you? By God, you think little of me!'

Channon recoiled. 'The whole ship will hear you.'

'Let them!' But Robin lowered his voice and threw the bolt to lock the door. 'Since you'll not believe a word I say, I must show you in deeds. Take off your clothes.'

Again, Channon recoiled. 'Robin?'

'I said, take off your clothes!' Not content to wait for Channon to comply, he stripped the larger man with sharp, jerky movements and tossed down his own linen and hose. Naked, he clenched his fingers into Channon's arms and thrust him onto the bunk.

'Robin?' Channon whispered hoarsely. 'Must you punish me?'

Surprise stopped Robin's hands. 'What?'

'If you must discipline me, I'll submit, but tell me what I am being punished for. Scepticism and pessimism never warranted punish-

253

ment, in any man's ship.'

'Punishment?' Robin's hands gentled. 'You're as foolish as you are lovesome. I wouldn't hurt you, least of all in bed. But I *will* leave my mark on you. You'll know now, if you never did before, what Guillaume knew at a glance.' He took Channon's shoulders with surprising strength. Nothing about Robin was boyish now, his slender body was like steel.

Channon caught his breath and for a moment tensed as if he would struggle. Robin would not allow it. Hands like talons did not ask but demanded, pressing Channon into the bunk. Raw sensuality blazed in Robin's face. He knew to the second when Channon surrendered.

The dark head lowered in submission and Dermot relaxed, as if he needed to relinquish command. Responsibility wearied him. Now, Robin turned him easily onto his knees and lifted his hips. Channon's buttocks spread, and he moaned.

'Mine,' Robin whispered. He slipped his hand between Channon's thighs, worked his genitals almost ruthlessly but denied him release, until Dermot groaned.

By the bed was an oily salve, left for Robin's scalp. It would do. Silent, acquiescent, quivering, Channon held the pot. His head snapped back and forth as he was probed deeply, with perfunctory gentleness. The muscle clenched about Robin's fingers reminded him of a man's vulnerability, and he resolved to take care as he swallowed the blinding lust and nudged into position. The blunt head of his cock lay against the slick, yielding anus, and Channon was not even breathing. This time he would know he belonged.

He drove himself inside in one long, relentless lunge. Channon was taut as a bow, rammed without respite until he came, and still Robin moved in him, hunting with bewildering power. Dizzy, Channon rode it out, relishing his pleasure, pain, even the moment's subjugation, and the eruption of Robin's coming, with a sense of wonder. He was the cause of this passion, a tumult that had maddened so gentle a lover.

His nostrils prickled on the heavy scent of their musk as shaking hands released him, and he curled up to rest. Robin's green eyes opened slowly, and cleared. He lay slumped against the timbers, leaving Channon astonished, outraged, delighted.

'Mine,' Robin repeated as he caught his breath, and pressed a kiss to Channon's mouth. Channon groaned again as he was pushed flat, bathed and examined. He was sore, and grateful for a swab of the salve and a massage performed by leaden hands.

Weariness tugged at them both as Robin bathed himself, but it was a contented exhaustion. Discovering his throbbing head, he sank down, and as lust abated he began to feel ill again. He cradled his skull and swore. Channon had his breath back, and Robin murmured gratefully as Dermot began to rub his neck. He yelped as Channon found the egg-sized, bruised lump. Love replaced lust and he looked up contritely.

'Have I hurt you?'

'A little. I'll survive. It was... different.'

Pleased to see Channon's rueful smile, Robin forced himself wide awake. 'Whose are you?'

'Yours.' He palmed Robin's chest and pinched his nipples teasingly. 'How could I doubt! I wondered how it would be, to be fucked most forcefully beneath you, rather than loved tenderly.' He locked his fingers at Robin's nape and kissed him. 'Now I know.' Channon's eyes were a little glassy, confused, and his skin was clammy.

Robin's fingers slipped in a film of his sweat as they kissed. 'I've exhausted you,' he observed. 'Sleep, while you can.'

'I will.' Channon rolled over and put his head down.

He was limp, desperate for rest, Robin saw with deep satisfaction. For himself, Robin wanted water, fresh air and another tincture. His skull was splitting. Lust had been a complete folly, and he paid the price for it as he left the cabin. He had put on the minimum of clothing and his legs trembled as he knocked on the surgeon's door.

The tincture was vile. His belly heaved but he kept it down and was on the weatherdeck, breathing deeply, when he heard Drake's voice.

'On your feet, lad? You Armaghs are tough.'

'Merely stubborn,' Robin corrected as he thought of John and Hal. 'Can I do you some service, sir?' he looked along at Drake with shaded eyes.

'You might.' Drake's callused hands gripped a rope as the ship rolled. 'Recalde's bullion stores are already empty. My men have been rooting in the rubble and have come upon his documents. I had a man who spoke Spanish like a native, but he was killed a month ago. Now I have Recalde's papers and no good translator. You told me you speak several languages. Latin and French, I expect. Spanish?'

'Yes.' Robin thought back on his lessons with a smile. 'I'd be pleased to translate, sir. Do you require written copy, or to hear the documents read aloud?'

'I must hear the contents at once,' Drake mused, 'but if you would write a copy in the Queen's English, I'll be in your debt.'

'As good as done.' Robin watched the crew making repairs to the gun mountings on the weatherdeck. They smiled at Drake as if they felt a fondness for him. He was an honest man, strong on religion, and aboard his ships men were treated fairly, which was more than could be said of many vessels in Admiralty service.

As he followed Drake aft, Robin wondered what Sir Francis would make of the delicious sin enjoyed in the stern cabin an hour before. He would likely turn purple with apoplexy. Robin stifled a ribald chuckle. How many such acts were performed on this ship, in silence and shadows? He thought of Channon and smiled privately as Drake offered him a cup of ale.

The documents were bundled loosely. Robin sorted them, arranged them by date, then by category. 'His personal letters, the manifests of various ships, garrison requisitions, tallies of stores and provisions, and a schedule of shipping expected to pass this anchorage.' He looked up. 'Where shall I begin?'

'The shipping, and tallies of what was stored,' Drake said shrewdly. 'I've no interest in the bread and wine coming in, but read off the cargoes loaded for Spain.'

'Gold,' Robin hazarded, and Drake's smile was impish. 'Well, eight ships are listed on the year's schedule. The *Santa Rosa* came just last month. You saw her?'

'We sank her.' Drake drained his cup and poured another.

'The *Valiente* and the *Osadia*, in company, in January.'

'Gone before we arrived.'

'The *Maria de Huelva*, next month, or the month after, probably to take out whatever should have been in their storehouses at this time.' Robin referred to a second document and arched a brow at the admiral. 'A mule caravan brought sixty thousand ducats' value of gold over the Isthmus ten days ago. You found nothing of this?'

But Drake shook his head. 'The storehouses were despoiled, nothing was left save a good measure of pistol shot in the walls. There's been fighting.'

'Privateers,' Robin guessed. 'Several are loose in these seas. Any one of them might have the cunning and audacity to come into a port already stricken with fever. I wager, their lookouts saw the caravan arrive. If you want that gold, hunt down the privateers.'

'You're guessing,' Drake said bluffly. 'It could be a goose chase.'

'A *golden* goose chase,' Robin added, and returned to the papers. The letters were neatly written, tersely brief. He read them quickly and at last, coming to a sheet dated no more than two weeks before, he frowned. 'I believe this tells the tale you have been waiting to hear. This letter was for His Majesty, and is abject. Recalde begs humbly to explain that the gold from Puerto Veneno, ported over the Isthmus by Capitan Leandro, was looted from his hands under the guns of a privateer, and assures His Majesty that his soldiers fought with courage but were outnumbered, due to the fever. The privateer flew a red flag.' Robin set down the letter. 'Hubert Guillaume flies a red flag. There is your gold.'

Drake's mouth tugged down. 'Is another mule caravan due?'

'Not until August, when the *Natividad* and the *Santiago* arrive for the cargo. Bad weather could delay them till September.'

'Too late.' Drake shook his head emphatically. 'We've lost several vessels already, and our presence here is no secret, if it ever was. The Spanish are not fools, Robin. They'll do as I would, in their place, and gather every warship in fighting trim from the Antilles to Vera Cruz. If I await the August caravan we'll be sunk — if the Yellow Jack does not take us first.'

The letters crackled as Robin folded them. 'Home, then?'

'In a day or two. We must make repairs before we can tackle the sea. But I'll move offshore, away from this cemetery.' He stirred, opened a leather-banded chest and produced a folio of writing materials. 'Could I prevail upon you for a list in English of the shipping and cargoes?'

'A pleasure,' Robin said, when in fact his head throbbed and his eyes protested. But the work diverted him from his faint nausea and it was not difficult to copy the lists.

He was occupied until mid-afternoon, and dined with Drake's bosun on pickled pork and melons. Channon must be awake, he thought, and returned quietly to the cabin. But Dermot was still asleep, still hot, his skin drenched with sweat. Surely the cabin was not so hot. The stern-port was open over the bunk. Robin shook him by the shoulder.

'Dermot? Dermot!'

'Ah, Robin.' He woke groggily and struggled up. 'Forgive me. You were most demanding and I did try to please you.'

'You were my delight.' Robin dampened a cloth and wiped Channon's burning skin. 'You're so hot,' he said quietly.

Channon acknowledged vaguely as he luxuriated in the cool cloth. 'The day is blistering and this cabin is an oven. Let me get on deck. Fresh air will blow the cobwebs from my head.'

It was hot, but not as overpowering as he thought. Robin frowned as he watched Channon pull on hose and shirt. He was unsteady, as if half drunk, but the sea wind calmed him and Robin said no more. The furious mating must have been more wearing than he had realised. He chided himself as he drew Channon to the side, under the forest of lines, well clear of Drake's gunners.

'Damn — I hurt you, didn't I? You're paying the price for my lust.'

'Whose brain is maggoty now?' Channon retorted, 'If this were my ship I'd kiss you. As it is...' He glanced over his shoulder. 'I think Sir Francis might keelhaul the both of us, so words must suffice. 'I'll spread you and have you, when we can rise to pleasure again, and we'll be at evens. If I walk a little stiffly for the moment, there's good cause!'

'Good enough.' Robin smiled. 'Sit in the shade, I'll fetch you a cup of ale.'

'Sit?' Channon smiled wryly. 'I'd rather stand, m'dear!'

The lookout shouted from the mast as Robin returned with a pitcher of brown ale. A boat pulled out from the beach and the bosun signalled for Drake. The Master Thief stood in the waist, stout and commanding, and to his surprise Robin saw four panniers he recognised passed into Drake's care.

They were opened, and Drake oathed as he found a weight of gold coin, vellum and butterflies, a man's pipe and kerchief.

'Hal's things,' Robin sighed as Drake folded the vellum. 'Butterflies, birds and beasts were his reason for being here. He was no spy. He left these for me, and they are for my own son, with your permission. The gold coin you have here is what you saw loaded aboard the *Swan*. His ransom.'

'And no doubt a good part of Master Edward Blythe's fortune,' Drake said bluffly. He gestured for the bosun to repack the panniers. 'Since your brother is dead, Master Blythe may have his fortune back. Our holds won't notice the loss, but Blythe would.'

'I am grateful,' Robin said honestly. 'Will you keep these things for me, with your own valuables?'

Drake agreed as he returned to his gunners, and Robin joined Channon, who lay in the shade of a single flapping canvas. He drained the pitcher of ale while Robin watched, and wiped his mouth.

'Not ready to sit yet?' Robin teased, 'Do I apologise?'

But Channon laughed. 'Would that I were so cherished every day! You have your coin and butterflies, and *El Draque* has Recalde's papers, if not his gold. We ship out of hell with this tide, then stand off to make repairs. See this sheet? It'll soon rip clean away. North, to take on water, then... England.' He closed his eyes. 'We shall be free again. I believe.' Was it a vow?

Brow creased, Robin said nothing. Channon lounged in the shade as the crew made ready to sail. The arm flung over his eyes could have masked grief, foreboding or a throbbing head.

He was restless, while the men went aloft to set canvas, and as sunset bloodied the horizon he stood in the stern and watched Puerto del Miel fall away. He held his weight on his forearms on the sun-hot wood, but Robin saw him sway, and his feet dragged as he returned to the cabin to dress for dinner. With the safety of a locked door they dared touch. Channon was clammy, sweated, and Robin stirred to dread.

'Christ, are you still pained? What have I done to you? Are you griped in the belly? Dermot!'

Channon blinked owlishly. 'I am just over-hot with the weather. And I'll worsen with this confounded doublet I must wear!'

'Let me examine you,' Robin began.

But Channon fended him off. 'You want only to lay these rapacious hands on me again. I must keep a sharp lookout, or be fucked again before I am aware of it!'

Robin forced a smile but was fretting. He had tried to make sure Channon was unhurt, and found no damage he could see, nothing to account for this feverishness. Then Channon laughed rudely at him and cuffed his head.

'I like you contrite and guilty!'

'Oh, enough of your nonsense,' Robin said, flustered as he set about dressing.

Bathed, shaved, his scalp salved and his lace tidy, he stood back for Channon's approval. Channon wanted to kiss, but when Robin embraced him he murmured in surprise. He was hot as a forge, as if he would soon catch alight. He was surely sickening, but Robin knew Channon would never allow the physician to touch him.

He closed up the cabin as Dermot stepped out. Drake's quarters were larger but still cramped, with little headroom. The table was laid with sumptuous fare — fowl, fish, cheese, fresh and dried fruit, black bread and pastries. Robin discovered himself famished and ate well. He spoke seldom, and divided his attention between the food and his lover while Drake read the English translation of Recalde's papers.

The work was praised, which pleased Robin, but he remained intent on Channon. Dermot had not eaten, but he drank a great deal of ale. The wine was excellent but he refused it. His thirst was unquenchable... he was ill. Robin recalled his own thirst, the morning after the scourging. His back burned with remembered pain, and he did not hear Drake speaking to him until Sir Francis called his name loudly.

'Master Armagh, what troubles you?'

'Forgive me,' Robin said quickly. 'I am preoccupied. What did you ask, sir?'

'I asked the strength of the privateer, Guillaume. Since you were his prisoner, you know this better than any man.'

They had shared the strategic lies in private, and Robin had the story straight. 'He has a French *galleasse* of forty-eight guns. She's the old *Pandora*, seized when she grounded on the coast. A slave crew mans her oars, and he has all the powder and shot he has looted from ships like the *Swan*. But he is just one ship, sir, and the *Pandora* is slow and clumsy. If you see her red flag, sink her!'

His vehemence startled Drake, and he laughed. 'You have a score to settle with the man! I imagine it tried you sorely to be his prisoner. You have Channon to thank for your liberty.'

'And much else besides,' Robin admitted. As the others returned to their discussion of Recalde's documents he leaned closer to Channon. 'Dermot, you're sick. There's a good surgeon aboard. He treated my head and I would trust him to examine you.'

It was the wrong advice, he knew it the instant he spoke. Channon would never allow it. He put his fourth cup down with a clatter and a little ale spilled. Drake's pilot and the two gentlemen adventurers looked sharply along the table at what they took for loutish behaviour.

'Our apologies,' Robin murmured with a smile. 'My companion has not been at sea for a long time. He forgets that ships have the unfortunate habit of rolling.' The explanation produced a general chuckle, and the gentlemen were appeased. 'Also, he's unwell,' Robin added as he noticed Drake's continued attention. 'I think the roll of the deck disagrees with him. His stomach is turned.'

'A breath of air,' Drake said bluffly. 'Or will I summon the quack?'

'No!' Channon stood, both flat palms propping him on the table as he swallowed repeatedly. In the light of a branch of candles Robin saw the colour drain from his face and leave it grey, waxen. 'My thanks, but no. I am a little unwell, sir. I shall be — shall be quite all —'

And then he toppled sideways in an untidy sprawl at Robin's feet. Drake came about the table as Robin knelt and tore the lace from his throat.

'Is he overcome?' Drake had watched Channon drink steadily, but four cups of mild ale never finished a man of Channon's weight.

'He's burning,' Robin said tersely as he bared Channon's breast, 'and has been since afternoon. He's blazing with fever, unsteady on his feet. He didn't eat, if you noticed, sir. I am not sure that it is the sea that discomfits him.' He swallowed, bit his lip as he felt the furnace heat of Channon's skin and looked up at Drake. 'Please, fetch your surgeon. I think he's ailing.'

A tense, pregnant silence followed before Drake's young pilot put the unspoken dread into words. 'Ailing? Fevered? God's teeth, we just came from a port dead of Yellow Jack!'

'It cannot be,' Robin protested, 'he's not yellow!'

'Yet,' Drake grunted. 'First comes the fever, then the jaundice and the spewing of blood. Then death.' He stepped back from Channon's body. 'Sir Oliver, fetch the surgeon. Master Armagh, get him to your cabin, let no one see or touch him. He has till morning, and if it is Yellow Jack he'll be put ashore. I'll not have plague on my ship.'

'Plague?' Robin could scarcely make sense of the word. He looked down at Channon's still, waxen face. 'It cannot be!'

'It can.' Drake sighed heavily. 'I've seen it happen. Worse than plague itself is the fear, the panic. You've just come from a charnel house, and that was on dry land. A ship becomes a coffin.' He looked from Robin to Channon and back. 'If he sallows by morning, then my prayers go with him, but he goes ashore. My first duty is to my crew.'

'But he is ill,' Robin whispered. 'Put him ashore alone, and he'll die.' Drake's expression was regretful but resolved. Robin closed his eyes. 'Then put me ashore with him.'

'And you too will die — alone, on these coasts? Suicide!' Drake's voice rose. 'What is his life against your own? Or do you think you owe him a debt, since he won your freedom from Guillaume? Perhaps you do, but he is dead either way. I see no need to sentence yourself with him.'

'I owe him everything,' Robin said quietly. Breathing was difficult and his belly clenched. 'If he sallows, we'll both leave you.'

'And be dead within the week!' Drake was exasperated. 'These hills are untamed. Indians and wild beasts will have you if the plague does not. What makes you think you can survive?'

'I have no assurance,' Robin admitted. 'But he deserves better than abandonment.' He stood and pulled his doublet straight. 'Perhaps we'll both die, but I'd rather end this way than let him perish and spend my years tormented by guilt, knowing I held his life in my hand.'

Drake shook his head sadly. 'The odds are against you. You command more courage than sense. But 'tis your life, to waste as you choose. Get him to your cabin, wait for the surgeon. And pray.'

No one would lay a hand on Channon, and somehow Robin carried his dead weight, unaided. The passages were cleared, no one saw him go by. Channon woke as he was set on the bunk, and Robin bathed his face. 'Shh, be still, rest now.' Did he hear? He was delirious, burning.

The surgeon examined him minutes later, and answered Robin's entreaties with a bleak expression and a shrug. It might be Yellow Jack, it might not. Only time would tell.

So Robin waited. If he had owned a shred of faith he would have prayed, but he could find none. He held Channon's head, bathed him and trickled ale between his lips whenever he half woke. The surgeon returned every hour, but even he could only watch. Once, Channon woke, caught the stranger's hands on him and lashed out. After that, Robin sent the surgeon away and sat on the side of bunk, watching for dawn and dreading what he would see. The night seemed a lifetime long.

By the first wan light of dawn the yellowing of Channon's skin was faint, but it had begun. His belly heaved, he spewed up the ale and a lot of blood. With daylight the surgeon returned and produced a knife and bowl. Robin caught his arm before he could begin.

'What are you doing, sir?'

'I shall bleed him,' the man offered.

'But he's already emptied his belly of so much blood. Has he not bled enough without his veins being opened?' Robin hesitated. 'Leave him for the present.'

Knuckles rapped sharply at the door and Robin turned to see Drake himself there. He was alone, and as he stepped into the cabin he closed the door behind him. In the light from the open port he saw the yellow of Channon's face and sighed.

'Aye, we'll leave you,' Robin said softly. He rubbed his neck, tired and sore. 'Will you give us a chance to survive, sir?' Drake's brows rose. 'There's a cove a little way east of here, just a few miles. We could be there by noon, or sooner. I know you want us off the ship at once, but what harm is there if Channon stays locked in here with me, while you take us to Bahia Zarzurro? Do you know it?' He looked away. 'Put ashore in Puerto del Miel, we'll surely die. The cove is safe, with fresh water.'

Drake sighed as he mulled over the proposition, and at last agreed. 'We have the wind at our bow and will make slow time. You're costing me a fair effort, Robin. But I dare say I can afford it.' He frowned gravely at Channon. 'What will I tell your woman and Ned Blythe, when I ship back without you? That you sacrificed your life for an Irish mercenary soldier?'

If Drake told Ned Blythe, it would get back to Blackstead soon enough that the old sins lived on. Robin Armagh was back with the male lover for whom he as flogged. William and Sir Richard would mask their disgrace and say nothing to Ned or Jen. Robin studied Channon's lax, sallow face. He smiled sadly and turned back to Drake.

'Tell my wife and Ned that I owe Channon my life; that Robert Armagh pays his debts, and with God's grace he may live.' He stretched his cramped spine. 'Will you return the ransom to Ned? Tell him how Hal died. Take the butterflies also, for my son. To my wife, take my affections. I'll write a letter if I can. She'll spurn me after this, I know, and I cannot blame her for it.' He shrugged. 'If I am to be an outcast, so be it. Jen will be happiest without me... and I?' He looked into Channon's face. *Without him, there is nothing for me.* Robin forced his mind to practicalities and confronted the surgeon. 'Tell me, how long before I know if he'll live or die?'

The man made scornful noises. 'Few survive, only the very strong-est, and not enough of them to count on one hand! If he lives two days after this, and if you can break his fever, he may survive. Otherwise he'll boil his brains in the oven of his skull, pour out his blood through his belly and mouth, and his heart will fail.' The man seemed to take pity on Robin, and touched his shoulder. 'Pray, lad. It'll do as much good as aught else.'

Pray? Robin had forgotten how. A pail of water was left for him and the cabin locked up from the outside. He heard commands on deck and the ship heeled over as she came about. The bosun shouted to the riggers, all sail was hoisted but the wind spilled and headway was as slow as Drake had promised.

Channon burned. The pulse in his throat beat like the wings of a captive sparrow. Robin stripped and sponged him, but could do no more. He clung to one hope. In three days the *gallizabra* would return to Bahia Zarzurro, and then Pasco and Valdez would help him.

If he survived.

Driven hard, the ship butted through the long Atlantic swell. The morning was a century long and the cabin was hot. Channon twisted, shuddered, at once sweated and frozen. Robin's bones cramped with fatigue as he marked the time by the watches and the patch of sky framed in the stern-port.

No one came to the cabin, save to fetch more water. Robin stripped and bathed, and stretched out on the deck to doze. Channon knew nothing as the wind turned westerly, but Robin felt the change in the movement of the ship. She made better speed, and in the early afternoon he began to listen for the order to cut sail and drop anchor.

Coral spurs just a few fathoms under the keel caught the anchor, and Robin dressed hurriedly. A breeze stirred through the open port as he struggled to get hose and shirt onto Channon. Drifting, deliri-ous, Dermot was mercifully lost to the world.

Footsteps announced company and Robin was not surprised to see Drake and his surgeon as the door was unlocked. No one would touch Channon, and Robin and the elderly doctor managed his weight between them.

'There's a boat for you,' Drake said bluffly, 'and the tide is running in.'

He was still annoyed, convinced Robin was making a grievous

mistake. As Robin hoisted Channon's shoulders over the side, into the boat and stopped to catch his breath, Drake held out a long barrelled wheellock, a poke of gunpowder, a bag of lead shot and wadding.

'Take this. It'll not hold off Indians or Spaniards, but you can bring down a bird and feed yourself. Till you run out of powder.'

'Thank you.' Robin panted as his gear and Channon's was brought up. He had their weapons, their cloaks, and to the wheellock was added an axe, a pail, a coil of rope, a tinderbox, two blankets and a bag of dried fruit and limes.

'Last chance to change your mind, lad,' Drake warned. 'When you see that sail on the horizon, 'tis too late to call us back.'

But Robin was already in the boat. 'My mind is made up, sir. And I am grateful to you.' He offered his hand, but with a pointed glance at Channon, Drake declined to take it. Robin nodded. 'Tell my family what became of me.'

'I will,' Drake promised. He shook his head over Robin with a mix of exasperation and reluctant admiration, then cupped his hand to his mouth and bade the lads hoist the boat over the side.

Robin held tight to Channon as it lowered away. He stirred fretfully as it hit the water. His skin was the colour of old gold now, and blood flecked his lips. Robin looked up at the larboard rail where Drake stood watching. The burly figure waved, but even then the anchor was up and canvas caught the wind.

The tide ran inshore, as Drake had said. As the galleons turned north-east, dwindling into the distance, Robin ran the oars through the locks and began to pull with the current.

Only then did he realise how completely he was alone.

Chapter Twenty-Six

In the evening, when Channon began to shudder with cold, Robin built a driftwood fire. He had threshed in delirium every moment since the boat pulled in through the forbidding heads into the tiny cove, and cried out as he was lifted onto the sand. The boat lay beached on the pebbles above the tidal area, and Robin's first concern was fresh water.

The oars had blistered his hands, and he soaked them in seawater to clean them. Channon lay on their cloaks with both blankets over him, as the moon rose. His skin seemed hot enough to fry an egg, and panic clenched Robin's belly as he began to doubt that he would even live out the night.

Only the strongest survived. Channon had proved his strength time and again, and he was still young. He had every reason to fight for life. Robin ran cool, fresh water between his lips, and his belly emptied again. Old and new blood poured out of him, and Robin washed it away with seawater. Fatigue drained him, and when Channon slept at midnight he slumped down beside him to rest.

Gulls woke him as they dipped over the water, and he jerked awake, astonished to find the sun on the horizon. The sky was blue and clear. He sat, aching and thirsty, and blinked at Channon, but Dermot was still asleep. His skin seemed a little cooler after a night's rest, and Robin took the opportunity to strip and plunge into the cold shallows. The chill of the water stole his breath and invigorated him.

But the cove channelled heat as the sun rose, and soon it was punishing. As Channon began to burn Robin tugged him into the now tepid sea, cradled his head and shoulders and let the ebbing tide strip the fever from him.

They must have shelter soon, or the sun would scorch them. Robin took the axe into the woods that rooted just above the sands and cut down three of the straightest saplings be could find. Set up in a tripod, lashed together with rope and draped with the cloaks, they made a shelter which withstood the wind and kept the sun off Channon.

Robin had never done manual labour and his hands bled. He soaked them in sea-water and bound them with strips cut from the hem of his shirt. Hunger gnawed at him, and he loaded the wheellock and watched for a bird large enough to make a meal.

A marsh fowl came foraging for shellfish in the silt. The shot sent the startled gulls wheeling as Robin waded out to gather the bird. Plucked and gutted, it spattered over the fire. The flesh was dry and fishy but edible.

The stream running off the cliffside was no more than a trickle, but it had eroded a deep channel in the rock. Robin guessed it ran perpetually, and it was the purest water he had tasted since England. He filled the pail again, drank his fill and coaxed water into Channon's mouth. This time it stayed down and hope bloomed as Robin lay in the shade with him to rest.

Three times in the afternoon, he cradled Channon in the tepid shallows. All he could do was keep him cool, give him water when he could stomach it, and wait. Channon was strong, he had every reason to live, if only his delirious mind did not believe he was on an English ship, bound for an English port. Robin dozed wearily as afternoon became evening. The *gallizabra* would return on the evening tide in three days, but to Robin it might have been three years.

'Try, Dermot,' he whispered as he lounged in the shallows, holding Channon's head against his shoulder. 'Try, damn you! You've always been a soldier — fight now!' For a moment the brown eyes opened. Even their whites were yellow, but Robin's heart squeezed. Did Channon know him, was he aware? Then he was gone again and Robin shook himself hard. 'Imagination,' he said hoarsely, tiredly.

That night they slept on a bed of palm fronds, and at dusk Robin gathered enough driftwood to feed the fire till morning. With evening Channon began to shudder again, though the night was not cold. As the trembling began Robin heaped both cloaks and blankets on him, and crawled in beneath them to share his own body heat.

The fever was no worse but Channon grew steadily weaker. He had spewed so much blood from his belly, Robin did not understand how there was a drop left in his veins. If he died, it was the loss of blood that would take his life, and Robin wondered how many men were killed by their own surgeons, who insisted on the common remedy of bleeding them, after they had already bled themselves almost to death.

Numb with fatigue, he was seduced by sleep. His arms were about Channon's chest, their legs were tangled and he was sick with fear and exhaustion. How long he slept he did not know, but animal instinct jerked him awake and he looked into Channon's face in the firelight.

His eyes were open, and for just a moment they were clear, and his hoarse voice was sensible. 'Robin?' he whispered as clumsy fingers stroked Robin's stubbled cheek. 'My lovesome, bonny lad,' Channon whispered in his soft, lilting Spanish, and then was gone again.

Tears stung Robin's eyes and he surrendered to harsh sobs that brought a kind of release.

The jungled hills were filled with wild beasts and the night was impenetrable beyond the ring of firelight. It seemed no other soul was alive in the world, and fear cramped Robin's chest. Only once had he ever before been so alone, and that memory haunted him now. He had waited at the gates of Blackstead, mounted on an old gelding of no value. He waited only long enough to see the coach go by. Channon looked out and lifted one hand as if he might touch. The moment was as final as the severance of death.

Death itself was Robin's enemy now. Dawn was pink and gold, but he watched it wearily, unable to see its beauty. This day, and the night to follow, would be the final struggle for Dermot.

'Fight,' he whispered as he held Channon against him and felt the quick, erratic beat of his heart. 'Fight for me, you black Irish ram! Leave me again and it'll be the death of me, I'll not go on without you.' There was no response, nor had he expected one.

As Channon began to shudder again Robin crawled toward the pile of driftwood to feed the hearth. A day and a night, he thought as he swam in the cold shallows not long after dawn. It seemed an eon, and he wished absurdly that he knew how to pray.

The world was an ocean of deep, burnished blue. For some time he thought it was the sea, but it could not be. His head was pillowed on something warm and soft and he was looking up, not down. He felt no pain or sickness, but he was too weak to move.

It taxed him even to turn his head and examine his pillow, but what he saw brought a tired smile to Channon's mouth. Robin was bare, and he had been naked so long even his hips and legs were tanned like pale copper. He lay with his head on a mound of sand while Channon's own cushion was Robin's belly.

Their bodies were in the wash of the sea. Every sailor's instinct told Channon it was slack water, between tides. It seemed they lay in a tepid bath, a restful and beautiful feeling. Channon stretched. His muscles trembled and he struggled to gather his wits.

He remembered Drake, the English galleon, his questioning... his total subjection to Robin's dominion, a bewildering experience for Channon, who had never before genuinely acknowledged another man as his master. Then, nothing.

Sickness? He shuddered, his inside spasmed, and as he saw the colour of his skin he knew the truth. Yellow Jack. His belly was a void, empty. He must have spewed blood until Robin gave him up for dead.

But it was over. His wits swirled dizzily but even in this groggy state he knew the ship was gone and they were alone, naked as children at play. Robin was asleep, his face drawn beneath his tan and a light beard. It had been an ordeal for him also.

Channon swallowed on a dry, taut throat. Robin had stayed with him while he had jaundiced and bled? Then the little fool had honoured his promise, that he would allow no surgeon to lay hands on Channon.

'Oh, Robin.' He turned over weakly and buried his face in the sun-hot, salty breast. He felt the heavy beat of Robin's heart, felt him stir, stretch, and envied his strength. His lips pressed one plum-coloured nipple, which tasted of the sea, and he lapped blindly at it.

'Dermot?' Robin was hoarse. 'Dermot?' His fingers shook as they knotted into Channon's hair to lift his head.

'Who else, if not?' Channon croaked, and was content to be propped against him. 'What became of us? The last I knew, we were for England, with a decent wind. This is the cove, Bahia Zarzurro.' His eyes obeyed him and he made out the cliffs, the mud flats, the tiny waterfall. Robin's arms tightened painfully about him. 'Gently, sweeting, for a while. I am delicate, remember.'

'Delicate?' Robin demanded as he slid into the water and floated with Channon's head on his chest. 'You are as strong as an ox, or you'd be dead! It has been three days. The ship returns for us tomorrow, but they may not allow us aboard at once. You are still yellow. Better to stay ashore till you are fully well, perhaps. I don't know how a man catches the fever. Surely I should have it, since you've been in my arms all this time! If I am well — and I am, though weary — then the plague panic is for nothing. Still, Pasco and Valdez will take no risks with the crew, and neither will I.'

'Captain Armagh,' Channon teased fondly.

Robin scooped water over his shoulders and rubbed his neck. 'I knew hours ago, you were mending. You kept down a mouthful of fresh water and your fever broke in the night. I simply waited and kept you cool.' He gave Channon a rueful look. 'You're yellow as old parchment, which looks most odd! How do you feel?'

'Weak, dizzy, and so tired,' Channon confessed. 'Drake is gone?'

'Halfway to England, I imagine!' Robin yawned and dipped his head into the water. 'I gave the ransom and Hal's things to him, for Ned and my son. I wrote a letter for Jen, but I said all the wrong things, and I know she'll spurn me... I went to my death in the Americas for the sake of a mercenary Irishman, rather than return home to her.'

'To your death?' Channon turned over in the water and draped his leaden arms about Robin. 'You feel alive, my lad. Gloriously so.' His cheek lay on Robin's chest and his eyes closed. 'I hear your heart. You've paid a high price for me, Robin. Tell me how to earn it.'

'Love me,' Robin whispered. 'And grow strong. Can you eat? I shot some birds earlier. The flesh is dry but not too unpleasant, if you've the stomach for it.'

'Not yet.' Channon accepted Robin's hands to come shakily to his feet. 'I've seen Yellow Jack kill lads who seemed to be half mended. They hunger and eat, and then bleed from the gut until they are gone.'

'As if the gut is wounded,' Robin mused, 'and must be well healed before it will hold food, else the wound reopens?' He held Channon as he staggered.

'I'll eat tomorrow, or the day after,' Channon panted as his thighs spasmed and his head spun. He leaned heavily on Robin as he tottered into the lee of the shelter. Sweat coursed from him with even that exertion but as he sat his wits began to clear again. 'You eat,' he told Robin. 'You're looking like a wraith.'

The breast of a pigeon, a gourd of water, a handful of dried figs, a piece of fish, a slice of lime. Hardly a feast, but Robin fell on the food as if he was famished. Channon drank a little, and the nausea was gone. Robin watched him like a hawk while he drank again.

Then Channon found himself pushed flat in the warm sand and rubbed from head to foot, to work the blood back into his muscles and life into his bones. He lay on his back for his breast to be massaged, intent on Robin's bare, beautiful body, which was thin and hard now.

'You've lost flesh,' he observed quietly.

'As have you.' Robin's hands began to stroke instead. 'You are lean as a boy, as you were when first I knew you.'

'*Te quiero*,' Channon whispered. He held open his arms and Robin lay down beside him. They were both lightly bearded by now, and it was odd to kiss. Channon stroked Robin's back. 'You should have let Drake's surgeon attend to me. It has been an ordeal for you.'

Robin snorted. 'Drake cast us adrift,' he said with rueful humour.

'You cannot have plague on a ship. You're yellow as gold leaf, even now. It'll take days to fade. You fell at my feet by the admiral's table and by morning were like a primrose.' He flushed. 'At first I thought I'd injured you, fucking you as I did. I'll never have you in such passion again. The agony I endured when I thought I had hurt you!'

'Robin,' Channon remonstrated, 'you forget, I am a grown man. It was without compare, you were my master as surely as if I was collared by the neck like a dog. It would not have been sweet to surrender to another, but it was you and submission was my whim.' He brushed Robin's mouth with his own. 'For you, I'd give everything, as well you know.'

If he expected smiles, he was wrong. The spasms racking Robin were nearer grief, his release, after exhaustion and fright. Reviving little by little, Channon summoned his strength and held him while he wept. At last Robin's tousled head lifted.

'What must you think of me? No sooner do you wake than I weep over you.' He struggled to his feet and fetched the pail of water. 'Drink, then let me rub you again, and sleep. The ship will be here tomorrow eve, and I'll not have Pasco and Valdez accusing me of your abuse!'

The sun rose quickly and Channon was content to do as he was told. He lay in the shallows, watching Robin with lazy, passive pleasure as he speared for fish with a lance he axed out of the forest.

How Robin had changed. Where was the cream-skinned, innocent boy who knew nothing of life and less of love, and who came to Channon trembling with fear? Robin was a man now, strong and prideful. Channon loved him as much for his courage as for his gentleness and affectionate ways. And he credited himself as the tutor who had made Robin the man he was.

As the fish spattered over fire Channon's appetite revived but he still refused to eat. Robin had found fresh fruit in the hills, and Channon chewed the flesh for its juice, spat out the pulp and swallowed only the sweet liquid. His belly felt sore inside, and some instinct told him, wounds within must heal before it was safe to eat.

He felt reborn, and in the afternoon he swam a few strokes as Robin dozed in the water. Gulls wheeled overhead, startled from their nests in the cliffs, and he wondered what had roused them.

A moment later he knew.

Voices echoed hollowly from the rocky walls, coarse laughter and

271

singing. Channon heard French and Portuguese, the rhythmic splash of a longboat's oars, the rumble of wood in the oarlocks. He pulled himself back to Robin and shook him. Robin woke with a start and Channon pressed a finger to his lips for silence.

'We're not alone. Listen. Frenchmen, a longboat. Hurry.'

Before the boat was through the narrow heads they had dressed, and Robin pressed a pistol into Channon's hands. Channon shook his head slowly. A single shot was only enough to make men vengeful. Robin had the wheellock, but that also gave them just a single shot.

Five men were in the boat, all of them armed with two or three pistols apiece. As the craft slid into the shallows Channon saw their barrels.

'They've come in for water,' Robin mused. 'They may not find us in the forest.'

'They would.' Channon gestured at the camp, the shelter, the blackened hearth, the remains of the food. 'They'll see this and hunt us like beasts. I'll not be hunted, Robin. If this is where we end, so be it, but I'll not die like a fox.'

'Christ!' Robin's fists clenched. 'No pagan god would bring you through Yellow Jack then give you to death like this. You look dreadful, Dermot. Sit, before you fall.'

In fact, Channon's trembling legs forced him to rest. His head spun and his heart raced. He sat in the shade with the pistol in his lap and watched as Robin went to the water's edge.

The men shouted to him as the boat pulled in, but though Robin answered their French was beyond Channon. He followed not the words but the tone, and he knew at least one voice. It was Raoul Leblanc, and Channon swore softly. Leblanc was the mate and master gunner of Hubert Guillaume's *Pandora*.

Five pistols levelled on Robin and he held up his hands. Leblanc and two others hopped into the shallows and splashed ashore, but the others turned the boat back to the heads, where the *galleasse* waited, to inform Guillaume he had unlikely captives. Robin backed up a step at a time and spoke quietly in Spanish.

'They know your face, Dermot. Have no fear, they'll not lay a finger on you, nor will Guillaume, I promise you.'

'Guillaume will gut me like a haddock,' Channon whispered, 'as he has wanted since we shared moorings on Isleta de Natividad and he sent that harlot of a boy to seduce me. I answered his taunts with

272

a fist in his mouth that night, and he's neither forgotten nor forgiven. He'll have me for it, Robin, and you with me. I am so sorry.'

'And absent-minded,' Robin said drily. 'Look at your skin! Keep your mouth shut and groan. They've already seen the look of plague about you — I told the mate you're dying, and I myself am sickening. We were put ashore at our own request, to spare the others. They'll not approach us. See the mate's face? We affright him, captives or no! Do you know the man?'

'His name is Leblanc,' Channon whispered. 'He is a savage.'

'Yet he frets for his life.' Robin sat on the soft sand beside Channon. 'They've gone for their captain. They think we might even have tainted the water here! Say nothing, let them think the worst.'

The longboat was quick to return. Guillaume stood in the bow, arrogant in white lace and black hose. His shirt gaped to his waist, displaying a smooth, brown and muscular breast, and the long yellow hair cloaked his shoulders. He was beautiful, young, strong, a predator.

Yet even he would not come up the beach. He stood on the wet, hard-packed sand, salt drying on his boots, and laughed in Robin's face.

'Mon Dieu! So I was right,' he said in his thickly accented English. 'The mongrel has been mastered at last.' He dropped a mocking bow before Robin. 'And now he dies, eh? He is yellow as daffodils. And you, Armagh, you are sick also?'

'I grow worse each hour,' Robin lied bitterly. 'I'll yellow and spew blood soon enough. Save your powder, Captain, we are dead men, not worth the price of the shot to kill us.'

'And how are you here?' Guillaume gestured at the cove.

Channon held his breath and Robin said, more or less honestly, 'We were in the hands of *El Draque* for a time. He put us ashore to die, lest he taint his whole fleet. If you had a shred of decency you'd let us die in peace. We've nothing to give you now, Captain, not even our lives.'

For a full minute Guillaume frowned at him. Channon could almost see the corsair's mind working, and at last the blond head shook. 'Nothing so simple, from Channon,' he said banteringly. 'The mongrel has a mind like a snake. Give me your pistols, and the wheellock. Throw them — keep back from me, plague-dog!'

Without a word Robin gathered them and tossed them into the

sand. Leblanc quickly swept them up, and Guillaume seemed satisfied.

'Where is your ship?' he demanded. 'The *Roberto* cannot be far away. I know Channon too well. Tell me!'

Robin sealed his lips and averted his eyes. The pistol in Guillaume's right fist turned aside from his belly and drew aim on Channon.

'Tell me, or I put a ball in his leg. Then his arm, his haunch. He'll die sooner than you, screaming to God. Tell me!'

'All right!' Robin snarled. 'The ship returns tomorrow night, to this cove.'

'Ah,' Guillaume scratched his head with the muzzle of the pistol. 'And the *gallizabra* is shallow-keeled, she can enter this cove, where my ship cannot.' He gazed back at the high, forbidding cliffs. 'One way in, one way out. Ha! A trap. For me, a gift from God. For you, how very unfortunate. But you are dead men before the week is out, 'tis of no matter to you.' His tone hardened to flint. 'Sit with Channon. Say nothing, do nothing, and you live until your ship is here. You will summon Valdez and Pasco in, and then —' He made a throat-cutting gesture. 'I said *sit!*'

Robin sat and listened bleakly as Guillaume barked at his crew in guttural French. They were to leave a company of men on the cliffs, then take the *Pandora* east along the coast and conceal her. The *gallizabra* would enter the cove, lured in by her own captain and his companion, and snipers on the cliffs would cut down the crew without damaging the ship. Guillaume wanted the vessel. For once, the crew was incidental.

No one approached them, and in undertones Robin told Channon the corsair's plans. Channon's face twisted bitterly. 'Damn the man. Why could Drake not have been a few days earlier, and sunk him? If this is God's will, it defeats me.'

'Rest.' Robin drew the pail of water nearer. 'Sleep, and then think. They'll not touch us, not even to manacle us, so we have liberty of a kind — and a day in which to work.' He pressed Channon onto the blankets in the lee of the shelter.

Guillaume and Leblanc pitched their own camp on a slope above the trees, in concealment. In an hour the French *galleasse* had departed, and Robin watched with narrowed eyes as the snipers marked their perches in the rocks. Thirty men carried powder and shot into the crags, enough to fire many times. As night fell, preparations for the ambush were complete, and it was but a waiting game now.

The corsairs withdrew to their camp on the wooded slope, and firelight flickered through the trees as they roasted meat and fish. Channon lay on his belly, chin on his forearms, gazing at the cliffs.

'Either we signal the ship, or we lose her. A flag? We have none. A pistol shot would do, but they took our guns.'

'But not the powder.' Robin added. 'See?' He turned over a corner of the blanket to expose the hessian sack he had carried from Drake's ship. In it were figs, limes, tinderbox, the poke of gunpowder, shot and wadding for the wheellock.

'It might as well be sand,' Channon said sourly. 'What use is powder without a gun? Ah, Robin, this is a bad business. What have I brought you to?' He turned onto his back and rubbed his eyes.

But Robin's mind worried on. The night grew chill and they had no firewood. He thought to gather some, but before he had gone a dozen yards Leblanc's voice halted him.

'Where are you going?' A bark of coarse French. 'Get back with the living dead.'

'Firewood,' Robin said. 'He is frozen, as am I. I shan't approach you, but I must gather wood.'

A pause, then Leblanc's shadowy form retreated. 'Come any nearer and I'll shoot you dead.'

He spat into the sand and Robin passed on to fossic through the tidal sand in the white moonlight. Driftwood was plentiful and dry. Shells crackled underfoot and the sand was littered with gourds, which rolled down from the wooded slopes and lay like lost cannonballs among the pebbles.

It was their likeness to shot that spurred Robin's mind. He knelt, dumped his load of wood and turned a small gourd over in his hands. Its soft insides had rotted away, leaving it hollow. The neck was narrow, the skin thick and hard as iron. He searched his memory for all he knew of gunpowder.

It burned hot and fast, and when it was confined in a shell of cannon-shot or the breach of a pistol, it exploded on contact with flame. Drake had been generous, they had enough black powder to stuff the gourd. But the neck must be sealed, and how could it be touched off? Robin knelt in the soft sand, gazed at the moon and begged for inspiration.

Channon had begun to fret for him and was on his feet when Robin made his way back up the beach with laden arms. Flint and steel struck sparks and in the firelight Channon saw the collection of oddments Robin had gathered. He waited for explanations while Robin kissed him, tugged him to the fire and chafed his cold hands.

'I am no longer an invalid,' Channon protested. 'I am weak but I'll soon be well. Fresh air and clean water are the best medicinals I know. Why are you gathering empty seashells, eaten-out fruit, and stones?'

'Watch,' Robin invited, and set to work.

He turned over a flat stone, wet it and used it to hone the edges of several large shells until they were like razors. Tools, Channon guessed. With these, Robin shaved out the inside of the hollow gourd, insisting that it must be completely dry. He looked often into the east, watching for dawn. Light would betray him.

The sharp shells cut the shape of a plug from a piece of spongy corkwood. Fallen boughs littered the edge of the forest. Channon held the gourd while Robin packed it with all the black powder they had. The plug fit tightly and he dampened it just a little, enough to make it swell into place. Only a knife would remove it.

'A bomb,' Channon observed. 'We have no fuse.'

Robin threw a piece of driftwood into the fire. 'We need no fuse. When Guillaume's men take their places and the ship begins to enter the cove, I'll roll this into the fire. When the wood burns through —'

'It will explode like a cannonball.' Channon took Robin against him and had his bearded mouth. 'I always swore you were the cleverest lad I knew. Pasco said it was love talking, that you were a sweet young boy whose faults I refused to see. Now he'll believe. My *amante* is a scholar, which is above captains and priests.' He kissed Robin's mouth more gently. 'My men already know you as a master pilot. They'll learn soon enough who won them their lives and liberty.'

'I shall be content to leave this place alive,' Robin confessed. 'Let me bury the gourd in the sand under the blankets. Lie on it if the corsairs come near tomorrow. So long as we light a fire by evening, we need only listen for Guillaume's orders. And hope,' he added, 'that Pasco and Valdez act swiftly.'

'They are good men.' Channon set the blankets back into place. 'Trust them, Robin.'

'I trust you,' Robin corrected as he crawled wearily into Channon's

276

arms and put his head down. 'Sleep now. It is almost dawn.'

But Channon was wide awake. He was silent as Guillaume's men appeared with daylight. The fire was out. No one approached, save to stand at a safe distance and shout insults. Channon closed his ears. The corsairs called him Robin's cur, his catamite, a bedslave. Guillaume and Leblanc looked upon them only in passing as they ambled down the beach to look at the snipers' nests. Voices called from the cliffs. All was ready.

Robin woke at mid-morning, stiff and parched. He shouted for water, but Leblanc refused him.

'You want water, fetch it yourself,' the Frenchman told him. 'And walk by the rocks. Come closer, and I will put a hole in your English head, you understand?'

Cursing softly, Robin took the pail and climbed the boulders to reach the trickle of fresh water on the opposite side. Channon lost sight of him in the brush but he was not concerned. Plague was the best shield they could have wished for, like the liberty of the leper, who could pass through the most vile company unchallenged. Soon enough Robin laboured back with the pail and an armful of fruit. Now, they waited.

Afternoon was stifling in the cove. Annoyed in the heat, the corsairs gambled and fought among themselves. The prize was a little blond Dutch boy whose face was painted like a girl's. He wore lace petticoats and was drunk when they used him. He did not seem to notice the abuse. Guillaume was bored with him and had given him away like a hand-me-down.

His new boy was a tall, willowy Spaniard with doe eyes and bronze earrings. If any man set a hand on this youth, Guillaume would lop it, so the Spaniard was his loyal lapdog, and would do anything for him. Until Guillaume inevitably grew bored once more, Channon thought bitterly, and beautiful Zacarias was also given away.

The sun was down behind the landward hills long before sunset, and as Guillaume shouted for the snipers to take their paces Robin seized his last opportunity to gather driftwood. The fire burned low as it had all day, as if Channon was feverish and chilled despite the afternoon heat. Since the corsairs thought him half dead, no one questioned it.

The marksman were scrambling up the cliffs when Robin said quietly, 'You have the gourd to hand, Dermot?'

277

'Bruising my ribs,' Channon whispered. He was still curled on the blankets as if he was half conscious, though in fact he felt greatly recovered. 'The *Pandora* must be a good distance away, or our men would see her on the way in. So the reckoning is only between us and the snipers. They'll wait till Valdez trails oars to stop. When she is dead in the water, slow to move or turn, she'll be easy game. They can rape her as they choose.'

'So our warning shot must come when she's still moving,' Robin mused. 'How long will it take the fire to burn through the gourd? It is a wager, Dermot, you know that. The only wager we have left.'

Channon smiled faintly at Robin's worried face. 'Roll it into the hearth when you see the bow appear through the heads, and if you know how, pray.' He gave Robin his hand. 'It won't be long now. The tide is rising fast. Pasco and Valdez will want high water to be clear of the mudbanks.' He kissed Robin's fingers. 'No matter what happens, know that I have always loved you.'

Robin answered with a smile and began to stack wood into the hearth.

The sky had flushed with rose and gold when the lookouts on the cliffs shouted for Guillaume. Channon did not understand the harsh, bawling French, but Robin touched his hand and nodded. Guillaume retreated toward the wooded hill above the beach. He paused only to fix Robin with a glare and draw aim on his heart.

'Here is your bargain, Armagh,' he said in English. 'When I have the *gallizabra* I shall leave you and your bedslave to the grace of God. Live or die at His will, not mine. But if you speak a word of warning before the fight begins, I shall have the price of it from you when it is finished. You do not look plagued to me, so remain silent and live, or by Christ, I will drown you like a rat.'

He marched away, and Robin began to breathe again. 'Words,' Channon said quietly. 'You said once, words are not worth dying for. Be ready... Robin!'

The high prow of the *gallizabra* had just appeared from the craggy narrows between the headlands. Robin glanced quickly at the woods above them, and bowled the gourd into the bright burning fire. Then he stretched out flat and hid his face in the sand. Channon sprawled beside him, heart pounding his ribs, and they waited blindly.

They heard the creak of timers and hawsers, the splash of oars, the cries of riggers cutting sail. She was through into the cove in moments, manoeuvring carefully so as to avoid the mud, submerged boulders and sands. In minutes she would be dead in the water, and now Channon held his breath.

The concussion was stunning as a wave of heat swept over his back and blazing fragments scattered the sand. It could have been a cannon shot, and at once Channon heard Valdez's voice, shouting up to his own lookout. They would see nothing, no gun emplacements. Now there would be chaos, Channon knew.

A crackle of pistol fire began from the cliffs, too soon to be effective. The ship was still under way and every man aboard was alert to the ambush. Guillaume would be insane with fury, but the same explosion that alerted Channon's crew sprang the trap too early.

The ship still had forward momentum, and oars trailed on the starboard side to bring her about with that nimbleness that earned the *gallizabra* such respect. Gunners scrambled to ready the cannon and marksmen began to fire up into the cliffs before the deck guns had been cleared.

Men fell from the crags, plunging into the water a hundred feet below. A rattle of sporadic pistol fire burst from the slope where Guillaume was concealed and Channon counted seconds. With the swiftness born of fear, he had sometimes seen his men rig for a full broadside of ten guns in under two minutes, but that brief time could seem like a century.

Then the heavy cannon roared, ear-splitting in the confines of the cove, and rock splintered away from the crags. Guillaume's men pitched into the water, some screaming, some silent, among the falling stone. The pistol fire from the woods ceased and Channon dared lift his head.

He saw Valdez in the bow, searching the whole cove with keen, predatory eyes, but as abruptly as the scene had begun, it was over. Channon waved one arm, and Valdez saw him at once.

'Dermot! Dermot, are you well? Who is shooting at us? Where are they?'

Channon stayed down. 'In the woods above the beach, pistols and long barrels, no cannon!' His voice barely carried across the water but the cliffs echoed it back. 'Come about and lay down a broadside into the hill!'

The oars pulled the ship about fast while the larboard gunners rigged to fire again. As the cannon came to bear, blazing shot ripped over Channon's head and pounded the hillside a hundred yards above him. Robin clamped his hands over his ears and swore as the peals of thunder reverberated off the cliffs.

Then, silence. A boat splashed into the water by the *gallizabra* and Channon came warily to his knees. He saw Pasco and a company of six men, heavily armed, and waved.

'Who is it?' Pasco shouted as the boat beached. 'A trap?'

'Guillaume.' Channon stood, weak and dizzy. Robin offered his shoulder, and he was glad to lean upon it. 'He came in for fresh water. We were here and he saw the chance of an ambush.'

'Dermot, you're sick.' Pasco stopped short, several paces away. 'You're yellow.' Fear hushed his voice.

'I was sick,' Channon corrected tiredly. 'Yellow Jack. I am half mended, for which thank Robin. Get up on the hill before Guillaume's marksmen shoot us dead!'

'Dermot.' Robin tugged him about toward the woods, and Channon oathed quietly.

They were coming down, many limping, some bleeding profusely. Hubert Guillaume was hurt. Blood oozed across his chest from a deep gash in his shoulder, but his face was dark with fury.

'So,' Channon said acidly as the corsair halted before him. 'The day is ours.'

'And my crew?' Guillaume asked. 'Many of us are dead.'

'As happens when a battle is lost.' Channon spoke mildly but the words cut like a knife. 'Bury your dead and nurse your wounded. I'll take the boy slaves from you.'

He counted Guillaume's survivors. Forty had come ashore to spring the trap. Nine remained, and most were hurt. The Frenchman wore a sullen face as the boys were led away, but held his tongue.

'If I chose,' Channon said in the same mild voice, 'I could chain you to an oar, as you have chained so many. I could give you to my men for sport, and throw your dead body over when they were done.' He cocked his head at Guillaume as the corsair's pale blue eyes narrowed. 'I was never a vindictive man, nor a murderer, Hubert. If you're to be judged, let your own crew do it, not mine.'

With that he turned his back on Guillaume and walked dizzily to the waiting longboat. Robin studied the corsair for some moments, but said nothing. Channon was right. A commander lived on his wits, his charisma and victories. If he failed, his own men would butcher him and choose a new captain from their ranks. Any captain prospered so long as he was feared or respected, and if that respect wavered privateers looked to their own fortunes. They gave allegiance to no flag and had no code of honour save their own, a brutal honour among thieves. Guillaume had led his men to disaster and they would deal with him more savagely than the pistol ball or the noose he would receive aboard Channon's ship.

At the water's edge Pasco approached Channon warily. 'Dermot, you're yellow as ripe corn. Are you sure you're well?'

In answer, Robin took Channon into his arms. 'If it were plague, would even I touch him? He was ill unto death when Drake set us ashore, but he is recovered.' Pasco was about to press for the story but Robin held up his hand. 'Later. He is still weak, and I am not the best myself. It's been difficult since the Frenchman arrived. The *Pandora* will be here tonight, expecting a victory... we could linger, Dermot, and sink her.'

'Another time.' Channon said tiredly as he stepped into the boat with the dazed slaves, and sat. He gave Guillaume a mock bow. 'Peace and long life, Hubert,' he taunted. 'I don't believe we shall meet again.'

The boat pulled back to the ship, and Pasco shouted to Valdez and Orlando. She came about slowly. The tide was high but Valdez was concerned about the fallen rocks, which had tumbled into the mouth of the cove. He stood in the bow to watch her through, as slowly as she could manoeuvre. Channon would not rest until he saw the open sea.

The cliffs of Bahia Zarzurro dropped astern as the sails caught the wind, and only then did Channon fall, belly down, on the divan in their cabin, and lie like the dead. Robin sat beside him, rubbing his back as he gave Pasco and Valdez a brief account of their struggle. Channon heard every word but could scarcely prise open his eyes. Mate and pilot were grave, silent for some time, and Valdez shook his head over them.

'Many would call you mad, Robin. You should have died.'

'He would have done, had I let Drake beach him alone in Puerto del Miel,' Robin retorted. 'Is it madness to love him?'

'Perhaps.' Valdez smiled as he studied Channon's still faintly yellow face. 'What course?'

Robin paused in surprise. The mate was asking for orders. 'I am not your captain,' he said quietly. 'But I think it is safest to head for home.

281

Drake is gone, Guillaume's affairs are in disorder and Dermot is far from well.'

'Home, then.' Valdez winked at him and closed the cabin door.

Tired and sore, Robin bathed in a pail of water on the chart table, forced a comb through his hair and frowned at his reflection in the polished silver hand-mirror. The man looking back was bearded, drawn and blue about the eyes. He razored his face carefully, drank a cup of sweet wine and settled on the divan beside Channon.

It was a long time before Channon woke. Without opening his eyes he pulled Robin against him and held on. 'We're under way,' he groaned. 'What heading?'

'Rio de San Francisco,' Robin told him. 'Listen.' Valdez was shouting orders. The oars were idle and the deck was at a shallow angle as the ship rode the wind. 'Come and take a breath of sea air.' He coaxed Channon to his feet.

'You shaved,' Channon said abstractly. His fingertips explored Robin's smooth jaw. 'I liked your beard.'

'Did you?' Robin rubbed his cheek across Channon's own, soft one way, coarse the other. 'Silk and hedgehogs! Go out and breathe, blow the last sickness out of you.'

'Upon your order, Captain.' Channon smiled.

'If need be. I only want you well.' Robin would not be mocked. Channon caught and kissed his neck, but for the first time he protested. 'You're in no condition to be a lover to me.'

'I shall be, soon. Be patient.' Channon stretched, pleased to feel the first returning thrill of health and strength. He chuckled as Robin stroked him intimately. 'Allow me time.'

'As long as you need.' Robin embraced him gladly.

A knock announced Pasco. '*Capitan*,' he said through the closed door, 'our table is laid, if you would dine with us. The men are eager for your stories. And we have a tally sheet for your attention. We ransomed a little merchantman for her silver and tobacco, just yesterday. Not a fortune, but satisfying. She sailed back to Havana.'

Channon released Robin with a sigh. 'Let me bathe and dress. Tell them I'll be there shortly.'

'Unless you are... otherwise occupied,' Pasco's voice mocked with ribald good humour.

'We are not!' Robin said sharply, with some final thread of English propriety.

'Not *yet*,' Channon added. 'I think I could break my fast now, but I'll likely disappoint you in bed.'

'Sleep and grow strong,' Robin chided as he poured a bowl of water and tested the edge of a razor. 'All else can wait.'

Chapter Twenty-Seven

Channon slept the sun across the sky and woke again at sunset, when Robin had just begun to fret for him. But when he came to his feet, eager to appease his bladder and bathe, he found himself almost recovered, and healthily hungry. He was only a pale shade of gold by now, which was almost indistinguishable from the brown tan of his skin, and even his eyes were clear.

He gave a grunt of satisfaction as he peered at his face in the mirror, and when his empty belly rumbled he called for Nicolas to fetch a meal. Pickled pork and onions, black bread and salted fish were brought to the cabin, and for the first time he dared eat more than a few bites. Robin watched with a worried frown, but Channon knew he was mended.

With a decent meal inside of him he felt almost well, with only a troublesome weakness in his legs to remind him of the sickness. Valdez said he had been lucky, but Channon would have said, *blessed*, for Robin's presence, without which he could not have survived.

The moon gleamed on the calm surface of the sea. The storms had gone, the wind had died down and the oars worked at a slow pace, pulling them homeward. Channon stood in the stern, gazing at the stars. He revelled in the warm hardness of Robin's lean body against him until he became aware of a movement behind them.

It was the youth, Zacarias, clad only in white hose which were rolled down around his sharp hip bones to display the slender beauty of his body. He wore no trunks, and his groin was hardly concealed by the snug, soft garment. His hair, which was grown long as a girl's, was loose about his shoulders. As Channon and Robin turned toward him he dropped to his knees and bowed his head.

'Yes, boy, what is it?' Channon asked in Spanish. 'And stand. You're not a slave here, there are no slaves aboard this ship.'

Still Zacarias remained on his knees, though he lifted his head. 'Captain, tell me what you want of me.'

'What I want?' Channon frowned at him and then looked sidelong at Robin. 'We've no task for you to do. When we reach our anchorage you may do as you please. You can likely turn your hand to something useful. What were you trained for?'

But Robin had caught some note in the boy's voice, or a light in his eyes, and laid a hand on Channon's arm. 'I believe he means, tell him what you desire in return for his freedom. He wishes to make restitution.'

Zacarias looked down at his body and his back arched intriguingly. 'I was well trained, for your bed.' He pulled back his shoulders and palmed the flat, boyish planes of his chest, little brown nipples displayed between his fingers. 'I've nothing else, Captain, and I am in debt. Let me pay you in what coin I own.'

Soundlessly, Channon groaned and slipped his arm about Robin's waist. 'You owe us nothing, boy. My bed is not empty, I have no need of such service.'

'I know.' Zacarias' eyes flickered to Robin. 'Then let me serve Señor Armagh. Oh, please, let me give you something. I have only myself to give.'

The offer clearly startled Robin. Channon leaned back on the timbers, which were still sun-warm, and regarded Robin's face in the flickering light of several lanterns. 'Well, Robin? Will you have the boy?'

'Will I?' Robin shot him a wary look.

'He's beautiful and willing,' Channon said, teasing, though Zacarias would not know it.

'I know someone else, just as beautiful and willing,' Robin scoffed. 'No, boy, we've no desire to make a whore of you, and our bed is busy enough. Besides, you must have seen enough of that duty to last you a lifetime. Guillaume would not be a gentle master.'

The boy stood, and in the shifting night air passed his hands over his body, which prickled his skin, made his nipples hard as pebbles and swelled his groin. 'Guillaume is a pig,' he whispered. 'I know you'd treat me fair and gentle. If ever you desire me, I am yours at your whim,' he added softly, regretfully, 'for I shall be in your debt forever. Only one thing more could you have done for me.'

'And what was that?' Channon slung his arms about Robin and set his cheek against his hair.

With a grim look Zacarias drew his finger across his gullet. 'Many times I prayed for the blood of Hubert Guillaume to slick my hands. I thought you would kill him.'

'And were disappointed when we did not,' Robin added. 'His own crew will have made away with him by now, and better them than us.'

'Perhaps.' Zacarias rubbed his arms against the slight but growing chill. 'He has the quicksilver tongue of a snake, and he knows many secrets. 'Tis how he keeps command so tight in his fists.'

A thread of curiosity began to spin itself, and Channon's brow creased. 'What secrets?'

'Only Guillaume and Leblanc know where the gunpowder is hidden,' Zacarias said. 'Kill them, and the *Pandora* is without the means to fight. And only they know where the richest of the spoils are hidden — kill them, and the diamonds and emeralds and sapphires are lost.'

Channon digested all this as he rubbed his cheek thoughtfully over Robin's hair and watched the beautiful youth with interest. 'How long did you share Guillaume's bed?'

'Six months.' Zacarias closed his eyes. 'I was taken off a merchant-man. The captain was my uncle, we were bound for Cartagena, but that God-cursed *galleasse* lay in our path.' He looked away. 'My uncle was killed, and I... Guillaume took me for his own.' Little shame roughened his voice now, he seemed merely resigned, though angry.

'And Guillaume took you hunting with him often?' Robin could guess what was in Channon's mind.

'When he would be at sea for more than a few days.' Zacarias closed his eyes. 'Guillaume is a hungry man. Like the wolf he must be fed, often.'

'Then,' Channon went on, 'you're privy to more of his secrets than he'd care to lose.'

The boy's brows arched in puzzlement. 'What is it you desire to know?'

'Can you read charts?' Robin asked more plainly. 'Do you know where Guillaume's anchorage lies?' A little thrill of excitement shook his voice.

'My uncle taught me to read charts,' Zacarias said with a sting of pride he could not have felt since the day his ship had been sunk. 'I never let Guillaume know I had the skill, so he never hid his maps from me.'

'Then you *do* know where his safe haven lies!' Channon stepped forward and caught the boy by the shoulders. 'Valdez!'

Footsteps announced the mate. 'What is it, Dermot? We are well on course.'

'Fetch the charts to our cabin,' Channon said tersely, 'and fetch Pasco, too. This boy is about to earn his freedom in fresh-minted coin you could not have imagined!'

'Guillaume's pretty little whore?' Valdez was surprised.

'And who better,' Robin said quietly, 'to know a man's secrets?'

Several lamps and a dozen candles lit the cabin, and the charts were unrolled, weighted. Zacarias fidgeted and wrang his hands, clearly discomfited. His eyes strayed to the bed, as if he would be much less agitated to simply lie down, bury his face in the pillows and spread his legs. Little more had been demanded of him in months, it was second nature now and he must grow accustomed to freedom.

'Here, and also here,' Channon said tersely, 'we've run Guillaume's gauntlet recently. Here he sank the *Rosamund*. We know he stops at Bahia Zarzurro for water, and we've shared moorings with him on Isleta de Natividad. So we surmise that his safe haven is no more than a week's voyage distant. What do you know, boy?'

If Zacarias had been lying it would have been obvious in his hesitation or blundering about the map, but Robin had been watching him since the charts were unrolled. His eyes had brightened, and skimmed from the Antilles to the Isthmus. He clearly recognised the shapes of islands, the form of the coasts. Hispaniola, Dominica and the great lagoon of the Caribbean Sea.

He pounced at once and a long forefinger stabbed repeatedly at the chart. 'Here, it is here, Isla San Carlos!'

Robin looked up over the table at Channon, Valdez and Pasco. 'Have you ever been there?'

But Channon shook his head slowly. 'It was marked on our charts as a rock in the ocean, with no fresh water, nothing worth our time.'

'It has water,' Zacarias said smugly. 'Leblanc found a spring, deep in the caves, two years ago. It has headlands like pincers, like crab claws, you can't sail into the harbour, for they guard it. From the sea you can hardly even observe the way in.' His eyes gleamed in the lamplight.

'But you, little tyke, you know a way,' Channon guessed.

286

A grin split Zacarias's face from ear to ear. 'Guillaume would kill me if he knew I could read charts. I know the back door into Isla San Carlos — you can crawl up its arse like a leech. But no one knows the island is Guillaume's. From the sea it looks like a barren rock, as you said, and he doesn't guard his arse, for where is the need?'

'Wait!' Valdez held up both hands to stop him. 'Dermot, what are you planning? Do I understand that you wish to raid Guillaume's safe haven?' His face was disbelieving. 'In the name of God, why, when just days ago you enjoyed the devil's own luck, and slipped through the man's fingers!'

With a glance at Robin, Channon pulled up a chair. He sat and steepled his fingers on the charts. '*El Draque* attacked Puerto del Miel looking for gold and was sorely disappointed. Drake found only Recalde's documents. Robin?'

'I translated them,' Robin went on thoughtfully. 'A mule caravan had lately come over the Isthmus from Puerto Veneno, laden with gold, sixty thousand ducats' value, and the bullion was stored, waiting for the *Maria de Huelva*, probably a *gallizabra* out of Havana, due next month. Long before we reached Puerto del Miel they had come under the guns of a privateer who flew a red flag and defeated the garrison easily, as if he knew the port was three parts dead of Yellow Jack.' There he fell silent and cocked his head at the boy.

'He knew,' Zacarias said quickly. 'Recalde had started to send boats down the coast to draw water from Bahia Zarzurro. Who would drink the water in a den of plague? Guillaume captured four men from the barrel boat and flogged them for the truth. Taking Puerto del Miel was easy.'

'As we rode in we saw no damage from a cannonade,' Channon mused.

'There was none,' Zacarias agreed. 'I was on the *Pandora*, anchored a little way eastward, when he took Puerto del Miel. At night Guillaume sent Leblanc and Barthelemy with thirty men, they went ashore west of the harbour and approached from the forest. They shot down the guard and walked into the town when the men who could still stand ran into the hills like frightened goats, to save their own skins. Then the *Pandora* went into the harbour and they brought the gold out by long boat.'

'They went into a plague port?' Pasco recoiled.

But Valdez readily accepted what he had been told. 'For sixty thousand ducats, easily won, there's few men wouldn't take the risk.'

Zacarias's nose wrinkled. 'They had remedies, such as the Indians know. Body and limbs, kept all wet with sea water and lamp oil. You piss on a kerchief and breathe through that, and upon leaving, bathe straight away in salt sea water. No men from the *Pandora* grew yellow, though Guillaume said privately, to Leblanc, he would shoot dead and throw to the sharks any man who did. I heard him.'

'I see.' Channon sat back and studied Robin's face.

So much made sense now. The few people who had survived in Puerto del Miel hid behind closed shutters, and the guards were so anxious that even two shabbily dressed soldiers of fortune were disarmed and arrested.

'So Drake's gold,' Valdez went on, 'is on Isla San Carlos... and you desire to take it, Dermot.'

A shrug, and Channon reached for a jug of wine. 'This lad knows the secrets of that island. Sixty thousand ducats, won easy, as you said.'

'And vengeance,' Pasco added. 'How long have you chafed at that French mongrel? He's been baiting you since he sent that little trollop into your bed, on Isleta de Natividad, and that's two years!' He looked at Robin. 'My apologies. Do you know of this?'

'He told me. Guillaume sent a boy called Luc to seduce him, when you shared moorings,' Robin said indifferently. 'It is of no matter to me, Emil. More important is what this boy knows.' He stood behind Channon, both hands on his shoulders, and pinned Zacarias with a look. 'You described San Carlos as having a guarded harbour, impervious to attack.'

'Aye, and an *unguarded* arse,' Valdez added.

'Help yourself to wine, boy, and explain,' Channon challenged. 'You desire Guillaume's blood with more reason and more zeal that I own, but we'll not go into San Carlos blind. What is this secret?'

The wine was old and sweet, looted off a merchantman, and Zacarias savoured it as if he had not tasted anything so good in a long time. 'Caves,' he said simply. 'Sea caves, on the side of the island that is fortressed by cliffs. They run along the waterline, birds' nests around them. No one knows that they go up through the whole island and come out where the fresh water spring rises, above the lagoon. If you know the way you can go through in an hour.'

'And you know the way?' Channon leaned back in his chair and covered Robin's hand with his own, on his shoulder. 'Tell me how you know.'

Zacarias's eyes widened. 'You think I am lying to you? I would not! I owe you everything!'

'Hush,' Robin coaxed. 'We know you're not lying, but do you think we've lived this long by being reckless?'

He took a breath, wiped his mouth and cleared his throat. 'I was a prisoner, but how can you escape from an island? They didn't lock me up or guard me, and when Guillaume took the ship out without me for a few days I could roam where I fancied. Men wouldn't be seen with me, for fear of Guillaume's anger. No one was allowed to fuck me, my arse was only for Guillaume and he'd cut the balls off any man who defied him and touched me.' He might have sounded self-satisfied, but Zacarias seemed merely relieved that his nightmare was over. 'The caves are cool in the heat of day. I was bored, so I took a lamp and started to explore, and I chalked my way on the walls so as to find my way back. I thought that the secret store of powder and the diamonds and emeralds must be in the caves. If I found them I could woo men like Fernando and Pierre, they'd kill Guillaume for me and set me free in gratitude.'

The story was sincere and Channon was impressed. He stood, hands on hips, looked from Robin to Valdez and Pasco and back again. 'If we approached the blind side of the island by night and entered through the caves, a handful of men might disable the harbour's defences.'

'What *are* the defences?' Robin asked shrewdly. 'And how many men are on Isla San Carlos?'

They were all looking at Zacarias, and the boy's brow creased in thought. 'Not counting the *galleasse*'s slaves, no more than a hundred men and boys, and of those many are but doxies. Bumboys — ' his voice dropped — 'like me.'

'Many of the fighting men were killed at Bahia Zarzurro,' Valdez added, warming to the scheme. 'Guillaume's crew has never been so delicate. And I'd wager, strike free the slaves and bedboys, and they'd be pleased to fight with us.'

'And the harbour defences?' Channon pressed.

'Four heavy cannon lifted from the hulk of a galleon,' Zacarias told him, 'set into stone mountings, pointed at the headlands, where a ship must come through.'

'Ah.' Channon rubbed his hands together, a small expression of delight. 'Spike those to split themselves wide open the instant they are fired, and San Carlos is defended only by the *Pandora* herself. And if her slaves were of a sudden cut loose, her fangs would be drawn. Robin?'

Robin cupped his hands at Channon's nape, massaging lightly there as he met Channon's bright eyes. 'We need to know much more, but... I smell something sweet about this. With Guillaume's cache in our holds we could be bound for Spain before the year is out.'

'Spain?' Zacarias said eagerly. 'You are for Spain?' Then he remembered his manners and flung himself to his knees. 'Oh, take me home. Please God, take me home.'

'You're from Vigo or thereabouts, by your accent,' Channon guessed. 'You have family left?'

'My father had five ships, I was to command one of them one day,' Zacarias said bitterly. 'I was on my third voyage, learning my trade with my uncle, when...' He looked up at Channon with wide, imploring eyes. 'Take me home.'

'One day, and soon, I think,' Channon said thoughtfully. 'For now, we'll bid you all good night.' He gestured at the charts and Valdez quickly rolled them. 'As Robin says, we need to know much more.' He smiled. 'But it smells sweet as honey.' He kissed Robin's mouth lingeringly as Valdez and Pasco stepped out.

It was some moments before they realised Zacarias was still in the cabin, hovering beside the divan. He had rolled down his hose until his groin and buttocks were barely covered, and as Channon noticed him he bared himself to the thighs and lowered his head.

'I was well trained,' Zacarias mumbled as he displayed a boyishly slender cock, small but ripe balls, and then turned and bent forward to show his pale, peach backside with its dark inviting cleft.

Amusement and reluctant affection were at odds with Channon's slight annoyance. He reached over and dealt the boy's rump a smart swat. Zacarias jumped and sprawled on the divan, panting, but Channon jerked his thumb at the door. 'Show me how excellently you were trained by following my orders to the letter. *Out*, boy, have some supper and find a lad of your own age to wriggle with for pleasure. How old are you?'

'Fifteen,' Zacarias struggled to his feet and rolled up his hose. 'All but two months.' He hurried to the door and dropped a deep bow before them. Then he was gone.

Exasperated and amused, Robin sank onto the side of the divan and looked up at Channon. 'Was I like that?'

But Channon shook his head as he set aside his clothes and snuffed the candles for the night. 'You were eighteen years old when I met you, very nearly a man; a scholar, prideful yet needful. You needed to be liberated, a service I was delighted to provide.' He stepped into Robin's arms and nuzzled his neck. 'I might be a lover to you tonight, if you coddle me and be gentle.'

'Then rest and let me attend to you.' Robin pressed him onto the bed, fluffed his pillow and stood in the light to undress.

Naked, wide awake and feeling much more himself, Channon watched with lazy, admiring eyes. Still, his cock was reluctant and he grasped it firmly, demanding that it stand up as Robin straddled his legs with a quick, easy erection Channon envied. Not until Robin's own hands began to stroke did he begin to feel the first real thrills of excitement, and then he lay back and let Robin do it all.

A salve gleamed on him, root to crown, and Robin lifted up to take him inside with a grunt, a curse, a long sigh. Channon stretched from shoulders to toes beneath him and watched as he began to rock and ride. That unmistakable man-musk prickled the nostrils, and Channon smiled as he filled his hands with the very jewels of the Armagh clan. Robin paused to rest, panting, gleaming with a film of sweat. But he had his wits and said teasingly, 'Did you desire Zacarias?'

Channon refused to be teased. 'No. He's almost a child, he has been a bedboy so long he knows nothing else. He is less beautiful, less willing and skilled than my *amante*, and I am not in love with him. Why should I desire him?'

The green eyes warmed and Robin leaned down to kiss. The bulk inside him shifted, arousing a gasp as Channon's hands slid down his taut spine, cupped his wide-spread buttocks and explored between to discover the hot, slick place of their joining.

'Besides,' he murmured breathlessly as Robin began to move again, 'Zacarias is more useful for what he knows. And *that*,' he added as he firmly grasped Robin's own cock, 'has nought to do with *this!*'

Chapter Twenty-Eight

Before the lookout shouted that he had seen the mouth of the Rio de San Francisco, Channon's colour was normal and his appetite as healthy as Robin's own. Robin was still weak with relief, still fussing over him, which earned him many a chuckle and the occasional teasing slap to his backside.

But Channon was preoccupied, and when Valdez asked if the *Roberto* would be putting out again to hunt after they had taken on fresh food and water, he made negative noises.

In the cottage by the river the lamps burned till the early hours, the night the ship tied up. Before Zacarias was allowed to lay down his head he had drawn a map of the whole island of San Carlos, sketched the caves, marked the fresh-water source and the cannons, and recounted everything he knew of the loose, careless routine Guillaume's crew followed.

When those men returned from a successful expedition they were drunk and debauched the whole night, and indisposed the day following. Zacarias squirmed on his chair as he told this, and Robin frowned deeply. On such occasions, when Guillaume's passions ran hottest, a bedboy's duty would be difficult. He caught Channon's eye, and Dermot sighed quietly.

The best time to come upon San Carlos was directly after some ship had fallen prey to the *Pandora* and her crew was insensible with wine and whores. Zacarias agreed to this without hesitation. If the guns were disabled and the slaves cut loose aboard the *galleasse*, Isla San Carlos was as helpless as a day-old kitten.

They let the boy go then, and Robin closed up the shutters. The plaster-walled cabin was quiet and private. He had come to think of it as home, and gave it a rueful look as Channon went over his papers a final time.

'I'll be more homesick for this place than ever I was for Blackstead or Ned Blythe's house,' he said self-mockingly. A shutter banged and was latched. He leaned on it to look at Channon, who sat at the table. 'You promised me Venice, Rome and Florence after we've discharged our duty in Spain.'

'I did.' Channon folded the papers and weighted them with a

lamp.

'Promise me something else,' Robin insisted. 'That we'll return home, here, when Venice and Rome have grown stale, and like prisons.'

Channon stretched his back and smiled indulgently. 'Would you relish a house like the Governor of Havana's residence, right here, where this cabin stands? And two or three *gallizabras* flying our own flags, plying between Havana and Santander upon our business, so legitimate that we must pay taxes to the Crown. No more privateering, unless we long for the thrill of danger.'

Robin's eyes widened. 'Is it possible?' Yet he knew it was. The storehouse along the river was filled to the rafters and they had Guillaume's hoard almost within reach. Robin swallowed hard and for a moment allowed himself to dream. Channon was waiting, wearing a faint smile, not mocking but unashamedly, unabashedly affectionate. Robin cleared his throat and slipped both his hands into Dermot's, on the table. 'I'd like all that very much.'

'Then you'll have it,' Channon promised. 'Guillaume has left us a rich legacy which should be ours for the taking.'

'You speak of him as if he were dead,' Robin observed.

'If he's not, he has more lives than an alley cat,' Channon said drily. 'He led his crew to disaster at Bahia Zarzurro and they'd swiftly settle with him, and with Leblanc. We'll meet another captain on that island.' He drummed his fingers on the folded papers and his brow creased. 'And still, we must know more before we dare run that gauntlet.'

'Sail by and use your own eyes,' Robin suggested. 'Isla San Carlos is but three or four days east of us, lost in the labyrinth of the sea. God's teeth, little wonder no one has stumbled over it — there are more islands and islets than ants on an anthill!'

'We'll go soon, in a few days,' Channon said thoughtfully, 'while the weather is favourable. We need news of the *Pandora*, where she is, who commands her, what fate befell Guillaume. I'll show you Isleta de Natividad.'

'Where you share moorings with other corsair ships on occasion, and those captains should have news of Guillaume.' Robin began to undress him, as if Channon were still unwell. 'Dangerous?'

'Not since this ship and crew forged a reputation that's widely respected,' Channon said grimly, and caught Robin's head to kiss.

✧ ✧ ✧

The July sky was burnished blue and in the afternoon the sun beat down with a ferocity Robin had never imagined. August would be even hotter, Channon told him, but in September the rains came and it could deluge till Christmas.

A mile offshore the temperature dropped and the wind freshened, but it was still hot enough. Robin was pleased to strip naked with several of the other men, stand in a hooped wooden tub and pour a pail of water over his head. He was tanned almost all over, the colour of a fallow deer, and Channon watched him with idle admiration as he bathed. Other eyes watched too, but while Orlando and Valdez, and even precocious young Zacarias might savour Robin's good looks, they knew better than to approach him.

The *gallizabra* turned east as she left the river, and before her were the islands, reefs and shoals between the Isthmus and Cartagena. These could be dangerous waters, for the privateers were hidden in coves and inlets too numerous to be charted. Even warships stalked their prey cautiously. In the open sea Channon would have set every scrap of canvas and made good speed, but travelling into these regions he chose stealth, and had the crew stand by both guns and oars.

Twice they saw sails at a distance, and both times stole swiftly into the lee of rocky outcroppings that thrust like spurs from the ocean. Those vessels flew the flags of Spain and King Philip, and from their speed and sail plan Channon knew them as *avisos*, dispatch boats quite capable of carrying news from Havana to Spain in twenty-eight days. *Gallizabras* were not so plentiful that the old *Esmerelda* might not be recognised on sight even now, and the danger was very real.

Two days east of home, she cut speed again and the crew manned the oars. Robin had been dozing through the heat of afternoon, stretched out near-naked under a canopy in the bow with Zacarias and the Dutch youth, whom he was teaching both Spanish and English. The boy spoke only his native tongue and some broken French, and was fettered by language. He was sober now, blond and pretty, at once disturbingly wise about men yet amusingly childish. Channon found him a troubling creature and hardly knew what to do with him.

294

As the timekeeper's hammer began to beat and the oars dipped into the water, Robin roused and padded barefoot in search of Channon, who was in the stern with Valdez.

'We're under oars, Dermot?' he asked curiously.

Channon gestured to the larboard bow. 'We'll come upon Isleta de Natividad before long, and I'll have the guns manned too.' He looked Robin up and down with a perplexed expression. 'Never did I imagine I would insist upon this, but — put on your clothes.'

Robin laughed rudely. 'I disbelieve my ears!'

'He means,' Valdez elaborated, sharing their humour, 'Natividad is filled with wolves... and one among us is a tender young lamb.'

'Indeed?' Robin was hardly surprised. 'In that case I'll wear sword and pistols, as well as my clothes.'

'And stay close by me,' Channon added soberly, 'or you'll likely have to fight. They don't know you, Robin.'

'But they do know you?' Robin's brows arched and he cocked his head at Channon. 'What wildness have you been up to?'

'Not wildness, Robin,' Valdez said softly when Channon declined to answer. 'Survival.'

'Dermot?' Robin set a hand on his arm.

He seemed to force a smile and touched Robin's face with his knuckles, and before he could speak the lookout called from the masthead with a sighting of the island. Robin hurried aft and dressed swiftly in fresh linen, his leathers and the first shirt that came to hand. Into his belt he thrust a pair of ivory ball-butted pistols, and then buckled on his sword.

'Better,' Channon said drily as he stepped back on deck. 'And *that* is Isleta de Natividad.'

It was a tongue of land with a saddle-backed hill and a natural harbour of clear, blue-green water at one side, but Robin saw nothing special about it until they were much closer. Only from the eastern approach to the craggy, jungle-clad islet could one see the steeply sloping beach of yellow sand, so ideal for hauling a ship out of the water for repairs in a place where no boatyard or slipway existed. A carrack lay beached while a dozen men daubed her keel with a fresh coat of stinking black tar, and a small frigate stood off, awaiting her turn.

The last sail dropped and the *gallizabra* floated into the cove under oars. Her anchors pulled her up quickly, before the water began to shallow. Above the beach was a cluster of two score buildings, thatched with palm fronds. Robin shaded his eyes and saw a market-place, longboats upturned and fishing nets drying in the sun; a mongrel dog yapping at two tethered donkeys, and a string of half a dozen men with ebony-black skins and manacled limbs, sitting in the shade of the palms above the beach.

'Slaves from the Guinea Coast of Africa,' Channon said quietly as Pasco shouted for a boat to be lowered. 'There's nothing to be done for them, Robin, they're someone's property, and have been since their own chief sold them. Did Hal tell you that?'

'That the Guinea chieftains sell the surplus young men of their tribe for labourers?' Robin sighed. 'He heard that from John Hawkins, but how hard I find it to believe.'

'Yet each Guinea tribe captures slaves from the others along their coast,' Channon added. 'So did the Irish raid for slaves in Saint Patrick's day, and you've read of the Greeks! The practice of slavery is as old as time... and as wicked as sin.' He gestured Robin toward the boat. 'Come ashore, stay close to me and keep your eyes wide open.'

'You smell trouble?' Robin hesitated, one hand on the side of the longboat.

Channon gestured at the beached carrack. 'That's the *Marianna*, I knew her at once. Mateo Alvarez took her and sold her crew, a year ago.'

'Alvarez,' Robin whispered. 'I've heard you speak of him. A cut-throat, you said.'

'So I did.' Channon stepped into the boat and beckoned Robin beside him. He smiled thinly as he gestured at his own sword and pistols, and the five armed men who accompanied them. Before the boat lowered away he cupped a hand to his mouth. 'Emil!' Pasco waved and Channon went on, 'Have the gunners take aim on that carrack. At the first pistol shot, smash it to driftwood!'

Standing in the middle of the boat, Robin made wry noises. 'You have Alvarez over a barrel — his ship is your hostage before we even set foot on the beach.'

'And the bastard will be assured of it without a word from me,' Channon affirmed. 'Today he'll be polite. He'll show my *amante* his best manners, or he knows he'll row home in a longboat.' Their own boat swung overboard as he spoke, and he grasped the side to steady himself. 'Mind,' he added cynically, 'next time our positions could be

296

reversed, so it would profit us also to be polite!'

The boat hit the water with a heavy jolt through the spine. Robin took the tiller as Channon ran the oars through the locks, and their escort of five men shinned down by the ropes. Then they were away, and behind them the *gallizabra* swung a little about her anchor lines to present the broadside of her starboard guns to the *Marianna*.

Several dozen men lounged above the beach, watching suspiciously. Alvarez's crew would be among them, and Robin saw a young lad run swiftly into a low, squat building which fronted onto the market square. As the longboat rushed through the gentle, lazy breakers and its bottom ground up onto the fine sand, he saw a figure appear in the deep, blue well of shadow under the overhanging thatch of palm fronds.

'There,' he said softly to Channon, 'the brawny man in the hat. Would that be Mateo Alvarez?'

Channon had seen him a moment before. 'A whoreson brute, but handsome in his way,' he said acidly. 'A bastard from the gutters of Corunna. He was flogged once too often, and led the mutiny on the *San Esteban*. He wears his scars like a banner, brags of them as if he's the only man who has ever felt the sharp end of a lash.' Channon stood carefully as the waves thrust the boat higher onto the sand, jumped over and gave Robin his hand. 'Pay Alvarez no mind. His noise is like an empty wine jar in the wind.'

Yet the man's eyes were as shrewd as a crow's, predatory, and Robin felt a tangible menace about Alvarez as he walked with Channon, off the soft sand and into the upwelling of early afternoon heat which cloaked the shoreline. Haze rippled about the hillsides above the tiny town, where a flock of green and scarlet parrots squawked and swooped. Sweat prickled Robin's sides. He plucked at his shirt and cursed the snug fit of his leathers.

He fell into step with Channon as they came up into the shade, and he saw that the building where Alvarez stood was a tavern. The beery smell of old ale issued from within, where someone was playing a mandolin and a pan of onions had just begun to sizzle. Several of the privateer's men sat in the shadowed corners within, but though their pistols lay naked on the tables in obvious warning, no one approached.

Mateo Alvarez was small. His head was only level with Robin's chin, but his shoulders were broader than Channon's, he had a chest like a plough horse, and while the girth of his arms and legs was astonishing, there did not appear to be a pinch of fat anywhere upon him. He was burned almost as dark as those Guinea slaves, and his eyes were nested in creases. He was ten years Channon's elder, if Robin was any judge; his curly black hair was still abundant, but showed a liberal sprinkling of silver. He wore a thick gold ring in his right ear, but where the ring in the left would have been the lobe had been torn away in a fight, likely by the ring itself. He wore not a gentleman's hose but the working man's breeches and boots, a thick leather belt into which were thrust twin pistols, sword and dirk. His face was as wary as Robin would have expected.

'The plague dogs have returned from the dead,' he growled by way of greeting, in gutter-accented Spanish.

'A ruse, Mateo,' Channon said smoothly. 'Guillaume was easily gulled, that day was ours.'

'So I heard.' He grinned insolently at Channon, showing surprisingly good teeth, and doffed his wide-brimmed, brown leather hat with mock civility before Robin. 'Hubert was always simple-minded.'

'Pickings have been good?' Channon asked guardedly. 'The last I saw of you, you were hunting with Guillaume.'

'The hunting's been like shit,' Alvarez told him. 'You don't leave much for us, Channon.'

'You never risk the dangerous waters where the best game runs,' Channon retorted.

'In a leaky *carraca*?' Alvarez snorted, and his narrowed eyes skimmed lustfully over the *gallizabra*. 'We hunt with Guillaume for the safety of his guns, 'til we can seize a good ship.'

'Like the *Roberto*,' Channon finished. 'Get your eyes off it, Mateo, that one's not for you.'

A rumbling laugh answered him, and Alvarez tilted his head at Channon, though his eyes flickered to Robin. 'So Hubert was telling the truth. I called him a liar.' He stood aside to allow Channon to step into the tavern.

Robin was on his heels, and three of their armed men, while the other pair remained at the door to keep watch. A single pistol shot, and every man here knew the carrack was driftwood. Robin was not concerned.

The tavern was dim, smoky, companionable. Ship's planking had been sawn up to make benches, tables and a long tap-bar where several kegs stood. A grossly fat, toothless old Portuguese was drawing tankards of ale. The onions spattered in a skillet on a brazier nearby, and a drowsy, honey-skinned young *zambo* stirred them with the tip of a dirk.

'What truth did Guillaume tell you?' Channon asked as he took a cup and passed a second to Robin. He was trying to appear indifferent, and perhaps only Robin knew the truth. Dermot was eager for news of his old enemy.

'That you've taken up with a mate. A *bed*-mate,' Alvarez elaborated as he threw down his hat and perched his muscular buttocks on the edge of a table. 'An English gentleman who fucks Channon like a boy and gives him orders on his own deck.'

For a moment the silence was pregnant and heavy, and Robin held his breath. Channon looked into his cup, lips compressed, and Alvarez was clearly waiting. This was the wrong time and place for an eruption of fury. Robin swallowed hard before he produced a ribald chuckle and thrust his hand at Alvarez in greeting.

'Good day to you, Captain,' he said in his accentless Spanish as Alvarez briefly clasped his wrist. 'I'm Robin Armagh, and Guillaume told you but half the truth. Aye, Channon has a bedmate, but his companion is just the pup you see before you. Dermot was ploughing me when I was a skinny boy. He finds that pleasure in me still, though I'm a man grown.' Deliberately, he tucked himself into Channon's side. 'Give the captain orders on his own deck — and suffer a strap-smarted rump?' He laughed derisively. 'By God, Guillaume could tell a good jest, I'll give him that. I know what a lash feels like, and I know how to mind my manners.'

'You?' Alvarez's dark eyes widened. 'The English rose has been whipped?' He chuckled fatly. 'You also tell a good jest.'

'Do I?' Robin looked sidelong into Channon's wary face and tugged loose his shirt. The linen pulled over his head and he turned to display his back. 'Lessons are often painful, Captain. One flogging was enough for me, and if you imagine I'd attempt to command Channon on his own ship, how wrong you are.' He tugged his shirt to rights and slipped an arm about Channon's waist. 'I'd sooner have kisses. I know how to earn those too, and 'tis not with quarrelsome words.'

Tension almost froze Channon's spine but Alvarez was persuaded, the moment was smoothed over. He drank, belched and wiped his mouth, and at last Channon found his voice.

'Who captains the *Pandora* now?'

'Hubert, who else?' Alvarez gestured for another cup.

'Guillaume is alive?' Channon took a step forward. 'The survivors of his crew did not gut him like a fish?'

Alvarez's black, bushy brows arched. 'Almost did they cut off his cock and stuff it up him... but not quite. Next time he won't slither around them like a snake.' He shrugged indifferently. 'He stopped here two days ago to repair sails. I've been here a week, with a *carraca* that takes water like a colander.'

With a long, quiet breath Channon sat on the bench behind him and stretched out his legs. He looked blindly at the toes of his boots and seemed oblivious of Robin's hand on his shoulder. Alvarez had his nose in his mug.

'Guillaume was bound for home?' Robin asked carefully.

'So he said.' Alvarez made a face. 'Now, he dare not turn his back on his own men. One day, soon maybe, they'll nail the mongrel to the deck. They lost friends at Bahia Zarzurro.' He looked at Robin as he spoke. 'You wish him dead?'

'Channon has a few old scores to settle.' Robin tried the ale, found it warm and bitter. He set down the cup and gripped Dermot's shoulder tightly. 'Captain?'

At last Channon stirred. 'We'll doubtless meet again, Mateo,' he said curtly to Alvarez, and as he saw the other man's eyes covering his companion's body with growing interest he took Robin under a possessive arm. 'This is another thing you can take your eyes off, for you'll have none of it.'

'You'd fight for him?' Alvarez licked his lips. 'An appetising morsel, this one.'

'He fights for himself,' Channon snapped. 'He's a man, or are you sightless of a sudden? Lay a hand on him, and you'll learn how painful lessons can be.'

'You stole Hubert's bum-boy.' Alvarez chuckled crudely. 'He wants your balls, Channon. He swears he'll pay a hundred ducats to the man who trusses you like a pig for slaughter.'

Channon smiled thinly. 'A bounty on my balls, eh?' His right hand cradled the butt of one pistol. 'And what price do you put on yours, Mateo?' He paused, watching Alvarez's eyes narrow, and then gave Robin a gentle shove. 'We'll be leaving now. If you meet Guillaume, tell him to come and truss me himself... if he has the belly for a fair fight.'

The crew of the *Marianna* hung back as Channon, Robin and their escort strode onto the soft, hot sand, and there Channon stopped. At the waterline, hands on hips, he glared about the ramshackle privateers' town. Robin felt Alvarez's eyes on him, intent and hungry, and shivered despite the heat of the sun on his back. These men obeyed no law but their own, and when they broke it only men stronger than themselves could exact any penalty from them.

'See the house, there,' Channon said tersely, 'by the marketplace. I was trading pearls and gems which we had in abundance, for powder and shot which were scarce. I bedded under that roof just a single night, and Guillaume could not forswear the opportunity to bait me. I'd had a cup or two of wine and barely was my head on the pillow when a warm little body slid in between the sheets with me — all soft, thin limbs and uncut hair, so that I thought it was a girl until he got my hand between his legs.'

'The likes of Guillaume and Alvarez would have called it a good jest,' Robin hazarded. 'Perhaps you should have laughed.'

'I was more disposed to anger at the time,' Channon said tersely. 'For I was wanting you, and had by then begun to despair of ever setting eyes on you again.' He strode away toward the boat, speaking over his shoulder. 'I had my plans, though. You'd have waited another year at longest before you thought you saw a ghost at the door of Ned Blythe's shop.'

'You'd have risked a voyage to England?' Robin sounded dubious.

Channon lifted himself into the boat and took the tiller. 'A Hollander would have brought me in, and I can pass for an Irishman when I set my mind to it.' He braced himself as the boat was shoved out into the surf. 'There's nought to be gained from dwelling on the past. Let it be, love, and fret for the future instead.' He paused. 'Alvarez liked your looks. If you meet him in future, be wary.'

'I will.' Robin deliberately half drew his sword. 'You've never seen me fight in earnest. One day you might. I'd wager I have Alvarez's measure, for he's much older than you and much shorter than me, though, by God, he looks strong as an ox.'

'Stronger,' Channon corrected. Right hand on the tiller, he rested his left on Robin's knee. 'What you said to soothe the situation when he began to taunt was well spoken, but a cruel deception. I'd never leather you, nor any man.'

'I know that,' Robin said drily, 'but Alvarez doesn't, and I'll warrant he keeps discipline in his own house with the strap. Dermot, I said what I knew he'd best understand. The guile was for him, not for you.'

'Aye.' Channon took a deep breath of the warm, languid sea breeze, leaned over and kissed Robin's mouth deeply as the long-boat pulled back toward the ship.

'Do we go hunting, or do you want to sail for home now?' Robin asked when he was permitted to speak once more.

'Neither.' Channon was brightening with every stroke of the oars. 'We'll sail by Isla San Carlos and compare what we see with Zacarias's drawings.' His teeth worried his lip for a moment. 'I think I must settle with Guillaume very soon. He's been the thorn in my side for years and is more dangerous now than ever. If he bolsters his position with his crew once more he'll surely become my nemesis, and now... I've so much to lose. Fear grips my belly like a fist, for he knows where lies my one weakness. You.' He looked bleakly into Robin's face. 'I'd sooner kill you myself, quick and clean, than let Guillaume have you.'

'So we are gunning for a corsair,' Robin guessed as his pulse quickened and his heart beat heavily at his ribs.

From some unexpected reserve Channon produced a smile. 'If you're game for it.'

Robin mirrored his wry, reluctant humour. 'I am, Captain.'

Anchor chains rattled up as the longboat was hoisted back aboard, and with a shrewd face Pasco took orders to steer for San Carlos, which lay a day further east, through the labyrinth of scattered islands.

Would Alvarez, next time he saw Guillaume, tell him that Channon was gunning for him? Robin believed he would, but the news would come as no surprise to Guillaume. This rivalry was too precarious, too dangerous to continue, and Guillaume was no fool. The time of reckoning was long overdue.

The wind was a gentle north-westerly and the sky remained fair, cloud-scattered but bright. Crews stood by the *gallizabra*'s twenty cannons at every moment, but they had still seen no sails late the following afternoon, when Valdez called from the bow that he glimpsed a spur of rock in the sea that was the Isla San Carlos.

'Cut sail!' Channon bawled. 'Come starboard and put us in the lee of that sugar-loaf, we'll skulk around by moonlight!'

The sugar-loaf was the crest of a mountain, breaking the surface of the water just higher than the masts of a ship, inhabited only by screeching seabirds. San Carlos lay five miles eastward, and from the masthead the lookout could see clean across the barren rock to Guillaume's safe haven.

Satisfied, Channon sent for a meal and sprawled on the divan to eat while the sun sank westerly. Not until the last trace of daylight was almost gone did he give Pasco the word to up-anchor.

The moon was like a lantern and the stars blazed so brightly, Robin fancied he could read by them. Every light was doused on deck, and although crews manned both guns and oars they approached San Carlos with the ghost-like silence of the wind. Zacarias was on the larboard rail, straining his keen young eyes as they ran in closer, under the cliffs.

'There!' he said suddenly, pointing. 'See where the caves come out into the sea at the bottom of the crags? I found my way right through, and swam there! My chalk marks must still be on the walls. 'Tis an hour's walk through the black bowels of the mountain, and then up into the daylight and air on the hill, where the caverns open in the forest above the lagoon.' He turned to Channon, wide-eyed and earnest. 'I tell you only the truth, Captain.'

'Because you long to see Guillaume squirming at your feet,' Channon said quietly. 'Oh, I believe you, boy. You've every reason to connive at his death. Valdez, take us well out and then swing about the island.'

'They may see us if they've posted lookouts,' Pasco warned.

'They'll see a sail in the moonlight, too far away to be recognised,' Channon amended. 'And even if Guillaume saw us and knew us, what of it? He'll not come out and fight, for he knows we'd chop him to driftwood; and if this boy is right, even Guillaume is ignorant of his own back door.'

Zacarias smiled, white-toothed in the moonlight. 'No one knows the way through, Captain, I swear it.'

'Good enough,' Channon said softly as the *gallizabra* passed by San Carlos, well seaward, and began to come about.

And there, as Zacarias had promised, were the crab's pincers of the headlands which guarded the natural harbour: high and rocky, with just enough leeway for a ship to make safe ingress under oars, though a vessel without the benefit of oars must be warped through by longboat.

It was like playing chess with the sea, Robin thought as he stood at the larboard side, forearms on the warm timbers, and studied the island. 'If the guns guarding the entrance were spiked, the explosions would be heard a good distance away. If this ship were waiting out here she could slip through heads, lay a broadside into the town and sink the *Pandora* if needs be.'

'And in the disorder,' Valdez added, 'we would sweep unchallenged through that land-locked little cauldron.' He nodded, satisfied. 'Aye, Dermot, I'll be with you.'

Channon looked from face to face, among the crew who had gathered about them. 'We crouch like a spider in a web and watch for the *Pandora* to return home low in the water under the weight of a looted cargo, and when Guillaume's men are blind with drink, as is their habit, we pounce under cover of darkness. A squad of men through the caves, with Zacarias to guide them... disable the guns, cut loose the slaves aboard the *galleasse*. San Carlos is ours.'

A thrill of excitement trembled Robin's spine as he listened to Dermot's low, beguiling voice. A chorus of 'ayes' answered the proposition, and Channon clasped a hand here, a wrist there. Last of all he clasped both Robin's hands, and Robin would not release him. 'Then, take us back to that sugar-loaf and drop anchor,' Channon said quietly. 'Sit me a lookout atop the rock, and settle yourselves to wait. All we need now is patience, and Guillaume is ours.'

How many men in this crew had been Guillaume's prisoners until Channon paid for their freedom? Many lads were rubbing bitterly at old, long-healed scars as they returned to duty. Channon's was not the only grievance which would be settled with the capture of Isla San Carlos.

In an hour they were alone in their cabin while the ship made fast to wait in the lee of the barren islet that had been marked on the chart as Sugarloaf Rock. Channon lay against the pillows and invited Robin into his embrace.

'This reckoning has been a long time coming,' Robin said against his neck as he nuzzled.

'With luck we'll be in Spain for Christmas,' Channon said abstractly. 'My family must believe me dead just as you did. Sweet Christ, it's been a lifetime.'

His arms closed tight and crushed the breath from Robin's lungs, but Robin did not protest save to say, 'You promised we'd return to Rio de San Francisco. I'll hold you to that pledge.'

With a quiet laugh, not a sound of mockery, Channon finger-combed the soft, unruly chestnut hair. 'I promised you much more than that, and I've never yet broken a pledge.'

'That's all right, then,' Robin said, muffled against Channon's breast as they began to make love.

Chapter Twenty-Nine

It was two days before the *Pandora* left Isla San Carlos in the first, feeble light of dawn. The wind was barely a whimper out of the north and she passed close by Sugarloaf Rock under oars. In the lee of the islet the *gallizabra* was well hidden. The morning air was so eerily still, the beat of the timekeeper's hammer and the crack of the lash carried across the water.

That sound made Channon's flesh crawl and his belly sicken, for it recalled to mind a thousand memories he longed to forget. For a blind moment the *Roberto* became the Esmerelda again. He saw Alonzo Corco's face, a visage without compassion or pity or even the simple charity of the faith he claimed to uphold. The red of blood veiled Channon's eyes and he drank a cup of wine to the lees without taking a breath.

'Dermot?' Robin whispered, but Channon would not answer.

He went into the bow, seeking any breath of air to clear his head, and Valdez held Robin back with hand on his arm. 'Leave him, lad. He remembers, we all do.' He stamped his boot on the timbers. 'This very deck ran flogger's red. The blood we spilled in the mutiny was but a drop more.' He smiled sadly, fondly, at Channon. 'Soon she'll be the *Esmerelda* again, yet you know the truth. She's happiest as the *Roberto* and will not be happy when she flies King Philip's colours once more.'

We might be in Spain by Christmas, Robin thought with a deep wrench of resentment, which he admitted was selfish. He had no desire to return, his ties with his family were painfully but thoroughly sundered. Drake would be in England in just a few weeks, and Ned Blythe's house would begin to mourn, while the grief of Robin's own loss was already half purged. But Channon felt the burden of responsibility, promises made almost seven years ago to a family that must believe him dead. Christmas of that bloody year, '88, he had sailed with Orlando Martinez from Cadiz, and it began; now, the end was at hand.

The sky darkened and lightning flickered in the west. It would be stormy over Rio de San Francisco. Rain slashed the horizon and the sea chopped with rolling grey waves. The deck heaved constantly and the *gallizabra* came about to put her bow into the gale.

For a day and a night the wind and rain confined them to the cabin, but Channon wore a look of grim satisfaction. He sat at the open stern-ports, cradling a cup of mulled, spiced wine as he watched the sky.

'Corsair's weather,' he told Robin as they bedded, late on a night so chill that the divan was thickly quilted and they pressed together for warmth. 'Ships sailing for Spain leave these shores over-burdened. They wallow even in calm seas, and when the waves are high as hills they spring timbers, rip canvas, shatter masts. When the storm clears the buzzards circle, looking for carrion.'

'Like the *Swan*,' Robin observed.

'And the *Rosamund*, and countless others.' Channon reached over him to snuff their candle. 'This storm is to our advantage. A few days, a week, and Guillaume will be back, laden. He has only to stalk the lanes between Cartagena and Santo Domingo and, now that Drake is well gone, evade His Majesty's warships.'

'Dangerous,' Robin retorted. 'A *gallizabra* out of Hispaniola could sink him before we can get our hands on him.'

Channon laughed. 'Then we'll be poorer only by the value of whatever was in his hold. Spain will hang Guillaume as a common criminal and disperse his crew as slaves among the galleys. Isla San Carlos will still be ours, and easier to capture with its complement of fighting men taken captive elsewhere.' He pulled Robin against him. 'Rest. I'll not say sleep, for the sea is too vile to allow it. Mark me well, Guillaume will be back. The devil takes care of his own.'

Five days later Channon remembered those words and gave Robin an impudent grin as the lookout signalled from the heights of Sugarloaf Rock that he had seen sails. The *Pandora* was approaching from the north. In her hiding place, the *gallizabra* would not be seen, and Channon rubbed his palms together gleefully.

Zacarias was ecstatic. 'Tonight they'll drink till they cannot see, fuck until they cannot stand, and in the hours between midnight and dawn —' he drew a finger across his gullet. 'I almost pity them. Almost,' he added darkly.

Robin frowned after the boy as Zacarias joined the friends he had made among the crew. 'He speaks like a hardened old soldier when he should still be a child. If he were my son I think he would frighten me.'

'But he's not your son,' Channon added. 'Zacarias is a survivor. He's seen the worst the world can do. He'll return to the Caribbean as a man, and be its master.' He drew his forearm over his face in the late-afternoon humidity as he performed the ritual task of disassembling and servicing his pistols. 'Have you looked at your weapons?'

'Not yet.' Robin was still intent on the tall, willowy Zacarias, who had beguiled the corsair and was now flirting coyly with Valdez. 'Are they sleeping together?'

'You mean, is Valdez fucking that boy?' Channon chuckled. 'I don't know. And if he is, Zacarias is content.' He leaned over to swat Robin's lean buttock. 'See to your weapons and fetch us a jug of ale.'

In an hour the lookout shinned down the craggy cliff face and rowed back aboard with the news that the *Pandora* had slipped in through the crab-claw headlands. Across the deck of the *gallizabra* the men were making ready to fight with grim determination. Some were original members of the crew of the hellship *Esmerelda*, four and five years out from home; others new arrivals from the *Swan*. They would be home inside of a year, and they counted themselves fortunate indeed.

The three longboats stood ready. Each would take eight men — six at the oars, one at the tiller, one crouched in the bow with a brace of pistols. Twenty-four men would go through the caves with Zacarias to guide them, while San Carlos lay in its drunken stupor.

By the moon, it was midnight when Robin and Channon supped with the crew on the foredeck. One could develop a taste for pickled pork and onions, Robin thought, amused at himself as he listened to the division of the night's work. Pasco would command the ship. After the longboats were away she would sail windward of the island and lose an hour at least before doubling back to stand off the headlands, there to wait for the signal.

That signal would be heard all over San Carlos. When the cannons which guarded the harbour split their barrels and erupted the roar would be like a galleon's full broadside. The task of spiking the guns and cutting loose the *Pandora*'s slaves, Robin had fully expected Channon to take on himself, and he was not surprised when Dermot said, 'I'll take Valdez in my boat — aye, and Miguel, who's the best shot among us. Six loaded pistols, and a lad of your own choosing to reload for you, Miguel.'

Robin tied up the neck of his own leather poke of powder and thrust his pistols into his belt. 'We ought to up-anchor shortly. It's past midnight, and if we'll be an hour or so on our way through the caves —'

'We?' Channon echoed, and turned Robin with a shuttered expression. 'No, Robin. Not you.'

'In God's name, why not?' Robin demanded.

'You're not a soldier, you never were,' Channon began.

'Good enough to ride into a plague port with you, nurse you through Yellow Jack, and reason the means of liberation for this ship!' Robin said loudly. 'But for me, every one of you would be Guillaume's property, or dead, or wishing to be dead!' He lifted his chin. 'I may not be a soldier, but I've done my share.'

'But not tonight,' Channon rasped. 'I don't want you in danger's way.'

'The captain's boy, am I?' Robin demanded, and shook his head slowly. 'No, Dermot, I'll not be that.'

Channon glanced about into the faces of his friends, and took Robin's elbow to urge him swiftly into the privacy of their cabin before they could begin to argue in terms which were very personal. Robin's face was firm and his mouth compressed as the door latched behind them. Channon took a calming breath and chided himself for the moment's annoyance. He had been the commander so long, he had begun to forget that there were men who took orders and others who gave them; and Robin Armagh was fast becoming one of the latter.

He swallowed his exasperation and gentled his voice. 'Robin, no.'

'I'll remain on the ship,' Robin said levelly, 'on one condition. You send Valdez and Pasco through the caves and remain behind, safe, with me. Give the command to lay down the cannonade yourself.'

His terms made Channon groan. 'You have it in you to be infuriating.'

'As have you,' Robin said mildly as he picked up the sword which had been on the bed, and strapped it on. 'And since neither of us is going to give ground, why don't you see to your weapons and —'

'Robin, it'll be bloody,' Channon said brusquely.

'Like the fight on the *Swan*, where your men tried to hew me limb from limb, and I put down three of them before I was cut,' Robin said pointedly. 'You taught me to use a sword, Dermot. You know better than any man the skill I own.'

'For the love of God,' Channon breathed.

'You don't believe in any God.' Robin was on his way to the door, and in passing dealt Channon's neck a nipping kiss.

'Robin!' Channon slammed the door shut and leaned on it. 'You'll not go into danger,' he growled. 'This is my ship, and so long as you're on this deck you'll take my orders like any man!'

For a moment Robin's eyes widened and his cheeks coloured, not with passion, Channon knew, but with anger. He tilted his head at Channon and spoke in deceptively mild tones, but his words cut like a knife.

'What am I, aboard this ship? You called me the captain's *amante*, but you meant his *catamite*, didn't you? I take your orders, pose prettily in the peacock clothes and jewels it amuses you to drape about me. I warm your bed and spread my legs at your merest whim, and count myself honoured. Now you place yourself in danger's way while I loiter aboard and keep your sheets warm, ready to spread for you at a word? Is that all I'm worth in your eyes? Damn you! You told Alvarez I'm a man, I defend my own honour — was it a lie? You'll not fight for me, Dermot Channon, I'm not a maid, nor a man's pretty-boy. I'll do your bidding like the others, but if you tell me to tarry aboard like a catamite, there'll be no warm bed waiting for you, *Captain*. I go with you as your *amante*, your comrade, or I stay behind as a common member of this crew.'

The verbal assault flayed Channon bare to the bone. 'And next time I want you in my bed, I must order you there,' he said softly, caught up in admiration and delight as he watched the glitter of Robin's green eyes, the dignity with which he held himself. 'If I ordered you to bed, belly down and open wide, you'd spit in my eye, there'd be another mutiny on this ship.' He threw back his head and laughed. 'By God, I love you best like this, sparkling with anger and sharp as a dirk with outraged honour!' He snatched up his sword and opened the cabin door. 'Time's wasting and we're already underway. If you're in my boat, Valdez is staying aboard. Go and tell him to change his arrangements.'

'Then —' Robin caught his arm. 'You'll not tell me to stay behind?'

Channon's cheeks warmed faintly. 'I wasn't trying to shame you. Selfishly, because I love you and fear for you, I wanted to keep you safe, as I did when you were a lad of eighteen years.' He touched Robin's face with his fingertips. 'I wish you were mine to command. But even aboard this ship, though you call me Captain, you're not.' He looked Robin up and down and dropped a bow before him. 'I'll not fight *for* you, then. I'll fight *beside* you.'

'And there,' Robin murmured gratefully, 'is the difference.' He took a breath, and hesitated on his way through the door. 'I love you,' he whispered, and was gone.

In his wake Channon rubbed his face ruefully, feeling as winded as if he had been punched. Robin had changed more than he realised. The boy whose beauty and innocence would have seduced a saint was gone, and in his place was a man Channon found irresistible. He was magnificent, the jewel of his whole family, though they would ever know it. None of the Armagh brothers was Robin's equal. Channon was absurdly prideful as he made his way on deck.

Isla San Carlos was white in the moonlight, and with the tide at slack-water the sea was calm. The wind stirred fretfully about the crags where thousands of seabirds nested but no lights showed along the heights, which loomed above the ship like the battlements of a castle.

According to Zacarias's drawings this side of the island, directly opposite the lagoon, was uninhabited. The land sloped steeply up above the anchorage and the jungle grew thickly only on that single slope. The rocks below were honeycombed with caves, but no one ventured into them save to draw water from the spring, which rose in the mouth of the largest.

'Allow us an hour to go through,' Channon told Valdez as the boats were lowered away and the lads began to shin down the ropes like a troupe of monkeys. 'Another hour to disable the cannons and cut loose the slaves aboard the *galleasse*.'

'We'll be waiting,' Valdez promised. 'When we hear the guns explode we'll be swift through the pincers, and fire upon the town.'

'We'll hoist the *Pandora*'s mizzen flags as a signal that she's ours,' Channon went on. 'Don't fire upon her if you see them.'

'And if we don't,' Pasco added, 'we'll raze her to the waterline before she can turn her guns on us.' He offered his hand. 'Luck, Dermot.'

'Luck?' Channon shook his head but clasped Pasco's wrist anyway. 'Luck has nought to do with it, not this time.'

The first boat was away then, and he went over the side with Robin, hand over hand down the ropes until he felt the cork- bobbing little deck beneath his feet.

In the moonlight the caves appeared as blue-black smudges, and as they drew nearer a dozen lanterns were lit. With a creak of timbers and taut lines the ship swung away and leaned into the wind. In minutes she was beyond recall, and Channon's heart gave that odd, familiar flutter, part fear, part exhilaration, as it always did before a fight began.

The moonlight was like silver on the sea and he looked back, watching the ship until the longboats drew into the stygian blackness of the caves. The rocks stank of bird lime and the light of the lanterns roused a thousand bats. Channon ducked as they swooped low over his head, out into the night. Zacarias hissed through his teeth, crossed himself and pressed against Robin's back, either hating or fearing them. Channon protected his face with his hand and peered into the weird, leaping shadows.

'There's the ledge, as the lad said,' Robin whispered. 'Are you all right, Zacarias? You've been here before.'

'The bats,' he hissed. 'They don't fly in daytime. I never came here at night.'

'Then cling tight to me and shut your eyes,' Channon offered. 'We'll soon be through them. Are we landing in the right place to enter the labyrinth?'

Zacarias chanced a look into the light. 'Aye. You'll see my chalk marks. Go up through the crevice.'

The cleft in the rock was just wide enough to pass a man through, if he ducked his head. The bats whirled in the outer part of the cave, and Zacarias grabbed a lantern and dove through the crevice, knowing there were none inside. A pace behind him Channon looked about for Robin.

'Stay close,' he murmured. 'All of you — don't straggle!'

'And get lost in the bowels of the earth?' The stout little English gunner off the *Rosamund*, Jon Jago, was clutching a rosary in both brawny fists as if his life depended on the fragile beads.

But Zacarias was already moving, chattering excitedly as he found his way easily from one chalk scratch to the next. Underfoot the ground was a mass of fist-sized boulders, as treacherous as trying to walk on scattered cannon shot. Robin swore as he slithered, and grabbed Channon's arm to steady himself.

Soon they were scrambling over long, shattered slabs of stone, climbing steadily, and Channon could almost physically feel the oppressive weight of rock above him. He looked back to find Robin grim-faced, panting lightly. The others were strung out behind him, sticking doggedly to the light of the swinging lanterns.

'How far now, Zacarias?' Channon whispered. A raised voice echoed loudly, seeming to bounce like a ball from one rock face to the next and back again.

'Not far,' Zacarias swore. 'Two minutes, and you'll see the cave with the fresh-water spring. I know the way well from here.'

It was no idle boast. The youth no longer looked for his chalk marks, but scrambled from boulder to boulder, agile as a goat while men twice his age and size struggled to keep up. And then, without warning, he dropped flat on the rocks and held up his hand.

'What is it?' Channon went down beside him and snaked forward on knees and elbows.

'The cave,' Zacarias whispered. 'The spring, see? The cave mouth is just beyond. Put out the lanterns, or we may be seen.'

'You heard the boy,' Channon said over his shoulder, and as the lights were doused he crawled on into the large, open cavern, and caught a welcome glimpse of starlight.

Bats stirred in the rocks high above and Zacarias sprang into the open air like a rabbit. The spring of cold, clear water rushed out of a fissure in the boulders, and Channon stopped to drink before he followed.

He found himself on a steep hillside. Above, the crags were

precipitous, beneath him the forest thickened to left and right, and below it all was a cauldron ringed by cliffs. The cockpit sheltered the lagoon, a tiny quayside and perhaps thirty buildings. The *galleasse* was tied up at the quay. A few lamps burned aboard, but most of the crew would be ashore, revelling in celebration of their voyage.

'The guns guarding the entrance,' Robin said breathlessly as he emerged at Channon's side. 'Zacarias, where are they?'

'I see them.' Channon pointed across the harbour, where the heads came so close as to almost join, leaving just a narrow bottleneck through which a ship might pass. The four cannon were mounted into the rock, angled down, permanently aimed into the narrow passage. 'But I don't see the way up to them,' Channon mused, and grasped Zacarias by both his thin shoulders. 'Which way, boy?'

'There, and there.' Zacarias pointed not at the lagoon but into the forest, where pathways had been cut out and beaten flat by years of marching feet. 'You climb up by the rocks. I used to sit there and watch the *Pandora* sail home, and I would pretend I was blowing her to pieces,' he added with hateful fervour.

'Split up,' Channon said quickly. 'Three parties. One on each of the headlands. The third for the ship. Robin, Miguel, Jon Jago, Fletcher, Kemp, Ramon, Pietro, with me. The rest of you, spike those guns. Watch the ship, wait till you see the banners rise over the stern of the *Pandora*, and then blow those cannon apart. Move! And you,' he added, catching Zacarias by the arm, 'come with us. You'll show us the safe way down to the waterfront.'

The boy inclined his head. 'As you wish, Captain. At this hour any path is safe. They will have drunk wine and fucked boys and each other till they are nearer dead than asleep. Listen, you'll hear their snoring, fit to raise off every roof. Follow me.'

His rancour was boundless, and Channon looked sidelong at Robin as they followed him into the shadows on the steep forest path. 'Who would believe a body so small could contain such malice,' Robin murmured.

But Channon's face was grim in the white moonlight. 'If you knew Guillaume intimately you would cease to wonder.'

'Where will he be?' Robin asked softly of Zacarias. 'Where did you bed with him, ashore?'

'In that house, on the hill above the rest.' Zacarias pointed. 'With French carpets and Spanish wine and an Italian bed with Portuguese drapes and Irish linen.' He spat into the dirt at his feet, drew back the cape of his long hair and looked up at Channon with those wide, doe eyes. 'Will you kill him?'

'Not at once,' Channon said, wary of being drawn into the web of Zacarias's bitter enmity. 'We want his secrets first. Where is the better part of his hoard hidden? When he has told us this...' He gave Zacarias a push. 'Hurry, now.'

On the youth's heels, he and Robin padded blindly through the deep forest shadow, and as the trees began to thin Channon took a pistol in either hand. They stepped out onto a grassy knoll just above the buildings, where the scents of woodsmoke, old ale and roasting pork combined with the smells of the sea, sun-rotted wrack, old timber and tar. Any portside town smelt the same.

Yellow lamplight spilled from windows left unshuttered, and Channon listened intently for sounds of activity. In the house where Zacarias had served, a single voice sang to the accompaniment of a mandolin, someone moaned and whimpered in a deeply erotic rhythm.

'Their minds are filled with wine and sleep,' Zacarias promised. 'Six months did I whore here, and I know them.'

'This way down?' Robin gestured into the dark alley separating Guillaume's house from what seemed to be a tavern. 'The *Pandora* is tied up just along the quay.'

'Aye. Only tread carefully and you'll be safe. Slaves carried rocks from the cliffs to build the whole quay,' Zacarias said darkly. 'It was still not finished when I was first brought here. The boulders are full of their bones.'

Channon grasped him by the arm as Zacarias tried to go on. 'No further. There'll be fighting now. Do you want to get home in one piece? Then hide in the woods, and when you see the banners hoisted on the *Pandora*, when you hear the guns explode, lie flat on your belly and cover your ears. The *Roberto* will be through into the lagoon unchallenged, and she'll pound this quayside to pebbles. Go!'

He did not need telling twice, and the last they saw of him was his slim backside in white breeches, like a rabbit as he vanished into the shadows. Robin swore softly after him, and Channon checked his pistols.

'No use, I suppose, to send you after the lad, out of harm's way?' he whispered for Robin's ears alone.

Robin looked sidelong at him. 'Was that a jest?'

'It was,' Channon murmured, almost honestly. 'Then, stay close to me and let me guard your back.'

'As close as I must be to guard yours,' Robin promised, and primed the wheellock pistol in his right hand.

Hours before there would have been a continual din of drunken voices, laughter and music, but with dawn no more than two hours away the revels were spent. All along the quay men lay snoring, some naked, some half clad. A cat watched Channon pad silently by, but the only other eyes which saw the intruders belonged to a little black boy, chained by the ankle to a bolt in the ground; and he made no sound.

The *Pandora* rocked gently at her moorings as the tide began to rise. Her oars has been withdrawn and the blind sockets of her gunports gazed over the quayside and the lagoon. In the shelter of the cliffs the wind hardly stirred, and Channon heard Robin's whispered oath as they drew nearer the *galleasse*. In the still air she stank with the fetid smell of filthy bodies, excrement and decay.

Her slaves remained shackled to the oars until they died in service, with their dirt accumulated about them and in the bilges below. Many of them would be sick or dying, but many more would be new acquisitions, recent replacements, quite capable of taking up arms. Keeping them silent and still until the moment came to move would likely be the most difficult part of the night's work.

In the ship's moonshadow, Channon crouched down and looked all about, from the gunwales above his head to the quay and down the length of the lagoon. Nothing stirred. He thrust his pistols into his belt, pressed a finger to his lips for quiet and grasped the coarse rope of the ladder which lay against the curved timbers.

At turn-of-the-tide the ship was low beside the quay and it was an easy climb. Channon lifted his head up to peer over the side onto the deck, and saw the night watch at once. Two men sat drowsing beside a brazier; a naked boy was asleep on his belly at their feet among a litter of wine jars and clean-picked chicken carcasses. The guards stirred only to snore and belch, and slumped against the timbers again. Channon looked down into Robin's intent face.

At Dermot's nod he was climbing, halfway up the rope ladder before Channon swung his legs over onto the deck. Behind him came Jago, Fletcher and Kemp, the Englishmen; Miguel, Pietro and Ramon, the Spaniards — men of different countries and churches with but one thing in common. They were privateers, freemen, and ambitious.

The brazier was almost out. Channon trod carefully among the empty wine jars and drew a pistol from his belt as he approached the sotted guards. On his heels, with the same thought on his mind, Robin drew one of his own ball-butted wheellocks.

A swift crack of barrel and skull, and with a quiet grunt the guards sprawled senselessly among their refuse. If they lived to see morning they would be nursing sore, aching heads, but their chances of survival were poor. Channon's belly churned as he recalled the mutiny on the *Esmerelda*. When the slaves were set loose they were savage as wild animals and driven by an unquenchable thirst for vengeance.

'Will there be other guards?' Robin murmured as he stooped to examine the boy slave. 'This lad is drunk.'

'They are more pliant that way,' Channon said bitterly. 'Ramon, Jago, the gentlemen's cabins. Fletcher, Pietro, search forward, there'll be one, two, below decks. Miguel, with me. Robin, stay here and keep watch. Kemp, stand with him.'

'Where are you going?' Robin called sharply. 'Dermot!'

'I said *stay there!*' Channon hissed as he crept silently toward the centre hatches. 'I'm going to cut the slaves loose. You think they smell vile from here? Stay!'

The oar deck of any vessel rowed by slaves was dank, foul. Channon would never forget that stench. Alonzo Corco drove his slaves under the lash, threw those who broke to the sharks, and when the wind fell away the whole ship would reek of the oar deck. It was weeks before the *gallizabra* had been free of that foulness, when she was no longer the *Esmerelda* and Corco himself had fed the sharks.

Only one guard was on duty and he was asleep, slumped on the timekeeper's bench. The slaves dozed, moaned, coughed, by the half-light of four lanterns. As Channon let himself down through the centre hatch a few gaunt, bearded faces turned to him. Links of chain rattled, timbers groaned as the old ship began to move with the rising tide.

Channon lifted his pistol, deliberately drew aim on the guard's capacious belly, then glared into the watchful faces and pressed a finger to his lips. Heads wagged, eyes opened wide, backs straightened in anticipation. Englishmen, Spaniards, Hollanders — all manner of men were Guillaume's prey, and all hungered for freedom. In this very instant the taste of it was new and sweet on their tongues.

The butt of the pistol struck the back of the guard's head, and as he pitched onto his face Channon cast about swiftly for keys. They would be close at hand, since they were used constantly, when the dead and dying slaves were discarded and replaced with fresh meat.

A black iron ring with four stout keys hung on a hook in the timber beneath the hatch. Channon had only to snatch it down and toss it into the hands of the big, brawny Flemish lad whose eyes had never left him since he appeared.

'Speak English?' he asked softly.

'Aye — who are you? Queen's men?' Clumsy with haste, he forced the lock which held him and four others captive.

'Privateers,' Channon said quietly. 'Let them all loose, Jack, and tell them to be silent. If you want this ship and this anchorage for your own, tell them to shut their mouths and wait. Understand?'

The Flemisher gave him a gap-toothed grin. 'Understand. Privateer? Irish?'

'Irish,' Channon affirmed drily, and lifted himself back out into the air. He filled his lungs gratefully and dragged both hands across his sweated face. That stench would be hard to be rid of. Slaves swore the only thing that washed it away was blood.

Robin was waiting, and the others were with him as Channon returned. 'Five of Guillaume's men were aboard,' Robin said softly. 'All dead or witless.'

'Hoist me the mizzen flags.' Channon clasped Miguel's shoulder. 'And then duck your heads!' He gave Robin a grin that was indisputably smug. 'We have them.'

The smooth-worn old decking planks were cool. He tugged Robin with him into the lee of a great iron cannon, and from there they watched as Guillaume's scarlet flag was raised. The centre hatch lifted and a face looked out, but Channon had only to wave the man back for the hatch to close once more.

'Obedient,' Robin observed.

'Gift a man with his freedom and you win his loyalty,' Channon said shortly. 'There's no magic, merely gratitude.' He looked up at that scarlet banner and held his breath in anticipation.

The eruption from both headlands at once was like a full broadside, dazzling in the night as the cannon barrels split wide and spat blazing powder in every direction. With that sound, Isla San Carlos was crippled.

Voices shouted along the waterfront now, but all was disarray. From what snatches of Spanish and English Channon could grasp, most of the men who rushed to gaze across the lagoon thought there had been an accident with the guns.

'Damn, it's happened before, a mishap with the cannon,' Robin said under the confusion. 'The bastards are standing there, stupefied with drink, blaming each other!'

'Then they'll soon learn otherwise,' Channon said acidly. 'Where the devil is Valdez?'

'There!' Bobbed up just enough to see over the high timber side, Robin had seen the prow of the *gallizabra* coming through the narrow passage into the lagoon. 'She's under oars and they're cracking on a good speed. What a sight, Dermot!'

'And a better one to come.' Channon tugged him back onto the deck. 'Get down, Robin — she'll trail larboard oars and swing broadside faster than you know.'

She was already turning, cramped in the confines of the harbour, and Channon clamped both hands over his ears. Robin followed his example and they were crouched, heads down, when ten heavy guns roared, almost in unison. The cliffs, like castle ramparts, echoed back the uproar, and even the deck of the *galleasse* trembled under them. Along the waterfront buildings shattered and roofs collapsed. Men screamed and some fled. Others were dead where they fell.

Valdez had ordered his guncrews to reload, and Channon swore lividly as his ears protested the punishment. When he lifted his head once more little was left standing on the quay. Fires burned brightly, men staggered drunkenly about, too dazed to grasp what was happening, and of authority there was no sign.

Rubbing his ears as if they had been soundly boxed, Robin got to his feet. He waved across to men on the deck of the *gallizabra* as she came about once more, and seized Channon by both his hands. 'We have them!'

Channon was less satisfied, though he took Robin's hands readily. 'We have the harbour,' he amended tersely. 'But where are Guillaume and his mate, Leblanc? We came for them and their hoard, not to smash down a few buildings.'

'They may be dead already,' Robin warned. 'Part of the house where Zacarias served has been razed. If they were inside, your old scores may be settled for you.'

Before Channon could answer the centre hatches slammed open and the swarm of slaves clambered up in the free air. Ragged, bearded, lash-scarred and often emaciated, they were also jubilant and bright-eyed with a craving for destruction that must be satisfied, no matter the cost. Channon did not even attempt to stand in their way.

'You know where the curs keep their weapons aboard?' He asked of the Flemisher to whom he had given the keys. 'Then arm yourselves, and the port is yours — with one exception.' He raised his voice, a whipcrack of command, first in English, then in Spanish. 'Hubert Guillaume belongs to us! Understand?'

'You want the king of the rats,' the Flemisher said with that gap-toothed grin, 'you can have him. We take the rest!'

Like tattered ants they were all over the *galleasse*, armed in moments, and then over the side on the quay before the *Roberto* had nosed in behind the high stern of the *Pandora*. The boarding ramp had been let down and Channon stood at the bottom of it, fists on hips, watching the fires as he waited for Valdez and Pasco. Robin swore softly as he watched the slaves fall like hunting dogs on a man they knew. With axes and their bare hands they swiftly tore him to pieces.

'I told you it would be bloody,' Channon said quietly. 'You've seen nothing like this, Robin. I wanted only to spare you. Your dreams will be no sweeter after this.'

But Robin lifted his chin and drew his sword. 'If we came for Guillaume, why are we standing here watching the crows peck out the eyes of the eagles?' He turned his back on the carnage along the quayside, and without waiting for Channon he strode toward the white-walled, palm-thatched house Zacarias had pointed out.

One corner had been damaged by shot and the roof was torn away, but the house had not caught alight. Lamps were still lit in the parlour and beyond, in the bedchamber. The door was ajar but the only sound Channon heard as he stepped inside was a curious, rhythmic grunting and squealing from another room.

Standing on Persian carpets, looking at an array of pewter, porcelain and gilt-framed portraits that would have graced any gentleman's residence in Madrid, Robin and Channon, Pasco and Valdez, shared a perplexed glance.

'It sounds like wild pigs mating.' Robin edged closer to the bedchamber, took a grip on his sword and pushed the door wide with the toe of his boot. Channon could not see into the room, but moved swiftly a moment later as Robin lowered his sword and stepped into the light. 'What are you doing? For Christ's sake, boy, stop!'

The Italian bed with Portuguese drapes commanded the room, but the Irish linen was already ripped to rags. Zacarias knelt in the middle of it, a dirk in both hands, slashing and stabbing through the quilt and sheets, into the mattress. Goose feathers dusted his hair, bare chest and breeches like snow as he reduced the bed to tatters, grunting and squealing with every blow. At the bedside, Robin watched until he began to exhaust himself. He gave Channon a grim glance and plucked the dirk out of the youth's hands.

'Enough, boy. If a bed can be slain, this one is dead.'

With a whimper, Zacarias seemed about to dissolve into tears, but he scrubbed his nose furiously with the back of his hand and looked up at Robin and Channon. Robin offered his hands, and Zacarias grasped them to clamber off the ruined bed. Robin dusted the feathers from his hair and gestured at the open window, which was on the rear wall of the house, facing the forest.

'You got in that way? Was Guillaume here?'

'He was leaving when I came down off the hill. He and Leblanc. I saw them go, after the cannons fired.' Zacarias was shaking, even his voice trembled. Now, he would not look at the bed.

'You saw him leave — where did he go?' Channon asked sharply. 'This is a small island, where *could* he go?'

'The secret places,' Zacarias said breathlessly, and hugged himself to still his trembling. 'I don't know the whole way, I never found them, but I can show you where they ran.'

'Hurry, then, before they have time to conjure some trap we'll rue.' Channon gave Robin a bleak look. 'This secret store of powder, if it exists —'

'It exists, Captain.' Zacarias's eyes widened. 'I did not think. He would turn it against us.'

'Then, thank God one of us thought. Move!' Channon barked.

Zacarias snatched up his dirk and climbed out through the window. Channon thrust Robin through after him, but paused before he followed and turned back toward Pasco and Valdez, who were a pace behind him.

'Valdez, come with us. Pasco, take the ship out of here.'

'But Dermot, surely you want the cover of her guns,' Pasco argued.

'Guillaume's men could have hidden themselves all over this forsaken island.'

'With powder and shot to hand,' Channon added acidly. 'By all means put a crew on the *Pandora* and clear her guns to fire on the hillsides, but get that *gallizabra* out of here!'

'Aye, at once,' Pasco said hoarsely, as if untold possibilities had just begun to occur to him.

He was out of the house, shouting for a guncrew to stand by the *Pandora*, as Channon clambered through the window. In the bushes Robin and Zacarias were waiting, and as soon as Valdez was out of the house the youth took to his heels.

Chapter Thirty

The faint, powdery light of dawn had just begun to flush the eastern horizon and the moon was almost down. The mouth of the cave, Guillaume's secret, was so concealed by underbrush and boulders that unless one knew where to search, even in broad daylight it would never be seen. It was not high enough for a man to enter without stooping, and so narrow that a very large man might not get through at all. Bats flitted in and out, and Zacarias refused to go any nearer. He sat on a boulder, arms hugged about his knees, and watched owlishly as Robin discovered the assortment of lanterns, lamps and torches left just inside.

On one knee, Channon struck flint to steel and touched the tip of a wick to the smouldering tinder. Valdez kept a look out, back the way they had come, up a winding, precipitous path between the forest and the cliffs. Robin crouched by the cave mouth, listening intently.

'You hear them?' Channon whispered as he lit a second wick.

'I hear... something,' Robin said cautiously. 'Like tapping, or many echoes of a hammer stroke.'

'Voices? Guillaume?' Channon joined him at the tiny fissure in the rock and handed him a lantern.

'A whisper now and then.' Robin looked up into Channon's face in the yellow light. 'Zacarias, how did you find this place?'

'I followed them one night,' the boy told him. 'You can't see the harbour from here, the forest blocks all sight. The heavy loads of powder were carried up by slaves, deaf mutes, and they were blindfolded and led like mules. Guillaume would leave a guard on the path to stop anyone following, but I stole through the trees and came out again behind him.'

'If he'd known you had followed,' Channon said quietly, 'he would have killed you.'

'Aye.' Zacarias rubbed his arms. 'Kill him for me, Captain.' His eyes were hard as diamonds, glittering in the lantern light. That blood-lust in one so young was chilling.

'Since only Guillaume and Leblanc ever knew about this place,' Robin mused, 'then only the two of them will be inside. We'll not blunder into an army, Dermot. Two of them, two of us.'

Channon choked off a groan and took a grip on his lantern. 'You never looked inside, Zacarias?'

'Bats,' Zacarias said, hushed.

'Bats,' Channon echoed acidly. He drew a pistol from his belt and edged closer to the ink-black crevice.

For a man of his stature it was a tight fit, but once he was inside the cave opened into an enormous chamber which reminded Channon of an unholy cross between the hold of a ship and a cathedral. Every sound echoed and from somewhere far off they heard the steady drip of water. Robin was through a moment later and Channon stepped aside to let him see the long, vaulted gallery of grey stone.

The voices and tapping were from their right, where the cliffs above rose steeply like a castle rampart. On silent feet Channon stole toward that sound, with Robin like a shadow, not a pace behind him. Twenty yards, and the voices began to gain substance; ten more, and they could make out words, though Guillaume and Leblanc were speaking in French, which Channon had never properly understood.

A glimmer of light showed about a protrusion in the rock, and with great care Channon set down his lantern before they went any further. A pause, and the tapping resumed, louder and sharper now that they were so near. A hammering of metal on wood, then metal on metal.

Cautious, creeping like a thief, Channon slid to the very edge of the rock and peered around into the chamber beyond. He felt Robin's hand on his shoulder, smelt the companionable tang of gunpowder from their pistols as he blinked in the sudden comparative brightness.

322

Guillaume was bare-chested, clad in tight white breeches, a studded blue codpiece and black boots, his hair a tousled yellow cape over wide, brown shoulders. Not so arrogant now, Channon saw. Every line of his body betrayed anxiety as he watched his companion work. About his neck was the emerald necklace he had taken from Robin, the price of Charles Rothwell's ransom. The sight of it on Guillaume roused Channon to anger.

Similarly half clad, as if they had both woken and run in seconds, Raoul Leblanc was still hammering. A heavy mallet battered at obstinate iron pins as he hurried to change the mountings of a small brass cannon. The weapon was heavy enough to destroy a longboat or a group of men, light enough to be carried by hand. A keg of powder and a crate of shot stood beside the gun, and Channon swore softly. They could hold off a small army, since the path up to the cave was so difficult, the way in so small.

With a quiet shuffle of feet on the rock, Robin moved up to see, just as Leblanc threw down the mallet and wiped his face. They were done. The cannon was mounted, ready for loading, and Channon's heart thumped at his ribs.

The wheellock rasped as it primed, an unmistakable sound. Guillaume spun, so lithe and graceful, caught one glimpse of them and dove behind a stack of barrels and sacks. Leblanc was not so quick, but snatched up the pair of pistols which had been set down by his lamp. As he flung himself after Guillaume, Channon heard a harangue in barbed, biting French, and Robin grasped his arm tightly.

'For God's sake, Dermot, don't fire. The whole chamber is filled with gunpowder!' Carefully, he secured his own pistols and dropped them at his feet.

'Mother of Christ,' Channon breathed furiously, but his pistols followed Robin's and the sword rasped out of his scabbard. 'Guillaume! Do you think you'll walk out of here alive? Guillaume!'

A blond head appeared behind the casks and barrels; the point of a sword gleamed brightly. 'I might,' Guillaume said, terse, shaken, as if much of his arrogance had been stripped away. 'What do you want, Channon? What do you come here for?'

'Perhaps I came for you,' Channon said acerbically. 'You'll pay a hundred ducats to the man who trusses me like a pig for slaughter, so Mateo Alvarez told me. Perhaps you'd like to try your own hand.'

'Alvarez has a big mouth,' Guillaume said acidly. 'He swore you

323

survived the Yellow Jack, but I hardly believed. How did you get in here? San Carlos is a fortress!'

'With a back door,' Channon added, 'which you left wide open. Zacarias could not wait to tell us everything.'

Guillaume swore bitterly, French invective Channon could half follow. 'You do business with me?' he offered then. 'You come here to win a corsair's ransom, *oui*?'

'Maybe I came to break a corsair's neck,' Channon retorted.

'Emeralds, sapphires, Inca gold,' Guillaume taunted. 'Take me to Natividad, safe, and I'll tell you where it is.'

'Careful.' Robin's hand closed on Channon's arm. 'The hoard will be in this cavern, we need only to search to find it.'

'Master Armagh,' Guillaume said unpleasantly. 'Tell your *boy* to do business with me.'

Anger clenched Channon's belly and his knuckles whitened on the sword. 'To the devil with you, Guillaume. I'll not trade with you. I came here to knock you on your nasty arse, I care nothing for your fortune.'

'Dermot!' Robin's voice was sharp in the confines, but not for the first time Channon ignored him. The cavern was filled with gunpowder, no one in his right mind would fire off a pistol, yet Robin's face was pale with the fear that Guillaume was mad enough to try. Channon was furious enough to take the risk.

Sure enough, the muzzle of a pistol appeared above the casks, but before Guillaume could trigger it Leblanc screamed and knocked it from his hand. A sword rasped, clattered, and with the grace of a dancer, the arrogance of youth, Guillaume stepped out onto the wide, sandy floor of the cavern.

Younger than Robin, taller than Channon, prideful, vain, for years Guillaume had been a hawk among hares. Behind him was Leblanc, the master gunner, Robin's height and weight, Channon's age, swarthy as any Portuguese peasant, cunning as an old wolf.

'You're a fool, Channon,' Guillaume mocked. The tip of his sword described a circle in the air. 'You know I can cut you up. You've no legs for this work.'

A pace behind Channon, Robin watched the fine Salamanca blade shift in Dermot's grip. Guillaume and Leblanc stood shoulder to shoulder, neither willing to strike the first blow, though it was plain at a glance Channon was not fighting just one.

Anger compressed his lips as he felt out the muscles of his legs, felt the old pains, phantom aches from long ago. From the corner of his eye he saw Robin coming up at his left hand and every time-worn protest was on the tip of his tongue. He spoke none of them. It was very possible that neither he nor Robin would walk out of this cave alive, but if they died it would be together, comrades and equals, and the soldier in Channon was satisfied. Vengeance would soon follow, possibly at Valdez's hand. Guillaume and Leblanc would certainly not leave San Carlos.

'Two fools for one coin,' Guillaume mocked. 'Better than I hoped. You die here, Channon. You want Armagh to die?'

But he did not wait for Channon to answer, and the chime of swords was like bells between the echoing walls. Even now Channon was quick enough to surprise Guillaume, and he knew every move, honourable and underhand alike. Despite Guillaume's agility and speed he was still young, still learning, and in the first six blows Channon realised one truth.

In the arms and back he was stronger than Guillaume. If he could keep the corsair working hard until he tired, in the end that strength might be the deciding of it. In the end, he admitted bitterly to himself, it was all he would have. The Frenchman was nearer dancer than swordsman and so fast, it was often all Channon could do to hold off his blows. These were the skills with which Hubert Guillaume had won and kept his rank as a captain of privateers. The worst mistake any man could make was to underestimate him.

Across the cavern, again and again, Robin's sword chimed on Leblanc's, but Channon dared not take his eyes from Guillaume. He followed Robin's fight by sound, listening to every grunt and curse. He knew when Robin nicked the Frenchman and drew first blood; he knew when Leblanc got the better of him. Kegs tumbled, a lantern overturned and Robin sprawled in the sand.

Guillaume's blows were swift and hard. Channon felt the stress on his wrist as turned them aside. Before his mind's eye he saw another fight — himself, much younger and arrogant in that youth... like Guillaume, he toyed with the fish who had taken the bait in the afternoon shadows at Hampton Court. Fury balled up like a fist under his heart and he put his full strength into the return blows, for the first time driving Guillaume back, and back again, into the wall of the cave.

With a desperate flurry of cuts Robin fended off Leblanc, rolled and scrambled to his knees. His ears were still ringing and he felt the moist, warm trickle of blood. He had lost his footing when the lamp upturned, cracked his head on a barrel as he fell, and only animal instinct sent him rolling in the right direction while his sword thrashed Leblanc's away from his throat.

His eyes watered and his senses spun, but as he rolled he caught one glimpse of Channon. Guillaume was slithering along the wall, this way and that, and Channon followed as if they were joined in some bizarre dance. Neither was bleeding yet, neither was spent, and Robin swore as he got to his knees and turned his attention back to Leblanc.

Blood trickled from a scratch on the Frenchman's cheek and he no longer wore that taunting, infuriating grin. He was out of Robin's reach when he stooped to snatch up something that had been dropped behind the kegs. For one blind instant Robin was sure it must be a pistol, and his heart skipped wildly.

He launched himself with his sword angled to deflect Leblanc's, his shoulder aimed into the older man's middle, before he could fire. Too late, he glimpsed the object Leblanc had snatched up, and there was no time even to curse. It was a coil of rope which Leblanc swung, knee-high. It cracked like a whip, swiping Robin's feet cleanly from under him. His own momentum carried him on as he fell, and he barely saw the fist which crashed down between his shoulder blades.

The air rushed from Robin's lungs with a sound that curdled Channon's belly. Finesse was forgotten and the Salamanca blade hammered like an axe on Guillaume's sword. Hilts twisted, locked and wrenched, and sweat sprang from Channon's pores as they began to wrestle. Guillaume was no fool, he had known since the beginning that he did not possess Channon's strength. His feet hooked, grappled, trying to snatch away Channon's balance, and they turned slowly, gripped wrist to wrist, bone and sinew straining.

Even then Channon was listening, and he heard the dragging sound of a body being hauled across the sand. Robin had gone down a scant moment before, and now Leblanc was shouting at Guillaume. Channon could not grasp the words but the man's voice was whetted by urgency. Guillaume's eyes glittered, his teeth bared with effort and his neck was a mass of cords as he threw his weight against Channon.

The wrench might have splintered bone, but instinct made Channon release his sword. The force of Guilaume's struggling, suddenly unchecked, flung both weapons away, and Channon watched them skitter into the sand. The Frenchman was gasping, more winded by the contest of strength than he had been by the duel. He crouched, came up against the stack of barrels and poised to launch himself after the still bellowing Leblanc.

Channon was in his path. The collision knocked the breath out of his lungs but he closed his arms about Guillaume's smooth, sweated torso. Hard, lean, intensely masculine, Guillaume had skin like hot brown velvet. Close, he smelt of fresh sweat, musk and lavender, which Channon might have found attractive if he had not been fighting for his life.

Fists flailed and he blocked them with both forearms as they hit the ground and rolled. Guillaume was on him, fingers clawing toward Channon's gullet while Leblanc bawled from the stone passage. Every word echoed, re-echoed between the rocks, and as Channon knocked Guillaume's hands away he heard Leblanc scream the name of Armagh.

Anger surged through him, hot and acid. With a strength he had not known he possessed, he got his knees between Guillaume's and threw him off, and before the corsair could recover his balance and wits Channon's right fist battered into the side of his head, and then again.

A grunt, a lurch, and Guillaume pitched into the sand, insensible. Channon rolled to his knees, snatched up both his own sword and Guillaume's, and came to his feet, poised over the Frenchman's body. The tip of his sword drew a tiny trickle of blood in the hollow of Guillaume's throat, but Channon did not press home the thrust. Somewhere in these caverns was a fortune that would ransom the English Queen and King Philip both, and Guillaume knew where it was. Truss him, then, and leave Zacarias to design some means to extract the truth from him? In that moment of fury Channon would have been as merciless as the boy.

Leblanc was still bellowing, and the name of Armagh was on his lips again as Channon plunged into the rocky passage. The darkness of the grave swallowed him at once and he snatched up the lantern Robin had set down, what seemed an hour before.

The pistols they had left at the entrance to the powder store were gone, likely kicked away as Leblanc passed by, and Channon did not have time to search for them.

The sand at his feet was scuffed, ploughed deeply with drag-marks, and his heart quickened. If Robin had been dead Leblanc would have ignored the body, joined Guillaume's fight and flung himself on Channon. So Robin was alive, and Leblanc was shouting his name, and Guillaume's, with purpose. Channon dragged air into his lungs and chided himself bitterly.

He should never have brought Robin into this. He should have bound him hand and foot, gagged him if need be, left him on the ship no matter how he protested. They would have thrashed out their differences later.

His legs hurt, but they were only phantom aches. The wounds paining him had healed years ago, the knives he thought he felt were only in his mind. The ground under his feet sloped steeply up — this was not the way they had come in but he was sure he felt the stirring of a breeze in his face. Up ahead he glimpsed movement, a shambling, monstrous form, mis-shapen in the strange grey twilight. No, it was two men, one struggling to drag the other.

'Leblanc!' Channon's voice roared back off the rocks. 'Leblanc, set him down! Guillaume is senseless, you're alone!'

But Leblanc picked up his pace, struggling backwards around an immense boulder, and as Channon drew nearer he stepped into a sudden, unexpected flush of dawn light from a crevice which opened into the air.

In that moment of dazzled blindness he was vulnerable. He did not even see the pistol torn from Leblanc's belt, but he heard the shot, and the hoarse, startled calls of the gulls which echoed his own voice. Leblanc might have been aiming for his breast, but was greatly wide of the mark. As the pistol ball raked him pain and heat ripped through Channon's right arm, reached a stunning crescendo and died back to a slow, steady, knife-edged throb.

The dawn sky was pink and blue, fleeced with clouds, filled with gulls which rose from the cliff ledges and wheeled about Leblanc's bowed head. He stood on the edge, a hand's span from the dizzying drop, panting and scarlet with effort as he fumbled for his second pistol. At his feet Robin lay on his side, and to Channon's intense relief he was just beginning to stir.

'Come no closer,' Leblanc rasped in an accent so thick the English was slurred. 'I have something you want, Irish.' He aimed a kick into Robin's hip, and the blow stirred Robin more swiftly than a dousing with cold water. Leblanc held the pistol steady on Channon's belly, stooped and clenched his left hand into Robin's hair. 'You want him, you give me what *I* want.'

Very carefully, Channon set down both swords and held up his left hand. The right arm was afire, pressed to his side. The wound was bleeding profusely, but he knew even then that the ball had gone clean through the flesh. 'Name your price, Leblanc,' he said hoarsely. 'You know I'd buy his life at any cost.'

'No price is too much?' Leblanc panted, and wrenched Robin's hair hard enough to make him wince. 'You give me the *Pandora* and twelve of my men.'

'You can't run a *galleasse* with twelve.' Channon swallowed on a dry throat and looked into Robin's pale, twisted face. His eyes were wide and clearing, he did not seem badly hurt, and he had seen the bright new blood soaking Channon's arm and hand. Channon forced a breath to the bottom of his chest. 'I'll give you the *Pandora* and every man of your crew who's survived the night. You can have them, and welcome to them. I'll give you safe passage out of San Carlos, we'll not fire on you, nor will we pursue you.'

'Tell me why I believe you,' Leblanc snarled, and gave Robin's hair such a wrench that he cried out. 'You love this one, Armagh?' Leblanc shifted his grip on the pistol.

'I love him,' Channon said hoarsely. 'Set him down, let him be. You can have your damned ship and your crew. Hurt him, and I'll cut the price of his pain out of your hide, Leblanc.'

Slowly, reluctantly, Leblanc's grip in Robin's hair released and Robin slumped to the ground. The gulls were settling, the sun was on the horizon and the sea air was cool in Channon's sweated face. He clenched his left hand around the wound and his eyes raced over Robin, searching for blood or bruises, finding nothing.

'I'm all right, Dermot,' Robin said ruefully. 'I let him trip me, he whipped a rope about my legs and struck me witless.' He rubbed the back of his neck. 'Foolish of me.'

'To be duped by a trick you'd never seen?' Channon shook his head. 'There's a saying about old dogs, Robin.' He glared at Leblanc then. 'I must send a man to the harbour with a message. Your slaves have been loose since this began but my crew will recall them.'

329

Leblanc took two measured steps away from Robin and drew aim on his back. 'Armagh remains with me till you return. Cozen me and he dies, Channon. I've nothing else to bargain with, and nowhere to go.'

'Oh, I believe you,' Channon said sourly. He looked down into Robin's taut, wary face. 'Be still, say nothing, do nothing. He means what he says, and he wants to live.'

'As do we all.' Robin eased himself on the rocks and settled again. 'Be quick, for Christ's sake, Dermot.'

'I will.' Channon shifted his grip on the hot, aching wound and turned back toward the fissure which led through the caves, the most direct way he knew to the path where Valdez should be.

Movement, a flicker of white, caught his eye in the boulders by the edge of the cliff. For an instant he thought it was a bird with wide-spread wings, and then it moved again and he saw the youth's long, slender legs. Zacarias was half hidden, worming through the rocks at the cost of the skin of his elbows and knees.

Where he had come from Channon could not guess, but he saw the fist-sized stone in the boy's hand, saw him rear up like a snake about to strike and throw it with the full force of his arm. Had he hit Leblanc's head the blow might have knocked it clean off his body, but the throw was low. The knob of rock smacked him hard in the shoulder, bowled him off his feet, and with the shock of the impact the pistol discharged into the ground.

Seabirds filled the air in startled clouds once more as Leblanc scrambled up and clawed for his sword. Robin was on his knees, in possession of his wits and bright-eyed with some heady blend of anger, fear, exhilaration. As Leblanc's sword cleared the scabbard he dove out of reach, rolled and came up against Channon's braced legs.

It was Channon's sword he was after, and Dermot held his breath as he watched Robin rise. The hilt fit his hand almost as perfectly as Channon's own, and it had been forged for him. Robin cut the air to find the balance, worked his shoulders to loosen them, and placed himself between Channon and the Frenchman.

Leblanc dragged his forearm over his face and spat into the rocks. 'You have more lives than a cat, Armagh.'

Robin answered in stinging French, out of which Channon could pick only the many expletives. Leblanc's eyes widened as the goading taunts found their mark. His first blows were crude, without form or skill, while Robin was in command not only of his weapon, but of his temper.

Steel chimed, bell-like in the morning calm, and Channon stooped gingerly to pick up the sword he had taken from Guillaume minutes before. His eyes never left Robin as he and Leblanc circled, probed and cut, but even Leblanc had known for some time that Robin was his match. The basic skills Channon had taught him so long ago had been nurtured, cultivated.

The competence that had kept him alive on the *Swan* served him again today. Channon gripped Guillaume's sword awkwardly in his left hand — he would use it like an axe if he must, if somehow Leblanc got the better of Robin. But the Frenchman was breathless, beginning to panic as, like a conjurer, Robin produced every skill he had ever learned.

Breathless, Zacarias scrambled up from the edge of the cliff and flung himself against Channon. 'Where did you come from?' Channon demanded, fending him off.

'I climbed up above the cave, to look down over the harbour and see the battle. 'Tis the highest point on the island.' Zacarias pointed to the boulders above the fissure through which Leblanc had dragged Robin. 'I heard everything.'

'So you crept around, through the rocks, and tried to knock his head off.' Channon pulled the boy out of the way as Robin's blows gathered speed and weight. 'Ha! See that? My lad is angry, and quick. Did you desire vengeance upon Raoul Leblanc also?'

'Aye, Captain,' Zacarias whispered as he followed every stroke of the fight. 'I prayed to God to fetch him to death last night.'

'His death is an hour or two late,' Channon said drily.

Fear whitened Leblanc to the lips and his breathing was laboured. His worst and last mistake was a lunge for Robin's heart which was turned aside, and the tip of Robin's sword darted in beneath his ribs and up. He sagged to his knees and blood frothed his mouth as the sword clattered from his fingers. Robin stepped back, poised, panting lightly, as if he would not believe his victory until Leblanc pitched forward onto his face and was still.

Relief purged Channon to the marrow. He leaned both shoulders back against the rock and let his right arm hang limply as Robin turned toward him and offered him the sword. The ten-year-old blade, forged by the master, Quiepo, seemed a part of Robin's hand.

Channon shook his head and gestured at his useless right arm.

'Keep it for me,' he said, husky with affection, and gave Robin a nod of appreciation. 'You had a good teacher, Master Armagh.'

'When I was a boy,' Robin said softly. 'He taught me everything I know.' He cleaned the Salamanca blade, thrust it into his own scabbard for safe keeping and gave Channon his hand. 'Let me see your arm, Dermot, you're bleeding more than you know.'

'Am I?' In that moment Channon could not have cared. He turned a little, lifted his face to the dawn sky and took a deep, healing breath as Robin tore his sleeve away from the shoulder and peered at the swollen, messy wound.

'It could be worse,' Robin mused. 'The ball bypassed the bone, but you'll carry another scar from this altercation.'

'Like that in your side, won on the deck of the *Swan*?' Channon asked unconcernedly. 'What does it matter?'

'*Captain!*'

Zacarias had been standing over Leblanc, nudging the body with his foot and gloating over the death of an enemy. He spun now, scattering pebbles and raising the birds with his screech of alarm. Channon's heart pounded anew. The boy was intent on the crevice between the boulders, and in the split second before Channon saw what he had already seen, Zacarias launched himself.

The sun gleamed on the bronze muzzle of the pistol aimed between Channon's shoulders. Hubert Guillaume stood framed by the rocks, groggy and swaying. Blood oozed from his nose and mouth, and from a gash on his temple. His wits were slow, his fingers reluctant, yet still he squeezed the trigger.

The bark of the single shot jolted Channon like a blow. Robin snatched the sword from his scabbard, but before it was clear Zacarias had crashed into Guillaume's belly. Knocked back into the boulders, Guillaume dropped the pistol and sprawled gracelessly, tangled with Zacarias's flailing limbs. Channon heard Robin shout his name, and saw the glint of the boy's dirk, with which he had cut to tatters the corsair's magnificent bed.

The point gouged toward Guillaume's throat but Zacarias had not the strength to wrestle with the Frenchman. He was a slender fifteen years, and his side was a mass of blood. In the brilliant blaze of his rage he likely did not even feel the wound, but still it fettered him as he grunted and wept with the effort to drive home the dirk.

All this, Channon saw in a tenth part of a second, before Robin had even drawn his sword. Guillaume's fingers had closed on Zacarias's wrist, they would snap it like a twig, and with a roar Channon flung himself into the melee of thrashing limbs.

His left fist clenched about Guillaume's right hand, which was on the dirk, his fingers dug among the sinews and he heard the dry, brittle sound of yielding bones. Guillaume screamed as the dirk loosened in his grasp and slithered away. Channon rolled, seized Zacarias about the shoulders, lifted him bodily and pitched him toward Robin.

He felt rather than heard the snap of a broken link of chain, and as he thrust the struggling youth out of harm's way he saw that necklace of emeralds and gold, Robin's necklace, tumble from Guillaume's neck and lie forlornly among the pebbles.

His right arm was like molten lead, the hand was useless and he was slick with new blood from elbow to fingertips. Like a hammer, his left fist lashed toward Guillaume's face but the corsair was always just out of reach of the blow that would finish him. Scrambling, clumsy with urgency, he tore himself out of Channon's grasp.

The broken hand was pressed tight to his chest, his face was waxen with sweat. He stumbled as he got his knees under him, and threw himself back into the crevice, into the well of darkness. For some moments Channon lay gasping, clutching his arm as he blinked his eyes clear.

Whimpering with hoarse, laboured breaths, Zacarias lay on his side while Robin wiped his wound with the rag of Channon's torn sleeve. Channon forced himself to his feet and scooped up the necklace, and the sword he had dropped moments before. Guillaume's own sword.

'Hush, lie still,' Robin was saying to Zacarias. 'The wound is deep but the ball went through. There is an old man on the ship who will give you a cup to make you sleep and close it with an iron, but you must be very still, boy. Tell me how to get over the rocks, back to where we left Valdez.'

'That way.' Zacarias pointed weakly. His eyes were wide and glassy, unfocused on the sky. 'I wanted so much to go home. Oh God, shall I die in this place that I hate?'

'Not if you lie very still and breathe deep and even,' Robin insisted. He looked up at Channon, and his own eyes glittered with grief and fury. 'What became of Guillaume?'

'He went back into the caves,' Channon panted.

'Dermot, he has enough powder and shot to render half of San Carlos into rubble.'

'Aye, I know. Hold out your hand.' Channon shifted his awkward grip on the sword and clumsily dropped the necklace into Robin's palm. With a soft, anguished oath Robin thrust it into his shirt, for it must be mended before he could wear it again. 'Get over the rocks. Tell Valdez to hurry for Geraldo.' Channon dropped his voice. 'Safest to tend the boy before he's carried down, or he'll be done for.'

'No need to whisper,' Robin said bitterly as Zacarias's head lolled on his shoulder. 'He's senseless.' He eased the lad flat on the rocks and dragged both hands through his hair.

'Look after that child,' Channon said tersely, already moving.

'But what of Guillaume?' Robin gestured at the entrance to the caves.

'Old scores. Too many old scores.' Channon peered at his arm and grunted as he saw that the bleeding was sluggish once more. 'Fetch Valdez, let me settle with Guillaume. I broke the bastard's hand, he's as crippled as I am!'

Robin might have protested but Channon did not tarry to hear. His arm was raw, aching, but he had feeling in the fingers, he could use it if he must. The gloom of the cave swallowed him as he slipped carefully into the tomb-like closeness of the rocks and cast about for Guillaume. He stooped for the lantern he had left in the passage and picked his way with care, for every twist and turn offered an excellent site for ambush.

He saw nothing, but he heard the grunting and heaving of effort. Guillaume had returned to the powder store, and Channon pressed against the cold rock face, just out of sight. The corsair was dragging something heavy across the sand, and without chancing a look into the cavern Channon knew it must be the gun.

'Guillaume, what chance do you think you have?' he rasped as he put down the light and tried his right hand on the sword.

'Devil take you, Channon,' Guillaume panted, 'and your English cur.' Pain roughened his voice. 'You'll not have me!'

He knew what awaited him if he was taken prisoner. Would Channon give him to Zacarias, or to the slaves who had laboured at his oars, for sport? In his place, Guillaume would not have hesitated.

Channon took a breath and drove himself out, away from the wall, into the open.

In the light of four lamps Guillaume was struggling one-handed to load the cannon. Black powder had spilled about his feet from a keg he had crudely split open with an axe. He was ramming the barrel as Channon appeared. Wadding and loose shot scattered about him, torn clumsily from their crates as he rushed through a job that should have been done with great care.

Heart in his mouth, Channon lifted the sword and took a step closer, but Guillaume had seen him the instant he showed himself. He spun, eyes wide and wild, and cast about blindly for the pistol he had left on the head of a barrel. With his useless right hand clutched tight to his chest he was awkward, and the pistol defied his grasp. It almost fell, and as he lunged after it Channon saw the lamp tip over.

Glass shattered, oil spilled and as the naked flame licked hungrily along the sand the pulse in Channon's head beat like a drum. Blood roared in his ears as he sprang away, back into the rock passage, up toward the air and sky. He was almost through into daylight when, echoing among the rocks, Guillaume's voice gave a single banshee scream.

Then it seemed to Channon that the world overturned and tore itself asunder.

'He's astir,' Valdez said, as if from far off, or at the other end of a long, narrow gallery.

Then Robin's voice: 'Oh, thank God. I feared the worst.'

'As did we all, lad. He's an impetuous bugger when his blood's roused, but mark me well, there's no truer mate than Dermot Channon.'

'That much do I know,' Robin said ruefully.

Dust-dry nose and mouth, gritty eyes and aching ears greeted Channon, and with the first breath he took he found himself coughing fit to wrench his ribs. Robin's hands cupped his cheeks, held him while he prised open his eyelids and saw the morning sky. Above him was Robin's tousled head, with a worried frown, dark morning stubble on his jaw and dust in his hair.

'I am alive,' Channon croaked lucidly.

'And lucky to be,' Robin added in a voice thick with tears. 'By God, did you set off the powder? A foolhardy thing to do!'

'A lamp — he upset a lamp,' Channon fought himself awake. 'And I fled.'

'You were almost out.' Robin hushed him, held him.

His head was in Robin's lap and by the sky it was still early. He had slept less than an hour. Channon took a deep, calming breath. 'Guillaume?'

'Who knows?' Robin swabbed his face with wet ragging. 'Where that chamber was is now a pile of rocks. Guillaume fashioned his own tomb.'

With a wince Channon sat, fingered his throbbing ears and looked into Robin's anxious face. 'You dragged me clear?'

'I did.' Robin fiddled with the bandage he had wound about Channon's arm. 'There was not a bruise on you, yet you might have been punched.'

Channon had seen the like of it before. A galleon's whole powder store caught fire and exploded, and men died though there was not a scratch on them. He lifted his good hand and cupped Robin's face. 'Thank you.'

'I was merely afeard,' Robin said wryly, and leaned closer with a light, chaste kiss. His tongue flicked Channon's briefly, fetching a spark of life to the invalid.

'Zacarias,' Channon said hoarsely as wits began to return.

'On the ship. Geraldo sealed the wound with gunpowder, which I'd never seen before. He sprinkled it into the very blood and touched it with a flame. It flared up like a torch, with a vile smell of burning, then he doused it with wet rags and when I looked back the bleeding had stopped.'

'Then the boy will live?' Channon wondered as he held out one hand, to be assisted to his feet.

'Geraldo can't say so soon.' Robin helped him up and offered his shoulders. 'Lean on me, Dermot.'

'I feel rolling-drunk,' Channon said groggily, 'without having indulged in any of the joys of wine and boys.'

'Wine and boys?' Robin's arms were about him, holding him securely.

'Wine and... good loving,' Channon amended. He hugged Robin tightly and felt the bulk of emeralds and gold chains about his neck, beneath the collar of his shirt.

The chain was roughly joined with a knot of twine. Channon fingered the quick, makeshift repair and Robin blushed faintly. 'I've desired it every moment since I gave it to Guillaume,' he confessed. 'I never wanted him to have it, but on that day I owned nothing else to pay Rothwell's ransom.'

'Aye, it looks better on you than on Guillaume,' Channon said drily, and nuzzled Robin's mouth. 'What news of San Carlos? What befell this cockpit while I slept?'

'They found the gold store by the harbour,' Robin told him as he helped him to a boulder by the cliff, and Channon sat. 'Filled to the rafters, Dermot.' His eyes sparkled. 'The sixty thousand ducats looted from Puerto del Miel will be a tiny fraction of Guillaume's hoard. His crew is put to the sword... the slaves ran wild, it was impossible to call them off. Every one had grievances to settle. Valdez told me the whole harbour is red with blood. I've not been down there yet.' He looked away, out over the sea. 'The slaves have laid claim to the *Pandora*. Did you pledge the big Flemish sailor the ship and the harbour, if they took your orders for a moment?'

'I did,' Channon said unconcernedly. 'We've no use for either. A French *galleasse* is an aggravation of a ship. They can have Guillaume's surviving stores of powder and shot, and a twentieth part of his gold hoard. They can make their own way hereafter. The rest of the cache is ours.'

'Most is already aboard the *gallizabra*,' Robin told him, yet he frowned. 'Valdez told me that Pasco is eager to put to sea, lest we become trapped in this cockpit. The likes of Alvarez may well share the secret of this anchorage. They could be holding us to ransom tomorrow.' He gestured toward the lagoon. 'One narrow route of escape, easily guarded even by the guns of a leaky carrack.'

Channon stretched his good arm over his head. 'Wise,' he decided. 'Is Valdez up here?'

'Searching the rubble in the cave, though for what I don't know,' Robin said disinterestedly. 'I'll fetch him.'

'Better, help me get my feet under me,' Channon corrected, and gave Robin his hands.

They stood, pressed close, and Robin laced his fingers at Channon's nape. 'Twice, you bested Guillaume.'

'Prideful?' Channon teased gently.

'Very.' Robin kissed his neck. 'I hoped and prayed to see you master that arrogant whelp!'

He was about to go on but paused as shouts erupted from the rubble-strewn cleft in the boulders, where the caves seemed to have collapsed. Valdez was excited, and his cries were echoed by Miguel and Jon Jago. Robin stepped back and with a quiet smile took the place he seemed to have decided was right and proper for him, at Channon's shoulder. Channon lifted a brow but said nothing, and to his immense pleasure Robin winked one green eye at him.

'Dermot! Dermot, see here!' Valdez was shouting as he scrambled out of the rubble. His hands were filled with sparkling stuff that winked in the sun, and before he had his breath back he looped a great weight in gold and silver chains over Channon's wrist, each one heavy with precious stones. 'Emeralds, sapphires, diamonds, amethysts, gems I cannot even recognise,' Valdez panted.

'Where did you find them?' Robin held a diamond to the sun. 'We were in what I took for Guillaume's deepest retreat yet we saw none of this.'

'Fortune favours the virtuous,' Valdez said drily. 'We might never have found this hoard. 'Twas in a cleft in the cave wall, sealed in with rocks the size of cannon shot. We might have searched for days and found nothing, but the uproar which brought down the roof shook loose the stones. The passage is strewn with a king's dream of avarice! These few trinkets, I snatched up in passing.'

Tired, sore and aching, Channon handed back the winking gems, gold and silver, and leaned heavily on Robin's shoulder. 'Fetch out all you can by evening. Pasco is right, it'll not be safe to stay longer. We could be peering down the muzzles of Mateo Alvarez's guns.'

Valdez looked him up and down with a rueful smile. 'Dermot, you look dreadful. Go back to the ship, lay down your head, take care of your arm.'

'Upon your orders, *Captain*,' Channon said drily, making Valdez laugh, and allowed Robin to lead him over the rocks where Zacarias had crept.

The quayside was strewn with the dead, and Robin was tight-mouthed as they stepped onto the *gallizabra*. Guillaume's storehouse was steadily being emptied, while men laboured aboard, stooped under the weight of riches the corsair had looted from so many ships. Spanish, Portuguese, French and English coins; ingots smelted on the other side of the continent, fetched over the Isthmus by mule caravan, bound for Seville and diverted into this unlikely place.

Seville, Channon thought as Robin latched their cabin door, and he stripped off the tattered ruin of his shirt. On the chart table were a mass of linen strips, a basin of water, a box of salves. Geraldo had been here. He knew well enough that Channon must doctor his own hurts. No physician's hands had touched him since Santa Catalina.

Yet he sat compliant on the side of the divan today and let Robin unwrap his arm, bathe and salve it. The wound was clean, not so deep, and he disregarded it even while Robin fussed. At last, with a fresh bandage tied, he caught Robin's hands and fetched him down onto the mattress. Their heads lay on the same pillow and Channon groaned eloquently as he relaxed at last. Seville was on his mind, and as always Robin seemed to read his thoughts.

'You're taking us back, aren't you?' he asked quietly.

'Most of us have good reason to make for home, however briefly,' Channon said, just as quietly. 'But I also promised you we would return here.'

'A house like the Governor of Havana's, on the river, two or three ships like the *Roberto*... the *Esmerelda*, plying for us, so legitimately, we shall be taxed. We can be in Spain by Christmas, settle our affairs, and be applauded as heroes in the street in Hispaniola by next summer.' Robin smiled tiredly. 'Grand dreams, Dermot.'

'Not dreams,' Channon argued, 'when King Philip shall have but a fourth part of what we own, and will never know the rest exists! How long have you sailed with us, Robin? A few months. This crew has been planning for our return, and our freedom, for years.' He sketched a caress about Robin's face. 'You must learn to trust me, love.'

'Teach me,' Robin invited, hushed with feeling, and kissed him.

EPILOGUE:
Seville, January 1596

Fox furs, ermine and velvet kept out the bitter cold of mid-winter, but the air stung the nostrils with its chill and the acrid scent of woodsmoke. Robin held his cloak about him and watched the grey storm clouds gathering in the north-east. Thunder would peal by evening, as it had the whole night before, like gunfire from ships at sea. The sound trembled in his bones.

He stood on the hillside, looking down on the estate and watching for Channon's returning figure. Beyond the bleak winter woods the distant cathedral tower caught a ray of sunlight and seemed to beckon him toward the river on which stood the city of Seville. Duty brought Channon here, but little that was pleasant or happy celebrated his return.

A week before Christmas the *Esmerelda* dropped anchor in Santander. Robin stood back with Valdez and Pasco, held his tongue and wore a polite face as the ship was boarded. Garbed in the austere black doublet and hose, with white lace, they seemed the embodiment of Spanish nobility, and though King Philip's officers in Santander were shocked to see the *gallizabra*, they extended considerable courtesy.

Documents had been prepared weeks before: a complete and detailed account of Captain Alonzo Corco's command, which was ended by the plague that rampaged through the vessel, south of Valparaiso on the Pacific coast of the Americas. With the gentlemen decently buried at sea, command passed into the hands of the captain of soldiers. Channon produced his contract, signed in Santa Catalina and counter-signed in Corco's unmistakable hand.

Following this was an exhaustive account of the ship's privateering voyage, how she ransomed English galleons and corsairs, and stole back the very gold which men like Drake had only just looted from Spanish ports and vessels. Much was made of the *Swan*, the *Rosamund* and the *Pandora*, and the scenes at Puerto del Miel and Isla San Carlos. Many of the details could be corroborated by other captains.

The document was a thick wedge of papers, meticulous and correct, and its last sheets were a tally, coin by coin, ingot by ingot, of the enormous wealth that had been fetched home in King Philip's name.

A courier raced to El Escorial, where His Majesty was holding court, but in Santander the gentlemen privateers of the *Esmerelda* were wined and banqueted.

Tall, sombre, magnificent in the austere Spanish garb, Channon answered a thousand questions, told a hundred stories that had been woven on the voyage east. Every man left aboard knew the tales by heart and would repeat them as gospel fact. The Englishmen, who would be at risk in Spain, had been put ashore by night in the Scilly Islands, a modest voyage from home. They safeguarded the secret of their own fortune, left buried somewhere between Rio de San Francisco and Puerto del Miel, and on the subject of the privateer *Roberto* their lips were sealed.

While they waited for word from El Escorial a messenger hurried to Vigo, to the house of the merchant Marcelo Sanchez Mendoza, with the news that his second-youngest son, Zacarias, had come home. Zacarias had celebrated his fifteenth birthday, sick and ill, in the mid-Atlantic. The wound had poisoned, his blood burned and the flesh fell from his bones. But youth won out over death, and though he was painfully thin when he caught his first glimpse of Spain he was well enough to stand, cloaked and hooded, and look out on the roofs of a port he knew well. His father would hurry to fetch him, and Zacarias's story would tell of a French corsair, hard labour and liberation at the hands of a Spanish privateer.

On those evenings when Santander saluted the company, Robin dressed in the same black garb as Channon, and wore about his neck a heavy gold crucifix. He was known by the name of Patrick O'Mara, a Catholic mercenary soldier who had served Don Julio Recalde before the plague of Yellow Jack, and had joined the *Esmerelda* when she liberated the slaves aboard the *Pandora*, of whom he had been one. He showed his scarred back and in his perfect, accentless Spanish he avowed the Catholic faith of his fathers and told his own stories, each contrived to strengthen Channon's.

The courier sped back from El Escorial with orders for the gentlemen of the *Esmerelda* to present themselves before the King and Court. Robin's belly churned with some mix of exhilaration and dread. He cropped his hair in Spanish fashion, gave money to every priest who addressed him and was never heard to speak a word of English. His rosary clicked through his fingers without pause as they began the journey which took him into the very heart of Spain.

Nights were hardest, for he bedded alone and he sorely missed the intimacy he had enjoyed for a full half year. Robin resigned himself, put security before comfort and told himself over and over they would soon be free. Seville was full of ships, for hire or for sale, and many of the men from the *Roberto* would be chafing to leave.

The morning when they had stepped off the *gallizabra* for the last time, Channon left word with the crew: come to Seville in February or March, to the Cervallo estate, and be ready to sail in April or May. The men who were returning to wives and families shook their heads and clasped Channon's wrists. For them, it was farewell. But many more promised to be there, and Robin prayed for the day to come soon.

Spain was bleak in winter. Impoverished, despondent, the lowlands flooded, the minds of the people morose. But El Escorial, the extraordinary palace and monastery which Philip had built in the foothills of the Guadarramas, glittered like a jewel in the midst of drabness. The courtyards and gardens, towers and spires astonished Robin, though he remembered Hampton Court well. Monks rubbed shoulders with ministers and courtiers, and it was here, Channon told him, that the King had laid his disastrous plans for the war.

A coach brought them into the forecourt. Guardsmen in mirror-polished casques and breastplates escorted them into the hushed, ringing marble hall where at last Robin glimpsed the King. Yet again, he was astonished.

How small was Philip, how frail, with thin legs, white hair and beard, and deep creases in his face. He was almost seventy years old now, and Robin thought he had an unhealthy look. He was dying, though he might have another year or two to live. Robin felt no pity, for he could not forget the anguish, the death that this man had invited, the thousands of mariners and soldiers who had died, and those who had suffered, like Channon. Like himself.

Rheumy old eyes appraised Dermot as he was presented, and knelt. Channon held out the whole folio of papers, every word that had been written about the voyage of the *Esmerelda*, and the accounting sheet. When he stepped back Master Patrick O'Mara was called, and with a pounding heart Robin knelt at the King's feet.

Every word of the folio was read aloud, and from time to time Philip seemed almost inanimate; he only properly enlivened when it came to the tally of the gold and silver which was being fetched by wagon from Santander. Damn the man, Robin thought, he still had hopes of war, and victory! He spoke of the sea trade and the Channel, which was the quickest, safest route for ships, and his life-long dream of closing off the seaway to all vessels save those of Spain.

Robin looked not at Philip but at his ministers, and the ladies and gentlemen who had thronged the magnificent audience chamber to hear the incredible story of the *Esmerelda*. Their faces were stony, filled with the poorly masked horror that this old man could carry on his impossible dream. *Are they waiting for his death, which would end the nightmare?* Robin wondered as the final documents were read aloud. How many of these gentlemen, knights and nobility, had been taxed by Crown and Church until they were as poor as the Cervallos?

A small prize in gold coin was awarded to Channon, and a public commendation was posted for his crew. Patrick O'Mara received only a document which to Robin was both worthless and priceless, for it granted him the rights and liberties of a citizen of Spain. He was as free in Madrid or Seville as any Spaniard, and recognised as a loyal son of the Church.

They left El Escorial two days later. The *Esmerelda* was relieved of her precious cargo, her crew had gone ashore and the ship was being serviced before she would return to the Caribbean with a new captain. Channon heard this news with an unreadable look but Robin knew he was grieved. She had been his ship, and she would become another hellship as soon as a fresh crew of slaves was taken aboard and chained to her oars.

But now Channon's eyes were on Seville, and home. Twice he had sent letters, once from Santander, again from El Escorial, but received no reply. The north wind was like ice at their backs as they left the palace. Pasco and Valdez had family in the south and rode with them, but the rest of the crew had gone in a hundred directions.

Seville was bleak, blustery. The lowlands and marshes were flooded but work continued without pause in the shipyards on the river. While Pasco took charge of their baggage mules and looked up an old acquaintance, Valdez rode down to examine what hulls might be for sale. They parted at the crossroad above the city, where Channon turned west and touched his heels to the flanks of his horse.

For years Robin had tried to imagine the Cervallo estates, but in none of his dreams had he pictured them as they were that winter's afternoon when he followed Channon over the shoulder of a hill and into the lee of a sparse wood.

A dozen sheep, a milk cow and a donkey shared the graze where a garden had once been. Two pigs rooted in the tumbled wreckage of an arbour, and a finger of smoke angled up from one chimney, on the last corner of the house which boasted a sound roof. Elsewhere the slates were off, the windows were broken, timbers rotted, eaves tumbled down. The wilderness had encroached with thistles and briars, right to the west wall, and over most of that wing of the house the roof had fallen in completely.

Channon was silent, uncharacteristically pale, and Robin's heart squeezed painfully. 'It must have been beautiful, Dermot. I can picture it as it was,' he said, but Channon only sighed.

'Someone is living there,' he said sadly. 'I'll go down and see. Wait for me here, I'll be quick.' He turned a face filled with regret to Robin. 'I'm sorry. Had I known I was bringing you to this —'

'I would still have come with you.' Robin held out one gloved hand and was pleased when Channon took it, almost the first time they had touched in ten long days.

Half an hour later, the mare and gelding they had bought in Madrid were grazing along the side of the woods. Robin had stood in the cold wind so long that no amount of velvet and fur could keep him warm. He walked down the slope, away from the occupied corner of the house, as if he was afraid of what he might find there. On the other side, overrun with weeds and rambling vines, he found the family chapel.

Neglected, sad and forlorn, this more than anything told Robin the truth. Don Mauricio lay buried in the crypt beneath the altar, and for the chapel to be so unkempt meant that the Cervallos were gone. Perhaps Dermot was the last. Robin shivered and hugged his cloak about him.

Further along, he looked in through the windows and saw the

remains of a parlour, a library and dining hall, the rooms Dermot had described to him so often. A hint of dignity and beauty endured and Robin closed his eyes, picturing the house as it must have been. And Dermot, a lad of fourteen years, so fresh from the wilds of Ireland that the only Spanish he had was the few words his mother had taught him.

The wind made odd sounds as is stirred through the empty rooms, and Robin fancied it mourned. He walked on, kicking through the weeds as he circled the whole house. As he rounded the east gable, where the chimney betrayed an occupant, a rough-made wooden door creaked open and Channon stepped out.

'Here, Dermot,' he called quietly from the corner.

Channon turned toward him with a face like granite. Robin offered his hands but they were refused until the bulk of the house afforded them complete privacy. Then Channon tugged Robin against him and pressed his face into his neck.

'They're gone, aren't they?' Robin asked.

'All gone.' Grief roughened Channon's voice. 'A shepherd lives here, without anyone's permission. The poor sot was affrighted that I was the owner, come to toss him out.'

'Who *is* the owner?' Robin stepped back to look at him.

'The man said it still belongs to the merchant, Hugo Ortiz, who bought it in '88, after Mauricio...' He cleared his throat. 'Ortiz was beggared by taxes and the loss of one of his ships, two years after. This estate soon fell into a sad condition. Even had it been well kept, there's such poverty in Spain after the war, who'd buy it? The shepherd said he believes Ortiz is going to tear down the ruin of the house in spring, and put the land under the plough.' Channon drew off his gloves and took Robin's cold face between his bare hands. 'I wish I hadn't brought you here.'

'And I am glad you did.' Robin turned his head and pressed his lips to Channon's palm. 'Did he have any news of your family?'

'A little.' Channon leaned closer to kiss, luxuriating in the opportunity, and the comfort. 'Ten days since I've touched you,' he whispered against Robin's mouth. 'Too long.'

'Aye. Your family,' Robin prompted.

Channon stirred reluctantly. 'My cousins shipped out in the same month as I did, all of us hunting for a fortune. Neither of them returned.' His eyes glittered with tears but none spilled. 'No news of

345

them ever came to Seville. Of the three of us, I am the survivor. Their wives were declared widows two years ago. They remarried, took their children and went away, God knows where.' He paused and swallowed. 'There are no Cervallos.'

'Oh, Dermot.' Robin clasped him firmly and Channon's arms went about him, bruisingly tight.

'You grieve?' Channon asked against his hair.

'I grieve for you,' Robin said, husky with feeling.

'Then mourn for them,' Channon corrected. 'I have the world in my arms, don't waste heartache on me.' He drew back and looked into Robin's chill-flushed face. 'You're cold, likely hungry and tired, and it'll rain again soon. We'd best hurry. We'll take rooms in Seville till we find a ship that suits us.'

'Soon,' Robin breathed. 'These nights apart from you are trying.'

Thunder rumbled in the north as they walked back to the horses, and Robin shrugged up the heavy hood of his cloak. He had his boot in the stirrup when he heard the rhythmic thud of hooves on the path, and as he swung up into the saddle he saw Valdez's tall, rawboned grey horse coming around the trees.

'Dermot!' He waved. 'I thought I'd find you here.' He saw the house then, and swore bitterly. 'Good Christ, what became of your family?'

'Fortunes of war,' Channon said quietly as he mounted up and gathered his reins. 'A long and bitter tale, best told by a warm fire, over a cup of hot wine.' He lifted his face to the thundery sky and took a breath, as if to sweep the cobwebs from his head. 'I know the best taverns in Seville.'

'And do you also know Martin Vargas, the shipbuilder?' Valdez asked shrewdly as they turned back up the hill. 'He has an old carrack he is trying to sell. Her hull is sound, her masts are strong and her sails are under repair. She carries twenty-two guns.' Valdez's face creased in a grin. 'She's not what we're used to but she'd get us home if we can sail in April. Vargas told me the bullion fleet, six *gallizabras*, leaves Seville for Cartagena, late in the month. We can run under cover of their guns.'

'And in Havana,' Robin added, 'sell off the carrack and commission a decent hull of our own.' He looked sidelong at Channon. 'Pero Menendez would build us a *gallizabra* for the cost of twenty ducats a ton, and we can pay that price.'

346

A sharp, stinging rain had begun, yet Channon's bleak mood had begun to lighten. 'This carrack,' he said to Valdez, lifting his voice over the wind as they hurried the horses toward the city. 'Is she habitable aboard?'

'More or less,' Valdez judged. 'The gentlemen's cabins are clean enough. I looked her over thoroughly.'

'Then tell Vargas he has a sale, and when Pasco fetches our baggage, have it taken aboard.' Channon gave Robin a faint, wry smile. 'It may not be gracious living but I think you'll not sleep alone tonight.'

'Then a pox upon gracious living,' Robin said drily. 'You know I'd sooner be with you in a hut than alone in a palace.'

For the first time in weeks Channon laughed aloud. 'You may come to rue those words.'

But Robin would have none of it. 'We're going home, Dermot.' He gestured over his shoulder at the forlorn, forgotten ruin. 'This is no more your home than Blackstead was mine. There's no way back, for either of us. We knew that.'

A shadow crossed Channon's face briefly but was banished at once. 'Then we sail with the bullion fleet in April, and till then we bunk aboard the carrack. Together,' he added, perhaps teasing.

'Aye, together.' Robin held out his gloved hand and Channon took it. 'I said to you once, a long time ago, one day we would clasp and never part.'

'I remember.' Channon assured him. 'I swore you'd be mine, for good and all. Were those my words? I've never been free with idle promises.'

They were on the hill above the city, looking down on smoky, rain-veiled rooftops, the grey, sluggish river and a forest of masts. Seville smelt like any city, and a man could long for untainted air. Thunder rumbled on the horizon like a distant cannonade, and Robin's very bones shivered. Channon was watching him closely and Robin had the uncanny feeling that they shared the same thoughts. To be sure, they shared the same experiences, and pride thrilled him.

He thought fleetingly of the youth who had sat on the wall at Blackstead, looked out at the world and dreamed of freedom. Then he took a grip on the wet, slick reins and turned his horse with Channon's, down into the city of Seville.

Also by Mel Keegan:

DEATH'S HEAD

On the high-tech worlds of the 23rd century, the lethal designer drug Angel has become an epidemic disease. Kevin Jarrat and Jerry Stone are joint captains in the paramilitary NARC force sent in to combat the Death's Head drug syndicate that controls the vast spaceport of Chell. Under the NARC code of non-involvement, each of the two friends hides his deeper desire for the other. When Stone is kidnapped and forced onto Angel, Jerrat's love for him is his only chance of survival, but the price is that their minds remain permanently linked.

"Unputdownable. Keegan has taken the two-dimensional Marvel/ DC comic strip and made it flesh, and what flesh!" — *HIM*

"Definitely one for the determined SFer" — *Gay Scotland*

"A powerful futuristic thriller" — *Capital Gay*

ISBN 0 85449 162 7
UK £6.95   US $10.95   AUS $17.95

Also by Mel Keegan:

EQUINOX

Angel — the lethal synthetic drug so pervasive and deadly that it has built empires and torn down worlds. Equinox Industries is a commercial monopoly mining the gas giant Zeus, challenged by a growing faction for its environmental record, and suspected of manufacturing Angel. Enter Kevin Jarratt and Jerry Stone, joint captains in the paramilitary NARC force at war with the Angel syndicates, and lovers whose minds have been bonded together. In their second action-packed adventure, the heroes of *Death's Head* need their empathic powers as well as the 23rd century's technological wizardry to outwit their corporate enemies.

ISBN 0 85449 200 3
UK £6.95   US $ 10.95   AUS $19.95

Historical Fiction by Chris Hunt from The Gay Men's Press:

THE BISLEY BOY

Queen Elizabeth I was fond of saying that she had "the heart and stomach of a king", but to her grave she took the secret that she really was a man. When the young princess died as a child, her frightened attendants substituted for her a cousin, John Neville, with the same red hair and delicate features. Once the trick was played, there was no going back. The astonishing story of the boy from a Cotswold village who became England's greatest queen has been rumoured down the centuries, is local folklore in Gloucestershire, and is now reconstructed by Chris Hunt in the first person.

ISBN 0 85449 221 6   UK £8.95   US $14.95   AUS $19.95

GAVESTON

Medieval King Edward II reflects on his doomed love for the handsome young French nobleman Gaveston. "Hunt tells a ripping yarn, a mixture of romance and cautionary tale" – *Time Out*

ISBN 0 85449 184 8   UK £7.95   US $12.95   AUS $19.95

N FOR NARCISSUS

Set at the time of the Oscar Wilde trial, the story of Lord Algernon Winterton shows the dangers that beset the most respectable of English gentlemen when an old associate returns to stir up disquieting passions.

ISBN 0 85449 136 8   UK £7.95   US $12.95   AUS $19.95

STREET LAVENDER

Back in the foggy alleyways of Victorian London, sharp-mannered Willie Smith learns to use his youth and beauty as a means of realizing fabulous wealth.

ISBN 0 85449 035 3   UK £7.95   US $12.95   AUS $19.95

Gay Men's Press books can be ordered from any bookshop in the UK, and from specialised bookshops overseas.

If you prefer to order by mail, please send cheque/ postal order (payable to *Book Works*) for the full retail price plus £2.00 for postage and packing to:

Book Works (Dept. B), PO Box 3821, London N5 1UY
phone/ fax: (0171) 609 3427

For payment by Access/Eurocard/Mastercard/American Express/Visa, please give number, expiry date and signature.

Name and Address in block letters please:

Name
_____

Address
_____

_____

_____